Smile in One Eye.....

Sami Moukaddem

to herself
Eireen
Hartafan,

Love
Sami

First published in 2006 by
Sami Moukaddem
e-mail: sami@iol.ie

ISBN 13: 978-0-9553947-0-6
ISBN 10: 0-9553947-0-8

A CIP catalogue record for this book is available from the British Library.

Typeset by The Edit Room
Printed and bound in Ireland by ColourBooks Baldoyle Dublin 13.

Contents

AUTHOR'S NOTE

What you have in your hands is a work of fiction, based on my experiences of growing up in Lebanon during the civil war. In writing this book, I researched world events of the time, noted themes I wanted to portray, and let my imagination play. Before writing each chapter, I would note keywords to themes and then proceed to write with the promise that what came out would remain unaltered. I would read what I had written, correct spellings and grammar, but no rewriting, deleting or adding scenes, or reshuffling paragraphs. Only on very rare occasions would a sentence be reworded. It is an approach that trusts an internal process, surrenders to it, and is then led by it.

Welcome

Words

Omar's earliest memory of Lebanon is in his uncle's old Chevrolet. Sitting in the back, behind his uncle, feet dangling, body turned to the left, and both hands up to the elbows out of the window. His face turning to meet the oncoming wind, smiling against 100 km/hr, turning back to look at the buildings stacked on that little hill just on their way out of Beirut towards Tripoli. It would have been around 1972.

From early on, Omar had a fondness for certain words, especially when he hadn't yet fully grasped them. His uncle's car was pale brown, pale peach ... pale something, and the metal was a bit rusty, so they called it *Mtartaa*: beat-up, wrinkly, or feels as if it's falling apart yet still functioning. Although it wasn't really *mtartaa*, Omar made fun of it because everybody else did, using *mtartaa* as a term of endearment. He loved playing with the word — *mtartaa, mtartaa, mtartaa*. His uncle talked about buying a new car, but everybody was fond of this car whose character kept on growing until it really felt like it was a member of the family. Would you sell your cousin, really? Would you sell your cousin and buy a new one?

'I would,' Ziad would say, and then immediately afterwards would take it back. 'No, no, no, I wouldn't.' Omar would keep his back to the conversation, letting it be tickled by the banter: his cousin would sell him; his cousin wouldn't sell him; until his aunt would say, '*Wla Kalb*' (you dog), and Ziad would giggle like a hyena.

'See, I told you,' his uncle would say. 'He's like that animal I told you about; what do you call it?'

'Hi Eeena,' the two cousins would say simultaneously, and then they would take turns pleading for the story of Eeena.

'Again?' the uncle would say.

'Again.'

'Again?'

'Again.'

The uncle would pause. 'Again?'

'Again.'

Eventually the aunt would hit the uncle on the shoulder. '*Yalla*, come on ... get on with the show.'

'Ladies, and gentlemen...' And he would look back to see if there were any ladies in the back seat. 'OK, no ladies ... well, hang on, is Omar a lady? Maybe he's a lady!'

Here's where the aunt would yank him by the shoulder again. 'Stop that! You made him cry last time; you know he's not a lady.'

'Fine, OK, so ... well, maybe Ziad is a lady.'

'Your son a lady? How could he be a lady?' And then she would wave her hand dismissively. '*Yalla*, get on with the story.'

'Why couldn't he be a lady? I know plenty of girls born with no eh, and then, ehm, it comes out.'

Omar would come in: 'Yeah, but you're saying it the other way around because Ziad was also born with one.' He had heard this argument before.

Eventually, though, the story began: 'Once upon a time, there was this Eeena. Eeena, unlike our sons here...' And Omar would feel a warmth going through him from being so warmly tucked into the family. The aunt would smile, proud of her husband's big heart, and Ziad would refrain from rushing his dad into telling the story. 'Well, this Eeena was so strong, she had a moustache.'

'Last time, you said she had a beard,' Omar complained.

'Yes, my son, but that was much later on, when she became really strong. But in the beginning, in the beginning, she had a moustache. She was actually born with a moustache.'

The aunt started to shake her head.

'Actually, if I remember correctly, when she was born, she came out fiddling with her moustache, just like Chou Chou.'

'Who's Chou Chou?' Omar asked.

'You don't know Chou Chou?'

'Who's Chou Chou?'

The aunt smiled, shaking her head in appreciation of an old soul. 'God Bless him, Chou Chou was great. In the old times, Chou Chou was a great comedian, a great comedian.'

'He's dead now,' Ziad said.

Sometimes the uncle made promises not within his reach: 'He'll be on TV soon.'

Omar leaned forward. 'When? When? When?'

'Soon, soon. You'll see.'

She would try to level Omar's excitement. Ziad, used to his father's premonitions, would stay a bit more relaxed: 'He *might* be on TV at some time, maybe soon, but we don't know.' And she would yank the uncle's shoulder, warning him not to make any more unfounded announcements.

'Aufff, aufff, aufffff,' he would huff. 'This shoulder has the patience of the gods.'

There were words like '*yalla*' which never had to be explained to Omar. He had heard it used, as far back as he could remember; whenever somebody was in a rush and wanted to hurry somebody else, it would be a *yalla*. If they were in a real rush, it would be about three *yallas*. If he and Ziad were just dragging themselves about the place and annoying somebody, it would one big *yalla*, followed by a sigh. If he was recounting a story or trying to tell a joke he had half forgotten, the *yalla* would be said with a certain encouragement. With all its variations, it was never explained to him and he never had to ask; it was just there like the air.

When he was young, he never used *yalla* on anybody else because it was mainly the rest of the world that had to wait for him, but there were other words he just had to use so he had to understand them. He was told that in Lebanon, if you are a minor, or a young man, you would address a man who's your senior as *Ammo*. You can still use the term *Ammo* through to your thirties and forties, but you may want to use *Amm*; it just takes that edge off your being a minor and it keeps your respect flowing out of you. *Amm* means uncle; *Ammo* is when you are addressing your uncle directly. Literally, it describes your relation to your father's brother. Your mother's brother is *Khall*, *Khallo* to his face. But *Ammo* is the one you would use generally as a term of endearment for somebody with whom you have a warm relationship, or just out of respect. For Omar, it was difficult to judge who he was meant to have a warm relationship with, but he knew he was meant to have respect for everybody who was his senior, including people he and nobody else liked — so every man was *Ammo*.

The age difference was a tricky one, though. 'How many years older than me do they have to be before I should call them *Ammo*?'

'It depends,' his aunt said.

'On what?'

'Well, you wouldn't call your cousin *Ammo*.'

'Even if he was much older than me?'

'Well, maybe then, but generally no.'

His uncle shook his head disapprovingly. 'What kind of ridiculous talk is this? Calling a cousin *Ammo*! You're mixing the boy's head up.'

As the aunt tried to argue the possibility of specific situations where it just might be appropriate, a car unexpectedly pulled in front of them. The uncle shook his head and let a sigh out: 'Hffff ... *ya ammi*.'

Omar's eyebrows raised and then he pulled himself forward. 'How come you're calling him 'your uncle' when you don't even know him?'

'It's an expression, *ya akhi*,' the uncle said, addressing Omar as a 'brother'.

The aunt laughed cutely and shook her head in amusement. 'Now who's playing with whose head?'

'Don't worry,' the uncle said. 'With time, everything with time.'

'What with time?' Omar asked.

'Everything with time, everything.' On those occasions when he mocked himself as a wise old man, he tilted his head slightly forward while nodding to himself, and spoke with deliberation. 'Time. Reveals. Everything.'

Jamal, the uncle with the Chevrolet *mtartaa*, wasn't Omar's real uncle. He was Sana's husband. Sana was his real aunt, ten years his mother's junior. She could have been called *Ammti* or *Ammto* Sana, but she didn't want the term. The equivalent of *Ammo* just sounded too old for her. '*Ammto* is for the wrinklies. Sana is just fine; it keeps me young.'

'But my mum said I should have respect for you,' Omar said on a few occasions.

'Don't you worry. I'll talk to your mum when we get to Tripoli.'

Ziad sniggered in the back, testing the word 'Ammto', and took his time playing with the word, 'Sa... na'.

She smiled in amusement at his cheekiness and then turned to her husband, saying sarcastically, 'Listen to your son, the little midget.'

Eventually the story of Eeena would be told in one of its variations; Eeena would be born with a moustache, fiddling with it in ultimate coolness, or with a beard, ready for battle. She was so strong men feared her but also respected her. It was never clear what she did, what kind of battles she fought, or why, but the implication was always that she had a very well-established reputation — so well established that there was no need to talk much about how she had gained it.

Ammo Jamal would wiggle his way through his story, only on occasions giving Omar and Ziad any concrete events. It was the wiggling that he enjoyed most, having the boys suspended over nonsense; it was the banter, their pleas to take them somewhere in the story, that created the lively shifting in the back.

'And then what did she do?' either Omar or Ziad would eventually say.

'I think right now she's having a cup of coffee. I think she needs her break to gather her great thoughts together.' And the back seat of this old Chevrolet *mtartaa* would start bouncing in jovial mutiny.

Eventually it would make it to Tripoli. In those days, the trip took about an hour and a half — maybe two hours if the traffic was heavy, if there were any accidents along the way. They would leave Beirut at dusk, when the atmosphere was just light, travelling along the coast, side by side with a sun, golden yellow, disappearing into the sea, the sky changing from blue to red, pink stretching out on both sides of the sun until it sank into the sea, and slowly the horizon dimming from dark blue into almost black.

They would get to Tripoli and Omar's mother would be waiting on the balcony. They would have phoned her before leaving, and she would have calculated their approximate time of arrival, always leaving herself extra time to wait. She would hug Omar and Ziad at the same time because she didn't want to differentiate between them. In summer, she would have the *bouza* ready. Just the mere mention of that word would be enough to get both boys buzzing with excited anticipation over the creamy Arabic ice cream. Omar's favourite was raspberry and mango. Ziad preferred chocolate and vanilla dipped in pistachios. The adults smiled over the children's happiness, almost denying their own love for *bouza*. They said they loved it too, but the licking was slow. It never made sense to Omar or Ziad. How could they be so relaxed about it?

A child wakes up to a blank picture of whiteness. He stands up and looks around. Total whiteness. The ground holding him: white. Looks up: white.

Standing still, he hears no voices. No smells. He can taste only himself: no taste.

He looks around, looks up, down and then hears his own breathing. He knows he is there, here.

Time passes. Time doesn't pass.

The child knows everything around him is him.

Behind his eyes is the child. He senses his senses...

Everything around him ... and what's behind his eyes ... is one... is separate ... is one ... the child splits

Now the child is behind his eyes ... what he sees is outside him...

And now he hears a voice from above, a low voice, telling him to take out all the colours and smells inside him, and splash them out into the world. A big voice. A warm voice.

The child sits down. He hears himself breathing, the breath from outside, into inside, then outside ... then again ... again ... always ... outside into inside and inside to outside ... One.

What is behind his eyes and what does he see, inside and outside? But ... he breathes the outside ... into inside ... and then inside into outside and ... and...

Now the child hears a voice from below him, a soft high voice, tender. The voice nudges him to go ahead and put himself all around ... all over... 'Be you,' she says.

The child gets up, and the first smile in this universe is formed.

Home

It was rare that Omar stepped off his school bus, looked up, and did not see his mother waiting for him on the fourth balcony of his building. As he walked to the left side towards the entrance, his mother would start disappearing behind the two sliding glass doors. Omar either walked or rushed to the lift and then, if the lift wasn't already at the ground floor, he would start pressing the call button incessantly. Once in, he would look at the thin metallic step separating the ascending lift from the descending floors and would consider pressing it down to jam the lift. Unless he was with appreciative company, he wouldn't bother. Once the elevator stopped, he would push the heavy metallic door and walk to the right. He loved to press the buzzer and was often disappointed when his mother left the door open for him to waltz through. One time, though, he realised that he never ever had to be disappointed again; he could press it anyway, even if it was open. He tried it. He pressed the buzzer and walked right through. She didn't complain. She called him *Shaitan* in the warmest way possible. On subsequent occasions, every time he was called *Shaitan*, the word tickled its way through him from his head to his toes. By the time he found out it meant 'the devil', he felt only admiration for the guy.

From then on, it was facing an unopened door that left him wondering how to elicit a tickled response from his mother, but it quickly came to him: he simply had to ring it a few more times than necessary. Although he rarely got *Shaitan* to his face, her welcoming *yalla* had an appreciation of his mischief; receiving an impatient response was as rare as not seeing her on the balcony.

Into the hall and straight into the kitchen, and what's for lunch? He had a few favourite meals, and especially on those occasions when she had gone to extra trouble to get certain ingredients, she would not show him what was in the pot. She would rush him back to the sink just outside the kitchen, hoping that the whiff he got wasn't enough for him to make a guess, and then she would rush him again into sitting down at the right side of the dining table, as the top was reserved

13

for his father who might take another hour to arrive. She would sit in front of him, serve him slowly, and then follow every one of his bites while balancing herself so as not to rush him. She would always say that she was waiting for his father, and then wait for her reward: that he would finish his plate. The trophy was when he asked for more. On some occasions, he would ask for a tiny bit more because he knew from the way that she would spring up with extra life that it was making her happy. Asking for 'more but not too much more' was something that would take him years to learn.

After lunch, he could throw himself onto the couch in the living room or take himself to his bedroom. Whichever he chose, he would have to face his homework in the next half hour. After that, he could play with the 'blue demons' if he wanted to: do whatever he pleased. But there weren't any demons around. By the time Omar was seven, he was living with his mother and father, 53 and 67 years old respectively. There was an age difference of twelve years between him and the youngest of his two sisters and two brothers, who by then had all left home.

Facing his homework was not the worst thing in the world unless he had a quiz coming up. For those occasions, his mother would make sure that his neighbour, Karim, came over. Otherwise, it was between him and the desk in his room. He would get off the couch and drag himself with an affected bounce back through the dining room, past the sink, and through the corridor, passing a vacant room by now labelled the 'guestroom', past his parents' room, and then take a right to the 'last room', now fully his.

He would go through his assignments while occasionally raising his head to listen for his father at the door. When his father arrived, he would greet him as *Ackrout* — an ambiguous swear word, used affectionately, and for which he could never muster the meaning from anybody. His father would then rub his head and comment that Omar was growing up by the day. Unless his father has been involved in an incident that Omar could understand, as opposed to another negotiation with the farmers, it would be *yalla* back to the homework.

By the time Omar finished his homework, his father would be having his afternoon nap, which was sometimes interrupted by a particular neighbour who occasionally shouted at his son. The only time Omar's father came out to the balcony that was shared by Omar's room and his parents' room was to cut through his neighbour's shouting. One friendly but firm command — 'Stop, my fella' — and a crescendo that had been building for a while would suddenly stop in its track. When-ever that neighbour started shouting, Omar would be on the lookout, anticipating and hoping for his father's slow movements: shuffling for his slippers while trying to maintain eyes half shut, up to the handle bar of the balcony door, a slight un-oiled creek, and then the finishing line. He was fascinated by this process. Something outside his building could be stopped by something, somebody, in his apartment, and what was most intriguing was that he never saw that neighbour.

But for most of his homework, he would not be afforded this pro-cession; instead, he would move a hopeful gaze to the balcony and, if all was quiet, he would get up and proceed towards his mother and present himself as a problem that needed a solution.

His mother was usually either sitting by the glass door window in the dining room, watching the world go by, or on the same chair moved back to the dining table, organising the next day's meal. If it was an intricate meal she was preparing, she would ask him to help her, know-ing that she would have to redo his work; in any case, he never lasted long, and she would immediately present him with the second option: watching her. He would complain that it was boring. She would then go through all the things that could happen, such as his brother Amin dropping by and bringing something exciting, which she knew would be followed by 'Like what?' and then she would start negotiating as to what might interest him. Then, she might start to consider arranging for some of his wants to be met, but she had to spell out the limits. 'There is no *bouza* in winter. Are you crazy? Who would eat ice cream in the middle of the winter?' Even though he knew that some options were beyond her control, he would still go for the argument: 'We are not exactly exactly in the middle of winter; there *is* a tiny chance that they might have some from last year at the bottom of the fridge and they forgot about it. I like ice cream and if I eat ice cream in the winter, it's not going to make me crazy because I like ice cream and if I like it and I eat it, then it's better than eating something I don't like because my dad says that it is better to eat something you like if it's not good for you than eating something that you don't like that is better for you.' She would reserve her negative headshake until the end, then, with a smile to herself, she would say, 'Hefff, you've just made me dizzy.'

As these arguments dwindled, Omar would keep his ears out for any arguments from the neighbour, while negotiating the possible and the impossible. From then on, if it wasn't winter, he could hang in and out from the balcony, reporting on who might be coming into the building.

By six o'clock, his mother would say that there was 'something' on TV. 'Something' was 'anything' which was hopefully better than nothing. On random occasions of flicking between two channels, the Lebanese and the Syrian, Omar would come across something worth ringing Ziad about, and they would be all excited to be watching simultaneously in different cities. They would ring each other after the show and their mothers would be encouraging them to wrap up the call. On rare occasions, such as the time when Chou Chou was commemorated on a tribute, Aunt Sana rang and told Omar to turn the TV on quickly and said that Ziad would ring him after the show. On these occasions, they would both actively search for what made the adults think that they would be interested in it. With Chou Chou, they both tried very hard to find him funny. They couldn't understand what he meant although they could understand the words separately. They did see how he could be funny, though; it was his lightness, his hand gestures, and his nasally voice. Also how thin he was. Anybody who was thin was funny.

Aside from those occasions, the programmes they waited for were only a few: *The Muppet Show*, *The Love Boat*, and *The Bionic Man* on the Lebanese channel, and *Ghawar Al-Toucheh* on the Syrian Channel. *The Muppet Show* was sacred for Omar; he just admired how Kermit handled everybody with fairness even though he was the organiser of the show and could have been really pushy instead. How he put up with Piggy was beyond Omar. Gonzo he genuinely felt sorry for and wished that he succeeded with his cannon. Animal was funny but he rarely got the jokes of the two old men in the box. The stars on the show were more educational as he rarely recognised them.

The Love Boat he watched but didn't really want to enjoy because it was a bit sissy. However, both he and Ziad admitted to each other that they really did enjoy it.

The Bionic Man was the best because he could actually do all of these things for real. It was really possible if you had an injury to replace it with a better part of yourself if others, like the secret government, were willing to spend six million dollars on you! Lee Majors. Lee Majors. Leeeeee Majors. He could jump over school fences if he wanted to.

Later on, there was *The Bionic Woman*, which was a bit strange at first because she was so pretty, it didn't really matter all of these things that she did. Even that *tatta tatta tatta* music that came on kind of interfered a bit with looking at her face. They should have let others help her so that she wouldn't be upset or trying too hard, because she looked nicest when she was happy and smiled.

Ghawar Al-Toucheh was completely different because it was from their side of the world: a small guy with glasses and an overdone Syrian accent scheming around with the aid of a loyal-but-heavy-handed big tattooed guy with a Mexican moustache. They were funny, no matter what they did. The programme was under the small guy's name, even though it would have been no good without Abu Antar, the big guy.

There weren't enough channels to fight over. Omar sat through some of the Lebanese soaps that his mother loved but could not always make it through a full Egyptian one because they were just overloaded with sadness. His father wanted only the news and the political discussions. Friday night was the only night that everybody watched, waiting for the amateur stars either to make complete fools of themselves under the tongue of Omar's mother, or to be half good and be encouraged to move on with a dismissive *yalla* — there were exceptions, but these were exceptions.

In those days, it was a black and white television that was a big bulk of wooden furniture in the living room. Unless Ziad was visiting, there was nothing else for him in this room. On summer days, if he wasn't away with Ziad or one of his sisters, he would slouch on the couch right in front of the two sliding doors and let himself be melted by heat. But to Omar, that was doing nothing, and since there were no broadcasts in the afternoons, it was double nothing. Later on, he would get up and switch between sliding out to the balcony while crackling the plastic blinds and then sliding back in, through his mother's complaints that he was wrecking the blinds, until he reached his comics in his bedroom. To him, this apartment — his house in his building, as he saw it — was made of these three rooms: living room = TV + nothing; dining room = food; and the last room = his room. The rest were somewhere between accidentals and incidentals, so when his eldest brother, Khaled, who was studying medicine in England, visited with his girlfriend and gave her a house tour, Omar was quite taken aback by her reactions. At every juncture, smiles were followed by raised eyebrows and even opening of the mouth and, on one occasion, hand over opened mouth followed by a giggle and a quick look at everybody's reaction to see if it was OK to have laughed.

17

They started by opening the hall door to show her how thick that door was. Why was it that thick? Everybody looked at each other. 'Look!' Omar's father pointed at the quality of the wood.

'Oh.' An embarrassed smile, and then a nod of near understanding.

The clock in the reception room was from the Othmalli times, the Turks. Old, very old. The mirror over the cabinet supporting the phone? Everybody looked at each other. Omar's oldest brother raised his shoulder: 'It's a mirror, just a mirror.'

She nodded, then looked at it again and then smiled.

'What did she say? What did she say?' asked Omar.

'She likes it even though it's just a mirror.'

'Don't they have mirrors where she comes from?'

'To the right is the guest's reception room.' Khaled opened the two tall thin wooden doors but then closed them again, telling her that they would go around and end up in it. 'Go ahead, go ahead, show it to her now,' said Omar's mother with anticipated pride.

'No, no, later.' Khaled hated that room.

To the left was the corridor leading to the bedrooms, so it was to be skipped and left until the end, so forward past the wooden sliding door and the first thing on the left was the sink. 'That's for washing hands *before* eating meals.' Omar's father tried to piece together a few of his broken English words and explain one of the wise habits of the Islamic tradition of washing before eating, since the hands would be dirty, and, of course, also after. Omar's father then stopped and gently let a bit of silence cement his point of pride.

'In front and to the left is the kitchen.' Omar's mother smiled as she stood in front of a few pots — this was her territory. But before they went any further, she shrugged her shoulders and asked Khaled to explain that there was nothing to show here because everything produced was immediately taken into the dining room and then straight into their tummies. As Julie finished processing the translation, her eyes were growing sympathetically, until she looked at Omar's mother, oozing a mixture of affection and satisfaction as she extended her hand to pinch Khaled's cheek. 'Him,' she said, and then, moving her hand to rub Omar's hair: 'Like him.'

Khaled explained, 'She said I was like Omar once and because of her food I grew up to be me today.' Julie had understood.

Out of the kitchen, past a closed door, taking a left at the sink and into the dining room. On the mantelpiece, Khaled explained, were black wooden statues given by his mother's cousin as a souvenir of his time in Kenya, and the china in the glass cabinet also came from him from when he was in China. Omar looked at his mother, full of pride, and then at the china and then said under his breath, 'But we never use them.'

When Julie inquired about Omar's comment, a slight ruffle developed which led everybody past the two sliding wooden doors into the living room.

As it was still early spring, Easter to Julie, the Persian carpets had not yet been taken out for the summer. Persian — handwoven, intricately designed, best washed with tea (no sugar, of course), then hung on the balcony, dust beaten out of them with a big, strong, flat corn bat. The whole city did this within two weeks so it would be buzzing with different beatings, sometimes sounding as if they were echoing each other and other times as if they were competing for the firmest bang. And then, they all got rolled with white little preservative balls called Naftaline, and were put away until the next winter.

Above the carpet was a metallic chandelier also intricately designed, Julie's mouth opened in appreciation. To the right, the furniture was wooden but as they had been coming to the conclusion that it was time to change it, they were dismissive of it. Still, Julie noticed the curvy wooden handles.

Adjacent to the living room, past the two sliding doors that opened noisily but smoothly, was the guestroom. But before going in, Omar pointed to the long balcony that extended to both rooms. 'Later, later,' they said. He shrugged. The guestroom was boring; it was just the same as the living room but nobody got to go in it so it stayed shining, and there was uncomfortable furniture in it and there was stuff that was breakable and a silly painting of a small rotted boat that nobody would want to fish in in the first place. He followed them, and then went around them and waited by the two long, tall wooden doors to see Julie's face, surprised that they were back in the reception room, where they had started.

When they came out, Omar had to tell Khaled to tell Julie that they had done a full circle. As Julie smiled at Omar who was now standing in front of the starting point, she noticed that there was a closed door they had not opened for her. 'That's just the washing room,' said Khaled dismissively. But then his father added, 'Turkish toilet, old time.' Julie's mouth opened; she was interested. When they opened the door to show her a washing machine in front of a pearl-shaped hole in the marbled floor, she giggled. They told her that even though it was a modern building, they still installed these things for old-fashioned people; it was for doing kaka, but it had never been used since they had moved in. Omar's mother then smiled and told Khaled that if she liked this, she would like the *beideh*. 'The what?'

Back out, past the sink and a right turn into the bedroom's corridor; immediately in at the right was a cupboard built into the wall, where Omar's dead footballs lay alongside old screws, pliers and household junk. Then, to the left, a bathroom with a shower to an open marble floor and a drain under the sink — sorry, no *beideh* in this room — then, right behind it, was the maid's room. 'Sorry?' asked Julie. A helper in the house, who would be a live-in — somebody from the country — but they didn't have one at the time. In the old days, though, the family had gone through several to help raise the now-grown-up gang.

Just opposite was the guestroom, which had been prepared for Julie. Khaled, of course, would be sleeping in Omar's bed, while Omar slept on a mattress on the floor. Then, a few steps further to the left, was the parents' room, which was just that: the parents' room. Straight ahead and slightly to the right was the toilet adjacent to the last room, at the moment, but not fully, Omar's room. They opened the door and the curtains were closed to a shower that was open to a bath. In front of it was a sink opposite to a blue toilet, and, to the left of the toilet, by the door, was the *beideh*. It was slightly lower than the toilet, and a bit smaller, like a younger brother. 'When you are finished with your pooh-poohing,' Khaled translated, 'you move to it and you turn it on while adjusting the cold and hot water to your needs, and then, you use the toilet paper to dry yourself.'

That's where Julie opened her mouth, smiled, then opened her mouth wider, while trying to cover her smile with her hand. And then, when Omar's father said to her that she should try it later, that it would 'Tickle, Tickle!' she nodded and laughed almost hysterically while judging the reactions around her. Khaled smiled assuredly and told her that his father was the only one who used it, and that it was fine, that she should try it later, and nobody was going to be looking anyway.

Judging by her reaction, Omar wondered whether there were other things in the house that he hadn't fully appreciated. As he started his own tour in his head, his mother broke up the crowd: '*Yalla*, time for lunch.'

Child, now in physical form, between the earth and the sky ... having smiled, is now alive ... not just breathing ... but breathing with all life around him .... even with rocks ... harder to hear them breathe ... but they're on this planet, here, with him...

The voice from above told the child how with every breath taken in, every living being on this earth is taken in, shuffled and mixed with their insides, and out to mix a new universe...

The voice from below told the child how the stars are always reorganising themselves when no one is looking ... constantly ... in between the flickering of our eyes ... when we sleep, when we daydream and especially when we are celebrating, unaware of ourselves, the stars are moving, moving, moving about...

The Child looks around and multiplies himself upon himself upon the world...

Child looks around ... now shielded by concrete ... of man's own creation ... ants build themselves houses ... man, too ... and zebras and eagles and fish and monkeys and flies and mountains and sky, air, smoke, and the world moves between moon and sun..

Taste

Omar and Ziad had talked about this before: Pepsi was the best taste in the world, but since they both lived in the city, and since all city buildings were about seven storeys high, there was no way they could have their own Pepsi tree. Even if they convinced Ziad's aunts, who had houses with gardens in the country, it wouldn't really work. Ziad's dad said that Pepsi trees wouldn't survive in Lebanon, plus milking them would be too hard and would take too long; by the time the juice oozed out, it wouldn't have bubbles in it — they're added later on in the factory — so there was no point then if you couldn't pour it in a glass and quickly chase the froth.

Cool-Aid was more of a mystery. Uncle Jamal said that it was sneezed out in winter by a dragon that developed terrible colds; the sneezed-out debris would then be dried. But they didn't believe him. In any case, even if they could have had the source, Sana was convinced they would also need a sugar factory since it took about a ton and a half every time she made it. If they could have it, though, it would be the purple flavour; the rest they could give away to other kids in the world.

The love for Pepsi and Cool-Aid was not shared by others, though, and the divide between children and adults was made very clear through certain foods. Both Omar and Ziad were told separately that when they grew older, they would develop a taste for olives, but for now they would be bitter. Both reacted defensively by saying that they were never, ever, ever going to like them — sometimes adults acted as if they knew everything that was going to happen, and that was definitely not true.

What they did have in common was Arabic sweets. They didn't know anybody who didn't have at least one favourite sweet, but while everybody automatically knew what to order, Ziad and Omar had to re-ask for translations: 'Girl's twirl' was very thin, like hair, and came like a white ball, and it was dry, and it was sweet; 'Ladies' thighs' described crunchy thin pastry, dipped in syrup, and then with pistachios crushed in, and filled with 'ashta', a thin film developed on the surface of boiled milk which was in most sweets ordered through the

22

specialist sweet shops. The home-made ones also needed figuring out: 'Moon under the clouds' was made from milk and rice; 'Boiled' didn't make sense because all milk preparations needed boiling; still, it was the one with cinnamon.

Whether or not a dessert or a meal took a lot of effort to prepare, food was to be respected. Omar and Ziad could say '*Tfeh*,' the expression of 'spitting', to communicate their distaste about anything they wanted to, but not about food, especially not in the company of food. They had heard their parents say *tfeh* about certain places because they were unhygienic, and a few times under their breath when served in certain restaurants. When spotted by either Omar or Ziad, this would be an occasion for 'How come you can say it and I can't?' which would be smiled off by the grown-ups with half an admission of having let themselves down. But they had never heard their parents say *tfeh* in their own homes about their own food, unless it was a takeaway delivery and had not yet been taken in and treated as part of the house; such deliveries were inspected at the door and the verdict was delivered with a flurry of gestures: '*Yalla, yalla, yalla*; return this straightaway.'

Omar rarely got a *tfeh* directly aimed at him, unless it was in jest, and it usually alluded to something he had done rather than shaming his core. He was more of a *Tayyeb* (tasty), which was usually the conclusion of any of his family when they kissed or squeezed him. He would hear the expression to describe people as humble and down to earth, but when used on him, it was a measure of his cuteness. Amin, the younger of his two brothers, who was studying law in Beirut, would often tell him that the government was thinking of bringing in laws to control levels of cuteness; otherwise the nation could be in danger of chaos caused by distraction, and Omar should definitely be hidden when the law came in.

Omar's 'tastiness' was so established in the family that he regularly attempted to expand on his range; he was definitely sweet, most commonly described as made from 'honey', but he often suggested his own preferences — 'ketchup?' No, no, no. He was told that ketchup came in bottles; it was junk, whereas honey was mentioned in the Koran: 'rivers of honey'. 'Salty?' Hmm ... not quite; actually, Omar was so tasty that he could be eaten *without* salt. 'Bitter?' Ooooh, no way, God forbid! 'Bitter' was one of the worst descriptions; it was the most basic rejection of any taste — children shook their heads and scrunched their eyes in distaste when given something that was bitter. 'Bitter' was almost as bad as 'no taste'. He had heard some unfortunate people described as 'not having taste'. The only reason these people were not flicked like flies off the edge of the earth was out of politeness — a social duty. These people were not mean; they just didn't have character. This was not something Omar ever had to worry about.

'Not having taste' was also the worst verdict that could be declared about a meal. Omar noticed that when his family members described anything edible as 'tasteless', it was a reason not to continue eating it — with the exception of Amin who often took a bite of a fruit, or a dessert, and then came back to nibble on it, giving the same conclusion with every bite. It was the joke of the family when he did this, and while he smiled through this process, for him it was more than a joke. He really did try to push himself to like a dessert despite his initial reaction. Omar laughed fondly when his brother was described as having a 'sweet tooth' and it was remarked that it was a wonder he wasn't 'as fat as a barrel'.

Still, whether 'tasty', 'distasteful', or 'having no taste', food was to be respected, and the closer it came from the earth, the more respect it traditionally received, but whenever Omar and Ziad got together, these definitions had to be re-explained. The fact that the same oranges weren't ripe was still no reason for them to be used as soccer balls on the long balcony stretch. Even when the food had rotted, it was still to be dispensed with respectfully, and rotten grapes should not be thrown at speeding taxis. Exploding crisp bags were more of a dilemma because they had been processed through so many chemicals and it was harder to condemn such an event without smiling, but still, crisps originally come from potatoes, so it wasn't really on, although with packaged western foods, reading the ingredients often led to head scratching. Once, when Omar's sister read a number as an ingredient, the whole family looked at each other. It was a limit that had been pushed beyond the values they had comfortably ingested. Omar and Ziad rejoiced at being allowed to destroy a present of a small box of breakfast Rice Krispies that looked and tasted nothing like rice. Each little piece died a slow death and the audibility of its death was measured with precision: under feet with no socks made least noise; with socks on, they made more noise; then with sneakers; and the noisiest deaths were under adult shoes which had harder soles.

The child looked around in his world and from his house he saw trees and bees, honey and cheese, clouds sun and moon, mountains land and sea, and birds, dogs, some cats, a few flies, small birds and big birds...

... life, being lived...

... he reached out with his hand, cut a cloud in half, reached out with the other hand, cut an orange in half...

... on its own, a cloud tasted grey, orange orange, cloud and an orange tasted like a bit of the sun mixed with the surface of the sea on a calm day; shiny reflecting yellow but with the shininess feeling different, maybe fluffy...

The world is here — the child heard a voice inside him telling him of descriptions of himself in the world and of the world when taken in...

Smells

It was amazing how some things didn't smell. Whenever Omar fell and hurt one of his knees or scraped his skin, his mother would insist that he put some Mercurochrome on his wound so that it wouldn't get infected. He loved it because it was painless and it usually followed Spierto, a white spirit that did sting and had to be accompanied by a lot of blowing. But Mercurochrome was like the icing on the cake; it was dark red and it stained him like an American Indian. Considering how deeply it stained, and the very strong and admirable name it had, like a Comic Hero, it amazed Omar how it didn't smell. Well, it had a tiny smell, but it didn't really represent it — considering its potency, it could have had a much stronger smell. Instead, it was like Superman who had so many powers and could have been arrogant if he wanted to, but he wasn't.

Omar was told that the Phoenicians had discovered dye. Lebanese people who were originally Phoenicians had also invented numbers and then money and lots of other stuff that the Western world now benefited from without acknowledgement. Omar wondered whether deep inside, Superman, who was an American, knew this and was a bit grateful, even just every now and then, as he flew with his red cape flickering in the sky. He wasn't so sure about Batman. Batman couldn't fly; he had to drive his mobile and it would have been more difficult to think about other things when he had to concentrate on driving and at the same time answer all of Robin's questions.

Having gone through all his comic heroes, he went back to wondering about all the things that could have smelled if they had wanted to. Honey was mentioned in the Koran and, whenever Omar was sick, his mother would make sure he took plenty of honey because it was 'energy'; if it had wanted to, it could have had a really bad smell since it was a medicine and also since it came out of bees' bums — but God must have intervened. He wouldn't be wiping each bee every time it poohed its honey even though He could be in more than one place at the same time — if God was to do that, He would be wiping until the end of time and that was too much work because he had other things

26

to look after like starving children in Africa. God must have come up with a solution and Omar couldn't figure it out, but like many, many things, and especially things that directly had something to do with God, it was mysterious. He was advised that these things were not for figuring out, but more for being marvelled at.

So, apple and honey gave him a good kick to get better, and then at night, to help shift a cough, he would have Vicks rubbed all over his chest and throat. 'Shouldn't it be rubbed on the inside of my throat to really, really help?' he asked. When his mother was worried about him, she didn't handle his joking as well but on one occasion, when his cough was particularly coarse, she felt for him, so she paused, and answered him back: 'OK, maybe I'll make you a Vicks sandwich.'

He was delighted with her answer. 'I'll put honey in it as well; then I'll have double energy.'

'You won't sleep all night; you'll be dancing like the blue demons.'

Vicks smelled. It was a gentle smell. It came in tubes as well, and when his nose was really congested, his mother would try to prevent him from overusing it, 'You're not supposed to shove it all the way up your nose; it'll come out of your ear.' He couldn't figure out how he couldn't smell it when he was putting it directly in his nose, but when rubbed on his chest, it would last all night. He couldn't figure out how it worked either; it shifted things somehow, in some invisible way. It was another thing to marvel at. Vicks was a friend. Just like antibiotics, except that they were like heavy-duty friends that were meant to be called on only in serious situations. And they didn't smell at all, not even one bit; yet they did their job so well, just like secret agents.

When he was sick was the only time Omar was allowed to smell. It was mainly his hair that his mother sniffed, turning away and throwing out an exaggerated puff. 'You stink like the garbage collectors.'

When his black soft hair grew long, it curled. 'Amin says that I should let it grow until it's like the black basketball players in America and then I could store stuff in my head. He says that's where they keep their car keys.'

'Your brother would let you get away with anything; if only he could see all the things you do get up to.' No matter how long, though, if he was sick, he was to wait because having a shower would take energy from him. But it didn't bother him too much because he could never twist his head enough to be able to smell his hair.

When he got better, he was shifted into the bathroom in a ceremony that ritualised the end of his sickness. Coming out of the shower was a decisive moment of losing the privileged power where just the mere mention of a fancy would have been enough to have his mother jumping to fulfil his needs. 'You treat him like he's dying; you never treated *us* like that,' his sisters would say if they were visiting. 'Look at him; there's nothing wrong with him; he's just playing you.' And on occasion he did try to prolong his moment; he would shout, 'Is this the right shampoo? I think it's for old people.' It was the one his father liked.

After a long day of checking the crops at the outskirts of the city, his father would be sweaty, but Omar was to be discreet about it because his father preferred to have his lunch first, and then his nap, and then his news, and then his dinner, and then, as he put it, to soften him like a boiled potato, he would take a hot shower. By then, Omar would have long been in bed and he never remembered to tell his dad directly that there were other shampoos that he tried when he visited Ziad. It was his mother who did the liaising, and the messages went back and forward: 'Tell him that we need to get rid of this historic shampoo'; 'Tell the clove of garlic to stop philosophising'; 'Tell Mussolini to try new things'; 'Tell him that we are all at his service'...

After Omar had his shower, whether he had been sick or not, he would be received like a new person. It was another occasion for him to be kissed and he would be called over to be received like a present coming out of its wrappings. Kisses would be planted on him and the words pronounced: 'You smell like the Messekk!' He was being compared to a flower that opened in the spring but he never bothered to ask to smell a real Messekk. No matter how beautiful it smelled, it wasn't going to live up to the strength of the kisses he received — as Amin would say, 'Damn it, Messekk doesn't have a chance with you.' When they got out of the shower, his mother and father and other adults never gave each other the treatment he received.

Omar's parents took showers to clean themselves because people weren't supposed to smell of the beautiful things they loved. Omar's favourite smell was when his mother mixed minced meat with coriander, plastered it on long metal skewers and then put them over hot coal on the kitchen's balcony. 'Stand away, stand away,' she would warn. 'I don't want to have to change your clothes in the middle of the day.' Omar noticed that everybody loved that smell, and everybody loved the taste, but they weren't meant to smell of it. When all the beautiful foods were done with, it was time to say goodbye to them; the remains were packed firmly into plastic bags, and brought out through the hall door and then either down or up the stairs to the halfway point between floors. There, to the left side, the metallic hatch was opened, plastic bags put in, and you could hear them going all the way down, one by one. One time, Omar stuck his head in; he couldn't see a thing, but it was the foulest smell he could ever smell. He was stunned by it; all of those smells were so beautiful when they were in his house but now that they had been sent to meet lots of other beautiful smells, they all turned ugly.

He took his dilemma to his mother but she wouldn't entertain any discussion, her main aim being to dissuade him from ever again sticking his head in. 'This is the dirtiest most unhygienic thing you can ever do; you can catch diseases. The bottom is probably full of rats, and what if somebody was throwing their garbage from the floor above? It would hit you on the head; is that how you want to die?'

The only food that Omar was allowed to smell of was orange skin. On lazy afternoons, he would agree to eat an orange only if his mother was willing to take the time to peel it carefully with a knife, from top to bottom, without breaking her flow. What he would have then was a monkey's tail. Having held it up, smiling, he would bounce it gently at first. Eventually, when it broke, he would cut the tail into smaller sections and, while holding his hand against the window light, he would squeeze. Against a background of floating dust particles, a spray of tiny little wet bubbles would emit from the orange skin. He did it again and again, watching with tickled delight as the particles shot out and then fell down and disappeared. It was just like fireworks, except it was much, much smaller, and it was indoors, and it came from an orange, and it was *his* doing. To be hit by the wet bubbles was a good thing. His mother had told him that the Arab Bedouins who lived outdoors would use the orange skin as a way of cleansing their hands of oily foods. It was the only food that you could clean your hands with. That smell, was OK.

One day, you'll be able to smell the space between the clouds and the ground, although you might not know how you do it, or that you are doing it.

One day, you'll smell others' feelings without having to talk to them.

One day, you'll be able to blink and smell your insides in relation to the world outside although you might have come to think you are separate.

And one day, if you remember to smell from your chest, you'll be able to inhale the roots of a rock in a wall, see where it came from and even talk to the sea it once slept next to,

but soon,
soon you'll forget that all of this:
that in and out,
above and below,
and the space between you and me,
is you.

Soon you'll drift into sleep, and when you wake up, you'll start naming names, thinking thoughts ... squaring circles ... drawing lines away from your centre, as far as possible, hoping that you and the infinite can be contained.

Soon you'll forget, and you'll wake up in a world among your others, most of whom are unable to bear their own wonder.

Family

Throughout the year, Omar's sisters and his brother, Amin, would visit sporadically, taking trips during the breaks in their college year in Beirut, to replenish their souls with some home food, to touch base, or to 'let the head settle', as Omar's mother put it. Most visits were planned not to coincide with the visits of the others. It wasn't that they were avoiding meeting, for they naturally kept in contact as well as being prodded by their mother to keep an eye on each other should any of them become ill. If it happened that one of them was sick and another was visiting, the visitor would have to carry extra food back. 'Extra food for the sick?' the carrier would complain. 'It's not like somebody is dying in some back alley.' But eventually they would calm down and try to assure their mother that the dying would be saved. And eventually they would penetrate through her admittedly unreasonable but justifiable motherly instincts — but not without carrying the extras.

For festivities, however, with the exception of Khaled, the whole family would gather in Tripoli. During those moments when the conversation buzzed through double and sometimes triple crossings of related disparate topics, where an outcome was not going to be achieved, and, if it were, it wasn't going to matter, Omar's mother would get tearful. Nobody really complained that she was ruining a beautiful nonsensical moment, for they knew that it was her sense of unity that was incomplete. '*We're* here,' they would say. but they did tease her. 'Poor Khaled, like a squatter in England.'

'A squatter?' and they would have to restrain themselves.

The only reason Amin was studying in a national university instead of the expensive American University in Beirut where his sisters were was that the family funds had been depleted, which was also why Zeina and Laila were studying in Lebanon instead of somewhere 'outside', like London or Paris. They would tease their mother, and when one of them wavered as they tried to hold on to their 'don't get me started' stance, a look from one of the others was enough to remind them that ultimately it was their mother's heart that was on display, and for that

31

they had to restrain themselves. It was promised that, should they later have financial difficulties in finishing their college education, their eldest brother would help. Omar's case was not up for another ten years, but when the time came, Khaled was to take most of the responsibility, and if the rest were working and producing more than two pennies, they would chip in as well. With this issue tingling, hanging, rarely boiling under the surface, eventually their mother would rise out of her longing and throw them a 'Don't tell me you don't miss him too', and their teasing would scatter like dogs tired of a useless fight.

After a few moments of silent acknowledgement, the conversation would pick up into old and new topics, mixing the mundane with the half serious, taking routes and detours, often alluding in jest to the parents' carnal life. It would be a quick stop with a throwaway comment advising them not to have any more children and then, just to make sure that Omar was not extracting any negative interpretations, he would be described as 'the most beautiful mistake in the world'. It took him years to figure that one out, and, although he did not comprehend it at the time, it did give him the intended warm security of assurance.

Amin, the youngest of Omar's siblings, gave him nothing but praise. 'He could slay half the city and you'd still be OK with him,' the rest would often comment. Amin would add, 'And once I graduate, I would defend him too.'

'So that he could finish off the rest of the city?' they would push him sarcastically.

But he had no limit. 'Yeah,' he would say. 'And get you too.' And they would resign, smiling.

Zeina, the next one up, kissed him like he was a precious vase, or so Amin would comment. 'What are you?' she'd ask. 'His police?'

'Please don't change the subject; this is an observation about how everybody around you is an object.'

'A subject, not an object,' she would proudly correct him. Zeina was studying Sociology, and, according to Amin, she carried herself like a judging peacock, proud and cynical.

Laila was in the process of graduating as a pharmacist. She would be tired and quiet. When the family got together, they would jokingly ask her whether she had found the medicine that could perk her up. She would smile back. She fought with no one, and when she arrived, she asked everybody how they were. Once her mother had offloaded all

32

her concerns on Laila, and Laila had then assured her dad that she was really fine, she would gently ask Omar to come and sit next to her on the sofa and tell her every little detail of every little and big thing that passed through his life.

It was only on big occasions that Khaled flew over from London. For the rest of the time, it was his coming that was the occasion. He could stay for only one week, two at the most, and did all the extended family visits. 'Should've been a politician,' Amin would comment. 'Or a Sheikh,' Zeina would add, but Khaled never answered back, just held himself as if he had to do what he had to do.

With all the snide remarks and sarcasm that occasionally flew between his brothers and sisters, Omar was never a target. With visits to extended family members, Omar could not figure out why some-times his mother would come back angry and at other times casual. Omar was received in the same way on all these visits: *Oh look how much he's grown! Do you like school? Oh my, oh my, you're almost a man. Here, take some sweets.* On being offered anything on a visit, Omar was supposed to refuse. They would then insist; he would refuse; they would insist; and then his mother would say, 'It's OK, Omar. We're not at a stranger's house.' He would take one sweet; they would say to take more; he would say it was OK, he had enough; they would say not to be ridiculous and, if his mother hadn't said anything, he would eye her for help. 'Omar, take one more. It's OK'. 'Why one more? Let him take more!' Once they addressed each other, Omar would just sit in his chair and then he was either lumbered with more sweets or his mother would have negotiated him out of more sweets. At that stage, it was more important for him to be out of it — his mother had made him promise never to show her up as greedy because any sweets they offered, no matter how glittery the covering, she would get him later. 'He is *sooo* polite, and so mannerly,' they would say.

'Ah yes, he is.' His mother would shrug off the comment while retaining her pride, and then add, 'You should see him at home; he's a monkey.'

At home, visitors wouldn't get to witness his full monkey-ness — only a glimpse of it as he ran when called to present himself for a few minutes. On such occasions, he would get all the comments about the speed of his growing up minus the sweet negotiation. That was for him to witness the guests going through, and if they had a child with them, they would receive the full negotiation process before being released to play with him. Once the visitors were gone, his mother would be on the phone to her sister, Sana, or one of her daughters, and would go through some of the comments. It had to be explained to him that some of the comments were 'off', but she wouldn't go into further detail: 'You wouldn't understand; you're too young.' Still, on some occasions, he listened and tried to figure out what the problem was, but it usually took about five minutes to get the gist of the argument and he became content in not 'understanding'.

The only place where there was nothing to understand, and no negotiation about sweets, was his grandmother's. 'Take them all,' his mother's mother would say. He had a choice: he could if he wanted to. But his mother would suggest, 'Take as much as you feel like taking.' And he would take a few. It would have been too much work for Omar to take them all; he'd be stuck with them. He wouldn't have time to eat them all, and when he got home, they'd just have to go into the guests' sweet bowl in the guests' reception room, where they would join the rest of the sweets. Any special and rare sweets that his grandmother might have would be given to his mother in a plastic bag, and it was for her to carry and not for him to worry about.

There wasn't much to do at his grandmother's house but he really enjoyed the visits. It took a few years before somebody actually said why those visits felt 'nice' while the others were just different: 'There's great atmosphere in her house.' It didn't explain anything, but it made sense to Omar. What he did know so well inside him was that whatever she said to him, she meant; whenever she talked to him, she talked to *him* and not *about him in front of his mother*, and the easiest thing for Omar was that in her company, he didn't feel smaller. If he wanted, he could walk around the house, go into dark rooms with very old things that were so uninteresting they were dead, and from his earliest days, he would walk in aware that, although he would never do it, he could break something, say it was an accident, and nobody would be really upset with him. He knew that his grandmother would say that it was OK, that nothing lives forever and would tell him not to worry about it, clean it up, offer him more sweats, smile at him, tell his mother it was OK and then go back to the conversation. And it would all be true. It would be the same as just before he had broken the thing. It was easy.

Towards the end of the visit, his mother would ask her mother if she would come home with her for a short stay but she would always refuse. She lived in a flat in an area called Ibbeh on a hillside just above the centre of Tripoli. Grandfather had died when Omar was four-and-a-half years old and a neighbour kept her company. She enjoyed her house, she said, and her things were here. 'He really, really loved you,' she would say to Omar. 'If he was here today, he would be dying to see you.'

The times when she did come back with Omar and his mother for a week or two were already arranged beforehand. If she was sick, she would be pressurised to come down and stay with them — it would be stressed that especially now that Grandfather was gone, she was free to enjoy a change of scenery. It took persuasion from Omar's mother that nobody was going to be inconvenienced and that they really would love to have her. She would be placed on the soft couch for she was as skinny as Gandhi, and even sat the Indian way, just like him. She had asthma and she smoked, and she always sprinkled extra salt on her food, even though the doctor told her that it would raise her blood pressure. Salt was the main thing Omar felt he had in common with her. When she visited, whenever his mother automatically commented that he was putting too much salt on his food, his grandmother would tell her to leave the boy alone and immediately the attention would be taken off him and she would be defending herself about her own health. Omar would silently appreciate the sacrifice and enjoy his meal in peace. When he had finished his meal, he would wait until his mother was not looking and then pour some salt into his hand and take it to his grandmother who would draw out a handkerchief to put it in, hide it under her legs, and then give him a nod of mutual understanding.

'She has never harmed a soul in her life,' his mother would say, and everybody agreed. She would recount stories from when the family lived near her house — how Khaled would come to her during his school break-time and she would give him money and tell him not to tell his parents; how she used to sew Zeina's school dress because she was a real rascal and always got herself in trouble; how Laila was really quiet all along and what a sweet gentle soul she still was; and how Amin always stood up for his friends without being a troublemaker. Her stories revolved around shielding Omar's brothers and sisters from their parents' reactions when they were in trouble. It was hard to want to upset his grandmother, but when Zeina visited, he couldn't help being fuelled by her spark.

Grandmother said that the cinema had been invented in Egypt — at this comment, Zeina and Omar would snigger but would not argue with her, out of an obligation to appear respectful. She would end up shrugging them off for being ignorant and then become irritated with their arrogance. Zeina had a way of rising her grandmother and Omar's eyes perked up when she put things in a such a way that, although she was still smiling, she also knew that she was going to irk her grandmother. She would say things like: 'We all know that...'; 'I'm not saying you're wrong, but the fact is...'; 'Grandmother, let me tell you something....' Omar wasn't sure how these words worked but he developed an ear for them and kept on measuring the effect of each. What was even more potent was if Omar used them himself right after Zeina did; the first time he did that, he knew that he was protecting himself, since on the surface he was appearing to do what his older sister had just done and so he should not get a worse reaction; in the worst case, he could hide behind the age difference and play at not knowing exactly what he was saying — he was merely copying his sister because it sounded good. With most of these topics, it was measured teasing, and since Grandmother was so peaceful, it was fun to rise her, fun to push her into being somebody else — somebody like everybody else they know, who when pushed would get dirty — but she never did. At her most irritated, she would blatantly tell them that they had just raised her blood pressure, and, in not losing her temper, she would have proven her sweetness.

The only topic where she could be taken to her edge was religion. She was a holy woman, the only one they really respected as having a real relationship with God. This was her defining grace and her most precious topic, so precious that even Zeina would not dare approach. But Omar could. Omar knew that he was 'still only a kid', 'ignorant', and so it was justifiable to ask ignorant questions. What would start as genuine curiosity — 'Where does God come from?' — would end up being described as blasphemous, and since he wasn't getting any satisfactory answers, he would soon forget about trying to learn and move on to refining his skills in winding her up. 'OK, OK, if God was never born, and cannot die, and has no brothers or sisters, then who's going to entertain him?' 'What does he look like?' 'If he is so strong, then why doesn't he crush the devil?' The one question that he could always come back to was: 'But I still don't understand; how did he get here?' While it was true that Omar did not understand, by then it was way beyond the point. Grandmother's blood pressure would be up but it would have been hard to shrug off a boy's attempt to learn. Omar's mother would tell him not to ask any more questions but even she enjoyed seeing him being devious without being disrespectful. It was an art that was hard for anybody to achieve in any area and Omar was slowly being labelled 'crafty when he wants to be'.

Gandhi would be shaking. Without being too obvious, Omar would take on all the grandiose postures of a pompous philosopher: 'If it is so perfect and tied up, then how come it can't be explained?' But still, with all her sparked reactions, she wouldn't say anything directly shaming, and if she did, it would have no lasting venom — for that she would have had to fall from the level of saint and her landing ground was still higher than that of all the whole family put together.

Being a Moslem meant that one should pray five times a day, wash hands and face and feet before each praying and fast for the whole month of Ramadan — no food, no water, except at night, of course. Everybody else in the family skipped the daily prayers, and Omar's father only occasionally checked out the Mosque speeches on Fridays, but all fasted for the month of Ramadan. Grandma prayed every day of her life, and when she had grown too old to be getting up, she would pray in the special sitting position designed for sick and handicapped people. She persisted through all her life despite being married to Grandpa.

Omar was told that *Jiddo*, as grandfathers were called, did not worry about the end. He reckoned that 'it was all right', as if he had a special arrangement with God. 'Do you not remember Jiddo?' Omar remembered only the slobbery wet kisses. Towards the end of his life, Jiddo's chest was filled with cancer; every time he coughed, his lungs rattled. He had been smoking since he was a kid. His father died when he was young and he had to raise his brothers and sisters and that's why he smoked *aaaaalll* his life — Omar remembered all of that. For years, he believed that Jiddo's chest was filled with the little cancer insects and, at the end, they burst his lungs. Whenever there was a great film on, Amin would take Omar to the cinema, the advertising slides would come on before the film and one of them warned against the dangers of smoking — it had a little nasty bug with eight legs sitting next to words that were read out to Omar, and the whole slide just imprinted itself on Omar's mind. It was that bug, with zillions of others like him, that had made Jiddo pay for his smoking.

He didn't remember feeling sad when his grandfather died. All the women dressed in black, and the visiting men smoked and drank thick scalding-hot Turkish coffee. They were received in separate rooms in Grandma's house and nobody smiled in the beginning. Some women would occasionally cry but Omar's mother and her sisters cried only with each other after the visitors had gone. He dreamt of his grandfather three days later, and the dream was so strong that Omar wondered whether his grandfather had really died or whether he was somewhere else besides nowhere. People who did good in life would go to Heaven; people who did bad would go to Hell and burn again and again, forever. God counted everything. In the beginning, a child would be ignorant and could do ignorant things, and the impression was that Omar still had some ignorance leeway, but eventually he was going to be accountable for every little thing and, at the end, a little bit after death, all his good things would be put against all his bad things and the calculations would tell which way he was going. However, if a non-believer repented just before death and believed in God and became a Moslem, he would be allowed in Heaven. Now, Omar couldn't figure out how a believer could do good all his life and if he renounced God at the end, he wouldn't be allowed into Heaven. More confusing still, if a believer acted good all his life, then renounced God, didn't do that much bad stuff, and then went back to being a believer again, how come he was not allowed to come back and be accepted like a non-believer who wanted to change?

In all of this it was hard to figure whether Grandfather was going to make it to Heaven. They said that he shouldn't go to Hell but they were also not sure about Heaven. They said he would, but they didn't seem very affirmative about it. Grandfather never seemed to worry about it, they said, and that was worrying: it wasn't that he did a lot of bad stuff; it was that he wasn't scared of God. 'Maybe he wasn't scared of God because he knew he had done more good stuff than bad stuff.' Not quite; they feared for his casual attitude more than the calculations: his attitude could skew the whole thing into his being a non-believer and that would put all his good-doing in a different category. That last bit, whether a non-believer good-doer was better than a not-as-good-believer was not agreed upon by everybody. So maybe Grandfather would be spending extra time in Purgatory while all these calculations were being made. He would probably be sitting down smoking in the waiting area, but without the rattle in the chest, because when a person dies, all the ailments go away.

38

Grandfather was the last of the real old Makram family. Well, there were other Makram men left but they didn't carry themselves like Jiddo did. In the old days, when they owned more land, all the farmers would bow their heads, calling him, '*Beik, beik*' whenever he visited. Omar should be *verrrry* proud of being a Makram and if they had more land, Omar too would have grown up to be bowed to without having to do much, just for being a Makram. Omar wasn't so sure about the pride thing, though — he would prefer if the farmers dropped the bowing thing and if all would play with marbles instead. Later on, they could eat together and compare the most perfect orange monkey tails and then wash their hands with them and then do some more stuff.

'No, no, no, no. The Makram family is really old; it goes all the way back to Mohammad's days.' If you traced Grandfather's father's father's father's father and about twenty more fathers, you would end up with the second cousin of Mohammad, and that was extra super special and double reason to be proud of being a Makram. 'Proud' basically meant that Omar could feel that he has more of something than somebody else, or that he was just better than somebody else. What that 'something' was, Omar couldn't figure out and he wasn't so sure if he wanted to have it. Plus, if you traced a person's father's father's father's fathers all the way, you'd end up with Adam, and so originally everybody started from the same place. In any case, Omar wasn't so sure about having more of something which he didn't start with but was given to him because his grandfather's fathers had it and somebody else didn't have it just because his grandfather's fathers didn't have it, even if everybody, including the person who didn't have it, was saying that this was the way things were and that he really did have it and that it was his for the rest of his life. Omar didn't really want it.

the child looked around and saw flesh like his
eyes and faces like his looking at others and others like him;
would have thought everybody is looking at the same thing —
should see ourselves when we look at each other

not so, apples and oranges are different,
even oranges and oranges are different,
everybody has eyes, and eyes are for the seeing,
but eyes are different sizes, colours, and shapes,
not even the left eye like the right

some babies are born smiling, some shouting,
that's how it is, that's how it is,
and not all clouds are friends,
the sea is salty but not all parts of it so clear
one spot warm, one spot cold ... the same sea...

Sounds

Beebeep bebebeep beepbebebeep! Omar would lean on the balcony rail and admire the finesse of taxi drivers. Amin would often point, saying, 'Look, they have absolutely no reason in the world to beep, but they do.'

On one occasion, when Amin had come up to Tripoli in a friend's car, he let Omar beep the horn. It was one big sound even for a small car, and it felt like the whole world heard it and it came out in one chunk, so how did the taxi drivers do it? They all made different sounds even though it sounded as if they had the same horns. 'Experts, they're experts,' Amin replied, laughing sarcastically while shaking his head in wonder. Omar looked at him to explain what he was thinking.

'Well, they're not meant to become experts on beeping. A horn is just to warn somebody to get out of your way, you know; it's meant to be for emergencies.' Wow, and they had taken the time to become experts; they must be special people!

While still leaning on the rail, Omar would see carts being pushed slowly and lethargically with incomprehensible musical shouts coming out of the men's mouths. If it was morning, then it was mainly vegetables that they were selling; in the afternoon, it was more likely to be fruits. To amuse himself, Omar would often go in and ask his mother what it was that they were shouting about. Most of the time, even after she had told him directly what they were saying, Omar would need to take some time to decipher how the sound had mutated into what he was hearing. Sometimes his mother couldn't figure it out either and she would have to come out to the balcony and laugh in amusement at the discovery. One of the few sounds that he was able to figure out for himself did not make sense to him, 'Mama, what does *On the kniiiiiiiife you melon* mean?'

'You point out which red melon you want, or you go down to him, and he cuts it. If it is white and not red, it's not good, so you don't take it.'

Omar thought about it. 'But how does he know which ones are going to come out red?'

'He doesn't; that's why you point and then he cuts it.'

41

'And what happens then?'

'Well, he can cut you another one and, if it's red, then you take it.'

'And if it's not?'

'Then you don't take it. What? You want to get stuck with it?'

'But then he would have all these cut melons!'

'Do *you* want to take them?'

It didn't sound very fair to Omar, even though, like his mother had said, it was the vendor who was making the offer. They looked poor. They *were* poor, and they looked as if they pushed these carts all day.

At dusk, he would hear '*Kaaaaaak … kaaaak ya kaaaaak*'. There were two types of *ka'k*: a round, hollow, bready, oval shape, covered in sesame; and a smaller, circular, rich bread with four holes in it. For both, you'd use *semm'a*, a red herb, sprinkled on it. The smaller *ka'k* could also be filled with cheese, but Omar's mother dismissed all meats and dairy products sold on the street. He would ask his mother's permission first, and then he would wave to the vendor, or she would make a *sssssst* sound and the vendor would look up and stop. Omar would take the elevator and his mother would watch him stand while the vendor heated a *ka'k* on the coal. When Omar came in, she inspected it for freshness and then told him to go ahead. They'd sit on the balcony and he'd eat his bread. It was rare for her to ask for one for herself. 'No, no, you get yourself one,' she would say as if the vendor had only one left. Omar would ask her again and she would say that really, she didn't feel like one, that her stomach was blocked.

Later, the TV would be turned on, and if cartoons came on, Omar would turn up the volume. Especially if she wasn't watching it with him, his mother would ask him to lower it. '*Yeyyyy*, what's going on with all this racket?' she would say. Omar would beg her to watch *Tom and Jerry* with him but she could never get into them. 'Is this a rabbit?' she would ask.

'It's Bugs Bunny.'

'Baaaggs Bannie — what kind of a name is that?'

If anything, she liked Tweety. He hated Tweety. Tweety was annoying and Sylvester shouldn't take his time; once he caught her, he should just eat her and get it done with. But his favourites were Heckle and Jeckle, two magpies. Their voices, the way they talked when they talked, the way they … he couldn't explain it; he just liked them.

Cartoons were never announced; they were just fill-ins between shows if a programme finished early or they had run out of ads.

If Grandma was staying, he could never enjoy cartoons, and would definitely have to turn the volume down. And then she would be making comments that all that stuff couldn't happen. No matter how many times he told her that of course it couldn't happen, it wouldn't be enough for her just to accept them and watch with him. She made comments on cartoons and every other programme that wasn't in Arabic. 'Americans don't love each other,' she would say.

'Why? Why?'

'Because they're always saying "*I Love You*".'

'Doesn't that mean that they love each other?'

'No, no, no, no. If they loved each other for real, they wouldn't need to say it every time. All they say is "*I love you*" and "*I'm sorry*". "*I love you, I'm sorry.*" They say it like water; it just comes out of their mouths for every little thing. How could it have meaning?'

'*Yalla*, your bed time,' he would eventually hear. It was a curse he had to negotiate. On Friday nights, it wasn't so bad, especially if his sisters had just come in from Beirut. They'd be caught up in settling for the Friday-night talent show where they would tear the participants apart. Every now and then, there would be Zajal: a group of men would sit on a table, drinking arak, some not, and they would answer each other in improvised sung poetry. He could barely make out a word of what they were saying, and there was no point in asking for translations because it would take the next five responses and he would still not have got the overall point, but he loved the encouragement from the rest of the men on the table. 'Aaaaaah,' they would mutter loudly but not too loudly to overshadow the speaker. The answers were meant to outdo each other but even the person who was being responded to would often nod his head in appreciation. It was controlled gentle pride used to fight each other in a poetic way. Omar liked that. Once, Omar was nudged to go to bed and he answered in the same rhythm and wounded intonation: '*Pleaeaeaeaease* let me *staayyaayyayyayya.*' The whole family cracked up and he won himself an extra hour. Next time he tried it, they laughed but he got '*Yalla yalla*, it worked the first time, but you're not going to play us every time.' Still, he enjoyed the bantering which bought him more time, even if it was just bantering time.

In the morning, if Omar listened, he usually woke up to the sound of birds chirping, even though he lived in a tall building among other tall buildings. On a few occasions, he looked out to his balcony window

43

to see a bird land momentarily on the rails. Once, when Ziad was staying, they came up with the idea of a catapult. Ziad had a friend who had a friend who knew somebody who lived in the country who made them from metal hangers and connected a few rubber bands and even doubled them for extra strength. They knew that if they told their parents, they would try to put them off the idea, even before they had a chance to prove that it was really safe. Ziad's mother would say that she didn't want to give them a chance to prove themselves wrong because by then one of them would have hurt the other, themselves, or somebody else — it would be too late, so they told no one.

By the next visit, each had a catapult, and to personalise them, Ziad painted his red and Omar's blue. It took ten minutes of suspicious silence on the back balcony before Ziad's mother came out and asked them what they were doing. 'Nothing,' they replied, followed by laughter, followed by, 'Nothing really', followed by an attempt to be serious, followed by 'We just have these things and, eh, we wanted to hunt birds like Uncle Ahmad and Samer hunt when they go and—'

She smiled, looked at their catapults, smiled an older smile and said, 'Oh my, these are good. We used to have ones like these when we were kids but whoever made these is good. He must be young because it's a rotten job but he's into it; he's going to grow up to be artistic.' She sympathised with them and then asked them why they wanted to hunt birds.

'Because everybody does it.'

She said that it wasn't good enough that everybody did it — if somebody banged their head against the wall, would they do it? They pleaded without reason until she slowed them down and promised them that she wasn't going to take the catapults from them but said that she wanted them to think for themselves. 'It's true that some people eat birds,' she said. 'But let's face it: you're not going to get somebody to cook them. Second, at the most, you're going to hit one bird, but why would you do that? Now, why would you want to do that?' They looked at each other and shrugged their shoulders. Because it was fun?

'A bird is a little beautiful creature that harms nobody. Is it his fault that he sings so beautifully?'

There was a moment of silence. Suddenly the birds they had tried to hit were alive — little things, each with character and life; another person even if very little. And something in their heads opened up and

44

they knew that it was impossible to try to hit the birds again and to laugh and to hope that they would get hit. They looked at the catapults: so beautiful, so much potential.

'Don't worry about them,' Sana said, and then leaned over and kissed each on the head. 'You're little angels. I'm proud of you.' And as she got up, she offered to take them to the souk and get them each a music tape. 'In the meantime, don't do too much damage with these,' she warned.

It was a few hours before they would get to the souk and they knew that the music tapes were an offer to replace the catapults so they had to make the best of the catapults before they could no longer push things to the limit. They transferred their base to the long balcony at the front of their building, and armed themselves with as many different types of ammunition as possible: melon pieces, chess pieces, even sweets they liked, lentils, but not marbles, because they could really hurt the taxi drivers with marbles, and no oranges either because they were too heavy and they would just flop. Having gone through as many things as possible, they concluded that they needed something that was not heavy but was still hard and something that wasn't going to hurt: ice, but they got caught at the freezer stage by Omar's mother, and then Ziad's mother smiled and suggested they get ready to go to the souk before she had to explain the situation.

As they crossed the street, Ziad and Omar on each side of Sana, they waited and prayed that the next taxi would be a new Mercedes and not an old round one. Taxis went up and down the main street in front of their building and went all the way to the 'T'all' where they would get off. There, at the main square of the city, they would hear shouts for 'Beirut, Beirut, Beirut'. The owner of the garage would be trying to attract customers who were going to come to him anyway if they wanted to go Beirut. Sana smiled and told them to look at him, going up and down in front of the parked taxis, a character. Every person in the T'all was a character, she said, and she would discreetly point to everyone who caught her attention: '*Shooooooeee Polisshhhh*', a young boy crouched by his wooden set; '*Laymoon Laymoon Laymoon*', a wrinkled face squeezing oranges in front of a cart; '*Ttk tk ttk tk ttk tk ttk tk*', in perfect rhythm each time, the clicking of Turkish coffee cups — it was the only attraction that didn't have to be shouted for.

There was a shop only a few yards away from the square and they didn't really have to go into the souk, so how about it? Omar loved being

45

with his aunt and cousin. Shopping for new things was fine as long as they weren't waiting for her do some clothes shopping. Even if she was clothes shopping for them, they couldn't bear the waiting, the inspection of merchandise, being asked to try them on despite lack of conviction, waiting while she bargained with the guy, and then said she might come back if everybody else was worse than him and maybe he would have had more time to think and reconsider his price. This was different; there was no plan, and off they went into the heart of the city. Cars dented and dusty as if driving out of a museum; hustle and hassle over products they had no interest in; hot-air shouting arguments alongside a flurry of hand gestures — it was rare that an argument was 'real', but on these occasions, people would stop and men from nearby shops would calm either or both sides down: 'It doesn't deserve all this,' they would say. 'Plant it in my chin'; 'Stop, my uncle.' Sana would laugh and then move on while Ziad and Omar's heads turned back. They walked into the older parts of the city, first the jewellery section with jewellery shops one after the other and right in front of each other, and then into meat shops where meat hung with house flies occasionally being waved away only to come back two seconds later.

When they had had enough, their senses filled with rich facial expressions and crowding lethargy, they went back to the T'all. As it was Friday, they had to rush to the shops before they closed for prayers, and they finally got to the cassette shop. 'Something for the kids,' Sana said. 'A tape each.'

'Ah, the tasty ones are being treated today. Come in. I have everything.'

Sana smiled. 'May God keep you. I want a tape each; don't try to sell me everything!'

'Madam, I haven't even started.' He took a tape and showed her the cover. 'Johnny Holiday, the best French singer ever.'

'Oooh, he gives me the creeps,' she said, looking at a posed picture. 'Charles Aznavour touches my heart; take this guy away.' She handed him the tape then took it back to look at it one more time. 'No, no, no, no, something for the kids.'

As a man walked by, he extracted phlegm from the abyss of his throat, '*Mkkkkkhhhhh,*' and then '*Tfeh,*' right onto the pavement. The guy in the shop shook his head. 'The best music,' he said.

Omar and Ziad loved his comment. The man added, 'I have a tape full of spitting if you want.' Their eyebrows rose. He added, 'With an orchestra.'

Sana laughed. 'Please, you're disgusting me.'

'OK, OK, how about this? Boney M. Right now, they're the best band in the world.' And he put it on for her.

'Hmmm.' She shook her head. 'If they're the best band in the world, what am I going to give the other boy?'

'I was going to give you Abba, but if you don't think you can have more than one best band in the world, then I have just the right thing for you.' He took a tape out and played it for her. 'A voice like silk.'

She tilted her head backwards and dropped her lower lip in appreciation. 'This is nice,' she said, looking at the cover. 'Joe ... Dolan. Where is this guy from? I've never heard of him.'

'He's foreign. What more do you want?'

'OK, fine,' she said, and then tried to bargain with him. He told her that if she chose two more tapes for herself, he would do a price for her but not if she was buying only two; she told him that there was a shop in the souk where they had better prices; he told her that they didn't have his modern stock; she told him that she had just seen Demis Roussos and Julio Iglesias there; even a shoe shop would have them, he said, and asked had she not had enough of them; she handed him the money and told him that he was a difficult case; he took the money and told her that if she was going to be like that, she could take the tapes as a gift and she didn't really have to pay for them; she shook her head, smiling, and told him she didn't want to upset him, it was all OK, God would help all; he gave her the change and told her that if she didn't want to upset him, she could buy one tape for herself and he suggested Om Koulthoum; she took the change and asked him whether she really looked that old; he put the two tapes in a plastic bag and said that everybody listened to Om Koulthoum, from the smallest to the eldest, that she was the queen of Arabic music, and her voice could break glass; she put her hand in the bag, taking out Boney M, which she gave to Ziad and Joe Dolan which she gave to Omar, and then she gave the bag back and said that she didn't want to break any glass in her house, that she had some crystal she was really fond of; he said in a prayer-like fashion, 'May God keep those two kids for you'; 'May God keep you for us,' she said, and then she took a taxi home with Omar and Ziad on either side of her, with elbows resting out of the window.

Even if he stretched out,
he could not hold the world with both hands,
the world is so big

the child drew a painting
when it dried, he drew a painting over the painting
and again
and again
he was sure that over time the first painting would talk to
the one on top of it
and then they'd all be talking to each other at the same time
the world is like that, he thought

Places

Omar and his parents lived in the apartment and the apartment was his house and his house was in his building and, even though it wasn't *his* building, it was 'his building'. Isaac Newton had an apple fall on his head and that was how he discovered gravity and it was in the centre of the earth, but all of that was not important because apples were for eating and if Isaac Newton wanted to dress up in white tights and sit under trees, that was all right but Omar had no trees in his building and the centre of everything was his apartment, including the balcony, and the centre of the earth was not his centre because it was too far down and he'd never get to see it because there was too much digging and he'd burn when he got there anyway. The apartment was the centre of everything except on the rare occasions when he was upset with his mother; then his room was the centre of everything. He would lie on the bed with his *Turok* comics and he would end up in 'Lost valley' with Turok and Antar, shooting poisoned arrows at dinosaurs. They never found their way out of the lost valley; they got close to it a few times but they never got out — they only got better at protecting themselves. And they never made friends for long periods of time; they were always moving.

After the weekend, Omar had school. It was a blue bus that looked like a moving box and it was jam-packed with kids. Omar wished that his parents could have seen it by the time it was approaching school because it was really full then. Once, a car hit the back of the bus only a few buildings away from Omar's building and his dad went down to see if Omar was all right. It was only a minor hit but with so many kids on board, they could have been hurt. 'The school should have two buses, not one,' he complained. 'And they shouldn't be taking risks with children's lives. What if it was a truck that hit the bus? They would have been squashed like sardines — worse, like tuna.'

The bus driver had nothing to do with this, he said. 'Please go and tell the school,' he advised Omar's dad.

And Omar's dad did, but like everything else that had to do with institutions, they said that they would look into it and see what they could do but they were trying their best so they couldn't promise anything right away. In the meantime, Omar didn't always have a seat. It was about half an hour by the time all the kids were picked up and, on the way back, about twenty minutes by the time they got to his building. One of the older kids once said, 'Imagine if our homes were taken and the school too; we'd have to live in this bus.' Omar knew that it was very unlikely that that could happen because things like that happened only in *Superman* comics and not at all in *Batman* comics, but still, he felt suffocated and couldn't get off the bus soon enough. He saw the bus pass through all his familiar places: the 200 Street with all the trees, back towards the T'all but then avoiding it and going out of the city centre towards Zehrieh, and then past the river, passing by the cinema that had only Chinese Karate films, and everybody looked to see if it was a Bruce Lee film and, if not, then what first name did the star have to supplement his second-name Lee imitation, then up the hill, around a few corners, and there at the gates of the Ibbeh, in, and school is here.

American Evangelical School for Boys. There was a branch for girls in Zehrieh but the boys would never get to see it, they were told; they would remain separate until the end. At eighteen, they would finish school. It was a lifetime for Omar, more than ten whole years, so there was no point in thinking about what might happen after school since he didn't know how he was going to get through it in the first place. He knew that everything was going to get more difficult, and things were just about manageable now. A year ago, the whole class was taught by one teacher, all week, all year, but things had changed. And playground access had changed too: he could go to more places now; he could mix with the adults instead of being in the small compound with the metal wire around it. It was scary sometimes, and when he thought that one day he could feel comfortable, he felt wonderful.

During break-time, he would play marbles. He played with others his age and didn't like gambling. Some of the older guys, and even some of the guys in his class, were out to win marbles instead of simply playing. They were so good that they wouldn't know how to simply play; they couldn't; they would just win in two seconds. They would take over the game. They really played on their own. Everything about them was different. They had so much confidence, they were made from different stuff, and in class they were just the opposite: they didn't have a clue what was going on; they didn't look as if they would last for a long time. But where would they go? What were their homes like? Omar was scared of them. He also admired them although he didn't want to be like them. He thought about it: he couldn't be like them; they were made from different stuff, he thought again and again.

Omar knew that people came from different places, not just that, but they thought differently, talked differently, and argued in a way that was normal to them but strange to him. Looking out from the school yard, Omar would see houses in the distance with washing hanging on the lines. His mum hung washing on the line, but it was on the kitchen balcony, not at the front of the house. These houses had washing on every balcony. And the people shouted from the balcony at each other. Omar's mother would say, '*Ayieb, ayieb*, you mustn't shout; the neighbours will shame you.' If everybody shouted, then where was the shame? They looked as if they had a different type of freedom.

They looked as if they would watch those imitation Bruce Lee films. Omar's mother wouldn't entertain the idea. Whenever Amin came from Beirut, he would take him to the main cinemas on the city side of T'all, but not the ones in the heart of T'all — these were filled with rats, he was told. And the Hamra cinema had dirty films in it, so dirty that even the seats were dirty in a way he couldn't imagine. And when he went to the cinema, he would always sit in the balcony. It was more expensive, cleaner, and not so full of *Ze'raan*: troublemakers. It felt as if they were seeing a different film except when the film was so popular that the whole cinema was full; on those occasions, he would hear noises coming from downstairs, comical shouts at the screen, and the upstairs crowd would laugh in amusement.

The cinemas were good, but the ones in Hamra Street in Beirut were the best. Not only did they have air conditioning but you had to sit in allocated seats. But the most amazing thing was that they sometimes played movies for more than a week. This never happened in Tripoli where films were changed every week, no matter how popular they were. Maybe once a year, a film played for two weeks, but that was rare. Omar had seen *Airport* in Beirut with his aunt Sana, and it was playing for its *seventh* week and it was completely packed. People were different in Beirut. People dressed more 'chic-ly', and some of them spoke French.

'Why do they speak French when they can also speak Arabic and everybody else speaks Arabic?' he asked

Sana laughed. 'Precisely because some people *don't* speak French.'

'But why would they not want somebody to understand them?'

She laughed in amusement again before replying: 'To show off.'

'Show what off?'

'Themselves.'

'What do you mean?'

She laughed tenderly, gave him a kiss, and said she was glad he didn't understand; she was glad he didn't make for a natural snob.

'No, seriously, tell me,' he said.

She kissed him again. 'Seriously, you are so tasty, so cute.'

'No, no, seriously.'

Ziad casually said that the town was littered with people like that. Sana laughed at her son's comment. 'Let's enjoy the film and then afterwards we'll go to the Rawsheh and you'll see all sorts of people,' she said.

After the film, Omar was hyper. Was it really possible to have air going into an aeroplane and still be flying, and was it really possible for a small aeroplane to hit a big plane without the pilot seeing it coming because if it was him that was flying the plane, he would not be blinking, and would be looking as hard as possible every minute of his flying. Sana answered each question as she drove out of the busy Hamra Street. Once she got to the Rawsheh, she asked both not to disappear and promised them *bouza* if they behaved.

'And if we don't behave?'

She laughed, shaking her head. 'Fine, you'll get your *bouza* anyway, so go ahead, drive me nuts, but not so nuts you put me in an institution.'

They walked along the boulevard stretch separating the long curved streets with the palm trees from the long and endless sea. The two big rocks that stood high in the sea were the Rawsheh's rocks. Sana pointed, saying in wonder: 'Look how one of them has a hole in the middle of it.' It was hard to see it at night but during the day some divers had jumped from the top. It was an act of courage but they were also crazy because they could have killed themselves. Omar thought about courage and wondered what he would need to do to get people's admiration. The rock looked way too high. Maybe one day he wouldn't be afraid, or was it that he needed to have his head shaken and his brain out of place to be able to do something like that?

They passed by all sorts of vendors, selling corn, candy floss, music tapes, and, just like the T'all in Tripoli, '*Tt'tk, tt'tk*': coffee and tea. The poorer people came to Rawsheh to walk; they dressed for the occasion and still looked funny. And workers too. 'You're not going to hear any French here,' Sana said.

'They'll have wrinkles in their clothes,' Ziad added. 'And dust as well'.

On the way back , Omar drifted off in the back seat, eyes flickering into sleepiness, his full stomach reminding him of the sea which he could no longer see. He heard Sana giggling under her breath as she drove. 'You've run out of petrol, *Ya Habibi*, my love ... soon you'll be in bed.'

Their house also felt like 'his' when he visited. It wasn't his when he was in Tripoli, but when he visited, there was nothing could have made him feel like he was a visitor. It was OK to break anything as long as it wasn't intentional, and soon he would be sleeping in one of the two bunk beds in Ziad's room. Sometimes Ziad gave him his bed and sometimes Omar slept in the other bed, but once they had gone through the allocations and had played and giggled, it didn't really matter: he was going to fall down into darkness and float away into sleep.

Beirut was busy and he could still feel the busy-ness as he drifted off but the house was so comfortable with all the clutter in it, and even though his aunt had always complained about this state, it was the clutter that made it so comfortable. And it was Uncle Jamal's greetings that made it so warm: 'How are you, Taztouz?' 'How is the Beik?' 'How is the Maestro?' Titles that could have been denigrating had equal weight with old and traditional praises, and especially when he woke up with his hair all over the place and his vest hanging off him and it was suggested that he was Tarzan: 'How many crocodiles did you wrestle with in your dreams?'

On the way back to Tripoli, Omar would say goodbye to all his favourite places, from the shiny-floored croissant shops to the small bookshops with all the magazines displayed outside on metallic racks, to places he never visited but was promised by his aunt that he would on the next trip, past his sisters' dorms, his brother's little flat, and once he hit the wide road where he could see the mountains straight ahead, he knew that Jounieh city was going to come up on the left. The tunnel was going to come up soon and then he'd see the Telefreik cable-car lines extending over the highway all the way up the mountain, and if he looked back, he would wave goodbye to Beirut, one bulk of busy business on top of itself. From there on, he would watch out for the movie ads, sometimes badly drawn and sometimes made of real pictures. Jean-Paul Belmondo. Alain Delon. Clint Eastwood. Sometimes they stopped to get Omar's mum some bread from a place that made it so especially extra fresh that the plastic bags were hot. They'd get other doughy crunchy derivatives of bread but they didn't have the same important status as bread; they were more treats than anything else. Omar wasn't so crazy about them because they weren't so sweet, but still, he'd be encouraged to have one because they weren't as messy in the car as other sweets might be.

When Ziad took the back left seat in the Chevrolet *mtartaa*, Omar lost out on the sea view and instead faced the land.

'What's behind the mountains?'

'Villages.'

'And then?'

'More villages.'

'And then?'

'More villages, all the way up the top of the mountain, then obviously the mountain has to come down and then you have Bekaa' valley, really old ruins, from very, very long ago. We'll take you there when you get older. You wouldn't appreciate them now.'

'Why not?'

'It's mainly rocks.'

'Rocks?'

'Heh heh, see, you're already bored.'

'Just rocks? Nothing else?'

'You know what you'll enjoy in a few years' time?'

'What?'

'The caves of Jeita. They're amazing, all the stalagmites. It's huge, it's awesome, and they play concerts there. A German guy came over once and played all sorts of weird modern stuff with electronics.' They argued about whether it was really music or not; Uncle Jamal wasn't convinced that just because they brought in somebody foreign, people should lap it up. Eventually they agreed that it would be best to take Omar when there were no events on so that he could enjoy it as it was, as God created it.

'What else is there?'

'Eh, Saidon, also old ruins, but it's past Beirut in the other direction.'

'Do they have more than rocks?'

'Of course. It's a whole city. You could sit in a café by the sea — now that's a location.'

'Like the cafés in the T'all in Tripoli?'

'Yes, but without the backgammon. Well, maybe some, but they'd have more of the Argeileh, the hubble-bubble with the tobacco on top.'

54

'Yeah, yeah.'

'It's a great place to clear your mind from all the world's troubles.'

'And behind the mountains and behind the valley with the rocks?'

'Another mountain.'

'And what happens when it goes down?'

'Syria.'

'Syria?'

'The land of your TV programme, *Ghawar Al-Toucheh*.'

'And do they all talk like him?'

'*Shouuuu ya akheiii* ... yes, well, maybe not as extreme as him, but yeah, it's a different accent.'

'All of them?'

'What do you expect? It's a different country.'

'How is it different?'

'Well, they have their own borders to start with, and they have a different government, but they do speak Arabic and, OK, it's a different accent, but it's still Arabic.'

'And what happens if we keep on driving backwards, past Beirut and then to the city that has this great location, and then past it also?'

'Oh, eventually you get to Israel. That's the enemy.'

'Enemy?'

'Yes, of course. They took Palestine from the Palestinians and they've called it Israel.'

'Oh.'

'*Klaab*, they're all dogs.'

'All of them? Eh, isn't there one nice person among them?'

'Recently, Israeli planes dropped poisoned sweets in the Beddawi, . Kids ate some and were poisoned. You should be careful, very careful.'

'Where is the Beddawi?'

'Just after Tripoli; you should be very careful.'

'Do we ever go to the Beddawi?'

'No, there's no need to, unless you're going to Syria.'

'Syria?'

'Heh heh, yeah, it's to your right, past the mountains, and it's also straight ahead. It surrounds Lebanon, and in the south you have Israel.'

'And to the left?'

'To the left, you have the sea, as you can see; you and your God can sit down and contemplate it until your heart is full.'

the child still felt glimpses of wonder within himself but
no longer heard directly from the sky or the ground beneath him;
instead, he was busy filling up in his head from those who looked like him,
those who had been here before him.

Once the world was all his, even places so far he'd never get to;
others who looked like him had felt like him, but now he is being warned —
even those who are his age, whether they looked like him or not, those who
have had the same amount of time in this picture, not enough to have decided
on the colours, those and those associated with them, are not to be approached,
but closed to.
And the world, the world is not all his, no it isn't, you can draw a line between
a tree and a tree and tell them they're not sisters, watch their branches turn
away from each other.

Are You Lebanese or What?

'**A**re you Lebanese or not?' Omar still remembered this question clearly. He was in his building, the apartment, feet dangling from a couch, the family gathered, Amin, Zeina, Laila, his mother and his father. Khaled was in London, away. They were talking, arguing, joking. Amin had just insisted that anybody who didn't like falafel was not Lebanese, and the question was being posed: 'Do you like falafel or not?'

'Which one is falafel?' Omar asked.

'Of course, he needs to find out how you're measuring him,' Omar heard, and then he was told that falafel was made from chick peas, it was fried, you wouldn't eat it on its own; you'd have to have it in a sandwich, with tomato, pickle, tahini and coriander. Any of these missing and it was not a falafel sandwich.

'Ah, so it's not the falafel?' Amin was confronted.

'It *is* the falafel but not just the falafel.'

'Falafel was not even invented in Lebanon; it is an Egyptian thing. How could you be measuring and defining nationality based on something invented by different people?' Amin was cornered.

'It doesn't matter,' he retaliated with a smile. 'It is *one* of the things that you have to have to be Lebanese. In any case, now it's ours, and you can't invent everything from scratch; you have to take some things from around you.' And then he turned his attention to Omar: 'So, Omar, do you like falafel or not?'

Amin was accused of turning away from the argument and using Omar. 'Well?' he asked his younger brother.

'Eh, do I have to be Lebanese or not-Lebanese? Eh ... can I not be just ... eh ... a not an animal?'

Everybody laughed, and Omar's father shook his head in amusement; instead of getting an answer, he found himself being commended on aiming to be international, of the world — what a guy, great ambitions.

'Seriously,' Omar said.

'No, no, no, you can't. That's not the game.' Zeina had been fighting Amin hard on his definition. She was fighting on her behalf and on behalf of everybody who didn't want to like falafel and still wanted to be Lebanese; who was Amin, anyway, to decide these things?

Even Laila wanted to be in; she didn't want her right taken away from her. She complained, 'I like falafel, but what if one day I went off it?'

'OK, maybe because you're a woman, you don't have to like falafel but Abu-Ali just has to like—'

Before he could finish his sentence, Zeina was ready to pounce: 'I don't believe this guy.' She turned to Laila, saying, 'He's discriminating against us; doesn't he make you furious?'

Laila laughed to herself as Zeina shook her head, indignant at the betrayal. 'You're a disgrace to womanhood,' she said. 'It's women like you who keep us veiled.'

'There's nothing wrong with being veiled,' said their mother quietly.

'Nothing wrong?' Zeina was slapping her thigh in shock. 'Please!'

Amin looked at Omar and whispered loudly enough to be heard, 'They're crazy; none of them is veiled and they're fighting about it.'

'I used to be veiled in the past,' said their mother nostalgically.

Their father looked away and muttered under his breath, 'You did, when you ruled the nation of Islam.'

The roar of laughter had more to do with the surprise of their father being sarcastic, and when he turned again to their mother, everybody went quiet with a smile of anticipation.

'I did,' said their mother. 'When I was very young.'

Their father said nothing, just stared at her as everybody else developed a giggle. 'I did,' she repeated. 'Don't make me out to be a liar. I did when I was young. My father made me wear it to school, and now when I take a taxi, sometimes I wear a scarf.'

Very calmly and without supplementing his words with any facial expressions, he said, 'An Yves-Saint Laurent scarf!'

'That has nothing to do with it,' said their mother with a smile. Zeina agreed. Amin circled a gesture of craziness around his head to Omar.

Omar looked at Amin and then threw out a question to anybody who would answer it: 'Who is Abu-Ali?'

'How did Abu-Ali get into this?' asked Zeina.

Amin turned casually. 'Before you started all your women's revolution, I was saying that Abu-Ali has to like falafel,' he explained.

Zeina smiled to herself, thinking of how she was going to retaliate. 'And tell me,' she said. 'Why does Abu-Ali have to like falafel?'

'If you remember, that's if you haven't gone senile, we were talking about what—'

'Who is Abu-Ali?' asked Omar again.

Zeina turned quickly to Omar and said casually, 'He doesn't exist.'

Just as she was turning back to argue with Amin, her mother said, 'No, give him his time; tell him who Abu-Ali is.'

Amin came in with 'Abu-Ali is our national treasure. Without Abu-Ali there wouldn't be any Lebanon.'

'*Bala bal'la*,' said Zeina in a singing tone with her hands on her hips.

'What does *bala bal'la* mean?' asked Omar.

'Instead of swearing,' answered Laila.

'*Bala bal'la*,' said Omar, trying out his new word. 'So even I can say it?'

'Yes,' said his mother. 'But not all the time.'

'Why not?' asked Omar.

Zeina answered for her mother. 'Because you'll drive us deaf with it.'

'People,' said Laila, 'what happened to being Lebanese?'

As their father got up and went towards the balcony, he spoke to himself: 'A gang of jaw-crackers, that's what the Lebanese are; they'll talk about anything beside the point.'

'You speak as if you're not of us,' said their mother.

'Fine, my sister; *we* are a nation of word-chewers,' he responded.

Laila said calmly, 'There wasn't even a Lebanon fifty years ago.'

'What?' asked Omar in shock.

'Don't terrify the boy,' said his mother.

'It's true,' said Amin in a matter-of-fact tone. 'We were one big country called Syria.'

'Syria?' asked Omar. 'We were Syrians!'

Zeina automatically huffed as she shook her head negatively. 'We're definitely not Syrians.'

Amin came in calmly: 'It wasn't just Syria; we were one big country including Jordan and Palestine.'

Zeina interjected, 'And then the British and the French came and cut us up.'

'Why? What did we do?' asked Omar.

Everybody laughed. 'It's too soon for you,' said Zeina. 'You'll only hurt your head.'

'But,' said Omar, confused, 'I thought we were Phoenicians!'

'That as well,' said Amin calmly. 'But that was a long time ago.'

'And now?' said Omar.

'Go back to the falafel,' said his mother. 'It's better for him.'

'OK,' said Laila with mustered pride. 'Lebanon is the only country in the world where you can ski and swim in the same day.' She looked at Omar encouragingly. 'We have the cedar tree; it's very unique, very old. We have the Jeita caves, all the different foods — nobody cooks like us; it's very different from all the other Arabic countries; nobody talks like us.'

'Yeah, *bala bal'la*,' mocked Amin.

'All the different places,' continued Laila. 'We have the dabkeh dance; we have the Sherwal, the farmer's dress with the extension between the legs.'

'Yeah, so that they can go kaka in it,' mocked Zeina.

'Let's see, what else?' thought Laila aloud. 'Chou Chou. Well, we *had* Chou Chou.'

'You can make anybody Lebanese,' said Amin flippantly.

Omar's eyebrows raised. 'Can you make Charles Bronson Lebanese?' he asked.

Zeina smiled. 'He *is* Lebanese,' she said. 'He's from the T'all, the heart of Tripoli.'

Laila and Amin laughed. 'You're right,' said Laila. 'He does have that look.'

'Everybody is Lebanese,' said Zeina sarcastically. 'Paul Anka is Lebanese, Pele is Lebanese—'

'Paul Anka *is* Lebanese,' said Laila.

'Demis Roussos?' asked Omar.

'Oh no, he's like a barrel,' their mother muttered under her breath.

The phone rang. Laila casually extended herself and lifted the receiver. She greeted the caller, then suddenly gasped in shock as she put a hand over her chest. Everybody went quiet. As their father walked back in from the balcony and looked around in bewilderment, he asked, 'What happened? Have you run out of petrol?' As he saw everybody looking at Laila, he turned to her and waited as she put down the phone. She looked up and, with a shaky voice, said that a bus carrying women and children had been shot at. About twenty-six of them had been killed.

Omar watched his parents disbelieving their ears. Amin wasn't sure what to say. Zeina was talking a lot. Nobody was listening. She wasn't listening. Laila was scared.

Twenty-six killed? Women. Children. Bus.

'Why?' asked Omar.

'Maybe it's not twenty-six, but that's what they're saying.'

'When?'

'They were in a bus; they're Palestinians. Christian militias killed them. Small group.'

'Small people have guns?'

'You should cover the boy's ears; he's only eight.'

Soon he would ask, 'How? What is it going to mean?'

School to be off. Omar rejoiced, but it wasn't that simple.

'Is there anybody from the family going to fight?' No, it wasn't like that.

'We don't carry guns,' he was told, and it was unlikely — well, they hoped so, anyway — that war would come this way. They were in Tripoli, and this was happening in Beirut.

'But Zeina and Laila and Amin live in Beirut!'

They'll stay here for a while.

Ziad. His aunt and Uncle Jamal?

'They're OK now, but they might end up coming over. We don't know what's going to happen now.'

Amidst the confusion and fear, Omar stood up. Before going to his room, he asked, 'Do I still have to be Lebanese?'

Better get a suit; the child was urged to know his identity and stick to it, everybody wears one; it'll say which side you're on.

but I don't want to play; the child stood naked; not this game.

Please Come In;
You Can't Stand Outside

The Western

It wasn't possible to cover the boy's ears forever, so Omar was told that an extreme group of Christian militias, which was different from the army because the army had both Christians and Moslems and was meant to protect the country from outside invasions such as Israel, had killed a bus full of Palestinians. Extreme meant that there were other Christians who were not like them, wouldn't do what they did, but still liked them. Omar was Moslem. Palestinians were Moslems. The family was Moslem and they were on the Palestinian side.

The day following the bus massacre, the war broke out. 1975. It was Christians against Palestinians, and Moslems, not just the Palestinians, also against Christians.

Omar didn't know whether to be excited or upset.

'No, it's not like a Western cowboy movie. If somebody gets hit by a bullet, they die for real.'

'But Clint Eastwood gets shot a lot, and he hurts, but he still gets up,' argued Omar.

'There won't be too many Clint Eastwoods.'

'Is he Christian?'

'He's not Lebanese so it doesn't count.'

'So which side would he fight on if he had to choose?'

While it wasn't said directly in Omar's family, over the next few months, he heard from the occasional visitors that God would be on the Palestinians' side. Palestinians had been kicked out of their country. It had all been set up by the British and the French after the Second World War. Hitler had been killing a lot of Jews, and they were all stuck in Europe, so they were given a present of a country because they'd had a hard time. Now it was the Palestinians who were having a hard time. They were kicked out because the British and the French had given the Jews something that didn't belong to them. It was a bit like going out on the balcony and asking you which car you liked and then saying, 'Here, it's yours,' when it's not mine to give in the first place.

So, the Palestinians were armed and, at first, they were backing up the rest of the Moslems in the country but then the rest of the Moslems got their own guns.

'But why don't the Christians like the Palestinians if they have had a hard time?' asked Omar.

'The Christians got greedy; they want all the power even though they're the minority.'

Omar scratched his head.

'We used to be ruled by the Turks and then the French and the English came and destroyed the region and set it up unfairly so that we would be fighting each other later on.'

'Why would they do that?'

'Long-term nastiness.'

'And the Turks, they couldn't stand up to the British and the French?'

'The Turks butchered us too.'

'They left us coffee though. That strong Arabic coffee; that's from the Turks. And the red hat worn by farmers; that's from the Turks as well.'

'The Turks were Christians?'

'No, they were Moslems.'

'So how is God on our side now?'

Omar's father didn't like it when visitors talked directly to Omar about the war, explaining their version of events with blind assurance. He would go along with the conversation so as not to be rude but he would eventually throw in a comment to confirm to his son that he shouldn't be taking it all in. 'Son, you were right; it is like a Western movie.'

'Who are we?' asked Omar. 'The Indians or the cowboys?'

'Oh, the cowboys for sure,' answered the visitors.

Omar's father wasn't so comfortable with that. 'No, we're not the cowboys. Why? Because the cowboys weren't right. They actually took the land from the Indians; it wasn't theirs in the first place. And then they butchered them and treated them like they were the criminals.'

Omar wondered aloud, 'If we're the Indians, and God is on our side, does that mean we're going to lose?'

The guests shook their heads in amusement — the boy doesn't have too much logic yet; he's young.

'No, he's right,' said his father. 'You never see the Indians win.'

'Oh, yeah, maybe he *is* clever, but no, no, don't worry; we are the ones who are on the right side.'

Omar was also told that 'we' hadn't started the war; 'they' had. In school, and when he was playing near the house, whoever started a quarrel or a fight was to blame for taking things further than they should have been taken. Nobody was saying that they shouldn't disagree, but they were told not to swear at each other and not to hit each other. So for the Christians to shoot people — well, that was taking it too far.

'But the Moslems are doing the same,' said Omar.

'Well, what do you expect? Just stand there?'

This complicated things for Omar when he played in the street in front of his house. His neighbours wanted him to be Christian so that they could be Moslems. He hadn't minded too much in the beginning but after a while, he noticed that being a Christian meant that he was supposed to die. Another complication was that some of the neighbours *were* Christian. Whenever they were around, he wasn't supposed to play a war game with them because it would make the game real. They were supposed to hate other Christians, ones they couldn't see, ones they'd heard were causing problems, and his Christian neighbours on the third floor were not so bad at all.

This was also the case when his school moved from Ibbeh on the hill of Tripoli to Zehrieh where the boys would join the girls. It was said that the location of his school was unsafe and the girls' school was safer, so they were going to mix them together in one school. Omar was excited about this but wasn't sure how it was going to be with the other Christians in the class. Also, it was hard to figure out which Christians they were fighting with since not all Christians were fighting.

He was told that Tripoli was mainly Moslem. Whichever Christians lived in it were OK. The ones who were fighting were the ones in Zagharta, a village on a mountain above Tripoli. Beirut was different: it had both Christians and Moslems and there was fighting among themselves in, across and throughout the city. His cousin had the same difficulties when they talked over the phone. Ziad said that even though there were areas which were definitely Christian, his area, which was Moslem, also had Christians. He told Omar not to worry about school, as children hadn't been fighting each other and their parents weren't fighting each other either when they picked them up.

In the cowboy films, the Indians had big feathers and wore skirts, and the cowboys had hats and jeans. It was so easy for them. Omar had been hearing a phrase for a while now: 'Kidnapping on ID'. It had been said so many times and so quickly that he hadn't bothered to ask what it meant, but eventually he did.

'They' were doing checkpoint raids. 'They' would stop people and ask them for their ID. If the people stopped were different from the people at the checkpoint, they would be kidnapped. And then what? Well, killed.

Cowboys and Indians would not have had to go through all of this. It was much easier. They would spot each other from their different clothes from miles away and start shooting immediately.

While watching TV one day, Omar's mother pointed to a fattish actor and said, '*Tfeh!*' with spitting disgust.

'What's the matter?' Omar asked.

'This guy,' she said. 'The one you see in front of you. He's been collecting people's ears and making a necklace out of them.'

'For real?'

'For real. He is Christian,' she said.

'Not all Christians are as bad as him,' said his father.

Over the next few weeks, Omar would struggle with a question. Next time his brother Amin came from Beirut, he asked him, 'Do we do stuff as bad as the Christians?'

Amin said that it was most likely true about the actor and his necklaces; he had heard it from a few different sources. But it wasn't good to start thinking that we didn't do bad stuff either.

'Like what?' asked Omar.

Amin wasn't so sure how to answer this. He crouched to Omar's level, put his hand on his shoulder and told him that he had nothing to worry about; he wasn't doing any of this stuff and his conscience should be clear since he was out of it.

'Yeah, but like what stuff have we done?' persisted Omar.

'Look, it isn't a matter of "done"; the war is still not over. The main point is that you shouldn't be thinking in terms of "we". You are basically clean and you will stay clean until the end.' Amin kissed him and added, 'Your heart is clear and it will stay that way.'

'OK,' continued Omar. 'But what stuff have the Moslems been doing?'

Amin stood up, turned away, sighed, and said, 'Look, see how we have been fighting Zagharta? Well, whenever they catch one of them,

68

they cut their head off and stick it on top of an electric pole outside Tripoli for the others to see. Both sides are doing this.'

Omar went quiet. Amin looked at him, sighed apologetically and said he wasn't so sure how much to tell him because he didn't want his head polluted, but at the same time it was happening all around him and he couldn't protect him forever.

Omar looked up worriedly and said that he had never seen this kind of stuff in films before; cowboys and Indians just shot at each other.

Amin looked at Omar and frowned as he took in his comment. He then knelt and told Omar not to worry, that cowboys and Indians had done just as bad to each other. 'It's just that they're never going to show it in their films,' he said.

the boy looked around him and saw flat land in every direction, plain plane. far away were dark clouds, in every direction. near him was some light. there were others walking about. suddenly somebody stopped and said, 'Please come in.' the boy looked around then looked at the speaker; he saw no boundaries. 'Please come in, you can't stand outside.' the boy looked around again, and again saw endless nothing-ness. 'See,' said the voice again with a knowing tone. 'I told you, there is no outside, so please, come in.'

the boy looked around him again in every direction and then gazed upward. dark clouds were slowly approaching, in every direction.

The Black Phone

The phone weighed down heavily on the wooden cabinet in the reception hall of their apartment. It was made of thick solid material. Omar would feel its weight whenever he picked it up and pulled it to unravel the line connecting the receiver to the cradle. He would then rest it on his right shoulder and rest his left hand on the cradle while he struggled to turn the dial with the fingers of his right hand. The phone was black, black, black.

The phone was black because that was its colour, but it was also black because the lines were no longer connecting. At times, fighting would intensify in Beirut, and if Amin, Zeina, and Laila weren't all in Tripoli, their mother could not settle. Ziad and his mother and father lived a couple of districts further away, in a slightly safer area, but if the children were in Tripoli and Ziad's family still in Beirut, this meant that the fighting had got even worse and now they were no longer safe. Omar's mother would try dialling, with vengeance, and Omar's father would eventually tell her to move away because she was wasting her time and energy. He would then sit down and twirl the dial with long measured sighs. She would leave but then come back to stare at the phone and eventually swear at it. Omar would be brushed away while she was dialling. This was no play time; there were real lives involved here, she would tell him. He would wait in the hope that the line would connect, knowing that he wouldn't be given a chance to try, but when, frustrated and exhausted by her exertions, she was moved aside by his dad, Omar would feel as if he was doing the dialling with his dad, even if he wasn't physically doing it.

Once it was established that his mother wasn't going to come back soon, his dad would look at Omar while dialling, and tell him that he shouldn't blame the phone; it was only doing its job. His father would suggest that maybe he should get a glass of water for the phone because by now it would be exhausted. Once, Omar went to the kitchen and came back to surprise his dad. 'Fine,' his dad said. 'Let's put it next to the phone.' And it became part of the ritual.

The dialling would continue. If the line connected while his father was dialling, Omar would run to call his mother as there was a very good chance the line would get cut off after only a few words. She would run over but his father would hold on as she waited impatiently. He would be very brief but would not budge until he had been told that everybody was fine, safety-wise and food-wise. Then he would hand her the phone. He would then stand up, give her his seat, move over to the mirror over the phone, pick up the glass and drink most of the water, leaving a small amount for Omar to finish. He would then turn to her and remind her to sit on the seat she was standing over. 'Relax,' he would say. She would brush him off and tell him to move away. After a few minutes, he would point for her to sit down, and she would. She would stall, look at him, and then thank him with her eyes. A few more sentences and she would hand the phone to Omar and tell him to be quick because she wasn't finished. On many occasions, though, she wouldn't get to this stage. The line would be cut off and she would be close to tears because she wouldn't have had long enough. On other occasions, the glass would be held, about to be lifted, but not enough words would have been exchanged, and the hand would let go. Omar's father would try a few more times and then get up, leaving it to Omar.

Omar didn't like to give up because he was treated as a hero if he got through. He would immediately shout out in victory. His mum would make it first and his dad behind her. She would take the phone from him and, as he got up, his dad would hand him the glass of water. Omar would drink most of it and give the rest to his dad.

Once, when Omar was still dialling, his father came over to see how he was doing. He stood beside him, warming him with brief company. His mother came over and as she stood in front of the mirror, she started to pick up the glass to drink the water. Both Omar and his dad stopped her in her tracks as if the world was about to fall apart. His father took the glass gently from her and put it back in its place, telling her calmly that it was for later. She looked at him and then at Omar's wide eyes and told them that they were both mad.

There would be times, though, when the glass would be left to its complete stillness. After two hours of trying, Omar would get up. He would walk past it and he would be tempted to spill it, but he wouldn't, just in case that decreased the chances of the phone ringing on its own. By the time he got to the door, he would remember his father's words, that it wasn't the phone's fault. He would look back with apologetic eyes and try not to think like his mum. 'You have a black face,' she told the phone once. 'You bring only bad news. Give us something good,' she demanded. 'At least once.'

On one occasion, the electricity had been cut off for the whole night because the power plants had been bombed. Omar had been dialling by the light of the candle. Both parents had been shouting for him to give up, but he had persevered, and suddenly he stopped. He looked at the phone and felt that they were both in the same position, as helpless as each other; they were both in Tripoli, in a small place in darkness, hands not long enough to reach all the way to Beirut. The phone looked very dark, as black as black could get even though the candle was right next it and also reflecting back again from the mirror. Its bulk looked dead. Omar looked at the full glass and thought of slowly pouring it over the phone to revive it like a plant that hadn't been watered in days, but there would have been too much explaining to do if his mother saw him, and she might go nuts if she thought that he was breaking it. He hung up the receiver slowly, and then, ever so gently, he dipped his right index finger into the glass and brought it up, carrying one drop of water. He carried it slowly to the top of the receiver, made contact, and then withdrew his finger, leaving the drop on the phone. He leaned back and saw the drop tingling in the candle's rays. He leaned over and carried another drop, and again, and again, and one more time, until there were five drops in line on top of the receiver. As he leaned back, he saw his father standing by the door, looking at him; he hadn't felt him coming into the room. He took a breath and looked at his father. There was a non-judging silence. The room was as quiet as could be. Had the electricity been on, it would have been loud, even if nobody was speaking, but it was so dark and so late that the room had been halted into perfect stillness by the company of darkness.

His father walked slowly over, looked at the phone, and then at Omar. Omar didn't need to smile, and without a word being uttered, he felt that his father had understood.

the boy's dreams dreamt of a better place, a breathing space

Peter and Jane

The hardest thing about Arabic was that it was hard. When Ziad finally made it over from Beirut, and all the kisses and hugs had settled down, Omar got to lay out his books and share with Ziad many of the things that didn't make sense to him.

'Look!' Omar took out the first Ladybird book in the series. 'Peter, a whole page for Peter. See, nothing else, just Peter on his own.' He turned the page. 'Look, Jane. She gets a whole page for herself.' He turned another page and read out, 'Peter and Jane.' Then he looked at Ziad, opened his eyes wider to urge further anticipation from Ziad, and then turned the page. 'Jane and Peter.' He shook his head in disbelief. 'The luxury,' he said in a huff. 'Now why can't Arabic be like that?'

Ziad agreed. Even his Arabic teacher admitted that Arabic was much harder than English, and, while the English books started easy and got gradually harder, Arabic didn't start easy and it was important that they understood all along the way because it was only going to get harder, much harder then English would ever get. 'Now, why is that?' the boys asked. 'Why do things have to be so hard?'

Ziad's teacher said that Arabic was really old, that if you really got into it, there was so much beauty to enjoy. If they stuck to it, in six or seven more years, they would get to the poetry and it was just killing. The teacher caught himself with the expression and apologised to the class, he said that there was enough killing and he certainly hoped it wouldn't last that long. To lighten things up, the teacher then smiled and said that he had meant 'killing' in a nice way, but then he stopped himself, looked at the floor, and then apologised again. He said there was no nice killing — that was just not possible. There was a funny silence then, while the teacher looked at the floor and nobody knew what to do. Then somebody raised their hand and asked whether there was any killing in English poetry. The teacher then burst out laughing and the whole class started laughing, even though it was obvious that most of them didn't know what they were laughing at. But then there was another funny silence because the teacher kept on laughing, long after everybody else had stopped. Some thought that not all of his tears were from laughter, that he was also crying, but they couldn't really tell.

Omar said that his Arabic teacher wasn't like that. He had said that Arabic was hard and that was that. He said that school wasn't for pampering; that was the parents' job. But then the English teacher was much nicer, even though she was a bit wobbly in the head. A boy in class asked her whether all ladybirds were ladies and she said that they weren't birds and only half of them were ladies; they were insects. And then she was asked how come they were called ladybirds, and she said that English was like that; she said it didn't make sense if you looked at it very closely, and the names didn't describe what they were naming. But then the good thing was that in English you wrote what you said, whereas the written Arabic was completely different from the spoken Lebanese — almost a different language.

Ziad agreed. His teacher had said that throughout the Arabic world, from Morocco all the way to Kuwait, the Arabic that people spoke varied so much that you wouldn't understand what some of the others were saying. 'If we met a Kuwaiti, we wouldn't know what the hell he was saying,' Ziad said. 'But if we wanted to, we could speak in the written Arabic, so once we learn it, we could talk to all the Arabs if we wanted to.'

'All of them?' asked Omar.

'Yes, all of them.'

'What would we say to them?'

Ziad smiled. 'Please, come in. We're shooting; please shoot with us.'

'Yeah,' Omar said with a laugh. 'And then we could send them to pick up the Khartoush.'

Ziad suddenly remembered that he had brought some empty bullet shells to show Omar. He put his hand in his pocket and took out three empty Kalashnikov shells, and then he told Omar to close his eyes and put out his hand. When Omar opened his eyes, he smiled widely: wow! Ziad had seven empty shells; live bullets were very hard to get, but Ziad said that he had found one right next to the wheel of his parents' car. He hadn't told them because they would just have taken it away from him. 'If you put it in a fire, it could blow up in any direction,' he said. 'That's what happened to a kid on my street: he lost an eye.'

'It's always the eye,' said Omar.

'No, this was for real,' said Ziad. He had seen the kid. 'At first, he had a patch on his eye, just like Moshe Dayan, the Israeli bastard, but then they were able to get him a glass eye. He wanted his favourite marble put in instead of a glass eye — he had it ready and all — but his parents wouldn't let him. He still tries to collect live bullets; he's got more than anyone in the street.'

Omar shook his head. He had heard that the kids on his street had also tried to put a live bullet in a fire. 'But it didn't blow up,' he said. 'Must have been a stale one.'

Ziad picked up the Ladybird book and pointed to Peter. 'Look at him. I bet he doesn't know the difference between a Kalashnikov and an M-16.'

Omar smiled in agreement. 'Yeah, I bet if he saw one, he'd go back to wetting the bed at night.'

'Yeah, if he heard a Doshka, he'd probably shit himself,' added Ziad, then said that there were kids younger than Peter on his street who could disassemble and reassemble a Klashen and they should teach Peter how to do it.

Omar laughed. 'He'd freak Jane out, *'Mammy, mammy, Peter was going to shoot me and rape me.'*

Ziad laughed and then wondered what 'rape' was. He had heard the word a few times.

Omar wasn't sure. 'Probably shoot until the cartridge is empty,' he suggested.

'Oh yeah,' Ziad said. He had heard of that. 'Shoot until they've made a sieve out of someone.'

'Sieve?' wondered Omar.

'Like the one your mum uses to separate the rice from the water it's been cooking in,' explained Ziad.

Omar thought about it. 'Oh yeah, now I get it: the blood would come out and then you'd have only the bones and the skin'.

Ziad nodded his head in agreement and admitted that he hadn't seen a body with all the blood out yet; he had seen only a burnt body. Omar hadn't seen a burnt body but he had seen a burnt dog.

'A burnt dog?' wondered Ziad. 'That's strange, because dogs aren't Moslem or Christian.'

'Well, maybe his owner was Moslem or Christian,' Omar suggested.

'Oh yeah, that would make sense then.'

child looked all the way round: black; it must have rained tar
child lifted his head up, turned in every direction; the black clouds are not done

Heaven

Ninety-one. That's a long life. Omar's grandmother had had a hard year. She had been saying that the war had been closing her lungs in on themselves. She couldn't breathe as easily any more. She had been told that having asthma and smoking didn't help but she had shrugged it off. She had smoked all her life; it wasn't the asthma. The doctors could say all they wanted; she knew that she was going.

'Where is *Taita* going?' asked Omar.

'If she goes anywhere, it's going to be heaven,' he was told. 'But she's not going anywhere, not for a while.'

'Well, if she's not going anywhere, why doesn't she come over?'

'That's what we've been trying to do,' said his mother. 'We've been trying to convince her to come over and stay with us, but she doesn't want to.'

Lines within Tripoli weren't hard to connect, so he rang her. 'How come you're not coming down to stay with us? What's wrong with us?' he asked her.

'There's nothing wrong with you; you're the sweetest thing in the world and I love you more than anything, but I want to die in my home,' she replied.

'*Muuuuum,*' Omar shouted to his mother to come to the phone. 'She says she wants to die; tell her to come down.' He held the phone and waited for his mother. She arrived to an angry face. He no longer wanted to use the phone, and he passed her the receiver as if it were a dead mouse.

'You've freaked the boy out,' she said to her mother. She motioned to Omar to go to the living room but he didn't budge. She then looked back at the receiver and told her mother that Omar was not moving until she got a promise that she would come down. She argued, argued again, and then sat down and let the silence give her a few ideas. She looked at Omar, then went back to the same arguments until he tugged at her. She covered the receiver and asked him what he had to say.

'Tell her that if she really wants to die, then she can die, but first she has to come over and stay with us; I have some questions to ask her.'

His mother looked at him, thought about what he had just said, and then repeated it verbatim. She waited, then looked at him with tears in her eyes and then smiled. She arranged a time to collect her mother, and then hung up the phone.

She looked at him, held his face and told him that he was a genius. Then she said that his grandmother had agreed to come down but her wishes must be respected. 'It does look like she's going and it will be very hard for her if she doesn't have much company. Now, it's great that she's going to be staying over, but when things get worse, I have to bring her back to her house and stay with her until she goes.'

Omar understood. She said that the fighting could get worse and the houses in the Ibbeh were not as safe as the ones where they lived; she could be stuck there for a while but it had to be done. 'Are you OK with that?' she asked.

Omar thought about it. 'Yes,' he replied.

Omar's mother came back with his grandmother in a jeep. That was the best thing in the world, Omar said. 'Grandmother should have tried a Kalashnikov while she was coming down.'

'You think I can lift a Klashen?' she asked him as she slowly bent down to kiss him.

'Does that mean if you could, you would have used one?'

'Your grandmother is tired and shaky,' his mother said. 'We couldn't get a taxi to bring us down. It was beginning to shell and we were spotted by some young guys. Please, move over and let her rest.'

'OK, but I want to interrogate her later.'

Omar sat beside his grandmother as she slept and waited until everybody was gone. After over a full hour, he walked out slowly and checked that everybody was either asleep or very busy. He came back and gently pulled on her gown. Her eyes opened slowly and a weak smile formed on her face. 'I have to know a few things before the rest come,' he said.

She nodded.

'Why do you have to go to Heaven? We have honey here.'

She wasn't sure what he meant. He related having heard descriptions of Heaven mentioned in the Koran — that it had rivers of honey. She looked at him and sighed. Before she had a chance to say anything, he said that he knew how she loved salt and that the doctors had banned her from having it but that he would get as much salt as she wanted. He wouldn't tell his mother; he'd keep on getting her salt until ... until ... and he wasn't sure how to say it.

'Until I die?'

He shrugged his shoulders. 'Yeah. This way, you'll die happy.'

She sighed again. She had seen enough in her time. She had been through the First World War and the Second World War, but at least they had been world wars — countries fighting each other, not themselves.

He looked at her, not knowing what to say.

She said that what she heard about sniping really broke her heart: it was sick, sick, sick and dirty. How could they just shoot at people randomly? Others would run to pick up the wounded and they would get shot themselves.

He looked at her, not knowing what to say.

She said that she was going to tell him everything in her heart, since he had asked. If he really, really wanted to know, then he could know, and she saw no reason to treat him like a child.

Black Saturday had been the breaking point for her. She said that Black Saturday was when the Kataaeb in Beirut agreed to cease fire and everybody went to stock up on food, and they went ahead and slaughtered people just on their IDs. She said that she had seen enough.

Omar told her that she had heard these things, not seen them.

She said that she knew that they were true.

He said that he knew they were true too, and then he paused. She encouraged him to go ahead and speak. He said that there were people who were physically in the middle of the war, and that she wasn't so bad.

She said that it was true; she wasn't hiding behind what she was saying. 'My body is old anyway,' she said. 'I'm going to die soon enough. I could fight it if I really wanted to, but I just don't feel like it.'

He looked at her, not knowing what to say.

She looked at him, long and hard, and then said, 'OK, I'm going to promise you one thing: I won't let myself go before my time, but I'm not going to kill myself to stay alive.'

He thought about what she had said, and then smiled. He said that he got it.

She asked him to come over to receive a kiss. She held him and told him that he wasn't nine years of age; he was much older.

Over the next week, she became increasingly irritated with television. She could no longer stand those black and white Russian cartoons, or the Russian nature shows on the Syrian channel. She would rather have the TV off and wait until there was something better.

By the end of the week, Omar was asking his mother whether there was any chance he was going to get to see *The Muppet Show*. She said that his grandmother was sleeping through most things so it would be OK if he kept it low. She looked at him and said that he was lucky because he had no worries.

'What's wrong?' he asked her.

She hugged him and told him that he was only a kid — she shouldn't be telling him stuff anyway.

'What's wrong?' he asked again.

She said that his grandmother was insisting that she be buried in the village where she used to spend her summers as a kid, but it was near Zagharta: too dangerous. Omar asked why she didn't contact those jeep guys who had brought her down. She smiled and said that she had been trying to find some gun people to bribe; his father was asking around if anybody knew some decent gun people she could give some money to, but it wasn't easy: too many people with guns, but to find somebody you could trust was difficult. Omar said that he had heard that the father of a kid in his class was in a militia but he wasn't sure which militia; he had an idea where the kid lived from the pick-up and the drop-off of the school bus. His mother thought about it and then shrugged her shoulders. 'What am I thinking?' she said to herself. 'You're not even ten.'

'So what?' He looked at her with wide eyes. 'So what?'

Suddenly his mother jumped. He looked behind him and saw that his grandmother had been quietly making her way to the toilet.

'I've decided I'm going to be buried in Tripoli,' she said. 'At least the local worms will enjoy eating me instead of the Zagharta worms.'

Omar was silent, afraid of being heard until she came back from the toilet.

'Eh, look, we'll figure something out,' said his mother, looking unsure but still not giving up.

Grandma held Omar by his arm and told his mother that she wouldn't have the little midget involved with gun people for her death. Added to which, she had thought about it, and if it was so hard for everybody to get her to her burial place, how were they going to visit her?

That settled that. The day before Omar's grandmother was to be taken to her home, he made sure he got a chance to talk to her on her own. She could hardly speak but it was OK with him; she could take her time.

'Will I be seeing you again?' he asked her.

She didn't think so. 'When a person is gone, they are gone.'

He thought about this for a while, and then said, 'Even if you don't agree with it, when you get to Heaven, don't close the door behind you. Leave it slightly open, only slightly.'

'When a person dies, they die. I've already told you that,' she said. She wasn't going to fool any angels.

'Well, it might take them a few days to notice. In the meantime, I might be able to visit you in my dreams.'

She huffed, then said, 'Look, I've told everybody: no screaming like vagabonds when I die; wailing is for the Bedouins.' They were to mourn quietly without overdoing it. She continued, 'And you're not to wear black for more than one month, not a whole year. You promise me to tell them to dress in colour after forty days because they're certainly not doing it for me after that.'

He took her words in. 'So, I don't have to cry after you die?'

'No, you don't. Just remember me, and not like this, dying — like I was last year; like the times you drove me nuts and I loved you anyway, you hear?'

He heard but he had another question. 'How come you get to go and we have to stay here?'

'Don't be blasphemous,' she answered with weak anger. 'You're young; you're not done here.' She coughed, and then added, 'Maybe when you grow older, you'll stop the war.'

His eyes opened in shock. 'Me?' he said. 'The whole war?'

Her eyes closed. She said that she needed to rest.

He looked at her, then to the floor, and then muttered under his breath, 'That's too much homework.'

The following day, Omar's grandmother was brought to Ibbeh by his mother. Three days later, it was announced that his grandmother had died.

Omar didn't cry. On the second night after her death, he dreamt of her walking in the corridor; she felt alive to him. At the end of the third of forty days of mourning visitors, he wished she would show up and tell them all they were talking too much, drinking too much tea and not going back to their homes soon enough. He felt lonely for her.

for a while, with all the blackness outside him, even when it was in the clouds, the boy could still be white on the inside

with so many words and gestures around him, he noticed that he had his own; the boy saw this.

the boy could be separate.

if he could be separate, he didn't have to want to run as far as possible.

he looked around him; there was nowhere to run; away was further than he knew.

he remembered the voice that once said to him that he couldn't be on the outside; to see something, even just to hear about it would make it part of him.

there is just not a far away that is away enough to be away from it all.

he could turn away only with his back or his face, but not with his breath. others can pretend it isn't so, but it is so; his chest knows so.

Maths

After two years in the mixed school, Omar was both comfortable and excited to be in his class. He no longer wondered whether the girls felt infringed upon by the boys' arrival; they seemed to like it too. It seemed as if there was no chance of the boys going back to Ibbeh: it was now occupied by militias. Most of the teachers were all right. Omar didn't love to study — nobody did — but overall, the different subjects were manageable. They were nowhere near half as hard as it was going to get later on, he was told. The old school bus was long gone. The new one was smaller and had seats that folded out into the middle of the aisle as the bus got fuller. Whenever fighting broke out, school would be off; parents worried for the children, and teachers complained about difficulties in sticking to the curriculum, given the lack of stability. These concerns did not bother the children, though: they were happy enough that chunks from the curriculum had to be let go, and most reacted with excitement whenever they heard gunshots while they were in class. Only a few of the girls got scared as the class was dismissed and the school bus was made ready. The lucky ones were picked up by parents before the whole class was dismissed. Omar enjoyed staying and watching the teacher's face grow more concerned while the class fidgeted to the new gun sounds. The moment when the class door received a knock and the decision was passed on to the teacher was a beautiful moment of joyful chaos.

There were only two children who looked at each other in worry; they lived in the Beddawi, a bit out of Tripoli, further away than the school bus's reach. They joined in with the class's excitement but they couldn't lose the worried look as they had to make their own way home. If their parents didn't arrive soon, it could mean that they were having problems getting over, which meant that the longer they left it, the more problems they could have getting home. On the other hand, leaving on their own before their parents arrived meant that they could miss their parents and that was a big decision for them to make on their own. The next time the class met, there would be an exciting story of their creative manoeuvres as they missed the bullets.

'What kind of an education is this?' the teachers would say to themselves in front of the class. 'What kind of an education is this?' most children would have heard their parents say.

'Yeah, what kind of an education is this?' some of the children learnt to say back to both with a cheeky smile.

Omar had complained at home about a few subjects. The thing he was having most difficulties with was learning different meanings for words in English. If there was one word that described what it wanted to say, how come there were five other words that also described the same thing it was describing. His father would say that there were subtle variations. 'Subtle?' Omar would complain. 'Why do they waste their time on subtle; let them find new words.' Omar's complaints never went far because he had nobody to keep up the banter with, but one day Amin told him that he was going to explain to him some maths that he would not get taught in school for some time. He said that he would put it in a context that was going to make everything they studied in school seem stupid. Did he want that? Omar's dad shook his head in worry. But Omar had jumped at the offer; it was too late.

It was after a long, exhausting day. Amin, Zeina and Laila had all made it over from Beirut the previous week, and Omar could not understand why they all looked exhausted although they did nothing more than go out to the balcony. All they did was watch a very, very long procession of armed troops driving as slowly as they could all the way down Azmi Street while they talked slowly through loud speakers.

Zeina had hushed Omar when they were all on the balcony, and had told him she wanted to hear what they had to say. This confused him. For almost two years now, whenever they watched somebody on TV talk about politics, everybody would end up shaking their heads within a few seconds, especially when a guy called Karameh came on. He would go on and on and everybody would be sighing within a few seconds. Omar would ask what he had said, and he would be told, 'Nothing.'

'All of this is nothing?'

'Exactly. This guy is deliberately trying to dodge the questions and he won't stop either.' Zeina would imitate his dreary lethargic tone and make everybody laugh and then she would finish off her imitation with an intricate swearing.

86

Omar was also confused because he had been told that these troops were a collection of soldiers from all over the Arab world and they had been sent to bring peace to Lebanon after two years of chaotic bombardment.

'They're Syrians,' Zeina said, shaking her head as if in response to an unfolding disaster.

'What's the problem if they are Syrians?' Omar asked.

She looked at him, full of contempt. 'They're not bringing us peace, you'll see,' she said, and she went back to shaking her head.

Omar turned around to the other members of the family who were all on the balcony along with every family on every other balcony as far as the eye could see. 'Are they *all* Syrians?' he asked.

Amin shrugged his shoulders, unsure. 'Maybe 10 per cent from different Arabic countries,' he said.

Zeina shook her head again. 'They won't stay long; they'll go back and we'll be left with the Syrians.'

After the troops had passed on to a different street, everybody went back in. There was nothing more to see; everybody was exhausted. Omar was bright-eyed and bouncy. Amin took hold of him and sat him down. 'Let me cut your excitement in half and teach you some real maths, stuff they won't be teaching you in school,' he said. 'How about that?' Omar smiled at his brother's unusual gloominess. '*Yalla*,' he said. 'Why not? What else are we doing?'

'Basically,' Amin told Omar, 'the Maronites were beginning to lose the war against the Druse and Palestinians and the Shiites, so they called in the Syrians to help them.'

'Who's the Maronites and who's the Druse and who are the Shiites?' asked Omar.

'OK, you know how so far you've seen everything in terms of Christians versus Moslems? That's 1:1 maths; that's too simple. It's more complicated than that. Now, Christians are not just Christians; there's Maronites, and they have the majority of power in the government — the government as set up by the French a long time ago — and then there is Greek Orthodox, Catholics, Protestants and what have you.'

'What have I?' joked Omar.

'Not enough fingers to count on. The Moslems aren't just Moslems either; you have Sunnites, Druse and Shiites. Sunnites are the second most powerful in the government.'

Omar thought for a minute and concluded that Sunnites had the most power among the Moslems.

'That's right, but Sunnites are not the majority of Moslems,' Amin explained.

Omar was shocked. 'What?'

'That's right, just like Maronites are not the majority of Christians,' Amin told him. When Omar's eyes widened even more, Amin added, 'That's all maths all right, but it's called Fucked-Up Maths.'

Their father formed a pained expression at Amin's uncharacteristic language, but then a contemplative smile followed and he decided not to say anything.

'So...' Omar looked confused. 'So, if the Christians called in the Syrians, then, eh, what type of Christians are Syrians?'

'They're not Christians. They are Alawi.'

'What?' Omar was surprised again. 'What's that?'

'That's another type of Moslems,' answered Amin.

'So Arabs are Alaweieh?'

'No, most Arab countries are mostly Sunnites, but some are mostly Shiites.'

'Oh no.' It was getting too much for Omar's head.

'Oh yes,' affirmed Amin. 'And the Alaweieh in Syria are not the majority but they have the power. Well, Hafez Al-Assad, he's their President, converted to Sunnite after he took the power, just to make the Sunnites more relaxed, but he was originally an Alawi.'

'And are they more relaxed?' Omar wondered.

The rest of his family laughed — those who were listening and those who were only half listening. Amin answered, 'Nobody is relaxed.' And then he waited for Omar.

'Eh, who else is left?'

'Palestinians?' suggested Amin.

'They're Moslems, right?' asked Omar, fearful that the answer might cause him further confusion.

'Yes, mainly, but they have some Christians too. But the thing is...' Amin looked at Omar to see if he was ready. Omar tilted his head forward as if anticipating a disaster. Amin laughed. 'OK,' he said. 'I'll simplify it for you. Originally they were living in Palestine, what the West now calls Israel, and then the British and the French helped the Jews of Europe come over to kick the Palestinians out of their homes.

They slaughtered them, pierced stomachs of pregnant women, killed children, the lot, and basically drove them out. They fled to the neighbouring countries, which are Arab. Now, the Palestinians in Lebanon are not considered Lebanese, even though many of them today have been born here.'

'How could they be born here?' asked Omar.

Amin commended him on his question. 'Well, all of this happened over forty years ago. Since then, those who came to Lebanon have had children. Those children have never seen Palestine; they were born in Lebanon, but they're not given Lebanese citizenship. They're considered Palestinian because the plan is for them to return to their home — that's another story, but basically they're not Lebanese.'

'Do some of those kids want to be Lebanese?' asked Omar.

Amin commended him again, before explaining: 'The catch is, if they're Christians and they ask for citizenship, they get it, but if they're Moslems, they don't get it.'

Omar was taken back.

Amin continued, 'The government wants to increase the percentage of Christians and keep the Moslems down. Moslems already make more children than the Christians; there were more Christians forty years ago.'

Omar scratched his head in confusion. 'Eh, and what are we again?'

Everybody laughed. Omar's dad answered, 'We're Sunnites.'

Omar squinted his eyes. 'And what does that mean again?'

There was laughter but no one came forward with an answer. Omar looked at Amin.

Amin shrugged his shoulders. 'It doesn't mean anything,' he said finally.

Omar complained, 'After all that, it doesn't mean anything?'

The other members of his family either shook their heads or laughed. 'Poor boy,' said Laila. 'You've jumbled up his head.'

'Look,' said Amin with a cautious certainty. 'You're also an Arab, although there is quite a big chunk of the Lebanese people — like the Maronites and the rest of the Christians — who would rather be associated with the French and don't want to see themselves as Arabs at all. They see themselves as descending from the Phoenicians but they'd rather be associated with the French.'

'What?' Omar asked, genuinely confused.

'You've gone too heavy on him,' said Laila.

'I'll make it worse for you,' said Amin. 'Not only are you an Arab, but this thing about Arabs, all this unity, and all this stuff about saving Palestine and giving it back to the Palestinians — it's all mumbo jumbo. They're calling themselves one nation; they talk and talk about it, but each is for their own.'

Omar's face dropped. He was disappointed.

'I'll give you an example,' Amin said. 'Both Syria and Iraq are Ba'ath party, but they hate each other!'

'The people hate each other?' asked Omar.

'Well, the people don't start hating each other; the government comes down strong with all its politics and forces the people to follow like sheep.'

'And the Palestinians?' Omar asked.

Amin continued, 'The Palestinians want their own government but they're stirring trouble in the countries that have taken them in. In Jordan, for example, when—'

Amin's father interrupted him. 'That's enough,' he said. Amin looked at his father, who added, 'He's nine; you don't need to wreck his head in one go. Leave some for next year.'

Amin turned back to Omar and went quiet, not sure what to say.

Omar complained, 'No, I want to understand.'

Amin smiled. 'Russia backs up Syria, America backs up Iraq, and America and Russia hate each other.'

'What?' complained Omar. 'What have they got to do with this?' Everybody laughed. Zeina came over to Omar and patted his head, while addressing Amin. 'Give the boy a break,' she said.

Amin looked at Omar and sighed.

Omar looked at Amin and, in a quiet, decisive tone, asked, 'With the peace troops coming in, we have peace now, right?'

Amin leaned forward. 'This is the maths I was trying to get to,' he said. 'See how the Syrians came in today with all their guns and they said that they're going to bring us peace?'

Omar nodded his head.

'Well, when people heard the news that the Arabs had got together and sent us their forces, they felt as if they could breathe again, but they're breathing dust.'

Laila shook her head. 'Amin, finish this up; you're speaking above his head.'

Amin turned to Laila. 'No,' he said. 'He'll understand; you'll see.' And then he turned back to Omar, saying, 'You've been studying maths in school; you've been studying multiplication, right?' Omar nodded his head. '7 times 8, 9 times 5, 3 times 4 — that's all multiplication, right?' And again Omar nodded his head. 'Well, when you multiply the same number by itself — like 2 times 2, or 4 times 4 — that's called squaring. Have you heard of squaring yet?' Omar shook his head. 'Well, now you know, the same number by itself is called squaring. Now...' Amin paused to give Omar a breather and then continued, 'If you square any number by itself, it gets bigger: 2 times 2 is 4, 7 times 7 is 49, 5 times 5 is 25. Are you following?' Omar paused, then nodded. Amin went on, 'Except for 1. 1 times 1 is 1. And that's that. If you square 1, it stays 1. No matter how many times you square it, it will stay 1,' Amin paused then continued, 'Now, the Syrians came in with their guns to bring us peace. Everybody who heard the news sighed with relief, except, you know all these militias who have been fighting for the past two years?' Omar nodded. 'Well, they haven't given up their guns.' Amin paused and looked for a stronger focus from Omar. 'So, you tell me — you've got all those guns for two years and the militias haven't given them up, and now you have Syrians with their guns, so what do you get?'

Omar wasn't sure what to say.

Amin came closer to Omar and asked gently, 'What's guns times guns?'

Omar thought long and hard before saying, 'Eh, square one?'

Amin rejoiced; he kissed Omar on the head and smiled. 'That's right,' he said. 'We're back to square one.' He looked at the rest of his family and said, 'I told you he'd get it; he's my genius.'

Omar's face widened with pride and then, in a split second, he burst into tears. Amin, taken aback, didn't know what to do. Laila ran over and hugged him. Zeina came over and looked at Amin. 'Come on,' she said. 'There was no need for all of that.' Amin didn't know why Omar was crying, and Zeina got angry with him. 'Why do you think?' she asked. 'He gets what you were saying to him.' She shook her head. 'You made him understand too much; we're hardly coping with it ourselves.'

Amin held Omar's hand. 'I'm sorry,' he said.

Omar paused and said through his tears, 'It's OK, but I don't think I like this much maths.'

the boy remembered that he used to hear guiding voices, from below, and from above

the boy looked around; blackness had mixed with the colours of the rainbow
    the rainbow is not the rainbow it used to be; it's back now, bent, heavy, from carrying the weight of blackness
    but maybe black is not as black as it used to be; the boy wondered whether blackness was out to blacken the rest of the world or just force the rest of the colours to share their brightness

now it was muddy

muddy above, muddy below, muddy all the way round

the boy remembered the child: once there was no inside and outside;he was the centre to all
    the boy now wondered, as long as he didn't breathe in the colours — black, brightness, or blackened brightness — would he keep his insides clean?

Wedding

Laila wasn't going to wait until the war was over to get married; she might never get married, she said. Kamal Jumblat was one month dead when she decided for sure that that was it: there was no point in waiting. The leader of the Druse in the mountains near Beirut had been respected by the whole family.

'Who killed him?' asked Omar.

There was a hush. Everybody shook their head negatively. It shouldn't be said too loudly: 'The Syrians killed him.'

Kamal Jumblat had objected to the coming of the Syrians, and he was going on a visit to India, and he was threatening to resign and expose the whole lot of them. It was a sore point, a wound. He was the last of the good people. It was bad enough when the leader of any group was killed, no matter which group it was, because it was only going to leave things grossly imbalanced, but when you killed a respected leader, that was like killing hope.

'OK, so the Syrians killed Jumblat,' said Omar, 'but—'

'Shhh, not so loud.'

'What, in my own home not so loud?'

'Well, you can't afford to slip in the street.'

'It's as if they're living in my house.'

'Well, when they catch people, they take them to the Mazzeh — that's all the way outside Lebanon. There nobody gets to hear of you, and they have so many undercover people.'

'But why would they bother, just because somebody said a few words? So what?'

'That's how they work; in their country, nobody dares open their mouth. At least here, we're lucky; we come from a country with a history of free speech, the freest in the Arab world.'

'And now?'

'Now the gun rules.'

All of Omar's questions made sense to Laila. 'He's right to be naïve,' she said. 'No, he's not naïve; he's honest. At least he's still not blinded.' It

93

hadn't taken long for the Syrians to start fighting with some parties while other parties fought with other parties all together. 'When the war started, it was Moslems against Christians,' Laila said. 'Now who the hell knows who is fighting whom? Ah, so it's no longer cowboys versus. Indians. It's more like ... eh ... we'll tell you when we've figured it out.'

Laila was fed up. She had met Khalil about a year before. Within two months of meeting, they had got engaged. Now they had both graduated from college. He had been working in his father's pharmacy since his graduation. 'He doesn't have the greatest income but at least it's stable,' she said. 'People will always need medicine, especially in this war. He's a sweet guy. I would have married him even if he was Christian, but he's not, he's Sunnite, just like us — so there: no extra headaches for anybody. So why wait?'

'Marry him before he gets shot,' suggested Omar. Coming from anybody else it wouldn't have been funny. Still, his mother hushed him. 'No,' he added to his sister. 'Seriously, marry him before *you* get shot.'

Their parents looked at each other. There was little to argue about: the boy was right. Laila sighed in relief: she had both her parents' approval. She thanked them for throwing away their caution.

'You can't let this war stop you. It has stopped us for over two years.' She was happy, she said. This way, if she or Khalil died, at least they would die together.

And so it was set, and the day had come, and the house was due to be filled with people because it was the bride's family's duty to hold the reception. That was the tradition. You didn't argue about it, just got out of the way or helped.

'OK, OK, OK.' Omar had a few questions. 'Are we going to have any rice thrown?'

'Rice?'

'Like in the movies.'

Movies, movies — everybody wondered what he was talking about until Zeina figured it out: in American movies, when newly married couples were coming out of the church, they'd have rice thrown on them. That was where Omar would have seen it. 'No,' she explained. 'We're Moslems; we don't throw rice and we're not going anywhere. It all happens in the house. The Sheikh comes over and he reads from the Koran.'

'Boring.'

'What do you expect? A celebration?'

'Yeah, of course.'

'That's a different occasion. This is the one that binds them together.'

'Oh.'

'And why do you want to waste rice? People are dying of hunger.'

'Well, just a bit: the hard ones, the ones nobody can eat.'

'That's uncooked rice, you silly billy. When you cook it, you can eat it.'

'Well,' Omar added cheekily, 'if the poor are really poor, then they don't have pans so you can throw it because they can't cook it anyway.'

'Omar, please, show us the back of your shoulders.'

He lingered, trying to come up with another question.

'It means "leave".'

'One more question: is there going to be any wailing? Can I wail?'

'No wailing; wailing is for vagabonds. Anyway, you don't wail today. That happens on the other occasion, and you can't just wail; you have to have been doing it for years. You'd sound like a broken ambulance. Now please, leave; we're tense enough as it is.'

'What's to be tense about? He's not going to change his mind!'

Amin agreed with his brother in principle, but he suggested a bit of calm. When Omar received an acknowledgement that they, his sisters and his mother, liked to get tense over nothing, he was free to leave them alone. He decided that it was better to go to the balcony and wait for Ziad and his parents. Amin agreed and decided to accompany him and stay with him. The temptation for his little brother to go in and mess with them was too great to take the risk. Omar promised that he would stay and that he didn't need to argue; he was happy to have the company.

The first car that was spotted was Ziad's family car, the Chevrolet *mtartaa*. After the greetings, they made their way to the balcony. Laila was to be allowed some space. There would be no more guests for a while, so an easy atmosphere immediately developed between Amin, Sana, Jamal, Omar and Ziad. Omar's other aunts would come later, but Sana was the cream and that was all that mattered, according to Omar.

'Oh,' he added. 'And Jamal is the only in-law who matters, and so all who matter are here.'

Sana looked at Ziad and then back at Omar, meaningfully. Well, there was no point in mentioning Ziad, Omar said. Ziad was the one and only cousin he would ever have. Sana said that Laila's husband had a nephew and he would be bringing him to the wedding. 'We're not going to see him again,' Omar argued. 'So there's no point in mentioning him.' So, that was settled then. Then Amin coughed and quickly looked away with a smile. Oh, of course, Amin was the only brother in the world. Omar smiled, filled with affection. Khaled couldn't make it to the wedding; he was in the middle of his medical exams and he had no guarantees that he would be able to fly back to London. Laila had insisted on getting married in early June and there was not too much that he could do about it. But even if he could have come, Omar said, Amin was, and always would be, his hero.

'Oooooh!' Sana patted Amin's arm. 'Your place seems to be secure.'

'Yes, that's right,' said Amin. 'This has nothing to do with the war. Even if Khaled were here, he would have no chance with Omar. I literally pour love into him. I fill him up with it, like petrol into a car.'

'Well, one day Omar is going to finish school, and most likely he'll go to London, and he'll be around Khaled for quite a while,' Sana teased.

'That's it.' Amin looked at Omar. 'Eight years — that's a life time.'

'Yeah,' added Jamal. 'Khaled will have finished medicine. The war could well be over, and Khaled could be back here by then.'

Within a few seconds, they were in a discussion about the different parties involved and the implications of certain alliances, how things might develop, and the political announcements made recently....

Ziad and Omar slipped back in to do some teasing. They had heard these conversations before; they went nowhere. When they reached Laila, she had been crying. 'What's wrong?' they asked.

Nothing, she was just reminiscing, missing the old times when everything was carefree, and she was hoping that everything would work out. She was also very happy. She was glad of everybody being around, and even if Khaled couldn't make it, she knew that he had tried.

'He said he'll make it up to me later when I go on my honeymoon,' she said. And then she reached out for Omar and hugged him, and then Ziad. These were tears of joy, she said; they were different from tears of disaster.

'Tears of madness?' asked Omar.

She laughed her heart out and then hugged him again. She said that he knew how to make her better. 'That's it,' she said. 'I'm going to appoint you as the family doctor.'

The wedding went fine, really fine. By the time the guests started to arrive, Omar and Ziad were in the back balcony. They would be called every now and then to greet some guests and, on occasion, to help with the bonbons, or with passing some messages.

When Laila's in-law family arrived, Khalil's nephew joined Omar and Ziad on the back balcony. He was a quiet boy even though he was two years older than them. He said that he came from a village on the mountain near Beirut. It had been suggested to Omar and Ziad not to talk about the war — you never knew how you might end up insulting somebody, and this little fellow would have seen a few things, so maybe they shouldn't remind him of what he had seen. They were curious, but they stuck to their promise. They dug up all the movies that they had ever seen. Of the recent films, *Jaws* was the best. *Jaws* was definitely more scary than *King Kong*. Not only was the film scarier, they all agreed, but if it was real life, you'd be able to blow up King Kong in no time. If he came to Lebanon, everybody could take a break from shooting each other, and if they pointed their guns at him, they'd have him down in no time. Actually, the film was really stupid, especially since it was the new version. With all their advanced guns, did it not cross their minds to shoot him in the balls? Even if the hit wasn't lethal, anybody hit in the balls would immediately end up holding them with both hands and he would lose his grip on the Empire State Building and fall all the way down on his head. *Jaws* was more scary: he had no hands and no balls, and he swam. No matter how many times you blew him in the water, it wasn't going to do anything. He was clever; he knew where to live. Water, that was it: nobody could mess with you in water. Jaws was clever, real clever, not just talk clever.

By the time the more distant guests were fading away, they were told that they could go in and mingle if they wanted to. But they didn't need to; they were happy with each other. Later on, when it was time to go, Khalil's nephew told Omar and Ziad not to forget his name, Habib, and he would not forget their names either. When he had left, Omar and Ziad felt quite sad but it wasn't just because he was a nice guy. It was probably because he was a sad boy and he had made them a little bit sad even though he hadn't said anything sad.

When everybody had gone, Omar and Ziad went to Khalil and told him in front of Laila that she had been crying earlier on, but now she had nothing but smiles and that was because she was married to him. He laughed and asked them whether they approved of him. They said they did, that he was a nice guy, and also that he made Laila happy. She smiled and cried at the same time. Omar told Khalil that Laila had explained this before: these were tears not of sadness, just plain old madness.

97

the child learnt to extract smiles from the darkest of clouds,
it was the way he would tilt his head, or maybe tilt the sky a bit,
after a while, whenever he looked up,
he would usually find one

Insects

Brring Brring ... Brring Brring...

Lying flat across a couch, Omar let his mum get the phone.

'It's Ziad,' she said. '*Yalla*, get up! You're going to melt in this heat.'

It was a hot summer afternoon. The troubles had calmed down so it was possible to go to the beach but he needed somebody else besides his parents to bring him. They both claimed to be too old, so unless his older neighbour, Karim, offered to bring him, he wasn't going anywhere.

The first thing Ziad said was how much he hated all the *dibbaan*: the house flies. They drove him nuts, he said; they drove everybody body nuts, he added, in justification of his own hatred. Since the war had started, refuse collection had never been the same, and even though their apartment was quite high up, the *dibbaan* still got in everywhere. But Ziad had figured out a way to deal with them: foam on the glass window.

'But how do you know they're going to go and land on the exact spot you want them to?' Omar inquired.

Pause. 'OK, hmmn ... yeah ... I swear it's a good idea.'

'I know, I know ... but...'

Omar didn't want to rub it in; they both knew there was a problem.

Ziad sighed and then said calmly, 'I'll ring you later.'

'OK.'

'You work on it too!' added Ziad.

'Me?'

'Don't you hate them? Come on! You must hate them.'

Omar didn't respond. He didn't hate them. He had watched everybody else wave them off with extreme frustration, swear at them, and then swear at life altogether. But he found himself to be calm about them. He even experimented with letting them land on him to see if he could get used to them. But that wasn't possible; they tickled in an unnatural way, and he *had* to wave them off, but he could do it without boiling and adding to the irritation.

Ziad didn't argue. 'OK, fine, you don't have to hate them, but think about it and I'll ring you later.'

99

Brring Brring ... Brring Brring...

Lying flat across a couch, Omar let his mum get the phone.

'It's Ziad,' she said. '*Yalla*, get up! You're going to melt in this heat.'

'Allo,' said Omar.

'*Shou?*' asked Ziad: what's up?

'*Shou!*' responded Omar.

'Well, what did you come up with?'

'Eh...'

'Nothing either, huh?' Ziad asked acceptingly.

'I don't know. Eh, I don't think this will work, but if you put foam on your hand instead of the glass, whenever there's a *dibbaaneh* around, you can wave your hand all over the place. But I don't think it's going to work because I've been watching the way they fly, zigzagging all over the place.'

Ziad paused for two seconds and then said, 'I've got to go.'

'OK.'

Brring Brring ... Brring Brring...

Lying flat across a couch, Omar let his mum get the phone.

'It's Ziad,' she said. '*Yalla*, get up! You're going to melt in this heat. Maybe if you moved your little behind, you'd get some air.'

'*Shou?*' said Omar.

'I got one!' Ziad was all excited.

'Oh no.'

'I swear.'

'I believe you.'

'I swear to God, I got one.'

'I told you, I believe you.'

'You're a genius.'

Pause.

Ziad added, 'Come on, I got one.'

'I know ... but, eh, does that mean *I* killed it?'

'No, no, not at all. God will punish only me; you don't worry about it.'

'But I put the idea in your head.'

'But I asked you to,' Ziad responded with enthusiasm.

'Are you sure about this?'

'Definitely.'

A little pause and Omar said, 'Because I was thinking, if you put foam all over the glass, then you're bound to get ones going into it blindly while at the same time you could be catching ones of your own.'

'... I have to go.'

'OK.'

'Thank you very much.'

'Yeah, OK.'

Over a short period of time, Ziad's methods of catching and dealing with houseflies advanced to a point where Omar no longer felt comfortable adding his suggestions even though he was coming up with creative solutions. Ziad had been taking their wings off and letting them walk around; he had put them in the toilet bowl and watched them struggle in circles; he had dipped them in foam and burnt them, put them under a clear glass with a firecracker and watched them explode; he even thought of using a thin thread to hang them but it was obvious that it was going to take too much time. It had become clear to Omar that any good ideas he came up with were going to be carried out, whereas not sharing his ideas meant that the houseflies would be safer.

A few years before, Omar's mother had told him that her father used to say that ants feared God, that if you saw them on the street next to a tree, knelt, and shouted 'Allah' at them, they would scatter. Omar tried it, and then also tried '*Battikha*'. He went back to his mother and told her that ants worshipped neither God nor watermelons. Still, she told him to respect ants above the other insects because they were clean. 'They do gravitate towards food if you leave dirty dishes out at night in the kitchen,' she said. 'But they don't bring germs.' Yet she killed them when she saw them. 'Well, that's when they're irritating me,' she would say, but generally they were good creatures.

Houseflies, in her opinion, were not good creatures. Not only were they irritating, but they also brought germs. 'They land on shit, they like shit, and then they come to us,' she said. Quite often, they did irritate Omar, but he didn't want to get into having an extra reason to hate them; they were annoying and he wanted to leave it at that level.

Mosquitoes were also to be hated. It wasn't bad enough that the refuse problem brought houseflies during the day, but it also brought mosquitoes at night, so the nation was being tortured round the clock, day and then night, no mercy. For some reason, Omar was rarely bitten by mosquitoes while everybody else around him was complaining about the size of their bites. He couldn't quite figure it out, but the reason he gave was that he had made peace with them and decided not to hate him. He claimed that mosquitoes could sense this and that's why they respected him and left him alone; it was a mutual agreement. There were times when his mother or visiting sisters would show how many bites they had when he barely had one, and he would wonder whether there actually was an agreement. He became so confident that he would hardly use the repellent cartridges his mother gave him. It was only when a mosquito buzzed in his ear as he was trying to sleep that he would turn on the light, or put on the candle, and then try to kill it, not because it might bite him but because it wasn't letting him sleep. When his mother heard his hands clap against each other or smack against the wall, she would ask him from her room whether he had got one and commend him if he had. But as he turned off the light, he would silently apologise to the dead mosquito.

While houseflies and mosquitoes alternated shifts in torturing people, day and night, cockroaches could appear at any time. They didn't bite; usually they just ran away, yet people jumped in fear when they saw them. Like everybody else, Omar jumped when he saw one, and there was nothing he could do about it; it was an automatic response. Whenever his mother saw a cockroach, he would be on duty to kill it. He admired their speed and their character — the way they were built: two long antennae, one colour all the way, brown, and a crunchy skin that made them all-powerful only by virtue of being disgusting. He struggled with the idea of killing them, but with cockroaches he resigned himself to the fact that letting them be wasn't an option. They were super fast. Throwing stuff at them never worked; they just had to be stepped on. Once, when Omar walked into his building, he saw the concierge's son step on a cockroach barefoot. Omar stood back in admiration; he knew that he wouldn't be able to do that.

Houseflies, mosquitoes, cockroaches and ants. That was the extent of the insects that Omar had come across, and while in his heart he viewed them from a closer distance than most people did, it was still a view from above, looking down at lower creatures. Until, one day, a boy in his class cheekily responded to the teacher who was saying that human beings were mammals. 'My dad said that we're not mammals,' the boy said. 'He said that we're insects because we're dying like insects.'

The teacher didn't smile, but out of interest she asked him what his father did. He said that his father was a doctor in casualty.

The boy looked at his hands and feet, this
will all dissolve one day, just like everything around you
He felt his body, his breath, and also sensed himself as not only flesh
You're also more than all of this, he had been told.
You have a soul, a spirit, something, and it stays
Or goes, somewhere, some place, after all is gone

The boy wondered, when he scratched his head, did he scratch himself
He's like the insects; he'll be stepped on one day, or just gone,
Gone somewhere maybe here
the insects too

Maybe it's just that things come and go at different times, even rocks,
They couldn't go at the same time; there would be a jam

A Year

A year was just about to end. There was no electricity. It was near sunset; candles were just about to be lit. Omar's mother was talking to Zeina and Laila, his father was napping, and Amin had gone to visit a friend but promised to come back before it was dark. The phone rang; Omar went to answer it.

He must have been about five minutes on the phone when he came back, very casually. 'Who was it?' they asked. He figured it must have been two girls in his class; the first one lived three buildings away, and the second had a link to Syria. They didn't admit it; they said that they were ringing to do a survey. They kind of giggled when he told them that he didn't think it was for real, but he ended up answering their questions anyway.

'What did they want to know?' They wanted to know what he thought of last year and how he would like the new year to be.

'And what did you say?' He said last year was fine, and he wanted next year to be like last year.

'Oh my, with *aaaaall* the events that happened last year, it was fine!' Zeina put her hand on her chest in shock. 'They must have laughed at you.'

'Well, yeah, they were surprised.'

One of the things that Omar had struggled with during the year was the death of the Franjieh family. The Franjieh were from Zagharta, like the President. They were Christian, militant, and they had shelled Tripoli. Heads had been cut on both sides, and they were slaughtered by the Kataeb. The Kataeb had originally been their Christian counterparts in Beirut and other areas, but then they wanted to secure the presidency for themselves — the Jemayel family, that is — and so they slaughtered the Franjieh. Many people around Omar rejoiced; they had their own shame. The Moslems had started out with the Palestinians against the Christians, and the solidarity among the Moslems had felt good, but then they split, and it was doubly shameful especially that the Christians seemed unlikely ever to do that to each other. And then the Christians did this to each other: one family slaughtered another whole family, and now all were all as low as each other. Omar heard glad responses all around him: 'Let them have it; they deserve it after all the things they have done to us.' The best of all, he heard, was the way the rest of the Franjieh family reacted: they banned mourning in the village. They ordered their own people to wear white; their mourning was to be suspended until the Jemayel family died. It was an ingenious move to fester revenge. Now they were not only against each other, but it was until death. Beautiful.

On the way to Beirut, Omar had seen pictures of the slaughtered Franjieh family on the walls of a Christian village: the father, the mother, and a blonde girl who looked to Omar to be no more than five years old. She was gorgeous. This nobody argued about. Omar couldn't feel good about her death. They said that the family had been slaughtered, blood everywhere. Red everywhere. He couldn't imagine it, no matter how he looked at the situation, because her picture, her blond curly hair, was in his head. Only a few people commented that it wasn't her fault, but as Omar saw it, even if they had spared her and slaughtered her parents, she was going to be so sad anyway, and she would not have been able to erase the memory of the slaughter from her head. That's war! They deserve it! Let Fekhhar break each other! But she had blond hair.

Zeina was half-jokingly pretending to be angry with Omar. He had forgotten about her car. The previous year, she had borrowed money from the bank to buy a car, and it was stolen after three months, and she had still not finished paying the bank for it. 'Have you forgotten this?' she asked. 'Are you happy that this has happened to me?' She was also angry on Laila's behalf; she too had had her car stolen and the thieves had rung her and told her that if she paid them $500, she could get it back. 'And the cheek of them!' Zeina reminded Omar. 'They wanted her to go to *their* area to collect it. If she had done that, they could have taken the money from her and God knows what they would have done to her!' But Laila was smart, and got them to deliver the car to her. 'What an ordeal,' Zeina said. 'And you wish that on others, huh?'

Omar smiled; of course these things were not good.

'What about Miss Manzoul, your favourite teacher?'

Omar hated maths up until Miss Manzoul taught his class. She appeared to be strict, but she wasn't really. She talked back to the boys and laughed at them for trying to push her around, and for that they respected her, and she did it with humour when she could have bullied them. Omar felt that she really liked him although she wasn't the type to treat anybody differently. She was tough, in a soft sort of way. She came from a village near Zagharta, was Christian, and, like many people from the country, she lived in Tripoli. One day, there was a knock on the classroom door and the headmaster appeared. He asked if he could speak to her. She left the class and stood outside. She didn't close the door completely and the front two rows could see her. The headmaster said something very slowly and, although she never moved, the tears started to roll down her face. She nodded and then came back in. She took her books and her bag, and said one thing to the class before going out: she said that she was going to miss them. And they never saw her again. Later, they heard that her husband had been shot dead.

Omar didn't smile. He shrugged his shoulders lethargically. *Well, you forget this stuff*, he thought. Zeina saw that he was sad but didn't want to hug him in case he got more upset. She didn't want to change the subject either, though; he was old enough to deal with it. So she smiled and tried to put things in a humorous light: 'What about all these people who died all over the country? Do you think that they were using firecrackers?'

He shrugged his shoulders again; he didn't know these people so it was easy to forget about them. 'Plus, nobody seems to understand anything from the news,' he said. 'Things are so complicated and nothing looks like it's going to change so you just get used to it.' He shrugged his shoulders even higher. 'I guess things could be much worse,' he said.

Zeina laughed as if he was nuts, and it was hard not to laugh with her. 'How the hell do you think things can get worse?' she asked. 'You want them to get worse than this?' She pointed to the candles. 'This is New Year's Eve; we're supposed to be out having a party, ce-le-braaaaa-TING.'

Omar cracked up laughing. How the hell am I supposed to know?' he asked. He had never celebrated New Year's Eve; he had always been too young to stay up, and now he was old enough but didn't know. Laila looked at her mother and they both nodded their heads in agreement; the boy had a point. Zeina put her hands up in the air and smiled sarcastically: what the hell did she know? Maybe things were good and she just didn't know it.

Later that night, Omar was allowed to stay up if he wanted to. Laila went to bed after about eleven. Amin ended up moving to the bedroom as his mother kept on trying to dissuade him from reading by the candlelight as it was not good for his eyes. Their father kissed everybody good night and wished them a happy new year just as it turned twelve and bullets started sounding in the sky.

Omar rushed to the balcony for the view. Zeina and her mother followed. Flashes and dots of light moved across the sky in groups of five or six; sometimes they were too fast to count. These were bullets fired from Kalashnikovs. If they were individual lights, with a discernible distance from the next one, it was a hand gun. For some reason, the big bomb sounds that would come from the heavy artillery never flashed. It was a bit disappointing as the sounds were so big but there was nothing to see afterwards — like a huge thunder but no lightning. Amin joined them for the view. As he parked himself between Omar and his mother and rested his elbows on the balcony rails, he shook his head. 'Other countries celebrate with fireworks,' he said. 'We go for the real thing.'

They watched the sky being lit with showers of light from all directions, intermittently, at times sporadically, and every now and then it would quieten on all sides, and then suddenly a big bomb would sound, a flurry of lights would follow from all directions and another cycle would begin.

'Isn't it amazing?' rejoiced Omar.

Without turning, Zeina said that all of these bullets, even though they were not being fired at anybody directly, were eventually going to fall down. They were going to be furnace-hot pieces of metal, and if they hit anybody, they could kill that person on the spot. Omar looked at her, then back at the sky to watch the next sequences of flashing lights. Then he turned back to her, irritated, and said, 'Do you have to ruin everything?'

The boy looked at the world around him, as far as he could see.
The world is big, big and not his.

He looked at his hands: he had only two.
For now, for a long time from now, he would need a lot more than two hands.

He looked at his feet; what can two feet do?

If he could change the world and make it his, at this moment, he wouldn't know where to start.
He would have to start everywhere at the same time.

Arab

By the time Omar was eleven years old, he was allowed to walk to school and no longer had to take the bus. Others in his class had been allowed to do it for a year now, so it was time. He had to wait until the winter was over before beginning his mother's experiment: whether he could cope without the bus and still not catch a cold or get to school too tired. Omar loved spring. He would wake up at six o'clock, take his time in getting ready, have a toasted Halloum cheese in Arabic bread, with tea, no milk, five spoons of sugar, and then negotiate what he was going to wear for the day.

His mother was relieved that he could pick up one of his classmates along the way: Walid, who lived only a few blocks from his house. 'Just so that you won't get lonely,' she would say. Omar didn't like the way she put it; he looked forward to seeing Walid because he liked Walid, not because he was going to prevent him from being lonely.

'The same thing,' his mother would say.

'No, it isn't the same thing: talking to people just so that they can stop you from being lonely is not a good reason to talk to people.'

'Fine, whatever. Go and put something warm on you, and remember, if the walk is too long, we can go back to taking the bus.' And she would button that extra button, knowing well that he was going to unbutton it the minute she took her hands off him. She would kiss him and sometimes smell him as if she were smelling a rose. He would kiss her back and jokingly throw her an old people's phrase: 'May God keep you for us.'

If there was no electricity, he would use the stairs, and then, once out of the building, he would wave to his mother; after one block, he would be out of her sight. He would time it to be in front of Walid's house at seven. Unless it was raining, Walid would wave from the third balcony and be down in a few seconds. He had become friends with Walid only after meeting him on the way back from school and ending up walking together. At first, they didn't talk much, and when they did, it wasn't about much, but then, after a while, Omar took a few risks with swearing at different things, and, very soon afterwards, they were both talking about anything and everything that bothered them.

One thing that Walid seemed to have more of a sense of was politics. He watched the news with his father; Omar didn't. There had been quite a bit of talk about Anwar El Sadat, the President of Egypt, meeting Jimmy Carter, the American President, and Menachem Begin, the Israeli Prime Minister. Everybody — people, the media, the neighbours, and others — had been saying that Sadat was a traitor for talking to Israel. Omar had heard from Zeina that last time Khaled had phoned from London, he had said that peace could only be a good thing, and so Omar expressed that view to Walid. Unlike most people, Walid didn't put others down when they said something that was of a different opinion; instead, he would try to find the most gentle way of putting his own opinion, and on this occasion, his opinion was that Khaled had not lived in Lebanon for a long time, and maybe he was thinking too much like the British. Maybe over time he had forgotten that any American president, no matter what he said, was going to side with Israel, and so any talk was going to be messed up from the start, And of course, any Israeli of any kind was a total bastard so Sadat was not only licking ass but he was also being a traitor who was not going to get anything in the end.

Omar had heard some people say that Sadat had grown tired of the Arabs because they were full of talk: they sat on their asses making speeches about being Arabs but they didn't do anything.

'That's true,' Walid agreed.

'They're supposed to be freeing Israel and giving it back to the Palestinians so that they can be one nation, but they're really just separate countries, each on his own.'

'That's true, too.'

'So what does it mean to be an Arab?'

'That's right,' Walid said. 'Nothing. And if Israel invades in the morning, none of them are going to move their asses. They said they were going to send us United Arab Forces to help us stop fighting and the Syrians came instead and now they're robbing our cars.'

'Israel invade us?' Omar wondered. 'For real?'

'Yes, of course. Have you not heard? Just this morning, there was talk of them coming into the south.'

'Wow, no!' Omar hadn't heard.

'Yeah, that's right. Who knows how much they can do?' On balance, though, they probably couldn't do too much: 'There's too many guns around.'

'Hmmm, and what did you say about the Syrians? They're stealing our cars?' asked Omar.

'Yeah, don't you know? All the stolen cars are going to Syria.'

Omar told Walid that his sister Zeina had had her car stolen and she had only finished paying for it a while ago.

'Tell her she can find it in Syria,' Walid said with certainty.

'Arab Jarab!' said Walid with a smile. Omar had heard this phrase said so many times before: Arabs are lice. It rhymed so he hadn't paid that much attention to it, but now for the first time he found himself imagining the lice, individually and collectively.

Walid shook his head. 'No wonder the Americans hate us; no wonder they don't respect us.'

Omar didn't like to think in whole groups of people. He liked Clint Eastwood; he was an American. He loved Muhammad Ali Clay; he was an American.

'Clint Eastwood is just an actor; he doesn't give a shit about anything anyway,' said Walid.

'You never know,' was Omar's stand.

Walid shrugged. 'Muhammad Ali doesn't count; he's black.'

'But he doesn't come from Africa. His original name was Clay something.'

'And why do you think he changed his name? They don't treat them like Americans.' Walid paused before continuing, 'If they don't count them, then we're not counting them, so, name me one American person who likes Arabs.'

Omar was sure that they couldn't all hate Arabs. 'Most of them wouldn't have even met any Arabs!' he protested.

'They see it on TV and they believe it,' Walid said. He was sure of it. 'They believe everything they see.'

'They see what?' asked Omar genuinely.

Walid thought to himself and then smiled. 'That's just it,' he replied. 'I don't know!' And they both started to laugh.

Omar shook his head in amazement. 'Wow! They don't have anything to see and they just believe that they should hate us.'

'Oil,' Walid remembered. 'They're jealous that the Arabs have oil.'

'But they produce cars and TVs. And we don't hate them for it.'

'Yeah, but the Arabs control the price of oil, and that really pisses them off.'

'But we don't tell them how much their cars should cost.'

'Well, they want to control everything; they want everybody to be their slaves, just like the British, except the British are not so strong any more — they used to make slaves from Indians just like Americans made slaves from blacks.'

'How do you know all this stuff?' asked Omar openly.

'My dad is interested in everything: he's got books on history; he's got brilliant pictures of the Second World War — bombs being dropped, loads of tanks, Hiroshima. The Americans dropped a bomb there just at the end of the war.'

Omar had heard of Hiroshima; he had seen pictures of deformed babies born a long time ago after everything had stopped. 'And they call *us* Arab Jarab?' wondered Omar.

'No, *we* call ourselves Arab Jarab,' Walid asserted with a smile. 'And that's because we are.'

'We are not. Come on! We don't have to agree with it.'

'In Saudi Arabia, they cut people's hands off for stealing; they have all the women scarfed up and if they saw one with a skirt, they would beat her up; and the rulers drink alcohol whenever they want, behind closed doors, and when they go to Europe and America, they also do whatever they want. Hypocrites.'

'How does your dad know all that for sure?'

'It's not just my dad; everybody knows it. Ask *your* dad.'

'Wow!' Omar shook his head amazement. 'Zeina wouldn't last a second in Saudi Arabia.'

'Arab Jarab,' mused Walid to himself.

'If Arabs are Jarab, and Arabs are not together like they say,' Omar asked out loud, 'then what are the Lebanese?'

They both laughed.

Sometimes the boy looked into his world and saw nothing, blank plain blank

nothing

The World

Khaled had been meaning to come to Lebanon for some time now but even though they would have loved to see him, his parents dissuaded him. At other times, it was the news he heard in London that put him off. Rescheduling took longer than it should have because his concerns did not usually match those of his parents: at those times when he was thinking of coming, they told them not to, even though he hadn't heard any news of war in London; other times, they told him to come and not to worry even though Israel had invaded the south. It left him unable to make sense of any of it until finally it just happened that he had an opening to leave work for a week, the Israelis had withdrawn with no immediate threat to return, and his parents told him to come: things were fine.

For Omar, it was a double event as he was going with his parents to meet Omar at the airport and then, because of sleeping arrangements, he would stay with Ziad while his parents stayed with Khaled at his uncle's house, before they travelled to Tripoli the following day. The whole family met at the airport, along with Ziad and his family, and received Khaled to a symphony of chaos, each asking the same question — 'How are you?' — not expecting an answer but just fending each other off for a little contact. Afterwards, Omar made it back to Ziad's family.

Jamal and Sana sympathised with Omar on account of having to stay apart from his brother on the night he had arrived but Omar told them that they didn't have to; it was he who had asked to stay with them as he had been missing them. Sana kissed him for saying such sweet words.

'Please,' he tried to explain to her. 'I wasn't trying to be polite and talk like old people and say things that I didn't mean just out of obligation.'

Sana saw his sincerity, laughed, and told him that he was the most precious thing in the world, along with Ziad. Jamal joked away the sentimentality and told her that she was making an 'auntie' out of him with all this talk. They had a much more important job tonight, a man's job: the World Cup was on; it was the last game, and although Omar hadn't been watching, it was time for the boy to be indoctrinated. Omar had not cared about the soccer World Cup until this point, but having heard how Jamal

114

spoke of it, and witnessed Ziad showing enthusiasm not for the game itself but more for the way his dad created excitement out of nothing, Omar was ready to be overwhelmed by the third big event of the day.

When Jamal announced so definitely that he was supporting Argentina, Omar and Ziad decided to support Holland so that they could beat Jamal. They asked Sana whether she had a preference and, to their surprise, she said she did: she was also definitely supporting Argentina. In the first half, there were no goals, but still they jumped here and there and all over the place, mainly in response to Jamal's excitement. Second half, it looked as if there weren't going to be any goals either, and if that happened, it would go into extra time. Jamal explained to Omar that that would be only half an hour, though, with a break in the middle.

'And if still nobody wins?'

'Another extra time.' But Jamal reckoned that by then somebody would make a mistake out of exhaustion and the other side would win — Argentina, of course.

'No way! Holland!'

'Argentina, you'll see. God is always with the weak.'

'Weak?' asked Ziad. 'What's weak about them? They got to the end!'

'Weak as a country,' said Jamal.

'That's right,' added Sana. 'They're just like us, *ma'treen*, poor, down to earth without much, not like the Europeans who have everything from having ripped off other countries.'

Omar and Ziad looked to Jamal for confirmation of her logic.

He agreed with half of it. 'She's right about the top part of Europe, the ones with blond hair and white skinny legs; Europe that is on the Mediterranean, though, is not bad.'

'So, which one of them would you have supported had they made it — Italy?' asked Omar.

'The Italians are crooks, thieves — funny thieves, just like us, so, yeah, I'd support them.'

'Greece?'

'They have kebab, just like us, and hummus, just like us, but they'd never make it to the World Cup because they're too busy breaking plates and dancing on them after dinner, and when you grow up in such an environment, it's hard to produce good soccer players who aren't limping from all the cuts on the soles of their feet.'

Omar and Ziad's eyes lit up with laughter.

'OK, so it's not true, but they do break plates at some celebrations but that has nothing to do with them not making it to the World Cup.'

'Who else? Who else?'

'Spain,' said Sana as she fiddled with Ziad's hair. 'That's where we had this little garlic clove.'

'Really, is that where you bought him?' joked Omar.

Sana looked at Jamal with moist eyes, and then back at Ziad and kissed him on the head. 'This jewel cannot be bought,' she said.

'The Arabs once invaded Spain,' said Jamal. 'That's right; don't be surprised. We ruled too, except we were good rulers: the Spanish loved us. They themselves, if you ask them today, would say they are Arabs. Where else do you think they got their black eyes and black hair?'

'Yeah, Spain is excellent,' Sana agreed. They had lived in Spain for a whole year back in 1966. Jamal's brother was still there.

'Well, why would he come back now?' Jamal said. 'But yeah, he's still there, and one day we're all going to visit, and if you're not still in your diapers and can get permission, then you're coming too.'

'It's that good?' Omar asked.

'Look, take it as a rule,' Jamal said. 'Any country that uses olive oil is good; any country that doesn't is doomed; and any country that is considering it has potential.'

'Does Holland use olive oil?'

'No.'

The next time Holland had an opportunity to score a goal, the team didn't get the support of either Omar or Ziad.

'What about China?' wondered Omar.

'China is not like us but they never did us any harm. They're poor now; there's just so many of them. But when you're constantly squinting, how are you going to see the ball?'

Omar and Ziad loved it. 'India?'

'India is still tired from being ruled by the British. They have cursed them with that awful cricket, made them wear white as if they don't have enough dust in their country, but no, they don't play soccer; they're too busy learning how to beat the British in their own game.'

'Australia?'

'That's too far. By the time we send them a soccer ball and they receive it, the air will have gone out of it.'

'Russia?'

'Too cold. Nobody would want to play and, if they did, the ball would be constantly skidding on ice.'

'America?'

'America ... ahh ... they have baseball and their own games; they don't want to play with the rest of the world; they think they're it.'

'Who else? Is that it?'

'Is that it? Of course not; how could you forget?'

'Who?'

'Brazil: they're the real artists. Now, that is beauty. They don't just play to win and have it all calculated; they love soccer so much that people commit suicide every time they lose in the World Cup.'

'Suicide!'

'Suicide — that's how much they love it.'

Sana laughed. 'They're mad,' she said. 'God help them. They're very poor; they have nothing else — that's why they kill themselves.'

'They kill themselves and they don't even have a war?' said Omar.

And then Holland scored a goal. Omar and Ziad first jumped in joy but then felt confused and looked at each other. Who were they supposed to support now? Jamal and Sana were shaking their heads. It was a disaster; there were only a few more minutes left. Suddenly Argentina scored a goal and the four jumped up.

The game then went into extra time. No goals in the first half. Then Argentina scored. Jump. Joy. Good for them; they deserve it! And another goal for Argentina — the World Cup was theirs now; no way now could Holland hold against the new momentum of the Argentineans. And the last whistle, *teettt teeet tteeeeee!* When Argentina held the cup high, Sana's eyes were welling up. She said that the country would be happy for months — everybody, not just lovers of football.

Next day, Omar was allowed to travel in Khaled's taxi, as he was the youngest, didn't take up much space although he was half a man now, and he hadn't spent the previous night in the same house as his brother. Omar asked Khaled whether he had seen the game the previous night.

'Yeah, I did. Twenty-two men running after one ball, but it was good. The end was exciting; Argentina won by stamina.'

'No way,' Omar objected. 'Argentina's great. It's one of the few countries in the world that hasn't used us.'

Khaled didn't know what Omar was on about. 'Holland is not a bad country,' he said. 'The Dutch are quite advanced; their medical system is quite impressive. And stamina is not necessarily a bad thing to win by; there's in-built determination in it.'

'No,' Omar argued. 'Argentina won because they deserved it.'

'Not so sure about "deserve". Well, they won the World Cup, so they were obviously the best team, but God wasn't interfering.'

Omar was not happy with what Khaled was saying. He struggled to argue but couldn't find the words.

'There's no such thing as "deserve",' repeated Khaled. 'Look all around you — all the killing; you'd have to say that we deserve all of this. Well, you can argue that some people brought it on themselves, those who got involved, yes, but the rest, no way.'

Omar suddenly went quiet. For having a Lebanese passport, Khaled had been treated like a criminal in European airports. Even though he was a doctor, they had still searched their files for his second name. 'It's humiliating,' he said. 'Nobody deserves to pay for the mistakes of others.'

'We were once called the Paris of the East,' his mother cut in. 'Everybody had respect for us.'

'Including us,' added his father.

'God doesn't interfere,' said the taxi driver. 'He leaves us to eat each other like dogs.'

'Not even the United Nations interferes,' added Khaled.

'What's the United Nations?' asked Omar.

'Maybe there's no point in knowing,' answered Khaled. 'Obviously, if you live in a war-torn country and you have to ask, that's an answer in itself.' But he continued anyway: 'Well, the five strongest countries in the world, supposedly, set up a committee after the Second World War to make sure that no more wars occur.'

'Are we the first war after the Second World War?' asked Omar.

Khaled laughed. 'I guess they don't teach real history in school and it's unlikely that they will. There's been Vietnam, Korea, Northern Ireland, and you can keep on counting.' He shrugged his shoulders. 'With Vietnam, well, the Americans did what they wanted because they are the United Nations — they're in it; they're it.'

Omar was confused.

'Put it this way,' said his father. 'They're supposed to protect small countries, like us, even bigger countries, but you saw what happened. Israel came in for two whole months. And this is not just one country against itself; one country invaded another, stayed for two months, and, on the way out, cut down as many trees as possible, just to mess us up.'

'Cut down trees?' wondered Omar.

'That's right: our agriculture would suffer; less competition for them.'

Omar's stomach churned. He noticed that this was the first time that he really felt angry at Israel. He had avoided going with everybody's anger when they talked so generally about Israelis, lumping them all together, but now he finally felt something, at least towards those who had done this. Now he had a sense of how everybody felt.

The taxi driver turned his head. 'God is sleeping,' he said, and then turned back to the road. 'Maybe he's dead; who's checking?' Then he turned to Omar's father and apologised in case he had insulted him, adding, 'It's just when you see what you see, and as a taxi driver you see all there is to see, then you stop seeing what you used to see.'

Omar's father nodded with a smile. 'No,' he said. 'I'm not insulted. 'I used to worry what my body heard, but now I don't. What I hear is how it is for others, and, by the way, you could keep your phrase and make a song out of it; I'll certainly be singing it later.'

When they arrived in Tripoli, Omar found that Amin, Zeina, Laila and her husband Khalil were already there. Omar started singing, 'You see what you see; what you don't see, you don't see; see what you want to see and turn away from what you don't want to see.'

Amin asked him what he had seen that had him all hyped up. Omar turned to Amin and asked him a definitive question. 'Who did you support last night?'

'Argentina,' Amin replied. 'Nobody deserved it like they did. They creamed Holland, made mince meat out of them, made girls out of their pale un-hairy legs, got the third world all the way up to the first world and kicked their asses.'

Omar was rejuvenated; he gave his brother a high five.

After everyone had settled, Laila and her husband cleared their throats in unison to make an announcement. Her mother got up and before she said anything, she kissed her on the head. Laila slipped her words: 'I'm pregnant'

'Oh my God!' Khaled smiled behind everybody's excitement. 'You people are still bringing children into this world?' When Laila shrunk slightly into herself, Khaled immediately apologised. No, it was fine, she said; she had already thought about it.

Big fish eat small fish — that much the boy knew about the world, but do some fish eat smaller fish even when they're not hungry?

If enough small fish got together at the same time, would they be able to eat a big fish, or at least scare it away?

A big fish has to go nowhere to eat a small fish; it just stays with itself, doesn't even have to talk to itself, but it takes a lot for small fish to get together and plan against a big fish, and maybe, while some small fish are waiting until some small fish fetch more fish to plan against the big fish, they might end up eating each other, out of hunger, maybe even boredom, and also, since there are not enough of them in the first place, they might end up being eaten by a big fish. If two big fish come along at the same time, then the whole plan is definitely doomed.

Fish have a long way to go.

News

$\mathbf{A}$ day came when Tripoli had been under shelling from the Ibbeh where Omar's grandmother used to live. It was still part of Tripoli but the Syrian counterparts had been heavy-handed for the past nineteen days. Non-stop. School had been off for that period. Omar was happy at first but then it started to feel as if there was no end in sight. Studying was bad, and a break would be good, but he had been missing his friends, even his teachers. He made an attempt to watch the news, be part of everyone else's speculations; this way, when the fighting eventually stopped, he would feel that he had taken part in the fighting stopping, not directly, but at least have been part of the process instead of being out of it, just absent. He watched Karameh come on TV; he watched him dribble words endlessly, in circles, monotonously. He checked his Arabic with his parents. No, it was fine; there was nothing wrong with it; Karameh wasn't saying much as usual, deliberate dodging.

'But why?' asked Omar. 'If he doesn't know what's going to happen, if the Syrians are bigger than everybody else and they make all the decisions, why not say it like it is?'

'He's a politician; he's not going to tell you.'

'No other politician stretches the words like he does.'

'It's just the way he talks.' And then the electricity would be cut off; it would be somebody else's turn to get it. Omar could go out to the balcony and watch a bunch of houses two blocks away from him being lit. Then no news. Omar thought that maybe the other houses would be getting the news then, but then he thought it was the same no news he was getting.

On the twenty-first day of shelling, Omar heard from his mother that since this bout of fighting had started, there had been seventeen breaks of ceasefires. Omar laughed at first, then he saw it: if in a duration of twenty-one days, the two parties agreed, seventeen times, to cease fire, and then they broke it pretty much immediately, nobody's words counted — nobody's. Omar then made a vow to himself never, ever, to attempt to hear what was going on. If it came his way, then fine, he would hear it, but he wouldn't be arguing about it and trying to

121

configure anything because they — the ones who were at the heart of it — didn't seem to be in it.

He had heard that the Americans had a lot to do with it, but he hadn't seen any Americans around. 'And you won't,' he was told. 'You have to see the bigger picture; it's all the game, a big game — we're just the pawns.'

'Oh.'

'That's right. Things can't be figured on a local level. You can speculate, but the bigger picture is what counts.'

'And what is the bigger picture?'

'Well, basically the world right now is being fought over by the Americans and the Russians; they're the biggest and strongest countries in the world. Syria is supported by the Russians and Israel is supported by the US. All the different parties in Lebanon are being given guns one way or another through those two countries, and sometimes at the same time.'

'Huh?'

'That's right; just so that they continue to fight.'

'Why don't they just let them win?'

'It's not about winning at this stage; it's about letting the war continue; it's about having Lebanon as a ground on which to threaten each other about other issues that don't necessarily have to do with Lebanon. They'll blow up a certain embassy just to make a point; of course, they have us do it since we're here.'

'And where do you get all this information?'

'It's here, plain to see. Just watch what's going on, listen to the world news as well as the local news and link the two.'

'No, thanks.'

From then on, Omar bought the newspaper on Mondays. Monday was the day when movies changed in Beirut. He would flick to the ad page, cut them out and glue them in a book he was making. Some he would not be able to see if they didn't come to Tripoli, but at least he'd keep track; he'd know what was coming out; maybe one day he'd see them. Then, he would leave the paper on the dining table. To him, the paper was now empty.

Omar started to take films seriously after Laila made a comment about a series of films that were going to be shown on Lebanese TV. She said that Humphrey Bogart was a great actor, and it was a pity they were going to run the films during the week because he had school next day but that he should catch them at the weekend or if there were clashes and he knew for sure he wasn't going to have school next day.

'Why should I watch Humphrey Bogart?' Omar asked. 'His films are really old, he's dead, and he isn't going to be making new movies.'

'Films are not only plots,' she said. 'You should notice the acting; it's the bit that makes you feel as if it's real.' Omar hadn't thought of films that way until this point. She added that even if the story was not very good, sometimes a film was still worth watching if the acting was very good.

From then on, Omar made every effort to watch as many films in the series as possible. On the nights when the electricity was on and it was obvious that he wouldn't have school next day because there was renewed shooting, Omar would be allowed to stay up. On other days, when he did have school, there was no point in arguing about staying up, so he would wait until his mother and father went to bed, and then sneak out, close the door to the corridor ever so slowly, and put the TV sound as low as possible and then sit right in front of it.

At first, he wasn't so sure why he was watching a certain movie — not much fighting in Bogart's films, a lot of talk, and sometimes he didn't quite understand the subtitles. Still, he sat through two movies before he saw *The Treasure of the Sierra Madre*: three convicts in search for gold in an American desert. Not much fighting in it either, not physically and not verbally, but it was there, somewhere between the characters, and he felt it. After the film finished, he felt brighter; something inside him was awake in a way that he hadn't felt before. He had been engrossed in the film while keeping an eye on the door and the film wasn't short; it was about 12.30 by the time it finished but he felt that it had been worth it.

One night, having watched six Bogart films over the two previous weeks, Omar realised that the series was nearly over — only two more to go. He had sneaked out and the film had only begun when the phone rang. He wasn't sure what to do. To get up would be to expose himself. Most likely, his mother would come only as far as the reception room at the hall, and if he turned off the TV and the lights and stayed put, then he could go back to watching the film after she had finished. He opened the corridor door, heard her question why it was closed, and then heard her answer the phone. It was Khaled from London. To avoid exposing himself would be to miss the call and he didn't know when Khaled was going to ring again. He let her talk for a few minutes and then decided to go over before his dad got up; maybe, in her excitement, the whole thing would be muddled up. The minute he opened the

123

guestroom door and walked behind her, she interrupted the call and asked what he was doing. He said that he wanted to talk to Khaled. She asked him again what he was doing in the dark sitting room. He said he wanted to talk to Khaled and asked her whether she should wake his dad. He looked behind him and saw that his dad had woken up and was standing next to him. They all talked to Khaled but when the phone call was finished, there was a question to answer.

They went to the sitting room and sat down. Omar said that he had been watching a series of films by a really good actor, that he had got into films lately and he was getting a lot out of them. His mother said it was ridiculous to stay up until 12.30 when he had to wake up at six next morning. 'It's just not on,' she said. 'There are plenty of other things to do. This is just mad.'

But his father asked her to let him finish. She said he was talking nonsense, and it didn't matter what he said. He gently said that Omar should still have a chance to talk. Omar looked up, took his time, and then spoke very slowly and calmly. He said that there weren't too many interests that he could have — anything that involved going outside, like playing football, was going to depend on whether or not there were new clashes. There weren't too many friends whose houses he could visit because it wasn't safe after sunset. He felt imprisoned in his own house. The only time he went out was to go to school, and very rarely to Beirut, but even school didn't make sense to him: why was everybody studying when nobody was working? And if everybody before him, the previous generation, had gone to school and there was still fighting, what did school have to teach?

His dad waited until he had finished, again asked his mother not to rush and then took a gentle breath and spoke back to Omar in the same tone. He agreed with Omar that life had got tough, but it was tough for everybody, he said, not just for him, and the situation was bigger than everybody, so it had to be lived with. Things weren't good but that didn't mean that everything should be dropped; he still had to go to school because there was no better alternative. Maybe school wasn't educating him like he wanted it to, and maybe all the political leaders had gone to school before, but many of those who were holding guns were not educated. 'Some, the very few, are acting out of a belief, a cause, and the gun is the way for them,' Omar's dad said. 'But if you respect them and leave them out of the equation for a minute, what is left? The majority are a bunch of fools swayed one way or the other, for money, for lack of a clear head, and basically *Ze'raan*: lowlife crooks.

As a father, it broke his heart to see his son so disheartened, and to be unable to provide a better world for him. 'The fact that there is no sign of things getting better is even more heartbreaking,' he said but the fact was that Omar was twelve, and whether or not he was ahead of his years in his head did not change the fact that his body was twelve, so staying up past midnight when he had to get up at six next morning was not on. Omar looked at his father and saw that he had heard him, his mother too. 'It's a physical thing,' his dad added. 'You'll get sick. We can't say OK to that.'

Two weeks later, Omar's father carried in a big colour TV. His mother smiled knowingly — a surprise she had been holding for a while. She said that the TV was his, although he wouldn't be telling everybody which channels to watch and he still had to stick to his promise of going to bed on time — no more deception, but still, it was his TV. Omar appreciated the message. His father then added that in a year's time, the prices would have gone down a bit, and by then they would know whether to get a Betamax or a VHS. They were going to get a video recorder, and that way he could watch all the missed films.

When Zeina, Laila, and Amin visited, they each complained jokingly, in turn, and independently, that they had had to live with a fossil of a TV for so long, and now Omar had got a colour TV, just like that.

Over the next few months, Omar continued to buy the newspaper on Mondays and learn as much as possible about which movies he should want to watch in the future. Laila had told him of a film being made about the Vietnam War; it was directed by the same guy who had made two really famous films, each better than the other, and he had risked all his money on this film. If it didn't succeed, he was going to be in big trouble. She explained to him what a director did and told him that there was a really famous actor in it, and they had to bring him into a real jungle and he had asked for $3 million. Omar started to write 'Apocalypse Now' on his notebooks in class over the next three months. Lisa, a girl he fancied, asked him why he kept on writing the name of a movie he hadn't even seen. He told her that he was sure it was going to be great, and that he had been promised by his brother and sisters that, once it opened in Beirut, he could go especially to see it.

'Why do you want to see a film about war?' she asked him. 'Do we not have plenty of it?'

He agreed with her, but he just knew he had to see the film.

When *Apocalypse Now* finally opened in Beirut, it happened that there were no clashes either in Beirut or Tripoli. Omar kept on praying, asking God if he was going to die in the near future, to keep it until after the film, and a bit further, until they got home, so that it wouldn't be too much hassle picking him up in the street. Also, he didn't want his brother or sisters to be blamed or to blame themselves for an unrelated event. Laila was just about to give birth, Ziad had basketball training, and so Zeina and Amin ended up taking Omar. They had rarely gone to the cinema together, but for this occasion, they decided to make it even more special. At first, when the film started, Omar was unsettled because there were no credits in the beginning, but then, on the advice of Amin, he just watched the movie. It was nearly three hours long, and Omar was mesmerised in every scene. When they came out, Amin and Zeina said that they had headaches.

'Yes,' said Omar. 'Me too.'

Zeina nodded. 'Isn't that a sign of how real the film was?'

As they left the cinema, Omar wondered aloud why he had wanted to see it so much. Zeina flippantly said that he had wanted to see that they were not the worst, that there were far more horrible wars. He smiled. 'Maybe,' he said. 'Well, I haven't seen any women drop bombs from helicopters, and I haven't seen anybody as mad as Marlon Brando.'

When Omar asked about the Vietnam War, Amin started to tell him, but then, just as they were about to turn a corner, Omar asked the name of the actor whose character loved the smell of napalm bombs in the morning. They weren't sure. He asked if he could quickly go back to the cinema just for two seconds — maybe he'd find out his name from the pictures beside the main poster. Only if he ran, they both said.

When Omar came back, he was walking very slowly. Zeina complained that he had run in but now he was taking all the time in the world. Then she saw his face: white, completely pale. She asked him what had happened, but he wasn't very coherent. She asked him to slow down and collect his thoughts. With a blank expression, he said that when he came out of the cinema, he was just walking, and there was this woman with a baby — she was probably carrying the baby — and then suddenly the baby was in the hands of a bearded guy, and he was just walking off with her baby. She was going crazy and at the same time trying not to scream because she didn't want to make the

guy even crazier and she was silently pleading for people to help her.
Then, one guy, who didn't know either, came to the bearded guy, very
slowly, and then, Omar wasn't so sure how it happened, but the
bearded guy ended up giving back the baby.

Omar was pale. He could hardly speak. He tried again. He said that
for no reason, a guy took a baby from a woman, and he walked off. It
didn't make sense. And there was something about this guy that made
you feel like you couldn't talk to him because he was not crazy, but black
all the way inside him and all around him. He looked as if he could have
shot anybody, for no reason. Did Omar see his gun? No, but everybody
was afraid he had one. He was just ... Omar didn't know how to say it.

On the way back, Omar said that there was no point in trying to
understand anything any more; he had finally seen the sickness that
everybody constantly talked about. What he had just seen had nothing
to do with who was fighting whom, nothing to do with anything; it had
no reason; nothing could explain it. Square zero.

When they got to Ziad's house, Sana wanted to know what was
wrong with Omar. 'Was the film such a disappointment?' she asked.

'No,' Omar said. 'The film was amazing.' He tried to explain that
he had seen an incident that had contaminated him, had made him feel
nauseous. 'I felt filthy for being human,' he said.

When Omar had explained what he had seen, Sana shrugged her
shoulders. 'You'll see a lot,' she said. 'You'll have to throw it all behind
your back, into the sea; this is what war is like.' Then she took his
hand, and said that he shouldn't let these things affect him.

But how could he avoid being affected by them? He was not a wall.

Her eyes filled up. She said he was right, that two weeks ago, one
of her neighbours, who lived in one of the smaller houses in front, had
started screaming out of the blue. 'I can't take it any more, I can't take
it any more,' he had screamed, out of his head. 'He just lost it,' said
Sana. 'This is life; this is what we have to live with.'

Ziad had been quiet all along. He wasn't sure what to say, but when
Omar seemed to be getting better, he said that he had a joke for him: once
there was this Lebanese guy who had a dog that he really loved. Suddenly
he won the lottery. He decided to treat his dog, so he took him to Paris, and
showed him the Eiffel Tower. The dog became unhappy. So he brought
him to London, showed him Big Ben. The dog became even more
depressed. He brought him to New York, showed him the Empire State

Building, but the dog was getting really miserable. He brought him everywhere, showed him the best of everything, gave him the best of foods — caviar, the lot — and the dog just became more and more depressed. In the end, his owner got really fed up with him. He brought him back to Lebanon and threw him onto one of those garbage dumps on the street. The dog sat back, smiled, and said, 'Yes, this is the life of a dog.'

When Omar and Sana laughed, Ziad added that the moral of the joke was that Lebanese people should just accept that they are dogs. Sana looked at the floor, smiled sadly, and then nodded her head. 'It's true,' she said, giving Omar a kiss and telling him not to worry. 'You know,' she said. 'What can we do?'

A week later, Laila gave birth to a boy; she called him Samer. She gave birth in Tripoli so that if fighting started again, at least she would be near her mother. The baby looked so small to Omar — tiny. He didn't hear a thing or understand a thing, Omar was told. 'Maybe it's better for him. Hopefully by the time he hears things, they'll make a bit more sense.'

Over the next few months, Omar heard that there had been a coup in Iran. The Shah, who had been a dictator for years, keeping all the money for himself, had been overthrown by a Moslem leader, Khomeini. 'He should be good for the country,' Omar heard. 'Just applying the Moslem laws should immediately make things fairer for everybody. Iranians are Moslems but they are not Arabs; they are Persians.' Omar had only heard the name of the country before; he knew nothing more, but he felt good for them if they were getting justice.

He also heard from Zeina that a woman leader might win in England. She was very excited for the English; she said that it would be good because it was a woman. 'Women don't get to lead,' Zeina said. 'It will be good for England because unemployment is so high, and she'll bring her female sensibilities and take them out of their old imperialistic way of thinking, soften them a bit.'

Local news became even more incoherent. On one occasion, Omar's dad sent him to buy a newspaper. On the way home, Omar noticed that most of the paper was blank. When his father looked at it, he shook his head. No, it wasn't a printing error; it was censorship. There were probably criticisms of Syria. He bowed his head in desperation and sighed, saying, 'Now we are being silenced in our own country.' He told Omar to take the paper back to the newsagent. He said that he didn't have to get his money back, but it was important that he return it.

the boy asked, when you look at another human and you don't see his soul,
only darkness, is it that it is hiding, or can a soul leave a body completely?

the boy wondered, hoped: maybe one day a tear will revolt, it will say it no
longer wants to be sad,
maybe it won't, maybe it won't even cross its mind

when a person cannot bear what is around him, and he snaps, can
he come back later?

the boy learnt of rusting: it happens over time, slowly, hard to see; the piece of
metal
looks at itself one day and it finds that it has rusted
the boy wondered what was happening to him, what processes escaped his
vision?

Sex

'The facts of life' had been explained to Omar swiftly and his curious questions only half answered. It happened unintentionally, it was a few months after Laila had given birth to Samer. She was chatting with Zeina about how it was hard to 'do it' immediately after giving birth because she had stitches. There was a giggle around the 'it' part of 'doing'; even 'doing' sounded different from any other doing, so Omar wouldn't let it go. Zeina ended up looking at Laila and they took a decision together. They reckoned he was smart enough and it wasn't long before he would have to know — at the most, about a year before his classmates would know; that's if they didn't already know. Zeina said that the bees story was a very general way of putting it. 'For human beings, it's the same principle,' she said. 'But basically a man puts his "thing" in the woman's "thing".'

What thing? How? But how does it get hard? If a woman's thing is at her front, and when the man gets hard and it goes up instead of straight, then how is he going to get it in? What if he put it in the same place as the one where she pees? How can he tell the difference?

Zeina told him that maybe he should ask Amin all of these questions, but for the time being, he knew more than enough. Also, she was a woman and she should tell him only so much. In the end, he had enough to think about and had accepted her last point, but just before leaving them to each other, he looked at them, and asked Laila, 'So you have "done it"?'

She nodded her head positively, with an accepting smile.

He then turned to Zeina. 'How about you?'

She laughed at his mischief. 'No, not until I'm married.' And then she told him to get out.

Over the next few days, he was baffled as to how such a major thing had slipped under his nose for so long. He had wondered about it, but he had certainly not questioned it as much as he should have questioned it. At the first opportunity, when the phone lines connected again, he rang Ziad. Ziad said that it had been alluded to by his father but only in passing, and, as usual, jokingly. Ziad had been caught up more in how his mother was tickled when his father mentioned the bees thing than in what it meant. His father had been able to make jokes out of nonsense and even make them work, so, on this occasion, it had slipped by him that there was no double meaning attached. They both agreed that from now on, they should question everything about the world, even if the adults themselves didn't question it. Surely there were more discoveries under everybody's noses. What they couldn't quite figure out was exactly which part of the flower a bee stuck his thing in. And if bees 'did it' to flowers, presumably because flowers couldn't walk over to each other, then who 'did it' with bees? Maybe honey was mentioned in the Koran because it was a holy product that had come out of an insect mating with a plant.

A few weeks later, when Amin visited Tripoli, Omar threw a zillion questions at him. Amin said that he was tempted to leave Omar's bee theory intact because he hadn't heard anything as warped in a long time, but he decided to clarify it because this area was warped enough as it was. Amin answered as many questions as he could, as openly as he could, but he admitted that this area was not about making sense, and since Omar hadn't started growing pubic hair, and hadn't even begun to feel 'urges', they should talk about it at more length as time went on.

Omar ended up holding back on a 'thing' that Ziad had heard: that if he went to the toilet and rubbed his penis for about fifteen minutes, even if nothing happened in the meantime, eventually it would shoot a liquid that was not piss. Ziad hadn't tried it, but he was considering it. After a few days of deliberation, Omar decided to do it. He went in, locked the door behind him, stayed standing up, facing the toilet, lowered his pants, and then started to rub his penis. After ten minutes of rubbing, he heard his mother passing by, so he sat on the toilet, trying not to stop, she asked him what he was doing and he said, 'Nothing', then immediately afterwards realised that 'Nothing' was going to yield more questions so he added, 'Nothing, because I'm constipated.'

She made a sound as if sighing with relief, then told him not to exhaust himself trying; he could always leave it till later.

He said he was going to give it his best shot since he was already on the toilet — all the while continuing his rubbing. After she had gone, it dawned on him that the 'rubbing' couldn't be just about 'rubbing', that he probably had to concentrate on making the rest happen.

Ziad had heard that there would be a point where the top of his penis would get really red, and that's when he might feel scared and stop, but that if he crossed that point, it would make everything else happen. Omar looked down at his penis and it was very red. He had been rubbing for so long that it had been numb for the last while. Then he felt some fear — the fear of letting something unknown happen — but he persisted, and felt more fear, and remembered that he had to go on, and then, suddenly, he felt something happening in his torso part, and then a feeling took over from his testicles, to his penis, and involuntarily, he shot out above the toilet. He shot a second, a third, and then a fourth time. And then stopped.

Omar's mouth opened in victory; he had found a secret door and opened it. He felt a glow for having gone beyond the fear. He wasn't sure what was going to happen, whether something was going to go wrong — the way the tip of his penis got so red, it could have just come off. Over the next two days, Omar felt overwhelmed by what he had discovered, but he also felt powerful: he could trigger the overwhelming experience himself. He talked about it with Ziad as discreetly as possible over the phone but he wanted to see him face to face to feel freer to talk about it in-depth. They came to the conclusion that maybe Omar could try it one more time to see if it worked, but that then he should leave it until he felt the 'sex' thing. Ziad said that most likely he would have to wait as it was due to come on its own within the next year; that's what his dad had alluded to.

On the way to school with Walid, Omar opened the conversation about having babies. Walid shrugged his shoulders. 'When people get married, they have babies,' he said. 'It happens on its own.' Omar felt that it might not be right to tell him.

In class, Omar felt as if he had a powerful secret. Maybe there were some guys who knew it too, but there wouldn't be many, he guessed, judging by the way most of the other boys seemed to be going along with things in general. As regards Lisa, he was surprised that his new discovery had made no difference to the way he fancied her. He felt he had something extra that he had not had before, but maybe she had her own too. He had always wanted to hold her, put his cheek against hers, touch her hands, play with her short black hair, and he still wanted to do all of these things, but he knew that he would never be able to. The soft pain in his chest that he felt for her would always be there and it

132

was not going to be soothed, because boys and girls didn't talk in the playground. The older ones walked with each other but boys and girls didn't meet outside school. For as long as he could remember, it had never been safe to be out later then sunset. At the most, people walked up from Mulla Street to Azmi Street, and back again, and up again, and back again, and then home. Still, he didn't want to shut out what he felt for her, even though it was unlikely that he'd be letting any of this out of his chest. And he didn't want to put his thing in her thing. He wondered whether he'd want to when the sex thing came.

Within six months, the sex thing had fully arrived. Omar had been watching out for it and so it felt like ages. It happened to Ziad first. He didn't make a big deal about it until Omar talked about it and he knew that they had both arrived at the same point of obsession with women's bodies. The slightest magazine ad could be the trigger for sexual fantasy. What they really needed though was real sex magazines. It was much harder to get *Playboy* in Tripoli and so it was up to Ziad to open the topic with his friends and see how he could get some, at least one. The next time Omar went to Beirut, Ziad waited until they'd had dinner and then, when they were alone, he said that what he was about to give him was far bigger than the Indian ritual of cutting the palm, shaking hands, and becoming blood brothers. He produced a copy of *Playboy* and handed it slowly to Omar. Omar lowered his head, received the magazine with both hands, and pledged that he would dedicate his life to repaying this holy gift with another.

What became so difficult about the summer was the amount of free time Omar had. He could go to the beach only if there were arrangements to go with more than one friend, and he needed somebody who was a member of a beach club. The hot afternoons when he lay on the sofa in the shade of his living room were eventually going to end up in sexual fantasies. Omar accepted that he was going to masturbate once a day and he would take time in preparing for it, making sure that his mother was busy and wasn't going to interrupt him, but what he found difficult was that even when he didn't want to, fantasies would overtake him and he would end up masturbating more than once, and sometimes it even happened out of boredom. This bothered him. He had wanted to keep it purely as a treat. He had noticed that whenever he did it as a result of fantasies overtaking him, rather than him planning it, he always came quicker. He talked about this with

Ziad. It was as if his penis — now dick — had a life of its own, with a fully developed brain.

And then a conversation he had with a shop assistant from the furniture shop next to his house sent him into a further dilemma. He had known Munir over the years from just passing in front of the shop. Munir was three years older than Omar. At one time, he had stayed in the shop with his older brother but now he was old enough to open it and sit in it on his own. In a passing conversation, Munir ended up responding seriously to a jokey remark Omar had made. He said that masturbation was blasphemous, that each shot of sperm contained thousands and thousands of sperm, each one of them a life. It was like sending God's army down the toilet to their death. Omar wasn't so sure about seeing it this way but did not have the words to argue about it. Also, Munir had so much energy behind his speech that it felt more like a sermon, and Omar had decided a long time ago that there was no point in arguing with somebody who was preaching because it seemed that they never let anything back in. Still, even though he went on and masturbated later on that day, he thought about the comment before and after he came, and even a bit during.

A few weeks later, a talk with his brother complicated things even further.

Amin was over for a weekend visit, and while Omar always took every opportunity of being alone with his brother to ask him all his unanswered questions, it was Amin who approached him on this occasion. He said he wanted to have a little chat with him, a kind of a difficult area but he wasn't going to be giving a hard time about anything so maybe Omar would try not to interrupt him too much, just listen at first. Amin said that everybody masturbated, it was natural, but that the come itself was very nutritious, full of protein, and, at this age, Omar would need a lot of protein for his growing bones and muscles. Of course it was also natural that he was going to do it, but it was important to do it in moderation.

Omar admired Amin's effort to talk on a general level so as not to embarrass him, but still, he had a question, and he tried to phrase it without his mischievous smile: 'How many times is "moderation"?'

Amin was cornered. He shrugged his shoulders, and suggested maybe once a week.

Omar's eyes widened in shock. 'What? ONCE? ONCE a week?'

Amin shrugged his shoulders again. Well, maybe twice, three times a week, 'but not kind of every day'. Then he added that he didn't really want to be bargaining about this, but it was important for him as an older brother to inform Omar of the facts, and then it would be up to Omar to work things out for himself.

Between the image of thousands and thousands of spermy soldiers meeting their death in the toilet and the image of his arms and legs getting thinner and thinner due to loss of nutrition, Omar came up with a solution. He decided that next time he masturbated, he would come in his hand instead of a handkerchief, then he would taste the sperm, and, if it wasn't revolting, he would swallow it. There would be nothing lost — neither lives nor nutrition. He would be recycling, and if it tasted sweet, there might be no harm in masturbating all the time.

Sperm wasn't sweet or sour, and it didn't smell good or bad but was a funny neutral. It was like an awkward jelly in his mouth, and swallowing it was a weird medication. After the third masturbation, he decided not to swallow it again; it just took from the whole thing. And he wasn't getting used to the texture or the swallowing. He'd just try to drink more milk instead, eat better. As to the thousands of soldiers dying, well, even when a woman did get pregnant, she was getting pregnant by only one solider, not all of them. Munir's argument that it was all right when it was for a holy purpose just didn't seem right. He wasn't so sure exactly how it was not right, but just because he couldn't pinpoint its fault didn't mean that he should follow it.

When the summer break finished and he went back to school, there was a vibrant buzz in the class. During the break, the boys found themselves joking about nothing but sex. It was a quick acknowledgement that during the summer everybody had found or had been found by the great secret and was masturbating out of a natural duty to teenagehood. This was what all the allusions by parents and teachers had been about; an era of mischief was about to be launched. Omar and his friends felt that they had gradually become more vociferous over the years, but this was different: it was as if the universe had handed them the power for mayhem. They smiled, knowing that they were going to be giving the teachers hell from now on.

through the darkest blackness the boy was filled with a playful vibrant life,
a gift due by the order of life around him,
it coloured his eyes,
in his wonderment, he could see life in death

Education

When Omar met his friends after the summer break, it took only a few days for a new vocabulary to develop. Omar, having crossed into the 13-year mark, with a breaking voice, held his crotch and announced that no nation could stand against his mighty cock. Everything and anything was '*Airi*' — his cock in you — the sky, Israel, school, anything that breathed and every inanimate thing. What fascinated him most about swearing was how good it felt just to say the words, especially when the translations made no sense when broken up literally. Some were ingenious in their defiance of logic; his favourite did not even have any sexual allusions in it, but was a phrase he overheard just outside his school in an exchange between a carpenter and a passer-by who had stepped on freshly laid cement. At first, the carpenter let out a disgruntled noise. The passer-by by said that a sign should have been put up to warn pedestrians, and then the carpenter let him have it at the top of his voice: 'I'll make God not have created you,' he said. Most men swore, but the ones who crossed into blasphemy held a special place of respect in Omar's heart; they no longer just vented spleen but had given up all hopes of any worldly or otherworldly system that could made sense.

After a few days of trying out new swear words, Omar and his friends framed their world with more aptly fitting descriptions of how things really were: 'Israel has raped us in the south'; 'The Syrians milked us dry, wanked us to the maximum'; 'The Arabs avoid us like a whore's smelly pussy'. With a wide, accepting smile, everybody concluded: 'We're fucked and you can't unvirgin a virgin; once you're fucked, you're fucked.' It was only a matter of how long more. And there was no end in sight.

Over the first few weeks of being back in school, Omar found himself in a gang of four. Ahmad, tall and thin, lived in the Ibbeh near where Omar's grandmother used to live. Originally from Syria, he had still retained his accent but shared his friends' verdict of the Syrian President and the Syrian involvement in Lebanon: 'Fuck them for fucking us.' Jamil was short and stubby. Having repeated a few classes over the years, he was three years older than his mates. He lived in the Beddawi, just outside Tripoli, and was one of three in the class who struggled extra hard to get home when local troubles erupted. George, although holding a Christian name, was the son of two Moslem parents. When his father's best friend had died in a boating accident while studying in France, he had promised himself that he would keep his friend's memory alive. George claimed that the reason for his existence was to test people's prejudice: Christians who gave him a warmer smile when they heard his name were prejudiced bastards, and Moslems who felt betrayed when they heard that he was a Moslem with a Christian name were hypocrites. The sense of loyalty that developed among the four still left them open to messing with others and siding with other classmates if a teacher made an unfair comment. Omar still walked to school with Walid but when they got to the playground, Walid would join less rowdy mates.

In one of the geography classes, George raised his hand and asked the teacher what the point was of learning about all the different places in Lebanon since they weren't going to get a chance to see them. He said that Lebanon was so proud of the cedar tree that they even had it in the flag, yet he had never seen a real one because it had always been too risky to go to Ihden where they had been growing for thousands of years. Jamil then added that there was no point in memorising the map of the country since Israel reshaped it as it pleased and invaded whenever it felt like it. Omar then suggested that they memorise only half the number of the population as stated in the book, as by the time they finished school, enough people would probably have died to make it an accurate estimate. Jamil sarcastically turned around and asked them to keep quiet, saying that he was here to learn and they were wasting his parents' hard-earned money. The teacher paused for a minute, and then asked them if they were finished. Omar said that he wasn't, and that, in fact, if the teacher didn't mind, he would like a shot at changing the Lebanese constitution: a teenager's effort would still be more mature than the infantile version left by the French. The teacher sighed and asked him whether he would like to take it up with the headmaster. Omar's eyes glowed, he considered it, and then said, 'Maybe next year.'

During break-time, Omar brought it up as a real issue for consideration: why didn't they meet with the headmaster and offer him their own version of the constitution, just for the hell of it? Jamil figured that doing this would entail finding out the details of the current one. There was no need to pollute their heads further — why not just try to convince the headmaster that there was just no point in taking geography lessons since none of the details were guaranteed to remain accurate from one day to another? Ahmad reckoned that their stand should be that there was no point to any of their classes; if education made a real difference, none of the current politicians would be as they were today. George's angle was that if education did work, if it gave them any sense of pride, it was going to make their lives more humiliating. They looked at him. It was an interesting point, but how so? He reminded them of how ignorant the Syrian checkpoints had become: coming from Beirut, you could be waiting more than two hours just outside Tripoli; you'd think an accident was causing all this delay until you arrived at a gunman who would be looking away, eating peanuts, and then when he felt like it, would flick his hand to let you go, without even glancing at you. Jamil laughed and said that with his accent, he had got into Syrian cars and overtaken whole lines of cars; all you had to do was have a picture of Assad, and in seconds you could overtake a two-hour line. 'Just waltz through while you guys are waiting,' he said.

Omar nodded. Last time his uncle came from Beirut, he had been waiting so long at a checkpoint that it had become dark and he forgot to turn his headlights on. When he got to the gunman, he was asked seriously why he didn't have his lights on — was it because he didn't have enough petrol?

Jamil's neighbour had been beaten up because he opened his boot from under the steering wheel. 'What was that?' asked Omar.

'Seriously, my neighbour had got one of these new cars where you don't have to get out of the car to open the boot — you just open it by lifting a handle under the steering wheel — and the soldier at the checkpoint took offence that this guy wasn't getting out to do the honours for him, so he got him out of the car and beat him up in front of the whole line.'

'See,' George said, all of these stories confirming his point. 'It is more humiliating to be educated and then to be ruled by blatant, thick, donkey ignorance.'

Omar shook his head in wonder; even if they stopped right here, nothing in the world could bring them backwards enough to be on that level. In the end, they dropped their ideas of meeting the headmaster with any real plan. It looked as if they would be meeting him soon enough on a regular basis anyway — it would be impossible to keep on going while bearing the outside world, without getting themselves kicked out of class. They needed at least some entertainment.

At the end of the week, Friday night, after dinner, around eight, maybe nine, shooting would often start. It had become a regular occurrence that a bomb would explode after the eleven o'clock Friday prayers earlier in the day. Sometimes it would spur immediate fighting; other times it would remain quiet until the night, and then, amidst the quietness of candle-lit houses, the sounds of gunfire would be heard. Omar's ears would prick up. The possibility of new clashes meant that he might not have to do a certain exam the following Monday morning. With the regular school disruptions, previous assignments would pile up and the teachers would find it difficult to stick to the curriculum, yet they had to go through it, they would say; otherwise, the students wouldn't get to the next class.

Logic or no logic, though, the sound of bullets on a Friday night meant a potential break. Omar would listen, occasionally taking his eyes off his text, and would judge whether it was escalating. Once rockets were launched, it was an indication to stay listening although not yet totally abandoning his text; it had happened on quite a few occasions that he would leave his text prematurely only for things to clam down. The disappointment would be unfair; sometimes he would have left the text well into the weekend and, by Monday, while still hoping that there was no school, he would find himself in class under-prepared. The harder the subject, the more fervently Omar prayed for successive regular bombing, with little intermission between retaliations. Once, it crossed Omar's mind that these bombs could be falling onto some people's houses — they could be dying, and that's what he was praying for. He wondered whether his prayer actually made a difference, whether it was just an expression of a wish within himself, or whether he had truly, somehow, contributed to the launch of another bomb which would eventually, very soon, land on somebody somewhere. He held the frivolousness of his exams against somebody's life. He knew that he didn't want anybody really to die. He also knew that, to his ears, the sound of fresh bullets and heavy rockets on a Friday night had become sweet.

the boy looked into his world, sky and earth, sun and dirt, and asked:
why am I here?
the trees and the clouds were saddened by the question; they had tried their best
to be seen, link the boy to the life in life — for the boy to have asked the question,
the last natural cord must have been severed.
Amidst the vastness of all around him, the boy was now alone.

The boy tried to ask another question; if a caterpillar has to want to become
a butterfly in order for it to grow into one, then if a boy has to decide to become
a man ... but the question had answered itself.

Talk

On the way to school, Walid told Omar that John Lennon had died. He had been shot by a fan. John Lennon had said, 'Life begins at forty', and he was shot at forty, point blank. When they reached school, Omar ran it by his friends in the playground.

'Who gives a fuck?' was Jamil's attitude. 'Hundreds and thousands of us die and nobody makes a fuss any more.'

George had heard that Lennon's death was so significant because it represented the end of the sixties, but argued, 'Well, we're in the eighties; what happened to the seventies?' He was convinced that Westerners were missing a big chunk of their brains to be still stuck in a decade long gone.

'He's a beetle,' said Ahmad, with a smile. 'That makes him an insect; you can't take the death of an insect seriously. We step on hundreds of insects every day without even thinking about it.'

Omar said that he wasn't pretending that John Lennon was his father, but he did love the Beatles' music and even John Lennon's later music made him feel better; it took him away from all that was around him. And John Lennon was all for peace.

'The peace that the West wants to talk about is all about taking your clothes off, taking drugs, and fucking each other.' George was getting heated. 'Putting a flower in a gunman's rifle doesn't necessarily stop him from shooting you through your flower right into your heart. The sixties didn't make a fucking difference; they still support their governments who send guns all around the world so idiots like us can kill ourselves. There's no way we would be having a civil war without America and Russia; we don't produce guns and we don't even produce bullets.'

Ahmad smiled. 'Guys,' he said. 'You can't be fighting over an insect here.'

'We're talking about peace,' said Omar.

'We're talking about war,' said George.

'No matter what you talk about, it's not going to make a difference,' said Ahmad.

Jamil agreed. 'Nothing makes a difference,' he said. 'There's no point in talking about anything.' And the bell rang, and it was time to go back to class and ignore everything they heard, let nothing in, just pass it back out in the exams.

Omar continued to wonder what did make a difference. Later, during a history class, he saw that Lisa, who was in the row in front of him, had ingrained 10,452 km on her desk: the surface area of Lebanon. The figure had been frequently advertised recently by the army as a way of inspiring national pride. Many Moslems felt that the army had stronger affiliations to the Christians, and Lisa was Christian. As the class ended, Omar made a flippant remark about the uselessness of the army: 'If they had any significance, they would have stopped the war.'

Without fully looking at him, Lisa replied that nothing was going to get the country back if they gave up on their own army.

Omar said that the army was biased, and so was the constitution; it was unrepresentative of the people.

'Yes it is,' she agreed. 'Still, the army is another thing.'

'It isn't another thing, when 35 per cent have the highest power in the government; it's just not going to jell with the rest.'

'It isn't 35 per cent,' she said. 'It's 40 per cent Christians and 60 per cent Moslems.'

'No,' Omar said. 'It's actually 35 per cent. 40 per cent? When was the last time you counted?'

'When was the last time *you* counted?'

'The army will eventually split on itself, like everything else in this country.'

'Maybe so,' she said. 'But until it does, one shouldn't be treating it as of it has; that would be killing all hope.'

'Hope,' mocked Omar; he saw no hope. And the next teacher came in.

While walking home with Walid, Omar wondered about his exchange with Lisa. What was that all about? How come he was getting caught up in an argument with somebody who was never going to make a difference to the war? She was never going to use a gun, and neither would he, so why was he making her feel bad? What did the truth matter? Walid saw his concern and asked him what was up.

'Nothing,' said Omar. There was no point in talking.

Walid smiled with his usual gentleness. 'That's right,' he said. 'There's no point in talking. In fact, Nizar Qabbani's wife has been blown up in the Iraqi embassy bomb in Beirut. Let's see what confused poem he's going to come up with.'

'What was that?'

'Nizar Qabbani, the famous love poet. He's originally from Syria although he's been living in Beirut for ages, and his wife's from Iraq. And Syria and Iraq have been having this big political difference, and, as usual, other countries vent their anger against each other on our soil, so the Syrians planted a bomb in the Iraqi embassy and the whole building came down. So, his own country killed his wife, and, since he's a poet, what else can he do but come up with some poem about the whole deal?'

Omar was shocked by the harshness of it all. He was touched for Nizar Qabbani. He had never read any of his poems but he had seen a picture of him; he looked like a kind man.

'A poem,' mocked Walid. 'We can hardly understand regular talk.'

At home, Omar pushed himself through his homework. He didn't quite understand an old Arabic poem, although the teacher had gone through each line in great detail. He went to ask his father about it. He found him listening to the radio, shaking his head and huffing. 'Iraq and Iran are fighting each other,' he said.

'Over what?' asked Omar.

'They're both Moslem countries. Iran is not Arabic but Persian, but still, it doesn't make sense as they both claim to be against America.'

'What does America have to do with all of this? They're next to each other and America is all the way down the other side of the map.'

'Oil, selling guns, whatever.'

'Is there any point in understanding this?' asked Omar.

'You'll only hurt your head,' answered his father lovingly, as if encouraging him to stay away from the burdens of the world, and then he asked him what he wanted

'It doesn't matter,' answered Omar. 'It's all bullshit anyway. I'll just memorise the poem verbatim.'

Omar's father gently took Omar's book and squinted at the poem. Omar reached to turn the lights on, and then remembered that the electricity was off. He lit a candle and put it in front of his father, and then started to blow tiny streams of air into the flame.

'It's about a man, standing on a hill, lamenting the loss of his loved one; it was a common practice in the old times. It is a beautiful poem but admittedly difficult.'

Omar listened as his father tried to dissect the poem and explain the various possible meanings, and he was successful with most of it, but there were many words he was unsure about.

'What is the point in learning something that most people can't understand about a practice from a few hundred years ago?' Omar asked.

His father said that he wasn't going to get into a philosophical debate; he might end up twisting his tongue.

Omar stared into the candle. His father's ears pricked up to a news announcement on the radio. 'Listen to this,' said his father with a smile on his face. 'The Americans want to elect a second-rate cowboy actor for president.' Omar tried to figure out the metaphor. 'No, really. Reagan used to be a Western movie actor; he even used to fall off his horse.'

Omar tried for over half an hour to reach Ziad over the phone to share with him a real-life joke. When the line finally connected, Ziad had already heard the news. He was very glad: 'Let the Americans fuck themselves up; let it not be just us who are mad.'

'Now it's going to be a Western movie for real,' laughed Omar.

Ziad said that he felt a sense of comfort: 'Nothing anywhere makes sense, and that makes more sense than some things not making sense in some places while the same things make sense in other places, right?'

Omar agreed. If Ziad was saying that nothing made sense, it was only right that he didn't make sense in describing how it didn't make sense. Omar and Ziad lost each other and ended up laughing about it; they felt they were more on the same wavelength than if they had been trying to figure things out. They both agreed that all news should be announced this way, with a deliberate aim to confuse the issue — that way everybody would see how fucked things really were.

After dinner, and having gone to the balcony a few times to check which areas nearby had electricity, Omar resigned to bed. He went through the events of the day, reflecting, and ended up thinking of Lisa. He promised himself that over the next few days, he would make sure to have little contacts with her, jokes or comments about the class, just to make it clear that his intentions towards her were warm. There was no point in talking about politics; it could only make things messy and he didn't want to get caught in a battle of words that made no real difference in the outside world.

Then he thought of her hair, how smooth and soft it was, how he would love to smell it, touch it. He had fancied her for more than six months, but then the fancying had been dwindling away just lately; he would most likely start fancying some other girl very soon. All of these feelings went nowhere; they just roamed around his head, as he remembered little gestures, snippets of smiles, his chest sometimes softening, sometimes aching. He was surprised to notice that his thoughts rarely had any sexual content. At the most, he would think of kissing, coming close to her neck, breathing in her smell and wondering what it would be like to have her hand in his. He had just masturbated a few hours before to pictures in *Playboy* and *Penthouse*, dreaming up all sorts of fantasies and positions, but the two rarely crossed into each other. His friends, too, could conjure up the crudest swearing among themselves but they never aimed it at the girls they knew, only at ones they had no contact with. It was funny, he thought, maybe he never allowed himself any sexual fantasies with the girls he knew because even the most basic wishes, like wanting to touch her hand, or even tell her of his feelings, would never materialise. Maybe later on, when people went to college in Beirut, but as long as he was in school, in Tripoli, he would go to school during the day, come back around 2.30, have his lunch, study for a while, go out for a walk between five and six, and then, once the sun had set, the town would be completely dead, whether there had been recent fighting or not. He would not be going to any parties; he would not be dancing; he would not be alone with any girl he fancied, and the most basic dreams and feelings would have a roaming range confined to his head and chest.

A few gunshots broke his reflections. He listened. It was Thursday night; there was no point in getting his hopes up about school beings closed next day. Clashes usually started after the eleven o'clock Friday prayers at the mosques. Recently there had been car bombs on a weekly basis around the time people were getting out of the mosque. Sometimes clashes were held back until Friday night. In any case, he didn't have any exams the following day. It would be really fun to go in freely and wait for the gun sounds to develop and escalate, watching the teacher hold a class while waiting for a message from the headmaster to dismiss school. There was always a moment when it became clear to the teacher that he had lost the class's attention because the fighting had become quite serious, yet there would have been no decision delivered to the class. That was Omar's favourite moment — the teacher's eyes gave up, and he accepted the jeering of the students:

146

'Oooooh, what a beauty; that was a really heavy shell'; 'We must persevere in the name of education, even if we are learning about our own death'; 'Hey, I've figured out the pattern; it's after three rounds of bullets that you get a shell; here it comes, NOW'. The teacher would stand with a wavering smile, not in a position of authority to let the class go, although everyone knew that that was the inevitable outcome. And then, one way or another, chaos would ensue and all the students would run into each other. Omar and his friends would then take their time in going out of the class and hanging out in the playground, playfully jeering receptive teachers for having given up the cause or stalling them to share one last joke, until it became too dangerous to stay.

In his bed, Omar listened to further sounds and concluded that he was right: it wasn't really developing. He went back to Lisa's hair. His chest ached slightly at the thought of never coming to hold it against his face. And then he let himself sleep.

the child closed his ears to words and asked: what else is there to listen to?

Love, God and the Universe

When Amin graduated from law school, there was little to do, he said. 'What law? There is no law; it's in the hands not of people but of armed people. Somebody pisses you off, you take a gun to them, or you can choose not to take a gun to them.' He had promised Omar that he would come to Tripoli and spend time with him before figuring out what to do next. To Omar, Amin expressed himself delighted to have finished a task but said that he was not sure what the task was for. Still, as usual, Omar had a million and one questions to run by him, ones that wouldn't have gone far enough with his parents.

After a couple of days of settling in, Amin was approached by Omar with clear intentions; he wanted to figure the world out.

'The whole world?'

'Yes, plus God, and also, if we have time, the universe.'

Amin's smile broadened into a loving welcome.

First, Omar had noticed that if there was no government, and small people could take the law into their own hands, they were in the same position as animals: they could get as savage as they wanted to, but they were not really doing that.

Amin wasn't sure where Omar was going with his point. 'Isn't there enough bloodshed for you?' he asked.

'Well, besides the big stuff, the parties and the politics, the common man who has no political involvements can get anything he wants by just getting a gun and sorting it out, like going into a shop, holding it up, and getting himself a video, for example.'

Amin laughed. 'Hmmm, this has been happening every day, from small-time crooks to much bigger ones.'

Omar had heard stories, too. 'But considering how easy it is — even I could get a gun if I really wanted — it's not happening as much as it could.'

Amin thought about it and shook his head in admiration. 'OK,' he said. 'That's a beautiful way of looking at a piece of shit. Yes, it can certainly have more flies on it and well done to the flies that are being dignified about it.'

Omar's conclusion was that there *was* love and respect in people's hearts. 'Most people are just lay people, and they could easily join the rest, but they don't because they don't believe it's right to live life like that; they don't want to hurt others and they don't want to become savages.'

'OK, yeah, fine,' Amin agreed. 'What next?'

'Well, God really.' It was pretty obvious to Omar that none of this fighting was about religion. Even for the Israelis. 'All of these religions talk about loving one's neighbour, so all of their interpretations of their own religions are basically wrong,' Omar said and waited for Amin to interject, but he didn't. Omar had a few specific questions about Islam, and also one main question: 'Did Muhammad have more than forty wives? How could you marry up to four wives today? Who really wrote the Koran? Is it true that Muhammad bargained God from 100 down to 5 on the daily prayers? And does swallowing your spit break your fast?'

Amin shook his head, trying to figure out how to approach the answers, and then asked, 'Which of these is the main question?'

Omar said that he was holding the main question until these ones were answered.

'First of all, so many things have been said about Muhammad and it's hard to figure out what's what, but yeah, it has been confirmed that he certainly married more than four, and many of his marriages were more related to making political alliances. But whether he was to live what he preached is a different philosophical question. Maybe what he preached is there to be strived for, but everybody is human, even prophets.'

Omar thought about the answer and said that he liked it, and then he added that most of today's Moslems wouldn't answer the question that way, whatever their answer was.

Amin shrugged his shoulders. 'If they were here, they might even chop your head off for asking the questions in the first place, even though Islam encourages all sorts of questioning so that faith is deepened. But they're not here, so fuck them!'

'OK, what's with the four wives?'

Amin smiled lightly. 'A long time ago, tribes would go to war. Men would jump on their horses, go and fight, and about a quarter of them would come back. What you ended up with over time was a ratio of 4:1 of women to men, and you'd have all these women twiddling their thumbs. Today, nobody does it really, and Islam discourages it anyway. There's this story about Muhammad where he is approached by this guy who wants to

150

marry two yet wants to treat them equally, and Muhammad says, "OK, say you've been treating them equally all day and you're coming back into your tent with one on each side; which would you let in first?" He was trying to illustrate that it was impossible to be equal all the time.'

Omar liked the story.

Amin shrugged his shoulders. 'Most religions are lovely when you take them to their sources; it's just what common people do with them is so horrible, but anyway: next question?'

'How come you can still marry four today?'

Amin answered spontaneously. 'You're not really meant to do that. The Koran is also a civil law book and not just philosophical preaching and it tells you that you have to secure the first wife, so today you'd have to get her an apartment or a house — who wants all that hassle?'

Omar was glad. 'Still, what reason would you have to marry four?'

'First of all, women are not exactly stupid; today they'd just tell you to go fuck yourself — at least in Lebanon they would. But the point here is whether all of these laws should be updated for today's time, but that's a question that every religion is being challenged on today: how to adapt to the times. It's not just the institutions, though; a lot of people want to stick to the romantic times when their religions were first founded.'

'Why is that?' wondered Omar.

'People are followers; that's why there are very few leaders. In fact, you're meant to interpret these spiritual teachings for yourself and be your own guide, not be an absent-minded follower or a leader. No matter who you listen to, eventually you're meant to lead yourself and follow God. That's why they tell you there's one God and he's not in physical form.'

Omar pointed out that Amin had just referred to God as 'he'.

Amin laughed. 'Yes, but that's just it: even our language traps us.'

Omar hesitated before asking, 'Who really wrote the Koran?'

'Maybe Muhammad and Co., but the story goes that Muhammad was illiterate and it descended upon him when he was in a cave. It was direct from God and he found himself writing — so there.'

Omar wondered if maybe somebody had helped him out with it.

Amin shrugged his shoulders. 'The whole point with the Koran, as opposed to other religious books that were written after the prophet died, is that there was no tampering and no influencing. There are Moslems today who would rage that it's blasphemous to ask these questions even though the Koran itself says to go ahead and question — that's how you reach truth yourself, instead of following ignorantly. But that's the whole point: you have those who appoint themselves guardians of the truth and even if they have been asked to do so by others, they certainly haven't been appointed by God, but they forget that and go on declaring wars and laying down laws and giving the rest of the world headaches.'

Omar scratched his head.

Amin encouraged him to read the Koran for himself: 'It is a beautiful book; the poetry of it just knocks you out, and there's no need to put down other religions either. All of these books differ very much in style and have some great things in them; it's just that all of these people who end up calling themselves believers are not only completely following blindly, but they don't even know what they're following.'

'Why do they follow blindly? How come they don't question?'

'First, people are born into religions; they say that they have a choice about it but act as if they don't have a choice, like being born a boy or a girl. And from then on, they put the others down, saying they're better, just like as if they were supporting a soccer team. It's not just religion; people do it with their second names, their family titles; they do it even with things they don't really have a choice in, like being a male or female, and that's the funniest of them all: how could people all over the world end up putting the other sex down when they've never had a choice in the matter?'

'You're confusing me — they have a choice or they don't?' asked Omar, and then added, 'Of course they have a choice.'

'Whichever way you look at it, they put the other down for stuff they haven't even thought about; they haven't checked out the other or even themselves, so take it from there.'

Omar was silent. He was digesting all that Amin was saying.

'What else was there?' asked Amin.

Omar was slightly dazed by his brother's energy.

Amin smiled as if he had exhausted Omar, and then added that there was so much talk and he shouldn't worry about all of it. If he really wanted to know anything, he should go straight to the source; he shouldn't be worried about any bargaining about any prayers: 'Traditionally it is five prayers a day, and that includes washing of hands and feet, and that has been an excellent practice to introduce to Bedouins who hang out in the desert all day, getting themselves dusty.'

'And the fasting,' Amin added. 'That's a practice that is excellent for the body. It's not about torture, so this business about breaking your fast if you swallow is complete bullshit. You fast for a month and at sunset, when you break your fast, you don't eat like a complete savage either.'

Omar smiled.

'OK, so what was the main question?'

Omar looked embarrassed. Amin prodded him with an encouraging look. Omar said that he had been thinking of praying: he had heard the voices of the sheikhs chanting the prayers over the mosque speakers and quite often he had been touched by them; he wasn't sure why.

'So what's the problem?'

'Well, I'd like to give praying a go for a while but I'd hate it if I ended up being militant and hating everybody who wasn't Moslem.'

Amin laughed heartily. He bent forward and kissed Omar, saying, 'As long as you pray with your hear, not your head, everything will be fine.'

Omar let out a sigh of relief. His eyes were teary, as if a burden had been lifted. He thanked his older brother and said that he hadn't been able to talk to his parents about it: his mother would have told him everything that had been passed on to her about Islam, and his dad would have said that he should just stay as he was because he was great and any messing would be too much of a risk.

'Are there any more questions?' asked Amin with a soft smile.

Omar hesitated. Amin shrugged his shoulders as if to say that anything could be dealt with. Omar perked up and became earnest.

'If God created all of this, including the universe, who created God?'

Amin laughed. 'It is Abu-Ali who made all of this.'

Omar smiled. He knew his question was difficult but he wanted at least some discussion. Amin said that he had heard a joke about Abu-Ali that might help him: once they found Abu-Ali looking for something outside his house, so they stopped and started looking with him, then they asked him what he was looking for, suggesting that maybe they could help him. He said that he had lost his ring, and then added that he had lost it inside his house. They were bewildered and they asked him how come he was looking outside his house if he had lost it inside. He said that it was dark inside; there was better light outside.

Omar laughed, but then his smile faded. 'How will that help me?'

Amin wasn't sure, but he did know for sure that some questions were not designed for our heads to figure out.

'Was that what you meant by praying from the heart, not the head?'

Amin was taken back by Omar's connection. He said that he

153

hadn't approached the whole universe from his heart; it had been too big for him so he had dropped it, but now he could reflect on it.

'Was there anything else?'

Omar smiled. 'No, the universe will be all for now.'

Amin suggested they go for a walk and get some ice cream.

As they strolled up Azmi Street, Amin suggested that they walk for a while, aimlessly, and then on the way back, they could stop for the ice cream. When they turned at Monla Street, Amin noticed a music shop. They went in and Amin flicked through the records, asking Omar whether he had heard of Bob Marley, Santana, B.B. King. Omar hadn't even seen the covers before. The shop assistant played some of these records, and Omar wasn't sure what he liked most, so Amin suggested that he tape the live Bob Marley record. He paid the assistant and agreed that Omar would collect the tape in a couple of days when it had been recorded.

When they walked out, Amin remarked, 'Maybe one of the things that you were so touched by in the mosque prayer chanting is that the person is singing from their heart; they're singing what they believe in. That's different from just singing while strolling down the street or wanting to become a star. They're actually singing their cause. That's what people like Bob Marley or what the blues is all about. A Sufi poet called Rumi once said that there were a thousand ways of praying besides kneeling down.'

Omar wondered what a Sufi was.

'A Moslem sect. They're not political; they have no part in the Lebanese war. They're kind of frowned upon for being mystical — well, any deviation from the regular groups is going to end up being criticised.'

It wasn't until after Amin had gone back to Beirut that Omar started praying on a regular basis. He would get up early in the morning, wash his face, wash his hands up to the elbows, and his feet, and then fold out his praying rug in his room. Having come back from school, he repeated this and prayed a second time, and then three more times before bedtime. At first, he didn't tell his friends, not because he was hiding his practice but because he wasn't sure that it was a practice yet. When he told Walid on the way to school, Walid was slightly surprised: he didn't think Omar had it in him but he was pleasantly surprised. He said that his dad prayed every day and he had shown him how to pray. 'It can be really nice but five times a day is something completely different,' Walid said. In the playground, he got what he expected. George called him Sheikh Omar, and said the title really

154

suited him and he should start making contact with Iran for funding for arms and blow up the school. Jamil said that he should be careful when bending down as Abu-Ali might be behind him, and he had a reputation for fancying small boy's bums. Ahmad was very encouraging: he told Jamil and Ahmad to leave him alone, but he couldn't stop giggling to himself. Omar smiled through it. He said he was disappointed, but he had prepared himself for much worse.

At night, having finished his homework, Omar would turn off the main light, leaving only his desk lamp on. He would take out a big Koran that Zeina had brought him from Syria and would read for half an hour. There were few sentences that he could read from beginning to end and understand; he got the gist sometimes, but mainly he read on without understanding. His favourite time was when the electricity was cut off. Then he would place a candle next to his book and read by the flickering flame. On these occasions, his mother would insist he light more than one candle so as not to strain his eyes, but he would always refuse.

He listened to Bob Marley every day. He was touched by the music and the voice. He didn't understand the words and couldn't figure them out but Amin had told him that blacks were mistreated and he was singing to his people, and that was enough for Omar to know.

One afternoon, on a Saturday, as Omar prayed, reciting the sentences, the thought of going for a walk in Monla Street crossed his mind, and then he felt a release in his chest. He sensed a love flowing from him. When he finished praying, he stood still and felt a love for the whole world, for every person he had seen and not talked to. He then went for a walk, knowing that he might see incidents of shooting that might pollute him. He went to a music shop, flicked through some records, listened to a couple of albums and then asked the assistant to tape Santana for him. He met with his friends, jeered, joked, walked, and noticed that the sense of love was still present. On the way back, he crossed the street, looked up to see if his mother was on the balcony, and then went into his building. As the elevator took him to the fourth floor, he filled with anticipation, as if he were going to meet a visitor he hadn't seen in a while. When he walked in, he saw his mother in the living room and his father listening to the news. He went over and kissed his mother, and then kissed his father. She said it was a very sweet kiss but wondered what request was coming up. His dad took Omar's hand, and then pulled him down gently and kissed him on the crown of his head.

the boy looked through love and into the world,
he looked from his chest and out through his eyes,
he touched further than his hands could reach,
further than his eyes could see,
further than his own world, but did not cover the whole world

the boy saw that a wandering bee and an angry man,
a caught fish and a rock,
a piece of cloth, a fluffy cloud,
the emptiness in a glass cup — all have love inside them

Turning Inside Out

Death

The afternoon walks had become messy lately. Omar had got into a routine: when he came back from school, he would pray, and then, having had his lunch, he would lie on his bed for about fifteen minutes, reflecting on his day, and then he would study for about two hours. And then his walk. He would go to Monla Street and see who he bumped into. But recently, the air had been funny. Too many incidents where he would hear shouting between people he hadn't seen before, and then one of them would either shoot in the air or between the legs of the other. If they were with somebody, they might be persuaded to let it go, but most people around them would run for cover. Others would move only far enough away that they could still hear the conversation while just about sheltering themselves at the corner of an adjacent building, body half-covered by the concrete and head totally out. These incidents had become frequent enough to be expected on each walk.

Omar did not know anybody who had a gun and so he felt safe in believing that such incidents couldn't happen to him. It was safe to argue among his circle of friends, all of whom were wary of getting too close to anybody who might have a gun; they were observers. As the atmosphere got too thick to talk and too heavy to walk, they would often stand at the corner of Monla and Azmi, watching the traffic go by until it neared darkness. One day, as the traffic moved at turtle pace, a passenger in a car looked at George defiantly and said, 'What the fuck are you looking at?' It wasn't a question. George didn't answer; he looked away slowly. He kept his body still to show coolness, having learned over the years that if somebody picked on you and you acted like a coward, they were more likely to bully you, and if you went head to head and got stubborn, one skull of two was going to crack. It was a perfectly balanced head move from George and, after the car moved, there was a sigh of relief and a new understanding that being an observer had crossed into being a participant. There was a new layer of bleakness. Breathing was more difficult.

'You still believe in God?'

'Sure.' Omar shrugged his shoulders. 'I don't see what God has to do with any of this.'

Opinions followed: 'God doesn't care.'

'God has created animals. With the way people have become, even if God wanted to help, they wouldn't let him.'

'If God saw us, he would go blind.'

'With all the shooting, if God hasn't died from a direct hit, surely he would have died from all the stray bullets.'

George was the only friend that Omar went to school with. Amin lived in Ibbeh and Jamil in Beddawi; both were too far to go back home to if troubles erupted and one could no longer risk one half hour to the next.

Normally these conversations balanced seriousness with fun but what was being said now did not leave much scope for Omar to joke with.

'All we're doing is shitting on each other.'

Omar responded, 'Well, just because God gave us assholes doesn't mean that his job is to toilet train us.'

They didn't laugh, but they acknowledged that it was well put. 'You've completely given up on hope,' said Omar, trying to lift the atmosphere.

He was dismissed for being naïve. An older acquaintance sighed lethargically, saying, 'Have you not heard? Hope has been taking a beating on a daily basis. One day, they just came to cut its throat; well, it didn't even resist.' And then he laughed at his own conclusion: 'Hope has given up on hope.'

Omar was taken aback; he hadn't thought in that way before.

Others joined in: 'Yeah, not only has it bled to death, but its blood has dried up.'

'And you know what? As it lay bleeding, dogs peed on it.'

'That's right, for lying to us, the bastard cunt—'

And then suddenly a few shots were heard and George said that he had had enough; he was going home. The group broke up and Omar was left standing with the older acquaintance. He said to Omar that it was a good thing that Omar could see light; he wished that he could. The sounds of a few more bullets rang through and he smiled, gesturing that he was splitting. 'If you can get home with your smile intact, it will be an achievement,' he said.

At home, Omar wanted to talk to somebody. Zeina said that there was a German philosopher who had said that God was dead.

Omar's father shook his head negatively; not only did they rule the Third World, steal their archaeology and put it in their museums, but they wanted to steal God and declare him dead.

Zeina said that it had nothing to do with 'us'; he had said it in the last century and he was saying it to his own people.

Omar's father let a tired laugh out, saying, 'That's what greed does to you: you rule other nations; you get everything; and when you're done playing God, there's basically nothing left.'

Zeina and her father were not on the same wavelength. She was responding to Omar's interest in finding God without going through the traditional religions; she didn't want to get into politics. Either way, Omar wasn't getting a satisfactory answer. He kept on asking exactly what Nietzsche had said, what he really meant, but she couldn't tell him. The idea intrigued him, but after a while he wanted some substance, something to help him.

Later, he rang Ziad. He said that praying had turned into a battle recently. He simply didn't have the energy. He still wanted to spring up and have the flow he'd had a few months ago but it was like a battery that was dying. There was nobody to be inspired by. He didn't understand the Koran and he wasn't going to read interpretations because they were written by ordinary human beings, the same ones who were fighting. He wanted to feel God for himself.

Ziad wasn't sure what to say, which actually made Omar feel really listened to. At least he wasn't argued with, he wasn't offered a better way of seeing things, and he wasn't being dismissed either. Ziad was happy to be useless. He said that his cousin could ring him any time he wanted to talk about something that he too was lost about. Omar then remembered to ask him how he was. Ziad threw in an expression used mainly by the older generation: 'We're living, from lack of death.'

Omar said that it was worrying how everybody talked about death as if it were a friend. Ziad laughed and said that that was exactly what his dad had said a few days before — that there was more life in death than in life itself.

'But anyway, how is school?' Ziad asked.

'School is fucked up. Most of the teachers are good; they're trying to make us believe that we should study as if we're getting an education. It's great to see them try so hard; it's the only thing that prevents you from giving up. And the ones that have given up, well, they're the ones that are easiest to fuck with: you run a circus around them and you do it without guilt.'

Ziad said he'd like to come to Tripoli to Omar's school for a few weeks. In his school, they were still taking it seriously — they actually believed they were equipping the students with some tools to deal with life later on.

Omar laughed and said he wanted tools to deal with life right now.

The following week, Omar approached his Arabic teacher as he was leaving class and asked him whether the Koran could have been written by human beings instead of having descended from God.

The teacher lit a cigarette and said that he had thirty seconds to smoke it before he got to the next class so he didn't have too much time for a big discussion, but that didn't matter because his answer was short: in his opinion, in his own opinion, in his own personal opinion, no.

'Why not?' asked Omar, as he followed him out of class.

He took a long pull of his cigarette and then let the smoke come out of his nose and mouth as he spoke: because it was too difficult, he said, too intertwined, and mainly too beautiful.

As Omar walked back to his class, he realised that he no longer cared about the question but he had been deeply touched by the answer because his teacher was Christian. He didn't have to give such an answer, and moreover, he looked like an atheist, and he probably was one.

Over the next two weeks, Omar reflected on religion and all the people that talked about religion. He concluded that he had seen more of God in those who said they didn't believe in God then those who talked about God as if they have been given direct orders to tell others what the rules were. In the previous few weeks, not only had it been an effort to pray, but every time he became conscious of the words he was reciting, he had become distracted. The voices of people who talked about God were being elicited and he didn't want to hear them. He wanted quietness; he wanted that sense of love that had flourished in his chest a few months ago. But it was no longer happening; it was getting crowded and messy. So he stopped praying.

Now the only time that he was alone and he felt any sense of love was when listening to music. He was listening to more Bob Marley. 'Babylon by Bus,' the crowd cheered as if they were one. He didn't try to make sense of the words; it made sense as it was. Then Santana. Then Deep Purple. Led Zeppelin. B.B. King. Osi Bissa. Black Sabbath. His mother would pass by his room and see him sitting very quietly and absorbing as much volume as possible. She would smile and tell him that it was likely to damage his eardrums but she would never say it with enough conviction for him to do anything about it. He would ask her if it was too loud for her and she would say that it wasn't bothering her because she was sitting in the front room; she was saying it only for his sake. He would tell her that he liked it loud. She would shrug her shoulders and say that it was better than his being in the street. He would have no response to this comment, and then she would walk off.

At night, he would wait until his father went to bed and then put on a video if it wasn't more than two hours long. *Mad Max. Kramer vs. Kramer. Annie Hall. Superman. Cheech & Chong.* His mother warned him that he was becoming addicted to both music and videos. He looked at her blankly and asked her: 'What's the alternative?'

'I don't know, but you know...'

He waited.

She said, 'You know ... I don't know ... I'm saying it for your sake.'

He said that he wasn't disagreeing with her, but really, what was the alternative?

She said that it was just that he was living his life through music and video.

'So what's the alternative?' he asked again.

She resigned: 'I guess it's not doing you that much damage.'

After she had left, he thought about her comment. He *was* living his life through music and films; there was no other life to be lived. He tried to swallow but suddenly it was difficult.

In school, Omar would have loved to rejuvenate himself through sports, but the sports teacher was one of the most despised of all teachers. He was thought of not as malicious but as a waste of space; he wasted valuable time that could have been fun; instead of playing real games like volleyball, he would have the class doing pyramids for the parents' show at the end of the year. Games like practising riding a bike where the slowest person would win were completely meaningless to just about everybody in the class. Omar, George, Jamil, and Ahmad would do their best to sabotage such exercises. They had complained that they wanted to enjoy themselves but they weren't heard and so they decided to make the best of what was around, by pulling stunts like deliberately falling on each other during the pyramid exercises. When the teacher split them up, they still found ways to disrupt his plans until he divided the hour: if training was done properly, the whole class could play volley ball. It was an incentive that most of the class worked for, but for Omar and his friends, nothing could beat the sabotage. If anything, they got cheekier, by suggesting even more meaningless exercises that might delight their proud parents.

Conflict with all teachers was played out through roundabout mischief or head-on confrontation. Omar tried on a few occasions to challenge his teachers, without intending provocation, simply asking them to explain the purpose of certain lessons and even whole courses when it didn't make sense to him. The most honest answer he got was that it was part of the curriculum and they had no control over the curriculum. If he got this far, he would then question the school's agreement with something their teachers didn't believe in; at that point, he would be told that they could no longer entertain his philosophical discussions.

George never asked such questions; instead, he often asked simple questions after the teacher had been explaining a topic for quite a while or had gone over it in detail a few classes ago. New teachers would often fall for his innocence, but they quickly learnt to turn the question back on him. He would shamelessly claim idiocy, saying that he had fallen on his head as a child. It was hard not to smile back, especially when he introduced a subtle stutter.

Ahmad worked on his classmates instead, distracting them by blowing rice through emptied Bic pens, releasing marbles ever so slowly between the desk rows, and, on occasion, stepping on garlic cloves and then smearing the juice as he walked over to the bin and back by a different route, claiming that he didn't want to disrupt the same students twice.

Jamil brought in German hardcore porn magazines that were guaranteed to distract. Having failed three classes over the years, he was older than his classmates and had access to material others wouldn't have come across, but still he said he was giving education a chance. He generally didn't confront teachers but when he talked about being angry with a teacher, his threats were so strong that they sounded like bluff. On one occasion, when he received a fail mark in a test, he looked so disappointed that he just shook his head, turned to Omar, and said that the following day, the mark would be sorted out. Next day, as he got up during class, he gave Omar a wink while showing him the fail mark from the previous day. He seemed to have a quiet talk with the teacher and then came back to his seat. After the class, Jamil gave Omar a quick glimpse of the new mark — 90 per cent — and then smiled. The next teacher came in and there was no time to explain, but ten minutes into the class, the headmaster knocked on the door and asked for Jamil.

During break-time, Omar, Ahmad and George gathered around their friend who proudly said that he had gone up to the teacher, and told her that the mark 'wasn't right'. She had said that it *was* right, so he had gently pulled back his jacket, revealing the hand of a gun, and said, 'I think this mark needs to be reconsidered.' Jamil added with a smile, 'She immediately changed it, shaking in fear.' Silence fell among his friends. This couldn't be categorised as 'mischief'. Jamil had crossed a new line and they wondered to themselves how he was going to recover his ground.

Ahmad broke the silence with a laugh. 'Fuck her,' he said.

Omar smiled fearfully, and then asked Jamil what the headmaster had said.

Jamil shrugged his shoulders, then smiled weakly. He had been asked to consider leaving the school.

Ahmad said that he didn't have to: now that he had discovered a new way of passing exams, he could surpass them all as long as he didn't get rid of his gun.

Jamil shook his head, and said it was time to leave. He would probably finish the year, and maybe get a letter of transfer to another school, but there really wasn't any point. He had got tired of being discriminated against. He said, without accusing them, that Omar and George came from good families and they wouldn't be picked on, and Ahmad had a Syrian background so they would definitely stay out of his way, but he had had it. He said that he was still glad of what he had done: she would think twice before she picked on somebody like him in the future.

At home, Omar was sad that Jamil was not going to be finishing school with them. To Omar's surprise, his father wasn't judgmental of Jamil but shook his head in wonder at the whole situation. 'You're all supposed to be growing up with at least a bit of innocence,' he said. 'But there seems to be no trace of it left.'

Omar responded nonchalantly, saying that he hadn't seen any in a long time. 'Maybe Mother Nature has had herself an abortion,' he suggested. He surprised himself with his answer, but then shrugged off the topic as if it were an old issue. He was struggling with what Jamil was going to do. He couldn't see him finishing school, and even if he did, it was unlikely that he would get near college.

He wondered about the power of the gun. Had Lebanon been at peace, what would Jamil have done? People will always be discriminated against and within the school system there wouldn't have been much that he could have done; she would have subtly failed him again and again, and the headmaster would have backed her up even if he didn't totally agree with her. Jamil had had his say, in the only way that he could have it, but still it was not a way that could be encouraged.

That night, Omar watched *The Deer Hunter*. Laila had told him that it had won several Oscars a few years previously. She had said in passing that it had influenced quite a few of the fighters in Beirut. She was on the phone from Beirut at the time, and her baby started crying, so she didn't get a chance to finish her sentence. When he got to the scene where a captured American soldier was being forced by the Vietnamese to play Russian Roulette, Omar cringed. Later, when he saw the soldier willingly gambling, he remembered the man who had snatched the baby on the street after *Apocalypse Now*. A line can be crossed into madness. He wondered again whether it was possible to cross back or whether it was a dimension that you just stepped into and got lost in.

Next day, while telling a joke to his friends on the corner of Monla Street, Omar noticed three guys with Kalashnikovs walk past. When he got to the punch line, nobody laughed. He repeated the punch line and was about to explain the joke when George stopped him, full of anger.

'What's the problem?' Omar asked.

George explained: one of the guys with Kalashnikovs had made a comment as he walked by that he would like to slay them one by one.

'What's the big deal?' said Omar. 'They're just three guys with guns!'

'Did you really not hear the rest of what they said?' asked George.

'No.'

'They said that they'd love to press the trigger and see a few bullets go into the foot.'

Omar laughed. 'Whose foot?'

'*Your* foot!' They had been directly referring to Omar.

'Oooh!' Still, Omar laughed, saying that there was no point in getting so het up about it; they didn't know him, and they weren't really going to do it, 'So whatever!'

Everybody was amazed at how he had missed the comment.

'Well, you wouldn't want to be in tune with all that stuff,' said Omar.

Some of his friends commended him on staying apart from all the hatred while others feared that not being in touch with his surroundings could leave him at risk of walking into dangerous situations.

A few days later, as Omar was returning home from his walk, he saw a tall man shouting at another man who was slightly shorter than him. He had seen the taller man on a regular basis over the previous few months. His nickname was Abu-Abbass. He usually held himself with dignity without being arrogant. Whenever Omar met his eyes, they would greet each other, although Omar had been discouraged by most of his friends from greeting anybody he didn't know; they commented that these days anybody could be anybody, and anybody could go head to head with anybody. Omar held that he didn't want to lose his smile. He said that he wasn't going to say 'Hello' to everybody: with some people, it was obvious not to go near them, but he still wanted to give a chance to the ones he wasn't sure about. Then the shorter man pulled a gun on Abu-Abbass. Omar, about ten metres away from them, stopped in his tracks, filled with fear. Abu-Abbass, clearly not carrying a gun, came closer to the shorter man and said, 'Shoot! Let me see you shoot.' He stood defiantly, showing no fear.

The shorter man, with his gun still in his hand, in disbelief at what was happening, started to move backwards.

Abu-Abass moved closer and shouted, 'GO AHEAD, SHOOT me!'

The shorter man turned around and started to run. Abu-Abbass ran a few metres after him and then stopped. On the way back, he met Omar's eyes and said, 'Good evening.'

Omar smiled and replied, 'Lovely evening to you.'

As Omar turned onto Azmi Street towards home, he noticed the vibrations of fear throughout his body turn into pride and admiration. He had never talked to Abu-Abbass, and it was unlikely that he ever would, and however it had been possible to conjure up such full presence as Abu-Abbass just had, it was unlikely that he would able to tell Omar how to do it.

When Omar got home, Ziad phoned and told him that Bob Marley had died. He said that he had heard there were no other singers around who sang the cause of the black people like he did. After the phone call, Omar cried in his bedroom.

the boy was told that the soul is the bit that lives inside him, in between his flesh, it's his spirit,
his head is the bit that manages his flesh on this earth, it tries to make sure it's not eaten
the boy looked around, then inside him, then outside him, and then he asked, what does the spirit want?

The Beach

For Omar, the official end of the year was the end of the school year not the calendar year. For Omar's mother, this new year presented a new kind of worry. Going to school was a worry that she had adapted to as she felt she had no choice: 'The boy has to go to school; what can you do? Keep him in all day?' But allowing him to go to the beach was something that she had been delaying as long as possible.

She had her arguments: whenever they started their gunfire, Omar would have made it home from Zehrieh before they started their shelling — Zehrieh was near enough, only a twenty-minute walk, and it was still in Tripoli. Going to the beach, however, meant that Omar was going to go outside Tripoli.

'But Zehrieh is right next to the Beb Il-Tebbaneh, just at the front line!' Omar would argue back. 'At least going outside Tripoli, if it's no more than twenty minutes along the coastline, is safer.'

'If they start shelling, you're going to get stuck outside Tripoli, and then what would happen to you?'

He would argue that he wouldn't get stuck outside because he didn't have to pass through the main shelling areas. He would avoid the shelling by coming in at the entrance of the city and then straight home.

What if the shelling were very intensive? She had no way of contacting him. How could she tell him to come back home? Also, even if there were no shelling, what if he were stopped at the Syrian checkpoint at the entrance to the city and detained? Even before getting to the checkpoint, what if he were stopped between the beach and the Syrian checkpoint and robbed or kidnapped or something?

Up until that point, whenever Omar went to the beach, it had been arranged through somebody that Omar's mother knew — Karim, an older neighbour; Amin whenever he was in Tripoli; or even on a few occasions she had taken him herself, only to sit at a coffee table until he had had his fill. For every one of her arguments, Omar would object that she was 'just worrying', and she would acknowledge that of course she was worrying. But, she would ask, did she not have enough

169

reasons to worry? He knew that she couldn't keep him at home for the whole summer, especially since his classmates were being allowed to go the beach unaccompanied by adults. It was only a matter of time, and he put a great deal of effort into trying to convince her before he brought in his father and used Amin and his two sisters as softening influences. He did worry about her worrying but in this case felt that some of her worries were unnecessary. He would go along with her line of worrying and at times even contribute to it.

'What if I drowned?' he would say, trying to show her that there was no use in worrying because if you worried about everything, you'd snap. When she came close to crying, acknowledging that she did worry about everybody, from him going to school to his dad making it back from work to his brother and sisters in Beirut, he would appease her and tell her that it was OK, he wouldn't add to her worry; he'd just stay home until he was ninety and she could keep on changing his nappies.

It was when she asked who he could go with if he were allowed that he knew that he was close to his breakthrough. George was the only one of his school friends, whom she knew, who could go with him; he knew he couldn't tell her about the rest, the older friends he met on his walks in Monla Street. He had met them through the music shop that pirated tapes and they were all three to four years older than Omar and had dropped out of school. He toyed with the idea of telling her about them and even telling her that he now often went into the pinball shop. He didn't play the slot machines because that would have been just flushing money down the toilet, but he felt that the boy was no longer a boy and maybe she should just let him be. He had been growing fed up with her overprotection, and with being the jewel of her eye. One day he had seen a boy driving a car, although barely able to lift his head up to see over the steering wheel. He must have been ten, hardly eleven; it was an old white Mercedes, not that old. His own friends were beginning to learn how to drive but his family didn't own a car so he felt behind in so many ways.

While he didn't push her past her limit, he started to tell her of some of the things from which he had so far protected her. He told her that when ambulances went into the Islamic Hospital off Monla Street, which was only three minutes from his house, people would often run towards the casualty entrance to see blood-drenched bodies being wheeled in. A youth around his age had encouraged him to come along, saying that it was 'character-building' to see these things. Omar had gone along on one occasion, even running to make it in time, but his stomach had turned. As the body had passed by, he had wondered how long he would have to endure this feeling in his gut before his character would be built. He had decided that he didn't want this kind of character. He tried to tell his mother that overall he was balanced, that there were many foul opportunities he could have taken had he wanted to but he had not, and it was time that his mother started trusting him. On most occasions, she heard him and thanked her own lucky stars that he had not been a greater source of worry, with all that was going on. However, she said that if he had been that greater source of worry, she would probably have lost her reason. She acknowledged him but she budged only an inch at a time.

By the time he had made it to the beach with George and three of his walking companions, they were all determined that, until one hour before sunset, nothing was going to remind them that they had lives to go back to. They had Scorpions, Black Sabbath, Santana, Deep Purple and Led Zeppelin. It was agreed that the most convincing way to escape was through live albums; if they had their eyes closed, the cheering of the audience could take them there. They would toast under the sun, feeling sweat building over their skins and would be reminded that they had parents only when they took out the home-made sandwiches. After a few trips, Omar insisted that he could buy his own sandwiches at the beach; he had to insist that they *were* hygienic, and he had to persuade his mother that there was no point in letting him be if she wasn't really going to let him be.

On one occasion, when Omar was persuaded by George to try to swim across to another private beach to meet one of their classmates, he felt excitement rush through him as he slowly came out of the water. They had to find Bilal before they were spotted as non-members. Within two minutes of wandering around between sun beds, a well-dressed man in a shirt and pants asked very politely which cabin was theirs. Omar and George said that they were visiting a classmate but had forgotten his cabin number. The man suddenly contorted his features and escorted them out, crudely and bluntly, just a few words away from swearing. He blatantly refused to let them go back the same way they had come, through the sea. They had to walk barefoot on the scalding-hot asphalt of the main road until they made it back to their

171

beach, at first congratulating themselves on their achievement but very quickly admitting to each other that they had felt like dogs being kicked out. 'Actually, poor dogs,' Omar said. 'If they had enough money to have a cabin, the dogs would be elevated to humans.'

'This is the new Lebanese,' George said. 'Polite and "whatever you want, sir," until he figures out you're just like him; then you're a nothing.'

When they told the others about the incident, Omar felt resigned to the fact that a Lebanese person was nothing, probably had always been a nothing, but mainly was going to stay one big perfected nothing.

George agreed about being nothing but added that they shouldn't feel less than 'outside'. He had heard that in England there were riots because of how the blacks had been treated; the Lebanese were nothing, for sure, but no more nothing than those who thought they were something. After a while, they concluded that their worthlessness was not something to be ashamed about. Sitting like idiots on the beach as Israel shat on their heads, with its planes dropping bombs on Beirut because it felt like it, was a fact of life they could do nothing about. The big countries could squash the small, but with time, they were being squashed from the inside. England, who set up Israel in the first place, was having its own people kill each other because of football, a game.

George added that there had also been riots because the Irish had starved themselves on hunger strike. While Omar wanted to hear more from George, it was hard to make sense as the conversation was pulled in different directions: 'Looook, there's plenty of sand here; tell this Bobby Sands he doesn't have to starve himself; we can give him a feast here,'

'Tell him we'll be very happy to train him and give him a whole range of guns.'

'The Irish and the blacks should get together and invade Britain.'

Eventually somebody suggested that the Japanese and the Indians should get together with the American Indians, the South Americans, the Irish and the Blacks, at least half of the African countries, not the Gulf Arabs because their asses were too fat, Mongolia because 'why not? you might as well', and the Germans. 'Did you know that we, the Arabs, were the third at the bottom of Hitler's list, right after the Jews and the Blacks?'

'Wow, that's something. You know, I respect this guy for disrespecting us.'

As they packed their bags, George went through the tapes with a cynical smile. 'Oooh, Black Sabbath — I wonder where they're from?'

And then, 'Hmmn, Led Zeppelin ... I'm not so sure about these ... Deeeeeep Purple.'

Omar looked up amused, and another argument started: 'That's exactly the whole point; they don't represent Britain, not the Britain that screwed us. If anything, they're everything that is against the old Britain.'

'Have you heard of the Sex Pistols? Now if you want to piss off the British, you listen to them.'

'Scorpions are from Germany; they don't count as British. Michael Schenker has nothing to do with this,' said Omar with a smile.

'Did you know that originally the British sent all their criminals to Australia to get rid of them and just to fuck them back, they turned out to be better than them?' said George.

'Yeah, as if now they're jealous and they're saying to themselves, they should have kept them.'

'You know, that's exactly, exactly the point: England is such a fucked-up place that even their worst criminals get better when they leave.'

They continued their argument into the taxi until they got to the entrance to Tripoli. They could see a line of cars standing still for over 500 metres. They thought of leaving the car and walking the rest of the way but the taxi driver warned them that they would be questioned at the Syrian checkpoint as to why they had left the car.

'Because we don't want to wait' answered Omar.

Without turning his head, the taxi driver said as gently and firmly as possible, 'No, you don't tell them that.'

'But we only have towels; we can show them.'

The taxi driver let Omar finish making his points and then let an uncomfortable silence develop before looking back. 'Look son,' he said. 'I'm just trying to do you a favour. You can argue all you want but let me give you some experience. In this town, you don't breathe against a Syrian and you don't talk too loud in front of anybody. I could be a Syrian, or an undercover, so just swallow your pride and spare yourself.'

After an hour of moving the distance of one car every five minutes, they arrived at the checkpoint. The Syrian gunman was looking away. The taxi driver greeted him with a blessing, and then waited. After a while, still without looking directly into the car, the Syrian waved for them to move and the taxi driver drove off.

When they got to the top of Azmi Street, the taxi driver was willing to continue to their respective homes but Omar asked him to stop. The rest looked at him. 'I need some air,' he said. They decided to get out with him. Omar was so furious he couldn't talk.

George put his hand on Omar's shoulder and waited for his anger to diffuse while the rest threw comments that he needed to take it easy: 'That's how things are'; 'It's life, fuck them'; 'They won't stay powerful all their lives'; 'Yeah, they're screwing us; get used to it.'

'You know what's worse than being screwed by an enemy?' Omar said, still shaking. 'Being screwed by your own brother.'

He was corrected: 'Syria would be a sister.'

Before the conversation could get skewed, George looked at Omar with a gentle smile, hoping that Omar would calm down. 'And that's a mighty big cock for a sister,' he said.

Omar continued to look away, concentrating on holding back the tears. But then he laughed despite himself.

He looked at everybody fleetingly and said that he would see them the following day. George asked if he'd like him to go with him but Omar said that he was fine.

By the time Omar got home, he was very melancholic. He walked in to find Zeina watching the wedding of Charles and Diana in England. His mother, father, and Amin were also watching quietly. He let himself plonk on the couch and sat back, dazed. Zeina was the only one speaking, in measured sentences, every little while, each dripping with cynicism: 'Oh, God bless that marriage; may they both live forever'; 'Fine for you, all your jewellery and money you made from thieving and ripping off every country you occupied'; 'Oh yeah, please, take your time; walk slowly while the rest of the world starves, why don't you?' 'May you trip, fall, and break your neck'; 'Hmff, thick, cold-blooded, humourless; that's what you are.'

'We're no better,' said Omar. 'I've just spent an hour waiting for a donkey to let me pass less than 500 metres.'

'Syrians are not "we",' argued Zeina.

'Who's "we" then?' Omar asked.

His father let out a sigh and, as he got up to go towards the balcony, he extended his hand for Omar to get up with him. 'Son,' he said. 'There is no more "we". You think of "we" and you get yourself a headache, you hear me?'

Omar nodded , appreciating his father's efforts to comfort him.

'Seriously,' his father said. 'You need to get that "we" out of your head.'

the boy heard a faint voice: your soul is the bit that tells you what's not right in you

the boy held his stomach in pain

London

When Anwar El Sadat was assassinated, Omar heard mostly jeering and the opinion that he deserved it for selling out on the Arabs. Initially Omar argued, without being too convinced, that eventually there would need to be some sort of talk with Israel if the Palestinians were going to get anything, and that this Egyptian president looked like he was the only Arab willing to make that move. 'If that was his real intention,' was the response. 'That would be great, but let's wait and see and you'll see.' The 'selling out' came into it because it was believed that he was making peace with Israel only for the security of his own country.

'OK, what's wrong with that?' asked Omar.

'The Palestinians are going to get nothing out of it; basically he's saying to the Israelis, "Go ahead; take their land; keep beating them up and putting them in prison and keep on demolishing their houses."'

'So, are the Palestinians his responsibility?'

'It's just that if you're going to call yourself an Arab and start talking about unity and all of that, then you're just selling out.'

'So is the new Egyptian president going to stick to the agreement Sadat made with Israel?'

'Yes.'

'Well, that's one Arabic country that can't call itself Arab.'

'No, that's one Arabic country that officially can't call itself an Arab; they've all been duds for a long time now. Look at our country: they said they were sending us peacekeeping forces made up by the united Arab world, and they send us the Syrians who have looted half the country, if not more. The number of cars stolen and transported to Syria is just unbelievable.'

Omar's political questions were dwindling over time, especially as most of the answers were pessimistic and delivered in lethargic tones: 'Nobody is going to help out the Palestinians'; 'International what?' 'To be honest with you, I'm not sure either who's fighting whom any more.'

What did spark his interest a few months later was Britain saying that it was going to invade the Falkland Islands. When Walid told him on his way to school that the Falkland Islands were in Argentina, Omar didn't believe him. He even said that he was disappointed that his prank was so weak: 'Fine if you want to stretch things out a bit but make them next to France or even Spain but not all the way at the opposite side of the globe!'

'Actually, there is already a bit of Spain that England has made British,' said Walid.

'Today, in this age and day?' asked Omar.

'I swear.'

'Yeah, sure, and the Spanish are happy about it and don't really mind.'

'Seriously.'

'Yeah, seriously.'

'No, seriously.'

Omar kept on laughing and saying that he wasn't falling for it. 'The Lebanese are the best bull-shitters in the world but if you bullshit more than one thing at a time, you're going to lose it.'

Omar watched TV in disbelief over the next few days. 'Margaret Thatcher is going to send some soldiers from the top of the map all the way down to its bottom, and the rest of the world is buying this!'

'Omar, relax. Nobody is buying it, but it's going to happen anyway.'

A few months later, more happened. On 6 June, Israel invaded Lebanon but unlike previous bombings, it was becoming a real threat that Israel was going to continue into the south, possibly all the way up to Beirut. When Khaled rang from London and listened to his parents' concerns, he said that he might be able to help but did not say how. Two days later, he rang again and offered to pay for Omar to come to London with a possibility of enrolling in a boarding school. There was no other way; with his training, he would not be able to look after Omar and supervise his homework or his social life.

There were too many factors at stake for a clear decision to emerge naturally. Omar was in an American school with an American system; an English system might not be easy to transfer to. Omar had his friends here: 'Sure he's likeable,' his family said. 'But he might not be able to mix with the British.' He would be sacrificing the love of his family for peace and education; would he be losing out overall?

He talked about it with his friends. He said he would have access to all the music that he wanted: he'd be able to see Rainbow, Iron Maiden, Black Sabbath, Judas Priest, all live at his front door. The number of girls to screw — they'd be dropping at his feet; he'd be able to have whoever he wanted the minute he set foot on the soil. No more checkpoints, no more guns, no more bombings, no more Syrians — he would have total peace.

Amin was of the opinion that it wasn't a great idea overall; his gut feeling was that Omar should finished his school first, only four more years, and then go over. He admitted that he couldn't really explain specifically why overall it wasn't a good idea but said that it just wasn't.

Laila, in her usual relaxed way, suggested that he go over, try it, and if he didn't like it, he could come back. 'Sure he'd lose a year in school and would have to start where he left off. But overall it's just a year.'

Omar's father wasn't so sure. Omar's mother was not so sure either. Zeina casually suggested that Omar didn't have to decide yet. He could go over for a short break. 'Khaled should be able to bear two weeks of Omar,' she said. 'He could take him to visit a boarding school, see what he thinks, and look at their books. At best, he could come back with the books and work on them while he finishes the next school year, even talk to some Lebanese guys who have made the move.'

Everybody looked at each other and then commended her.

When Khaled rang two days later, he immediately thought it was a good idea. It might waste money if Omar returned and didn't take it up later on, but anything else might be too much of a risk anyway.

If Khaled had not been a doctor who knew somebody who knew somebody else, it was unlikely that Omar would have got a visa so quickly — or, indeed, got his visa at all. According to Omar's friends, he was a terrorist: 'You'll see when you get to the airport in London; George's older brother gets asked obtuse questions as a matter of principle at this stage.'

'Go,' they said. 'Before Israel finishes the whole country.'

When Omar rang Ziad to see what he'd like from London, he ended up worrying about the advancing Israeli army. Ziad told him not to worry. 'They can't just invade the capital of a whole country,' he said. 'There are limits; the world won't allow it.'

As revenge against the sports teacher who was still having them do mindless exercises instead of allowing them to have proper football or volleyball games, Omar decided to steal one of his worn-out leather volley balls, bring it to London with him and play with it in the park until the grass coloured it green, and then, just to mess with his teacher's head, sneak it back among the rest of the volleyballs.

When Omar arrived in London, he was prepared to be hassled about his passport. He answered the brief questions with eagerness and conviction while holding in his excitement at all the bright lights around him and the vastness of the airport; after all, he might not be let in. As he waited in heavy silence while the officer ran through a list of names, he saw from the corner of his eye an Asian family shaking their heads in controlled disappointment while holding themselves like cornered animals. And then suddenly, in a flash, Omar felt his stomach being released by the sound of stamping: his passport was handed back with a polite smile. 'Hope you enjoy your stay,' the official said.

Khaled spotted Omar before circling around with a trolley. From then on, it was a case of Khaled holding back while Omar framed every detail in a Lebanese context: 'They let you have a trolley,' he began. 'What if you take it home?'

'And what are you going to do with a trolley at home?'

'You can take it to the park and swing down slopes... Wow, look! A Ford — in Lebanon that's definitely considered a *mtartaa* car!'

'It's actually British-made; it's a newish model, smooth, you'll see.'

'Look at all these clouds, and we're in the middle of the summer!'

'Yeah, well, this is London summer.'

'Look at all these midget buildings. Are they all like that?'

'Yep, they have enough land; they don't need to pile them on top of each other.'

'Look at these ads: Wow, wow, wow, wow! Rainbow are playing!'

'Who's Rainbow?'

'Ritchie Blackmore, the guitarist from Deep Purple. Don't you know him?'

'Hmmn, no. We'll see.'

'Ooops, OK! Nice ass!'

'Calm down! You're here to check out the school.'

'We haven't had traffic lights in years. I can't believe you actually stop at them; where's the Lebanese in you?'

'In Lebanon, where he belongs. Not only will they stop you; they'll put you in jail.'

'Even if you didn't cause an accident and were able to swirl between the traffic?'

'And you think if everybody did that, there wouldn't be accidents?'

For all the English that Omar spoke in his school, when he met Julie back at Khaled's apartment, he clammed up. At first, even his 'Yes' and 'No' answers would sometimes get confused. She told him his

English was very good and said that she had taken the day off work to show him the area, and all the shops like WH Smith and Woolworth's. And later on, she would show him how to use the buses, and maybe his brother would show him how to use the tubes and take him to Oxford Street, Leicester Square and Piccadilly Circus.

Omar said that he had never been to a circus but what he really wanted to see was the park where people could get up and say whatever they wanted about Israel. She laughed and told him that a long series had just started on TV about the Jews, called *Holocaust*; it would be good for him to see it. Omar was fascinated that TV ran all day and said that his difficulty would be watching more than one channel at the same time.

At Woolworth's, Omar was told that the music he was looking for was called Hard Rock; they said that there was a bigger selection at HMV and Virgin. He went back to Julia and Khaled to see how soon he could get to those places and how far away they were.

'Don't you want to see the museums and Madame Tussaud's? The zoo is huge. And the changing of the guard?'

Omar paused. 'Yes,' he said. 'But I have to do my religious duties first, and there are people back in Lebanon depending on me to bring back some supplies; this is the only thing that can save them.'

Khaled said that a colleague of his called Marcus wanted to meet him. 'Maybe we'll go together,' he suggested. 'He'll probably know what you're talking about.'

The day after Omar arrived, a bomb exploded at Hyde Park corner. Marcus said he was sure that Omar had something to do with it. He was a white South African, and had come to London because he could no longer stand what his government was doing to the blacks, so he said he completely understood Omar's reasons for the bombing; it was the only way he could bring the world's attention to Israel's bombing of Lebanon.

Omar laughed, not sure if he was serious. When Khaled confirmed his friend's background, Omar was full of admiration that Marcus had made the big move to England when he could have stayed in South Africa and used the blacks as freely as he wanted to. Marcus brushed aside Omar's interest in his history and told him that he should stick to his mission: the IRA needed some training; blowing up horses in Hyde Park would only have the horses defect to the English side. Instead, Omar should tell them that they should collaborate with the horses so that they would throw the police off their backs in Northern Ireland.

Once Omar had been reassured about Marcus's genuineness, that he was on 'our' side, and that he really did appreciate the Lebanese and the Palestinian cause, Omar wanted only to talk about music. Did he really know John Bonham and had he really been asked by Led Zeppelin to attend his funeral? Did he really know David Gilmore and did he ask him why Pink Floyd had a whole album with songs of animal names? Would Ritchie Blackmore consider going back with Deep Purple? If they were friends once, there must be a way to be friends again!

As they walked towards HMV on Oxford Street, Marcus pointed to a man in a white gown, staring at a shop assistant as she served customers at a counter. 'Look,' Marcus said. 'One of your guys. He looks hungry.'

Omar retraced a few steps. 'He's just looking at her,' he said. 'He's not even buying anything.' He started walking again. 'He's not one of ours. He's from the Gulf. People from Lebanon don't wear white all over.'

'It doesn't matter; you're all the same,' joked Marcus.

A few minutes later, Omar shook his head. 'It makes one feel ashamed,' he said. 'No wonder they hate us.'

'Look,' said Marcus firmly. 'Don't let anybody make you feel ashamed. Up till 1905, you used to be able to buy a woman, right here, in London, for five pence. You'll see lots of stuff on TV about how the Saudis treat women like shit, and they do, but you have to be careful how it's used. You have to ask why they're showing this right now. The whole world is one messed-up place, but they're not showing all the bad things in an equal way. Everybody says slavery in America was a bad thing, but they go to South Africa and holiday there and support the system. They'll show the Holocaust and all that happened to Jews but they won't show all that the Israelis are doing to the Palestinians. Watch *Holocaust*; it's good to know what happened to them, and it's true, if not worse than what they show you. Your brother won't be telling you much of that stuff because he's tired of it all, but when you show something that happened forty years ago and don't show what's happening today, you're just letting the same thing happen again. Worse, you're just repeating the same thing while saying it was very bad the first time it happened.'

Omar watched *Holocaust* and slowly found himself immersed in it.

When Julie joined him, she said, 'See, these people have had it hard, like nobody else did.'

Omar wasn't sure what to say to her. He liked her. He didn't want her to be upset with him especially after she had taken him around when she didn't have to. Even if she had done it as a favour for Khaled, she didn't have to do it from her heart. He hoped that his brother would come in and say something so that he would know how much she was willing to hear.

When Khaled walked in, he just took the remote control and changed the channel, while putting his hand out to tell Julie to hold on before she reacted. He flicked it to the news.

She looked at him. 'Now you care what Margaret Thatcher has to say?' she said.

'Wait, Israel has reached Beirut,' he said. 'They're bombing it from the air and they're going in.'

A few minutes later, Omar saw Israeli planes blasting Beirut, and then the ads came on.

'It looks like you could be staying here for a while longer,' said Khaled, shaking his head.

'Why?' asked Omar.

'How are you going to get back? No airport.'

Suddenly Omar jumped. 'Where's Ziad?' he said.

For the next two hours, Khaled kept on pressing the automatic dial button on his phone, eventually promising Omar that he would try again really early in the morning before going to work, and if he heard anything, he'd wake Omar up, even if it was six o'clock.

Having turned off the light, Omar resigned to sleep as he knew that the phone might not connect for a couple of days. Then he felt Khaled peek his head through the door. Omar sat up slowly. Without putting on the light, Khaled said that he had spoken to their mother in Tripoli. Ziad and Sana and Jamal hadn't left on time; they were stuck, but they should be fine — there was a very good bunker in their building. He suggested that Omar try to get some sleep because there was nothing he could do about it. 'We'll try again tomorrow,' he said.

After Khaled left, Omar got up, kept the light off, opened the curtains and went back to bed. He looked up through the window at the sky. It was a clear night; he could even see the stars from his bed. He listened to the silence for a few minutes and knew that nothing was going to disrupt the sky, or anything in the city, for hundreds and hundreds of kilometres. Everything was going to stay as he was feeling it and sensing it at that exact second. As he closed his eyes, he saw the pictures of the Israeli planes. From the few seconds of footage that had been shown on TV, he knew that Ziad would be in the bunker of his building and that his building was going to be shaking every few minutes with each bombardment, until the planes went away, and then, when the Israeli army went in, who knew what would happen?

Next day, when the news came that the Israeli army had gone into the capital, Julie looked at Omar in sympathy. 'I've heard you have a relative in Beirut,' she said.

'Yeah.' Omar nodded, not too sure what he could say. 'He's my cousin,' he muttered slowly, adding, 'but he's my brother.'

On their way to visit one of the boarding schools that had been discussed, Khaled made it clear that it was a boys' boarding school. A mixed school would be too distracting and had risks with girls, and Khaled really couldn't take any more responsibility than he was already taking. He said his words, leaving no room for discussion on this topic. Omar wondered as Julie looked out the window whether she had been warned by Khaled not to interfere on this point.

When they reached the school, Julie said that she was going to stay in the car. When Omar came back from the meeting with the headmaster, leaving Khaled to ask a few more questions in private, he hovered around the car, first avoiding Julie's eye. She slowly got out and waited beside him without saying anything. After a few minutes, Omar looked at her with a red face, and blurted, 'Did you know that if somebody does something wrong, he has to go to the headmaster, take his pants down, and they smack you with a cane?'

Julie nodded. 'Yeah,' she said. 'It's kind of tradition in some schools.'

Omar shook his head with a determined but pained expression and then looked away. 'I'd rather have both my legs cut off and sell Chickletes chewing gums in the souk of Tripoli even if ten thousand bombs were falling on my head.'

When Khaled returned to the car, he handed Omar chemistry, physics, biology and maths books. On the way back, Khaled said, 'Yeah, it's a very old system; the caning isn't meant to hurt, but they still have it even though it's ancient. But then again, you're not coming here to start a riot; you're here to study and finish your education.'

Omar didn't answer. Julie said that maybe they should take their time and talk about it later.

Omar answered, 'No, I'm not here to start a riot, but I also want to be able to breathe.'

'Fine, maybe we should talk about it later.'

When they got home, Omar gave the books back to Khaled who refrained from taking them. He said that it had taken a lot of effort to bring Omar over, and the least he could do was give them a chance. Plus, it looked like he might be stuck in London and he couldn't just stay in the apartment. Omar said that he appreciated his effort, but if he was a burden on him, he could just drop him off at the airport. He got up to leave and Khaled stopped him, saying, 'And then what?'

'And then nothing. You just don't have to worry about me.'

To diffuse the situation, Julie swiftly offered to take Omar to the Zoo. 'There are a few zoos,' she said. 'We'll go to the nearest one; it'll be fun to see our ancestors.' As they sat on the second floor of the bus, they talked about anything other than their previous conversation. When they walked through the zoo grounds, Julie said that she didn't know the specifics of what had been said between him and his brother, but it looked as if the situation was bigger than Khaled; he could do only so much. She said that Khaled was not putting any pressure on Omar to make a decision on the spot. Since school in Lebanon or in England didn't start for a little while longer, he still had some time to mull over the situation. No matter what his decision was, he should still give his brother the courtesy of going through the books. In the meantime, he could enjoy London; there was so much to see by himself. And then, to lighten up, she suggested they queue for a camel ride; he could give her a few tips since last time she had nearly fallen off.

Omar smiled. 'Sure, the camel ride is a good idea, but I can't give you any tips. I've never been on a camel before.'

She was surprised.

He shrugged his shoulders. 'We don't have camels in Lebanon.'

She squinted her eyes, and said that she clearly remembered a TV series that had been on recently about a princess in Saudi Arabia, and, at the beginning of the film, they had shown a plane taking off from Beirut Airport, and in the background, there was a camel.

Omar smiled. 'Yeah, Marcus warned of those programmes.'

'No, seriously,' answered Julia. 'It was a good series. It was a long one, and there was a lot of money spent on it, same quality as the Holocaust one.'

Omar nodded knowingly. 'But Lebanon is the only Arab country that doesn't have a desert,' he said. 'Camels live in the desert.'

The boy heard a voice from his stomach; you're still you, just because everything around you is
different doesn't mean that you're somebody else.

And Back

A few days later, Omar approached Khaled slowly and gently. He sat in front of him in the living room and put the books on the table. 'Just like I said to you, but I'll explain,' he began. Khaled felt Omar's genuineness and let him begin. 'The biology is good; it's very clear. There's a lot of it, though. I'm not sure whether they'd expect us to memorise the whole thing, but at least if I killed myself, I'd be able to get somewhere with it.' He let out a sigh before continuing, 'The maths looks like I could manage it but I'm not sure how they teach it. Our maths teachers are actually very good. If they take the time to show us how these things work out, then, yes, but I'm used to our teachers. The physics is a bit of a problem. The physics in Lebanon is more equations than real-life examples of how physics works; it's more like maths. So I'm not sure if I can link my physics with this physics. The chemistry is like reading Chinese. Our chemistry has nothing to do with chemistry; it's like maths with symbols, and there's no way I would get this.' Then he shrugged his shoulders as if making a compromise. 'I'm going to take these books with me anyway; the biology and the maths might even help me in Lebanon.'

Khaled nodded his head. 'I've talked with the parents. They said that the only way for you to go back now is through Syria. They have to see who can go and collect you from the Syrian airport. They want you to think about things before you make a decision. I told them you'd already made your mind up. So, enjoy yourself for the next couple of weeks until we can figure this out, but mind yourself.'

Khaled was clear that Omar should not be late coming back at night — eight, nine at the latest, if a movie was long. So Omar had to negotiate: if Rainbow played after the other band who was playing with them, they'd finish at ten at the earliest. Khaled had warned him that concerts were dangerous: 'They take drugs; they get into fights; there are always ambulances at concerts, and, when getting home, sometimes there are organised gangs who want to hurt people who don't have white skin.'

Omar found out that the less important band was the support band and they always played first, so he rang Khaled at the intermission and said they wouldn't be finished before eleven. Khaled was pissed off, but told him to go ahead and watch his only concert. When Rainbow came on and Omar saw Ritchie Blackmore stand on stage, in his own skin and not just the pictures he had seen on the covers of LPs, he felt all his friends around him and started thinking just one thought as a rush went through his body, making him feel like one whole being: *this, what is happening, is real, and it is happening right now, and it is in front of me.* He looked around and couldn't understand why a lot of people were banging their heads forwards and backwards. He smiled. That's what they do, he thought, looking back to the stage and breathing it all in.

On the way back from the concert, when the bus conductor refused to believe that Omar was fourteen and charged him an adult fare, he felt humiliated that somebody would not take his word, especially over such a small issue. But then it occurred to him that all those films that were rated '18' that Khaled told him he couldn't watch were now open to him. *Dirty Harry* with Clint Eastwood and *Taxi Driver* with Robert De Niro were advertised as a double bill. Two days later, he borrowed his brother's overcoat and tinted glasses and sweated as he paid for his ticket. Every time the door opened during the first film, Omar would put his glasses back on for fear that they had come for him after the usher and ticket woman had both wondered to each other whether the person they had let in was really 18. Having watched all of *Taxi Driver*, he decided that if they had let him watch one film, they were likely to let him watch another film. And then, after Robert De Niro killed all those people and became a hero for it, he thought of all those films in Soho that he might be able to get in to see, although they might be difficult with sex films, so he borrowed his brother's hat and wondered whether a scarf would be too much and give his disguise away.

He couldn't believe how he could even go to sex shops and flick through magazines like everybody else did — and the range they had, the regular ones as well all those Asian and Black and German. Having gone through most of the magazines, he decided that just showing everything was not the best thing, as some of his friends had said. He preferred *Playboy* and *Penthouse* and *Club* because they had taste. The pictures looked nice and the women were much prettier even if they weren't doing anything.

After all this excitement, he realised that there was still a lot of time left in the day. Khaled was busy; Julie he saw at night; and Marcus had his own life. He took his volleyball to the park and decided he had to work on it to make it green just in case he had to go back to Lebanon suddenly. At first, he kicked the ball around but then he felt conscious of looking stupid, even though it seemed that nobody was looking at him. He knelt on the grass, held the ball, and rubbed it hard against the grass. When it became green enough to bewilder his teacher, he got up and started walking back towards the lake. As he passed a group around his age, chatting in front of the horse track, he decided to walk back and sit close enough to them not to be an intrusion but hoping that eventually they would talk to him. After about forty minutes of looking at them individually and together, and looking away and back at the lake, and then at his own shoes, and putting his walkman on and then off, he finally sighed and got up. As he got up, a roller skater whizzed by him, accidentally unbalancing Omar and knocking the green volleyball out of his hands. It bounced towards one of the girls who had black and blond hair. She handed it to him and smiled. He heard a black friend of hers mutter something that ended up making the boys laugh and the girls trying not to laugh. Omar took the ball with a shy, solemn face and she saw he was embarrassed. She shrugged as if apologetic for her friends and said, 'They want to know what you were doing with the ball earlier on.'

'I was making it green for my teacher,' said Omar in a serious tone.

She was about to repeat his words to her friends but then she stopped and looked at him again, giving him a chance to expand on his explanation. When she passed his full explanation to her friends, they burst out laughing and the black guy said that he wasn't a nerd after all. After they had invited him to sit down, they told him that there was no way he was going to meet people by just sitting around. 'People don't talk to you that way,' they said.

Later, one of the girls who had sallow skin told him that she was half-Lebanese but hadn't wanted to say it earlier on because she didn't know what he was like.

She ended up talking to him in Arabic and telling him that the last thing she wanted to be was Lebanese; she couldn't bear to go back and live there; she had left three years earlier and she couldn't stand the gossip of who knew whom, and it was obvious that for women it would get worse. He told her that he was going back as soon as the Israelis got out of Beirut or as soon as somebody could arrange to collect him in Syria. She said that she didn't even want to know what was going on any more; she'd had her fill. But she advised him that if he wanted to make friends, he'd have to know somebody — maybe sons of his brother's friends, or their neighbours or whatever; otherwise it was going to be impossible for him. He said it was weird how he looked like a nerd here when in Lebanon that's the last thing he would be. 'And friends? You just hang around for a little while before you're talking to somebody.'

She said her gang was OK — only OK. Most were much better on their own. 'But that's how it is and that's how it is.'

As they all left, he got up, too, and she told him it was likely that they'd be here again and they might bump into him, but it would be better for him if he worked on getting his own friends.

When he asked Khaled whether he knew anybody who was around his age, he became strained and said that he had been mainly involved with work; people around his age were like Marcus and didn't even have two-year-olds. He usually said 'Hello' to his neighbours, but they didn't have kids and he didn't know them well enough to ask them whether their relatives had any kids around Omar's age.

Two days later, Khaled said that when he had told his boss about Omar, he suggested that his son stay over on Saturday. He said it would be good for his son to meet somebody from a different part of the world.

'I'm Peter Smith.'

Omar wasn't sure what to do with Peter Smith when they were left on their own. 'There's a great film on TV tonight,' he said. 'Probably Hitchcock's best.'

Peter wondered whether there would be any objections to seeing an '18' film; it was supposed to be quite scary.

Omar was surprised. 'But it's on TV!' he protested.

As they played chess first, Omar remembered a remark made in passing when Peter's father had introduced them; he had laughed as he said that Peter didn't like to lose. Omar wasn't afraid that they were going to fight or that they wouldn't make friends. Within two minutes of meeting Peter, he had realised that it would be unlikely that they would meet again, so he counted the opportunities when he could have checkmated Peter and, after the fourth, he sacrificed his queen. When Peter missed the opportunity, Omar checkmated him. They both agreed not to play any more chess and chatted about their different school systems.

'So, you study when you're supposed to? Every day, for example?' asked Omar. 'And then when the time comes, you're ready for your exam?'

'Yes, well, how else could it be?'

After Omar had told Peter of the alternatives, Peter wondered how come they were not thrown out of school for all their mischief.

'If they did that, then all the schools would be throwing everybody out and everybody would just end up changing school,' Omar replied. With a smile, he added, 'And then, after a while, the same class would end up back in the same school where they started, so there's no point.' Peter looked at him blankly.

In the scene in the film where the angle changes for an overview of the stairs and Norman Bates comes charging in with a knife, both Omar and Peter jumped in their seats. Omar looked at Peter with a smile at having been scared and saw that Peter was scared of having been scared. After the film finished, Peter asked whether they were both going to sleep in the same room.

'Whichever you want,' answered Omar.

Peter said that he was likely to have nightmares after the film.

Omar had to be convinced by Peter that he wasn't joking. 'So you've never seen a real gun?'

Peter shook his head.

'Or a body?'

As Peter shook his head, he added, 'Please...'

Omar had been about to continue but he stopped; he understood that the request was genuine.

The following day, Khaled tried to be patient. 'This is all I can do,' he said. 'What do you expect? He's the son of a top surgeon.'

'If his dad is a surgeon, doesn't he tell him about all the people that he cuts up?'

Omar saw more footage of the Israeli bombing of Beirut. Still no news about Ziad and his family, but Omar's parents knew that the Israelis had surrounded the city and cut off electricity and water. Over the next two weeks, the Israelis went in. Omar walked more in the park, bought more magazines, saw more films and all the TV there was at night.

As Omar heard that Bachir Gemayel had been elected president, he looked at Khaled, and asked, 'How can the head of Christian party be elected president when they're in the middle of the troubles? He shook his head disbelievingly, and added 'And who could vote if the Israelis were in?'

Khaled explained that even before the war, the Phalangists had had their soldiers trained in Israel. Not only did the news surprise him as to Israel's level of involvement in the Lebanese war, which Omar had seen mainly as a civil war up until just a few months previously, but he was quite surprised that Khaled had any political interest.

Khaled said that he hadn't always been a sell-out, that there was a time when he had been in the Syrian Arab Socialist Baath Party. 'Not Syrian as in the same regime that is ruling today,' he explained. 'But related to much earlier — what existed before the British and the French doctored the region.'

Omar's eyebrows rose. 'And what happened?'

'I was arrested once, for speaking my mind, and look.' Khaled pointed at the television. 'No amount of talk makes a difference. Who would ever have thought that Israel was going to invade half of Lebanon and get away with it?'

'But you're a doctor now,' urged Omar. 'Your word will have even more weight!'

'And where do you want me to speak? At Hyde Park corner?'

'Anywhere. In your work.'

'Doctors don't change the law, or journalists, or historians; politicians do. So I'll save my breath. No, thanks.'

After much resistance, the PLO announced that they were leaving Beirut. It was unlikely that the Israelis would stay too long afterwards as there would be continued resistance to their stay, but it could still take some time. Omar's parents said that they would wait two more weeks and if the Israelis didn't withdraw, they would start making arrangements for Omar to come back through Syria.

Omar rejoiced when he heard that the new President had been assassinated.

'But he's your president,' said Julia, surprised. 'You're not even giving him a chance. And how can you rejoice at the death of a person?'

Omar said that this guy was responsible for the death of so many people that it was quite likely he would commit more atrocities, and in any case, there was no way that he had been elected legitimately. How could you have an election when another country had invaded your capital city? And then he thought and asked her, 'How many people in England would have preferred somebody like Hitler to have continued on living?'

191

She argued that there had never been a figure in history quite like Hitler.

'Maybe not,' agreed Omar. 'And I definitely didn't think that anybody could deserve what the Nazis did. I've watched *Holocaust* with you for the past five weeks and I'm glad of it, but if people only saw *Holocaust*, then nothing else is ever going to be bad enough. Also, do we have to have another Holocaust before anybody is going to say anything about it?'

Four days later, Julie let the tears silently roll from her eyes as she watched Khaled and Omar look at the television: under the supervision of the Israeli soldiers, the Christian Phalange had surrounded Sabra and Chatilla camps whose Palestinian soldiers had left Lebanon, and had gone in to kill over 1,800 people, mainly women and children. A young girl who had survived said that when she lay among the dead, she heard a voice announcing that whoever had not died should stand up so that they could be taken to hospital. There was a pause, followed by more shooting. She survived because she had already been shot in the leg and was too injured to stand up. After the scene, Julie asked Omar how he was.

He contained himself, but when he turned and saw her tears, he looked away so as not to cry. 'I accept we're shit,' he said. 'I accept we are less than scum. What I don't understand is how people who allow this and support Israel could pretend to have so much dignity.'

Over the next three days, Omar would try to get his fill of London as he prepared to fly back to Syria. He could see only three films in three days; he had previously tried to see two films in one day but it had left him remembering neither. On one occasion, when he went to see *Blade Runner*, the Indian usher who took his ticket from him came in and sat next to him. At first, Omar was surprised that the usher wouldn't have seen the film already, but then, a few minutes later, he felt the usher's hand over his. Omar froze; he wasn't prepared for this. He thought of all the things he could say while the usher's hands kept brushing against him. Then he got up and moved one seat. The usher waited a minute, moved next to Omar, and then started touching him again. Omar held his breath and then looked at him and said loudly, 'ARE YOU OK?' The usher didn't answer. He looked away and then when Omar turned, he got up and left. Omar sighed and tried to go back to watching the film. He tried hard to concentrate, knowing that, should the usher return, the right tactic would be just to be loud again.

As he tried to concentrate on the film, he kept on thinking about what would have happened if he had been four or five years younger.

As he packed his bag, he cut out the best bits of the magazines he had bought and tried to think of ways of bringing them back. He knew that if he were caught with nude pictures at the Syrian airport, he might be in trouble. He decided to insert them in between the outside cover and the hardcover of a big book on dinosaurs.

For his last night, he was invited by Marcus, with Julie and Khaled, to a 'better-than-McDonald's hamburger place'. Over dinner, Marcus asked Omar whether London had treated him well. Omar had not heard this expression so he thought to himself and said that London had nothing to do with him; he had tried as much as he could to get some things from London. The record shops and the bookshops were amazing, but he hadn't met many people. For him really to enjoy London, he would have to bring his friends over, even just for one day. Aside from that, he didn't know, but if people were just like Marcus and Julie, it was a great place.

'Yes,' answered Marcus. 'And then it would be 50 per cent South African anarchists and 50 per cent peace-loving Welsh Bambi people, and we'd just have to decide whether we'd let in any Lebanese doctors like the one you've just excluded.'

Omar objected with a smile, and defended himself, saying that he hadn't included Khaled because he wasn't English.

They all laughed. That was Marcus's point: there were so many people in London who were not English. He then went on to explain what 'Welsh' meant. 'Well then,' Omar said, 'I've probably met only about three English people, so I can't judge.'

At the airport, Julie hugged Omar, telling him that he could write to her if he wanted to. Khaled assured Omar that if he had any trouble with his passport on the way out, it was only going to get him back faster.

At the Syrian airport, Omar walked around, quite surprised at its modernity. He had been told that it was not much of an airport, but the shiny floors and the bright neon lights impressed him. The scenario Omar had been dreading happened just at the last check on his way out; he was asked to stop and open his bags and the only item that was approached was the large dinosaur encyclopaedia, which had nude pictures slipped in between the covers. Omar remained cool, trying to evoke in himself every James Bond film that he had seen. As the book was opened, he feared that the pictures would slip out. 'No hanky panky material?' the officer said, smiling, looking as if he was hoping that there would be.

'Just a book about our ancestors,' replied Omar, and then quickly corrected himself: 'I mean, *my* ancestors'.

'Good, good. You go ahead.'

Omar walked out, repressing a big smile until he saw Amin.

Through Syria, and then into Lebanon Mountains until Omar saw for the first time in his life the cedar trees. Amin was surprised that he hadn't seen them before. He was too young to have been taken skiing before the war started, and then after it started, it was a Christian area. He hadn't seen the cedars before this because of the war, and now the only reason he was seeing them was because the war had got even worse.

When Omar reached Azmi Street, his mother was waiting on the balcony just as she had waited on so many occasions when he was a child. He had a feeling he would see her but was still surprised. The trip from Damascus was not two hours but six, maybe eight, hours. He was greeted like a lost treasure that had been found. Zeina was there, and his dad, waiting in the background until everybody finished kissing him. They teased his mother that she had been going in and out of the balcony for the past three hours. Amin objected that he was more than a chauffeur and if he wasn't, then they should at least acknowledge him with a tip. Omar had a present for each and couldn't answer their questions quickly enough to satisfy the different curiosities: Wasn't their messed-up country still better than 'outside'? Did Khaled treat him well? Had he been too naughty? Did he spend every penny they gave him? Did he see the wax museum? Did it look like he had lost weight? Were the British cold with him? Was the weather really horrible? Was Julie still the same and was she taking care of his brother? They accepted all his answers until he said that he was impressed with the Syrian airport; it looked like the country was making an effort not to stay backward. He was scoffed at as if he were a fool: 'And how do you think they made all that money?'

'How?' asked Omar as if trying to figure out a puzzle.

'By ripping us off, you silly billy. Remember when Laila's car was stolen, and on top of that, they rang her to see if she wanted to buy it back!'

'Did those guys have a Syrian accent?' wondered Omar.

'No, they have the best of our dirt doing their dirt for them.'

After the rowdiness calmed down, they told him that they had a surprise for him. Ziad would be there in two hours; it was his first time leaving Beirut since the Israeli invasion and he was dying to see Omar. Omar calculated that he would have at least half an hour to see his friends and said that, if it was OK with everybody, he was going for a short walk.

'We've spent all this effort to get you back and now you want to leave us,' they teased, but they understood.

In the street, Omar was treated as if he was a gigolo. The more he told them that he hadn't slept with any girls — that in fact he had found it very difficult to meet anybody, let alone girls — the less he was believed. The topic was dropped only when he told them that he had seen Rainbow, but he hadn't seen any other bands. One glimpse of Ritchie Blackmore was enough: What was he wearing? How did he move? Did he close his eyes when he played? Did he talk to his audience? Did he look like he was missing Deep Purple?

Omar could stay for only about half and hour and then he had to return before Ziad arrived. He rushed back just in case they had arrived early. When Omar got near his building, he saw Jamal unloading his car. He kissed him and was told to hurry as Ziad had just rushed up and was dying to see him. Omar ran to the lift and it had just closed. He ran all the way up just in time to open the door of the lift. Sana held his face and Ziad passed by him as if jokingly avoiding him. Omar looked behind to see Ziad greet everybody quickly and then quickly go towards Omar's room without even turning back. Sana told Omar not to worry about going down to help Jamal, just to go ahead and see Ziad. Omar couldn't quite decipher her tone but went ahead.

When he got to his room, Ziad was standing at the balcony door with his back to the rest of the room. Suddenly Ziad turned around and said, 'They tried to crush us; they bombed the fuck out of Beirut; at first, we didn't want to leave; they told everybody to leave because they just wanted to bring the city to rubble; one night, the Israeli planes bombed us for eleven hours straight, and when they went in, they would stop anybody in the street; you know, they slapped Shafik, my neighbour, because he said the word "Palestinian"; with the back of his hand: WHACK!' Ziad gritted his teeth and continued, 'And it was the Israeli who was asking where the Palestinians were, but they wanted to *annihilate* the Palestinians; they didn't want the Lebanese people even to say the word "Palestinian".' He shook his head from side to side. 'The chosen people have chosen to erase the un-chosen people, as if they could get an eraser and erase them. For four weeks, no water, no electricity, as if we were dogs, and you know what? Not even one white flag. I begged my parents to let me get a gun. What good is it to read about it later in history? They just wanted to wipe us out, like this,' and Ziad extended his whole arm across Omar's table with all the LPs, books and other presents he had brought from London and swept his hand across, pushing everything to the ground.

Omar stood back; it was too late to save them from the fall. Suddenly Ziad realised what he had done, and put his arm near his mouth, not fully covering it, knelt on the floor, looked up at Omar with apologetic eyes, then started slowly to reach for the fallen objects. Omar went over, took him by the hand and moved him and sat next to him on the bed. Ziad started to shake, holding himself back from sobbing. When he looked up at Omar to apologise for throwing his stuff on the floor, he saw Omar's tears held back and then his own tears flooded. He sobbed and sobbed, his chest vibrating with a wheeze, while Omar sat next to him, sometimes putting his hand on his shoulder and sometimes taking it off so as not to crowd him. After about ten minutes, Ziad squinted his eyes towards the far corner by the balcony window and then slowly looked up at Omar 'What's with the green volleyball?' he asked. Omar smiled.

the boy looked at his chest in bewilderment and then asked, 'Are you still here?'

Withdrawal

When family relatives came to visit Omar's parents to greet him on his return, Omar didn't want to see them. He'd had enough of social customs; he hadn't invited them: 'They just want to drink coffee in my name and yak on, so why should I be used as a solution for their boredom?' But he did see them; he consented to meet them for a little while — that would be more than two minutes, his parents urged — and then he could go for his walk to meet his friends.

The first thing they asked him as they sat down was, 'Which is nicer — "here" or "outside"?' Although he wouldn't have considered going into details, he was happy to answer this question: with all that London had to offer, he would still miss his friends and just being 'here'. They commended him on his loyalty even though it was not quite clear who he could be loyal to; at this stage, just about every political group or militia had split against whatever allies they had. Without making an effort to engage him directly, they discussed what it was about 'our land' that had 'something' which you just wouldn't find 'outside', and towards the end of each of their sentences, they would look at him and ask, 'Don't you think so?' leaving room for one answer only. He would stall his answer before they went off on their own again. As the topic withered and the space between the words widened, they said, 'So, we've heard you're not prepared to be hit on your ass; good for you!' He looked at his mother with betrayed eyes and then back at them to shrug his shoulders and reply, 'Yeah.'

'Well, I wonder if they smacked Charles on his bottom when he was younger.' And again without leaving any room for his answer, they said, 'It looks like they did — that's why he walks like a fridge.' He said goodbye and told them he had promised to meet his friends.

'So, what did I miss? Fill me in; fill me in,' Omar enthusiastically urged his friends.

'Nothing.'

'You idiot, why did you come back?'

'You had a chance to escape and you didn't take it!'

It was the familiarity of what he knew, the comfort of what he had grown accustomed to. And there were only three more years to go at this stage — might as well finish them. He said that mainly he had missed his friends; it didn't look like as if he would be able to make friends like them. They all shook their heads. Each said that, given half a chance, he would never come back. They had had enough of this place a long time ago. He said that with all the war, there were still some things that hadn't been lost: 'Just the way strangers are with each other — there was something about London that was cold. Not just the weather.' And there were other things that he had heard but couldn't make sense of.

'Like what?' he was asked.

He couldn't get his head around 'the Chelsea smile'. He had been warned by his brother's friend about going to soccer matches. 'You're beaten just for supporting an opposing team. With the Chelsea smile, they come and hold you on both sides, then somebody else takes a knife and cuts a bit on each side of your mouth, and then somebody else kicks you in the balls and, when you scream in pain, your face splits open and you have a Chelsea smile.'

They were repulsed by it. 'But still,' they said, 'it's better than being here.' At least if he stayed there, he could choose not to go to soccer games, and anywhere else he wanted to go to, he wouldn't have to stop at checkpoints. He said that there were things that you just get used to and expected with war, but in London he just couldn't make sense of violence when you had a choice not to be violent. 'It's just that when the reasons are petty, like a soccer game, then it's more mad than the war.'

They said that he was the one who was mad for choosing the war — this country was way beyond hope and now *he* was beyond hope because he didn't even see it. Had he heard while he was in London how the new Lebanese government had been formed? 'MPs were taken at gunpoint in Beirut and forced to vote, and then, when Bachir Gemayel became President and was assassinated a week later, they thought it was the Palestinians who had done it, so, under the supervision of the Israelis, they slaughtered about 2,000 Palestinian woman and children, and then, guess who it turned out to be who slaughtered the President?'

'Remember the Franjieh family in Zagharta when they promised to avenge the slaughter of their family?' someone added.

Omar still remembered the poster of the blonde little girl with the curly hair.

'Well, they got them back real good.'

Omar shrugged his shoulders. 'Still, whatever.' He had no argument for liking Lebanon, but maybe he didn't need one.

When most of his friends had finished doing nothing, they decided to go back home. Omar thought he would go for one more stroll before heading back. As he walked up Azmi Street with George, while the usual traffic jam moved at a snail's pace, Omar heard a car beep. He turned to see a bearded man get out of the car in front of it. The bearded man shouted at the man who had just hooted at him — a middle-aged plumpish man with glasses, whose wife sat next to him. The bearded man then shouted for the other man to get out of his car. Omar saw the seated man freeze while his wife looked at him in bewilderment, her face quickly contorting in shock. The bearded man took a gun out and shot twice up into the sky. The man in the car remained still while his wife repeatedly shook her head, desperately urging him not to get out of the car. The bearded man reached for the door handle but the door didn't open. He moved back, shot one more time up into the sky, and then turned around, still shouting, and started walking back to his car. He got in and drove off. The street was dead still; pedestrians who had walked off and then stopped and had been watching were frozen to the spot. After a few moments, the couple in the car looked at each other blankly. The man then put his hands on the steering wheel and drove off very slowly, taking a left at the next corner.

George looked at Omar and asked, 'You still want to stay in this country?' Omar felt revulsion spread throughout his body. He stood still, feeling sick, but not knowing how to throw up; the nausea went from his head to his toes. He shook his head as if to shake off the incident and then stood, wondering whether he should walk forward or turn back.

George spat on the ground. 'Fuck this country!' he said and then looked at Omar. 'Just because he beeped him, just because he beeped him — that was his crime!' He was furious. 'And in front of the guy's wife too, humiliated him down to nothing.'

Omar remained still, frozen.

'And you want to stay in this country? Huh!'

Omar looked at George as if he no longer had any answers.

'Look, you go back home, this is not a walk,' George said.

Omar held his hand out, patted George on the stomach, and turned back.

When he got home, Laila had just come from Beirut with Khalil and their little son, Samer. They were surprised at their flat greeting and asked him how come he looked yellow. He told them of the incident he had just seen. He said that he had seen plenty of incidents but this one had got to him so much because it was over the most frivolous thing he could ever think of. As he turned to walk back to his room, Laila looked disappointed; Samer had been calling his name in the car all the way from Beirut and he was looking forward to seeing him. Omar turned his head, looked at little Samer and said he'd be back in five minutes. As Omar walked off, Laila asked him to come back and look at a newspaper headline about Israeli torture of Lebanese captives. She read aloud, 'When they asked for water, they urinated in their mouths.'

Omar stopped, turned back quite angry, and said firmly, 'Please, I don't want to hear any more.' As he walked off, he added, 'I don't want to hear anything any more.'

He heard his father ask, 'And the Arabs, where were the Arabs?'

Omar answered, 'In my ass.' He looked at his dad, trying to ensure that he hadn't insulted him.

Samer toddled over to him and hugged his leg, saying 'UP, UP, UP!'

Omar softened, and looked at Laila and asked, 'Can I take him to my room for just a few minutes?'

She smiled resignedly. 'Whatever would get you out of your black cloud, but don't be too long; we came to see you.'

In his room, Samer picked up objects randomly and handed them to Omar as presents. He took each object with a smile and began to exaggerate his expressions and treat each object as new. After a few minutes, Omar went to the living room with Samer and announced that he was the only person who made sense to him; it was a pity he had not spent more time with him before but from now on, he was going to boycott the world and listen only to Samer.

in the vast openness the boy went to a shop and said, 'I want to give back my identity; I no longer want to be me.'

'Go, go away, we are full up, and we'll never be able to get rid of what we have.'

Dislocation

The walks were becoming more and more futile, Omar admitted to his mother, but it was his only way of breathing, even if he felt as if he were filling his lungs with tar. Yes, he did play pinball; he openly admitted that he had become an expert at it. But it wasn't gambling; that he definitely didn't do and wasn't into doing. 'But pinball, well, the better you get at it, the less money you spend.' He had friends who had shown him how to sway the machines without tilting them. He had got so good that sometimes it was boring; sometimes he just handed over the machine to whoever was in line waiting to play. There were times when the owner would glance at them, knowing he wasn't making money out of this crowd, and if it hadn't been the type of town where one person might bring an armed scoundrel down on another over the smallest of things, he would have kicked them out a long time ago.

What else was there to do? Of all the things that could go wrong, at least he had kept himself intact. Videos. His mother had asked him hundreds of times, 'Aren't you sick of videos?' Sometimes he wouldn't even give her his classic answer to her question; he would just look at her and she would then throw her hands up in the air, saying, 'What can I do?' Sometimes she would smile and say, 'You're right', and then she would go over and kiss him, sometimes adding, 'It's just that with the movies, you go, you disappear ... I guess it's better than this place.'

It was Laila who had originally urged him to see *The Deer Hunter* and he had promised himself he'd see it again. It was about three hours long, though, and he wanted to savour it and make sure he wasn't going to be interrupted by his mother.

The first time he saw the film, he had felt as if he was in Vietnam, almost smelling the jungle. It was different from *Apocalypse Now* because he knew they were going to come back. He had heard about Russian Roulette, but he knew that Robert De Niro was likely to come out alive since he was the hero of the film. Still, the first time he saw the film, he wasn't sure the rest would make it. Even if the film wasn't real, it looked as if somebody had gone through what he was seeing.

When he had finished watching the film in his living room, he looked around and everything was dark. There wasn't a hiss. It had been their area's turn to be supplied with electricity, so no generators buzzed loudly. What stayed with him the most was Christopher Waken going back to play Russian Roulette of his own free will after he had been freed by Robert De Niro. Who the hell would come back to Lebanon in their right mind? Suddenly a thought crossed his mind; he felt almost jolted. But no, he wasn't like Christopher Waken; it wasn't as if he could have stayed in London; Christopher Waken could have gone back to the safety of his own home had he wanted to, but Omar had come back to what he started from.

Next day, when he rang Laila to talk to her about *The Deer Hunter*, he asked her about something that she had said in passing a while back. 'Are there really people playing Russian Roulette in Beirut?'

'Yeah, it was in the English papers.' Khaled had told her about it. 'And they did it for nothing.'

'What was that?'

'Some are playing it on their own, not because they gamble.'

Omar went silent. 'Yeah,' said Laila nonchalantly. 'This is what we've come to.'

Then she remembered Sana's neighbour who, a couple of years before, had started screaming out of the blue, saying that he could no longer take it. 'Well,' she said. 'He shot himself or jumped or his brain blew or something.'

'Something?' asked Omar.

'Well, he's dead for sure — dead or killed himself, one of them.'

When he rang Ziad to check the story with him, his cousin laughed. 'Yeah, like my mother says, these are the courageous people; these are the ones who have enough courage to let themselves go mad.'

When Omar asked Ziad whether he had seen *The Deer Hunter*, Ziad shrugged him off, saying, 'The Marines landed here a couple of months ago and they've bombed the fuck out of the Druse mountains until the mountains were shaking and you want me to feel for them?' Ziad affirmed that the only sane thing was to watch porn; it was the only time where you believe somebody was getting screwed and was having a good time at it. But life was tough: his parents didn't always sleep early.

Omar said that life has been more merciful on him: his parents did sleep early. In fact, life had really been looking after him in this area;

unlike Beirut, the video shops in Tripoli would not expect you to bring back any movies in less than a month.

'Wow!' Ziad was impressed. 'Sure, everything is pirated but in Beirut they treat their pirated films as if they were originals.'

'Life is funny,' reflected Omar. 'Once you get used to certain standards, it becomes very hard to change them. In Tripoli, people just don't accept that the owner of a video shop has a business to run and a life to live; they just keep the films they rent out for as long as they feel like it; there are lots of people who feel like keeping them for a month.'

As they talked, Ziad could hear bomb shelling in Omar's background. By the end of the conversation, Sana came on the phone and suggested to Omar's mother that they come down to Beirut for a few days. There had been predictions that things were going to escalate in Tripoli and since Omar's school had been off for a few days, maybe they should come down.

Omar's father didn't want to go to Beirut but he insisted that his wife take Omar. They would enjoy the scenery, he said. 'And I can settle my head in peace if I'm on my own. If it gets too bad, I promise I'll follow you '

The trip took only one-and-a-half more hours than the usual two hours in spite of all the manoeuvres the driver made to avoid certain checkpoints that might be kidnapping people. When they arrived, Sana had lunch prepared. Just after they sat to eat, at Omar's third bite, the building shook with an explosion. In a split second, the glass shattered into the living room and they heard glass fall out onto the street from the adjacent building. Within another split second, they realised that this was not a shelling but an explosion of a bomb that had been planted either in their building or an adjacent one, or a car bomb. They wondered why anybody would plant a bomb here; it wasn't a busy street; they faced side streets. And then they heard the screams of a woman. They all got up and walked out to the balcony. Omar gazed down to see a woman screaming while hitting her own head in lament. A few metres away from her lay the body of a child who was barely coming into his teens. He lay on his face while she screamed. Sana spoke in a broken voice as she looked at the woman. 'That's Hamid's mother,' she said, covering her mouth. Just before she continued, Ziad added, 'That's Hamid on the ground.'

'They're the concierge's family' Ziad explained to Omar. Omar felt the woman's screams run through him. He squinted to see what she was holding in her hand and he couldn't make sense of it until he looked at her son's body and saw that his left foot was missing. A wave ran through him, and then he felt his body sway slightly backwards. He gripped the rails and felt the woman's screams again. Her son's body was perfectly still and Omar knew that it was not going to move again.

After a few minutes, they went inside — to leave the people to themselves, as Jamal put it — but the screams were hard to bear when they couldn't see what was going on, even though they knew what was going on. Omar looked at Ziad who was eating at the table. Everybody was surprised that he could eat. Ziad looked blank and said, 'What can I do about it? I have developed crocodile skin; I don't feel anything. This happens every day. I don't see it every day but I know it happens every day.'

After much discussion with the neighbours, Jamal came in later and said that the bomb had most likely been planted by the owner of their own building. He had been wanting to raise the rent but there were no laws to back him up — he couldn't get rid of people just by telling them to leave. So he had put a bomb by the side wall to the entrance where there wouldn't be much damage to the building but it would be enough to scare at least a few. When Ziad heard, he fumed, 'I'm going to show the bastard.' He took a knife out and started rubbing it against the wall over the drawer.

Sana came over and looked at him. 'And who do you think has to live with these walls?' she asked.

By the end of the night, Jamal had vowed that for the first time he was going to consider his brother's suggestion to move to Spain and set up a business there. 'This country is fit only for dogs.' Ziad's eyes perked up, but then he suddenly looked at Omar with disappointment at the thought of leaving him behind.

Omar shrugged. 'What have dogs done to deserve such condescending comparisons?' he asked.

he shook violently, he rocked his head up and down ... he looked around and saw no one; he was alone between the ground and the sky. Everybody seemed to have left; the place was deserted.

He looked down at his chest, mouth foaming, and at the top of his voice shouted, 'Leave me, LEAVE ME, get out of me!' He gritted his teeth and raged, 'Leave me, I don't want you in here.' He beat his chest and scratched against it. 'Get out of me, just leave me alone; go out of me.' He shouted some more and then quietened.

Then, with sober eyes, he looked at the ground and said calmly, 'I don't want to belong to you, let me go, loosen your grip.'

He looked up to the sky and with the same tone said, 'You have collapsed on me a long time ago; I have clipped my own wings just to spite you; I will never fly in you again, ever.' He wiped his mouth and added, 'As of now, I have nothing to do with you; you are not above me.' He looked again down at the ground beneath him and said, 'And you're not below me.'

Slowly, he saw himself dislocate and drift off into nothingness.

In Between Nowheres

Negotiating Love

Omar would think of Rola's hair as he let himself sleep until he no longer saw himself next to her; he would drift into her hair, dreaming that he could live in it, even for a few seconds. He wondered what her neck would feel like, how soft it would be, whether she would shrink away in tickles and then lean back for more of his touch or whether she would stand still, close her eyes, and feel the ripples of his touch going through her. He knew that he would see her the following day in class: one row in front of him and two seats to the left. He was going to get glimpses of her hair to feed his memory. He might even brush against it but he wouldn't do it deliberately; that would be almost like stealing. And he didn't need to be like that with her; that would take things in a completely different direction. It would take him into physical flirting and that would be a quick death for his world of fantasy which could grow only if there was a physical distance between them. He wanted to keep this world: it lasted longer, it was richer, and it could grow bigger than any other doomed world. This world could embrace him, protect him from all the other worlds around him; it could shield him from confusing questions: 'The Americans and French and the what-have-you came in as multinational "peacekeeping forces" and Israel is still occupying huge parts of Lebanon — does that make them a peacekeeping force too or does that make the Americans a "forceful keeping piece"?' Just to sense how she moved took him away from realities that had become certainties: 'How many?' 'This one killed twenty-five.' 'No, I think it's twenty-three or twenty-seven.' 'We have at least one car bomb a week now; I was just thinking, you'll get one for sure after Friday's mosque prayers, but in Beirut you'll get more than one a week,' 'Yeah, here maybe every two weeks, maybe three. No, hold on, that's not fair, eh, let's say, every ten days.' Or her smile, which there was no way of catching every time it released itself into class. He knew that even with his eyes closed, there were things that he did which were almost going to guarantee at least a giggle: the nonsensical phrases he had been perfecting, or the out-of-place words that worked mainly through a mixture of timing and a delivery saturated in old Tripoli accent would often get him in trouble with the teachers when too many of his classmates laughed spontaneously. From then on, he would depart from trying to impress her individually, and the stage would get bigger. With the teachers he liked, he would take the extra step, turning the spotlight of fools on himself rather than making it seem as if he had got one up on the teacher; on one occasion when he was asked to open his mouth to show why it was bulging, he revealed a mouthful of multicoloured chalk that had been chewed and was most likely about to be swallowed for effect. 'I needed some calcium ... because of the hard times, my mother hasn't been feeding me too well ... the chemistry teacher said it was good for my bones; I was just trying to apply what he's teaching us ... if I'm doing it wrong, please show me how to do it right. I actually want to learn ... I want to learn because I want to become a good citizen, not just of Lebanon, but of this world, this rotating world that, that, that just keeps on rotating without getting dizzy. Seriously, and I mean it, how does it do it?' On those rare occasions when he was given the opportunity, mainly out of curiosity on the part of the physics teacher or the history teacher, to see how he was going to negotiate himself out of the situation, he would come out triumphant, knowing that he had won her admiration, which would enrich those glances that she often gave him.

With teachers he didn't like, he would win her admiration through completely different means: 'All I said was "Casablanca". That's all I said.' He had won the class's general admiration for creating a situation where there was almost nothing for his teacher — in this instance, the chemistry teacher — to pin on Omar.

'All you said was "Casablanca" ... and your classmates laughed?'

Omar let the tension build, and with the chemistry teacher it always felt as if it was him against the class, so Omar physically held himself as still as possible, trying to balance a position not of defiance — because as Omar had learnt from others, defiance had little success with any of his teachers — but a position as neutral as possible, leaving his teacher as disarmed as possible. 'Yes...' And he let an awkward silence develop. 'That is all I said.'

'And Casablanca is...?' leaving Omar the opportunity of humiliating him.

But Omar would not take it as he had decided that a short victory while strong was going to leave him far more inflexible than inflicting smaller humiliations until the end of the year. 'Yes, it is—' Omar responded on this occasion, and then let his teacher finish the sentence.

'... a city in Morocco,' affirmed the teacher.

Omar was often tempted to go against his tactics and embarrass his teacher as fully as possible, and on such occasions, it needed only a slight tilting of his head forward as if he were the teacher. And he might have uttered the words, 'Yes, as it has always been,' but he didn't. He remained as still as before and left the stage to his teacher, belly fully forward, tightened with a fuller inhalation to instil a firmer sense of dignity.

'I see,' the teacher went on, with full awareness of the alternatives. 'I guess it's a private small joke in the class,' and he breathed with a smile as if showing magnanimous generosity. 'I'll let it go,' he said and he turned back to the blackboard.

They had this chemistry teacher until the end of the year, and, if he didn't drop dead from their prayers for a heart attack, then two more years until they finished school. Omar's main forte with this teacher was taking a stand. The question, as he said to his friends, was: 'How do you stand right in front of a huge lump of fresh shit that is imposed on you for the next three years? Well, if you hold your nose tightly with the thumb and index finger of your left hand, you have the three remaining fingers left with which to cover your mouth to avoid swallowing all the flies that are going to be hovering around his highness. From then on, you no longer have to be contorting and squirming away from the smell and you even have the full use of your right arm to wave and show him that you're not affected.'

It was insights such as these that strengthened his connection with Rola. Even when he wasn't talking to her directly, and especially when he wasn't even looking at her but knew that he was within her hearing range, he enjoyed her laughter; at those times he earned it without even trying hard. Her laughter would often spontaneously ring in his ears later on at home, when he was on his own, fighting the weight of all the homework and the building pressures from all the missed schooldays due to new troubles. At times when he felt sluggish and heavy, he would invite it, imagine it, intercede with it to push away the gloom and the endless hopelessness that were slowly becoming a daily routine of the solitary hours that were inevitable if he were going to finish school. At times, especially when there was new fighting and he wasn't sure when school was going to be back, he pushed away his books, got up, declared a break until he felt lighter, and moved to the balcony. But there he never found her smile or the movement of her hair, not as long as he had his eyes open, and the more time passed, the more he tried to bring a sense of her in himself, the less he was left with. It was back to the metal of the balcony rails, an occasional taxi beep if anything at all, until either the fighting began all over again or a few more days of assurance before there was any movement in the streets. And then maybe, possibly, back to school, and finally, with an imagined but unexpressed exhalation of gladness, a refill of her being.

He seldom went beyond himself and felt overwhelmed but never felt freed from what he depended on to sustain him. 'Did you hear? There was a whole truck of bomb explosives at the airport in Beirut. It blew itself up into 248 Americans and 58 French.' Omar had got tired of wishing for peace and exercising the sense of love he had felt for all around him, regardless of where they came from. He allowed himself to take a break from who he was trying to be, working so hard at not hating, or shrugging his shoulders, but he had grown sick and tired of his lonely position. Vietnam was more than ten years old. He hadn't watched *Apocalypse Now* and *The Deer Hunter* to learn that war was horrible or sick or degrading or, even in a pure and simple child's language, a 'bad thing'; he had watched them because Laila had told him that the Americans were acknowledging that war hurts everybody involved, especially the civilians, and that the soldiers were civilians before they put on their suits, and when they returned back home, they returned to be civilians exactly like the ones they'd just fought against. Since the acknowledgment of the horror of war had been confirmed in Oscars for both films, Omar had hoped that no more troops would be sent in to more wars.

But then the marines were in Beirut. They came in again after the Sabra and Chatilla massacres, then left the Israelis to do whatever they wanted, and then fired at the Lebanese, and bombed the hell out of the mountains from their long fleet ships. Did they not watch their own films, and, if they did, what was the point in making those films if they weren't going to make a difference? He had tried to fight against the constant message that nothing made a difference — fuck them, let them die. He couldn't keep on holding his breath while the Lebanese died and the Americans took their time in not learning from the messages of their own films. Hearing the news that so many died in one go felt good — yes, it did! He surprised himself when he held his hands up; he wanted to bring them down but he smiled. A few minutes later, he hovered between being honest and his efforts to override his honesty, or refine it, or push himself to evolve into somebody else — he no longer knew what he was doing. There were some things that Rola's smile or gestures were just not going to reach.

Way into the night, past afternoons of monotony, no amount of fantasising was going to reach the hole that was developing in his gut. The only thing that took him out of that hole was watching some beautiful girls very quickly let themselves be teased into taking their clothes off — sometimes not even two seconds before they were putting a penis in their mouths or spreading their legs and moaning as they were licked, and then from top, from behind, below, until the man came, and then another scene. It was when they looked as if they were enjoying it for real and not just going through the motions that he felt engaged. It made him alive, although after he came, suddenly all of this strange life disappeared, even though the video went on with the same beautiful girls he had been watching just a few minutes earlier. Sometimes the desperation returned as soon as he went back to bed and closed his eyes, but sometimes it didn't. Sometimes he closed his eyes and let himself imagine that he was not of this life but that what he had just seen had happened to him. Although he would have preferred to have watched those movies before he felt his desperation emerging, they were the one thing that seemed to be stronger than painkillers — he found that out before a root-canal job.

So he kept his supply — at least five films at a time that he could fall back on should the two new ones he had just rented not have beautiful women, or be cheap, or just flat, un-erotic. He would specify that it was romantic porn that he wanted and he would try to guess the quality whenever the tapes came with a photocopied cover. But more often than not, he had to take the word of the shop assistant, and he made it clear that he did not want to see anything new or different. Once he was given a tape of sex with animals: women along a horse's big penis or a curled pig's penis or having sex with dogs. Another time, he was given a tape of men with transvestites. These sickened him. He had limits and did not want even to finish the films just so that he could say, 'Yes', he had seen these extremes. If anything, he concluded, such films were just like the wars he was living; he was almost certain that they came from the same place. It had surprised him that beautiful women would have sex in regular films and he wondered why they couldn't get regular paying jobs for the same money, but these other extremes he couldn't understand: why did they make them? Just like he couldn't understand how anybody could intentionally want to create a war.

It seemed that way in the back of his head was a world so far apart from the one that was being touched by Rola. There were times when he would see himself as he moved from one world into the other. At other times, he would just drift until he was touched by nothing. Maybe if he could really touch Rola, if he could be naked with her, love her, make love to her, he would live in one world. Even inside him there would be one core and not a torn one. But that was never going to happen. For a girl to lose her virginity was beyond contemplation; even just kissing her once was beyond contemplation. The amount of secrecy and planning just to create the privacy where he could have this one kiss would exhaust all romance. There was no such place in school, and the walks did not include her street. She lived three streets beyond his walking route and, like many people, she didn't choose that option. But most of all, it was never said that he fancied her or that she fancied him. It was a space left untouched.

He realised that within a few months, Rola might be replaced by someone else. The only physical difference would be the looks exchanged as he moved about; the rest was within him. For a fleeting moment, he saw that his existence was pathetic. As pathetic as being turned on, all over, by watching beautiful strangers have sex. Some things were beyond him. Beyond maybe even the clouds and the bees and all the seas put together. Still, Rola's hair was beautiful and her smile was beautiful, and for now, just for now, it made him breathe a different type of air from the air that was in the air.

Advanced Maths

Omar had been warding off much of the discussion around politics during his walks with his friends after school. Some developments intrigued him but he made as much effort as possible not to be sucked into discussion of them: 'Did you know that the Moslems in the army refused to fight Jumblat, the head of the Druse? And imagine, after nine years of war, this is the first time they ended up involved as a party!'

Omar would shake his head and then throw in a comment such as: 'The double live album by Rush is brilliant; Neil Peart plays his ass off.'

'Yes, that's right. The Palestinians have split on themselves — who would have believed it? Abu Ammar has been fighting Abu Moussa; it's a Syrian policy, a complete fabrication, you'll see. They want them to split so that they can come in their place.'

Omar had read a great quote by Einstein: 'If relativity is proved right, the Germans will call me a German, the Swiss will call me a Swiss citizen, and the French will call me a great scientist. If relativity is proved wrong, the French will call me a Swiss, the Swiss will call me a German, and the Germans will call me a Jew.'

'Oh, yeah, the bastard created the nuclear bomb so that the Americans could drop it on people who were already squinting so hard they could barely see.'

Sometimes Omar succeeded in diverting the conversation. 'No, no, you can't blame him for what the Americans did with it, but you know, we have an expression, "The weapon in the hands of the shit cuts"; you can't give a gun to a kid.'

There were few developments that Omar could get drawn into, but after the PLO pulled out of Tripoli and went to Beirut, a new party quickly began to develop in its place; it projected itself as a Moslem party.

Omar rejoiced: 'Excellent, they'll bring all the good and clean and wholesome honesty of Islam. No more shit for at least a while.'

His friends laughed at him. 'There is nobody who is clean. You can't trust anybody. Wait and you'll see.'

Then Omar was told that the few who welcomed the arrival of the new party were hoping for some showdown like the old days. They had heard that this group calling itself the Tawhid and its members had come in on horses, carrying swords.

'What? Who the fuck are they going to fight with horses and swords? Are they for real?'

Within three weeks, Omar heard that the Tawhid had come into El-Mina, the extension of Tripoli into the sea, and held members of the Communist party on the ninth floor of a building. The hostages had been told to say, '*La Illaha Illa al Lah, Mohammad rasoul al-lah*', the phrase that declares that there is no other God but God and that Mohammad is his messenger, thus declaring the speaker of these words a Moslem. Those who refused to say these words were thrown from the ninth floor. A chill went through Omar when he heard this news. Was nothing sacred any more? Every time he thought he had heard the worst of it, a new incident happened, a new twist on reality that would distort one more boundary. On the other hand, he was surprised that there were still principles left that could be deformed.

He had heard it through different sources with increasing confidence: the Islamic Tawhid who suddenly came out of nowhere had been brought into Tripoli by Arafat as a counter resistance to Syria. Arafat wanted to maintain a hold on Tripoli so that the PLO could come back later on. 'See, all the complications were very simple after all.'

One afternoon, when Omar went to rent a video, he took a side street that was at the back of a dump and met Tony, a friendly guy from school he had not seen in a while. Tony put his hand over his mouth as he talked and ended up showing Omar a scar at the side of his neck. He then opened his mouth wide to reveal two missing teeth and a disfiguration to his lower jaw. He said that being among the Christian minority in Tripoli, his family feared for their lives and had gone to stay in their village away from Tripoli until they figured whether the Tawhid were going to prosecute the Christians. One night when his parents were at the neighbours' house, Tony's friends had come over, and they had had a few drinks and ended up quarrelling over a game of cards. One of his friends had drawn out his gun and shot him. Maybe he didn't mean it because he didn't shoot him point blank, but still, he had managed to get a bullet through the side of Tony's neck and as Tony screamed while the bullet was going through his teeth, his mouth opened and it went out.

Tony shrugged his shoulders and said, 'And who would believe this if they saw it in a movie? And who knows where anything is at?' He added, 'I don't know. Maybe where God has put me: right here.' He took a gun that he had tucked into the back of his jeans, 'Look,' he said blankly. 'And I don't even know what I'm doing with this.'

Omar was surprised. 'And what *are* you going to do with it?'

'Nothing,' answered Tony. 'Have you ever shot with a gun?'

Omar had seen guns and handled them before but never shot with one. 'Here, try it. Shoot at the dump. There's nobody around.'

Omar slowly took the gun from Tony, held the grip, felt its weight, and pointed at the dump. He felt his body gently vibrate, knowing that he was not going to pull the trigger, but just letting himself feel the gun. He slowly brought his hand down and gave the gun back to Tony.

Tony tried to reassure Omar: 'It's OK. You can shoot one bullet; they don't cost that much.'

Omar smiled, but said it was OK: he had already felt its power; he didn't need to make noise and scare somebody.

'Who cares? People are used to it. Just one shot; nobody would notice.' Then he looked at his gun, staring at it for a brief moment before slowly tucking it into the back of his jeans. In an effort to conceal it more than he had earlier, he pulled his shirt down over it and said, 'You're right; who am I gonna shoot? If somebody pulls a gun on me, am I going to shoot them? Maybe I should just get rid of this thing.'

When Omar got back home, he did something he had been thinking of doing for a while. He took out an old metallic toy gun he had played with as a kid. It felt solid, it looked realistic, and it was a step up from the ones that came with plastic powder cartridges and looked more like cowboy guns. These were filled with individual golden bullets that had powder which blew into a flame through the gun's barrel as the trigger was pulled. If an extra bullet were put into the top of the barrel, the pressure from the triggered bullet, along with the emitted fire, would explode the second bullet and have it shoot off. It wasn't accurate but it could scar. He had never intentionally used it against anybody except once, when he was nine or ten, at the second day of Al-Odha celebration when he had shot his neighbour in the back and was shocked to see that it had left a black mark, ruining the jacket his young neighbour had just received as a present. It was one of the few occasions when he had got into serious trouble with his parents and the only time he had been in trouble with any of his neighbours.

He sat at his desk, put one bullet in, and rotated the cartridge as he had seen it done in *The Deer Hunter*. He put the gun to his right temple and felt the trigger. If the bullet was still live and the powder hadn't gone stale over the years, it was not going to kill him; it would burn his skin, maybe mark it. This wasn't *The Deer Hunter*; it was just *like The Deer Hunter*. But just as he had felt the power of Tony's gun without pulling the trigger, he felt that what he was doing was going to take him to a new place; once there, he would not be able to go back because he would have done something he had thought about so many times before but never allowed himself to do. The gun rested at his temple; he felt the trigger, and then slightly slid the gun so that the barrel was parallel to his skull — if he hit the bullet, at worst, it would burn his hair. He pulled the trigger. CLICK! There was no bang. Maybe a dud. He put the gun down on the table and felt a strange sensation go through his body.

He had gone half the way. He smiled. He had put one foot in doing it and one foot in not doing it. Then he wondered whether the bullet that was in the gun was still live. He went out to the balcony, adjusted the cartridge so that the bullet would be next, closed the gun, and shot straight. A BANG with a flame.

'What was that?' his mother immediately asked all the way from the living room.

'Nothing ... just a lot of nothing.' He put the gun back into the drawer as he felt his previous experience take a firmer place within him. He smiled. Funny how if the bullet had been a dud, it would have minimised what he had just gone through even though he was learning the fact after the event. But the bullet was not a dud. He had done something he didn't have to do again. To be honest, it was half a game. It was both: he had had a taste of being a person who would not really do such a thing and a taste of being a person who would.

He went in to reassure his mother that he was just checking something from his childhood.

'Aren't you finished with being a kid?' she asked lightly.

'Yes, I am,' he reassured her, then smiled immediately, saying, 'No, no, I'm not; that would be the end of me.'

As she looked at him, the phone rang. She paused in her conversation to let Omar know that Sana was coming to Tripoli with Ziad and Jamal the following week to say goodbye. After his mother had finished, Omar talked to Ziad; he was excited about their move to Spain. They were all packed. There was something half set up by Jamal's brother but he was going to let them stay in his place for two months until they settled. Omar picked up a tinge of sadness in Ziad's voice. Without referring to it, Omar assured his cousin that he wasn't being left behind; he had only two more years before he moved to London. 'Plus, from what I know, Spain's a great place; you simply don't have a choice but to look forward to it.'

Ziad said that the only thing that linked him to the place was Omar; otherwise he had just had enough and he simply didn't care what happened any more. He then casually told Omar that he had just heard that the Israelis were releasing 4,800 Palestinian prisoners in exchange for six Israeli soldiers who had been captured and held in Tripoli. Omar rejoiced; he hadn't heard such good news in a long time. After the call, he told his mother that he was going for a quick walk to Monla Street to meet with his friends.

When he met George and a few others at the corner in front of the familiar *ka'k* vendor, he told them of the brilliant exchange. George laughed and asked what was so good about that.

'Isn't it a brilliant negotiation?' asked Omar with a smile he had kept from political discussions.

'Israel captures Palestinians whenever it wants. They'll capture another 4,000 right next day. In any case, those 4,000 are going to be extradited to Algiers. If they are political fighters, that's like death to them. They're shipping them away from their country; it's not like they're sending them home.'

'They'll come back,' answered Omar, surprising himself that he was not letting the topic go.

'It won't be easy for them to come back. Maybe a few will weasel back in. What? Ten? Twenty? Fifty?'

Omar heard laughter from behind him, and someone said, 'You think it's good to exchange 4,800 Palestinians for six Israelis? Think about it; it's a confirmation of the worthlessness of Palestinian life. Here, calculate it … let me see … that would make … one Israeli worth 800 Palestinians.'

Omar's face dropped.

'Ha, ha! You still had hope of dignity? No more.' He was patted on the back. 'You've got to drop this hope thing of yours.'

Omar felt a chill going through him. He smiled despite his feelings and threw his hands up in the air, saying, 'OK, let's go back to square one.'

The following week, when Ziad arrived, Omar told him of his friends' assessment of the exchange. Ziad huffed sarcastically and said, 'Yeah, well, what is there to say any more?'

He was to stay for two days before going back to Beirut, and then the following week, his family would leave. Ziad and Omar decided that, for old times' sake, they were going to spend the next two days on the balcony, and perfecting their methods of finding the best objects to throw at cars. They knew that if they were caught, their mothers would have more or less the same reaction: 'I can't believe you're still doing this; you're sixteen years old; you're no longer boys; you're half men now.' They smiled all the more, knowing that they wouldn't be doing this again for quite a while.

What made a smooth splash no longer interested them. They looked at each other and started choosing heavier objects; whole large oranges made one hell of a bang if they smacked the middle of the roof of a Mercedes; firm apples looked too risky but Omar threw one and both were glad it missed; and then Omar came back with a half a large plastic bottle of mineral water. Before Ziad could stop him, Omar let it rip. It landed flat on the bonnet of a taxi and, worse, it didn't explode but retained the momentum it had built in the air and ended up making a huge bang. Both Omar and Ziad crouched on the balcony to avoid being seen. They couldn't tell whether it had dented the taxi but they heard the shouting of a man who got out of the car and threatened to go into the building. When the door bell rang, Omar and Ziad stayed on the balcony until they heard the door slam and then they slipped inside. Omar's mother said that it wasn't fair: they could have damaged the car; they shouldn't be doing these kinds of things; and, yes, of course she had lied — she had casually told the driver that there was nobody else in the house besides herself and her sister.

Sana looked at the boys and refrained from speaking, and then she smiled. 'OK,' she said. 'So you're going to milk the next two days, but be careful.'

They promised their mothers that whatever they threw from then on would be harmless.

They bought thin kitchen plastic bags that exploded immediately on impact if they were half full. It was just water, they showed their mothers; it was harmless. At around the fiftieth bag, Omar managed to land one water bag on the half-open window of a BMW. It exploded dramatically, splashing some of its contents against the glass and the rest inside the car. Having crouched down and waited for the driver to get back into his car and drive off, they decided to stop. No matter how hard they tried, they would not be able to top that hit.

When the time came, Omar and Ziad played the situation down, as if they were going to see each other the following week, while their mothers wept. Jamal insisted that the following summer, when they were all settled, Omar should definitely visit. And he should check out some of their colleges — why not think of Spain instead of London? Having watched them kiss his mother, Omar escorted them downstairs and helped load the boot. Then it was his turn, each embrace measured and stretched, except with Ziad — a mutual throwaway. They got it. Omar stood still, and the Chevrolet *mtartaa* moved off. Omar waited for a second and then quickly followed them to the road under the eyes of his mother. He then took a water bag from under his shirt and whacked it with all his might. It smacked right in the middle of the rear glass. The car stalled under Jamal's steering. They all looked back with a smile. Sana put her head out the window. 'Good one,' she called out, and her smile faded sadly as they drove off.

The Currency

Some said that it was after Arafat officially left Lebanon that the currency took a sharp plunge; others said that it was after the Marines were bombed that Lebanon got too messy for them and the US pulled out in more than a physical way. Omar had heard on so many occasions that they were just pawns in the hands of the bigger players. Lebanon could in no way subsidise such a lengthy war: over nine, almost ten, years. He had seen so many shoulders shrugged, so many hands open to face each other, empty, with the words, 'We just don't have the money.' There were moments when Omar was able to marvel at the grand absurdity of it all: the world's biggest powers, America and Russia, were playing out their conflicts in Lebanon, backing up different groups and planning car bombs against each other's embassies while the parties they supported had split against themselves, leaving the two superpowers scratching their heads. Israel came in, did its slaughtering, tried to erase the Palestinians, but couldn't. Syria who was supposed to be against Israel ended up putting pressure on the Palestinians too. Even the Palestinians split among themselves. And then, Arafat left officially, but they could be back as soon as you knew it. It seemed that confusion was the one thing that ran through from the lowliest man to the biggest powers in the whole world. In that sense, Lebanon was defiant — defiant in its own self-destruction.

Moments of wonder arose only when Omar overheard heated discussions on the overall political conditions, whether it was passing through the video shop, on his way out of the pinball shop, or whenever his father threw in the odd comment. For the rest of the time, he was busy shrugging off incidents and dismissing whatever new idiotic things the Tawhid were doing in the name of Islam. Wearing white and having a beard qualified you to have a gun, if not a machine gun, and to be official. Teaching of the Koran was enforced in Omar's school, an Evangelical American school. The Christian students had the option of not attending this class. They rejoiced in a hushed but friendly way, teasing their Moslem classmates. Omar tried to argue his way out of

224

the class with the headmaster when he made his announcement a week prior to the sheikh coming in: 'I like Buddha more than anybody else; we've been friends for so long and we've never fought about a thing. Seriously, can you tell them I'm a Buddhist?' The headmaster shrugged his shoulders. This had nothing to do with the school; it was imposed on them by the Tawhid and the most practical way to deal with it was to make the least trouble. If they started asking for a list of names of students, they'd pretty much be able to tell from their second names who was Moslem and who was not attending. It was just one hour a week and it was really not worth the trouble. The headmaster let the students vent their complaints in the hope that they would be diffused by the time they met the sheikh.

'Is he open to us teaching him about Islam? I know some gossip that I bet even *he* doesn't know.'

'Does God really want this or are they making things up again? Because when I was praying last night, I was not informed of any of this.'

'How come the girls don't get to grow beards, and how come they never get to be prophets? They seem to get away with everything.'

After a few minutes, the headmaster dropped his smile. 'Seriously, I don't want any of you to get into trouble. We've put up with messing but these guys are serious.'

The sheikh seemed to have surprising patience. There were a few who wanted to take the risk of messing with him. Omar begged George to stay back, although he could have got away with skipping the class on account of his first name being a Christian name. Ahmad agreed that he would try his best to find a way to mess but he was more at risk than anybody else in the class since he was Syrian and the Tawhid were fighting the Syrians. Direct heckling was too risky so they started with ambiguous distractions. George very calmly emitted a humming drone that rang through the class, while he pretended to take in what the teacher was saying, and even managed to keep it going, as he would deliberately drop his pen on the floor and pick it up without interrupting his flow. Ahmad came up with asking ambiguous questions with as innocent a face as he could muster, and, when the class was stopped, admitted that he wasn't really sure what he was asking about and agreed with the sheikh that the question itself wasn't clear — but that was why he was asking it in the first place and perhaps the teacher could help him ask the question. He suggested that perhaps every little while, the teacher could answer some questions without any students asking any, just to make sure that everybody understood. As the sheikh didn't know any of the students and was not going to be communicating with their teachers, Omar developed a stutter when he asked questions and ended up exaggerating it while his class laughed, and then he sat down angrily as if genuinely embarrassed by his classmates.

The girls grew increasingly worried that the sheikh did actually know what was going on and whispered that he might not be letting them know but he could end up sending armed people to their houses. After the first week, when no such thing happened, Omar, George, and Ahmad began to question whether he was a genuinely nice person: maybe he was a real Moslem. The girls reminded them that among the first few things he had said was that he did not want to force anything on anybody — that did give the impression that he didn't agree with the class being compulsory, and maybe it was the bluntest thing he could say without directly coming out and disagreeing with the Tawhid. 'Maybe he is sent by God directly; all the better reason to test him,' said Omar with a smile. He was warned again that he was playing with fire.

One day, on coming home from school, Omar walked in to see his mother crying and trembling every time she tried to speak. She shook her head, indicating that nobody had died, but still she could not be coherent, so he sat with her and she cried it out. Eventually she was able to tell him that a bearded man had rung her bell. She was immediately frightened when she saw him; he looked as if he was from the Tawhid and she was worried that something had happened to Omar. Then he said that he wanted to pass on a message in relation to Karim. When she told him that there was no Karim at this address, he asked where Karim lived. When she asked him why he was asking, he just slowly pulled open his jacket to reveal a gun tucked in through his belt and said, 'You tell him to just mind his own business.'

She told him, even though she was shivering, that there was no Karim in this building, and started to close the door. As he moved back, he said, 'You just pass the message, or else.'

She said that after she had closed the door, and since, she'd been crying, fearing that he might come back for her. What if he found out that Karim lived on the fifth floor and was fuming having gone around all the buildings looking for him?

'Maybe it'll take him a while to find out where he lives and he might come back next week,' she said, and, with that, she broke down again. 'How will I know? What have I done to be burdened with this curse? And what the hell has Karim done?'

While she had not had too much contact with Karim's family, she had always respected them. She didn't see him much any more since he had moved to the American University in Beirut a year before. She had always thought he was a nice boy. He occasionally used to help Omar with his homework, years ago, and had even taken him to the beach a few times, so what could have corrupted him to get into this? She had tried to contact his mother but there was no answer. When she suddenly caught a glimpse of Karim through the window, getting out of an old beaten-up red Peugeot, Omar immediately got up and said that he was going to go down and tell him what had happened, to warn him. Omar ran down the stairs and bumped into Karim as he was approaching the lift.

Karim smiled as warmly as he usually did but with a slight tiredness. When Omar said that he wanted to talk to him about something, Karim suggested that they go back to his apartment — his parents would not be in for a couple of hours — unless Omar really preferred to go back to his own place. In the elevator, Omar started to relay what had happened. As they went into Karim's apartment, he closed the door behind him and stood in the corridor until Omar said that his mother just wondered what it was that he had done. Karim half-smiled and motioned that they would go into the living room and sit down.

He said that there was a girl in his class from school, Safa, with whom he was friendly. He even fancied her, but when he was in school, you couldn't take it anywhere. In any case, she had been to America and she had tried horse-riding and liked it. She was now back awhile, and he was in Tripoli for the next two weeks on a semester break from his college in Beirut, and they had been in touch. She had wanted to go horse-riding, which she did every now and then in a place that wasn't even very nice — they had just about a horse and half a donkey or something. 'Anyway,' Karim continued. 'On our way back from the ride, we were walking home — there weren't any taxis — and suddenly this car pulled up, this old orangey peachy Renault or something, and there was another car behind it. In any case, two guys got out of the car and told me to get in. When I questioned them, they showed me their guns.' The men had told Karim that the car behind would take

Safa home, but they wanted to talk to him. He continued, 'They took me to their headquarters. About four of them came into this dingy room, all with beards — you know, the usual Tawhid — and they started asking me why I was with her; a man and a woman shouldn't be on their own if they're not married, and all of that, and they started citing the Koran all over the place. They told me it's forbidden in the Koran; that she shouldn't be riding horses because she could break her hymen and lose her virginity. Well, at first, I was very scared of them; I didn't know what they were going to do with me. They had guns and beards and the four in the room were all against me, but a couple of years back, I got into Islam. I read the Koran and a few different inter-pretations so I started arguing with them, using what I knew from the Koran. Well, it surprised the hell out of them, and very quickly it was obvious that they didn't know the first thing about Islam. Every time they said something or quoted something, I came back with more angles and more quotations.'

Karim lost his fear of the men and they didn't know what to do with him. After about an hour, they said that they would let it go lightly only because he seemed to be a knowledgeable Moslem. They drove him home and told him not to go horse-riding with Safa again.

'Oh, and this has just happened?' Omar asked. 'You're fresh from the story?'

Karim shrugged his shoulders and said, 'I'm just about getting myself round it.' Then he remembered Omar's mother and said that they should go down and reassure her that everything was fine, and thank her for trying to protect him.

As Karim repeated his story for Omar's mother, Omar became excited. At one point, when Karim took his time in telling how he had argued back with the men, Omar stretched out and grasped his jumper and told him how proud he was of him. 'I can't believe you fought them with their own weapons and won,' he said.

His mother smiled and told Omar to let go of Karim; she didn't want to have to get him a new jumper.

Karim tried to reassure her that the men would not be back; the whole thing was excessive and they had ended up looking stupid. 'Anyway, if they do come back, don't worry about it,' he said. 'Just send them up to me.' He said that he was extremely grateful to her for her effort in trying to protect him.

Omar's mother was difficult to reassure, though. She asked him a few times whether he had told her the full story and he swore that he had; these people had done worse things over smaller matters. Yes, she had heard.

A couple of hours later, Karim came down again and said that he had just found out something that would interest them. He had just got off the phone with Safa. It transpired that her neighbour from across the building had fancied her for a while, but she had refused to have anything to do with him, and when he saw Karim going up to her place a few times, he got all messed up. 'His uncle is in the Tawhid,' Karim said. 'So he set this up.' Karim told Omar's mother not to worry about it because Safa had eaten the guy's head off. She had confronted him on the phone and then gone over to speak to his mother. In the end, the guy was squirming like a little kid.

Omar was furious at how such a small, insignificant lowlife could cause so much trouble just because he couldn't handle his adolescent pimples, and could come down so heavy, all in the name of Islam.

The following day when Omar went to school, he was still fuming as he told his friends the story. He then took out a picture of Boy George, who, Amin had told him, was the latest sensation in England and was turning heads because of his image. Omar was determined that he was going to show the picture to the sheikh in the Moslem class later on, and ask him would he have any objections to teaching this guy if he wanted to attend his class. His friends urged Omar to back off, telling him that he could just end up taking things too far.

As they came into the classroom, Omar saw Ahmad talking to the sheikh, with a slight smile on his face. The sheikh tilted his head at what Ahmad was presenting him with and then nodded solemnly as he gently spoke. When Ahmad returned to his seat, just as the class was settling, he discretely slipped the Boy George picture back to Omar and stretched over to whisper in his ear, 'I showed him the picture and he was cool about it. I'll tell you about it later, but for now, back off.'

After the class was dismissed and they had gathered their books to go home, Ahmad waited for George before he talked to Omar. On their way out, Ahmad said that they had both decided to steal the picture because with Omar's vibes he would just have made a complete mess of things. In any case, Ahmad had honoured Omar's original intentions and had asked the sheikh exactly what Omar was going to ask him.

Ahmad laughed. He said that the sheikh actually looked at the picture and said, 'If he is interested in Islam, then he's very welcome, but it might not help him with his make-up.'

Ahmad asked if Omar had noticed that the sheikh spent a lot of time talking about how Islam encourages questioning and promotes openness. Omar shook his head negatively, still solemn. He hadn't heard a thing throughout the whole class. George then reminded him that it was he who had said that they shouldn't take things out on people who didn't deserve it; he should chill out and live up to his own words.

As they headed to the school gate to break off in different directions, Ahmad tried to change the subject. 'I still can't believe it: before the war, it used to take three Lebanese liras to make up one dollar, and then, after nine years of war, we needed five Lebanese liras to make one dollar, but now, in just less than a year, it takes one whole thousand Lebanese liras to make up one dollar. Now, how the hell could it stay still for nine years and suddenly take such a huge plunge?'

Omar smirked and said, 'Yeah, and your Syrian lira is getting stronger on our back.'

George reached out to take Ahmad's hand. 'My dear Moslem brother,' he said. 'Don't mind this heathen who is not aware that the only viable currency is the currency of God.'

Ahmad giggled. 'I'm not sure if I want to be in your club, but I have a better idea. I have connections; I'm sure they'll approve of you. We can set up a checkpoint at the gates of heaven and charge ungrateful ones like the one behind us.' He gestured towards Omar. 'If God is happy to be clean and not get involved, then that's fine by me, but we could have something going here—'

George interrupted, still keeping his back to Omar: 'Yes, yes, and we can also set up a checkpoint right in front of hell in case hardheaded people like the one behind us insist that it is the best place for them.'

Before Ahmad could speak, Omar intercepted, 'Yeah, and we can set up checkpoints all over and in between and you'll end up with Lebanon.'

Ahmad giggled. 'Yeah, minus the heaven bit.'

'Oh, and the God bit,' added George.

The Beginning of the End

When Khaled rang to tell Omar that he had been trying to contact certain colleges to see which ones would consider taking in a student from a foreign system, he also emphasised that his school results for the 1983–1984 year were likely to be more important than his results from the following and previous years.

'Now you tell me!' complained Omar.

Khaled didn't understand the problem.

Omar would have three more months both to shape up his school results and prepare for the first Baccalaureate. 'The first Baccalaureate I can probably do well by the time I get to it because it's set by the government and has nothing to do with the school, but the school results will take into account my exam results throughout the year; even if I kill myself, I won't get a good result.'

Khaled couldn't understand why Omar hadn't been studying since he had known that he was working towards the prospect of leaving Lebanon to go to a good college in England. In any case, he said, he wasn't going to argue about it. He told his younger brother that the reality was that he had three months to shape up and, if the worst came to the worst, when he was submitting his results, he would try to emphasise his Baccalaureate results over the school results.

When Omar told his friends of his new situation, Ahmad shook his head with a smile. 'What kind of a doctor is your brother?' he asked. 'He doesn't understand the predicament of the Lebanese student.' A flurry of comments followed on having lost all reasons to study: 'Are we going to give ourselves respectable titles so that the Syrians can humiliate us some more?'

A couple of weeks earlier, they had seen a student from the class above slapped by a Syrian gunman because he took his time in crossing the road. The guy came into school with a cheek so red it looked like it was about to burst. 'Or are we going to leave Tripoli for the Syrians and head for Beirut and set up practice and then be brought down to ashes whenever the Israelis feel like it?'

'Hey, hey, guys, before we talk about setting anything up, we still have to go to college. Do you think we'll make it through the AUB after the kidnapping of all the teachers? By the time we get there, we'll have to teach ourselves.'

Eventually it was remarked that Omar was the only one who would be leaving Lebanon; some might leave later but for now they should give him all the support they could.

Omar laughed. 'And what kind of support am I going to get from non-believers?'

Well, first, Ahmad could help him perfect his cheating techniques: 'I've been developing a system where you write your answers finely on small sheets of paper, thin enough to roll into your Bic pens. Depending on your questions, you look for the right pen and then get the little paper out by tapping the pen against the desk.'

Everybody laughed. 'So that's what all that noise was about the other day. Why did you persist in tapping instead of just breaking the pen?'

'Ah, well, you see, by then I'd got so much into the whole thing that I didn't want to disrespect the pen.'

George identified the main problem: they were all more interested in the method of 'not failing' than in passing. None of these suggestions mattered though: you could cheat only for the arts subjects, not the sciences, and, worse, you could cheat only in school; if you cheated during the Baccalaureate, they would kick you out and you would have to repeat your whole school year.

'The point is,' Ahmad said, laughing as he asserted a new point, 'Omar's brother should just know better than to make unrealistic demands of Omar. He should keep his mouth shut when he rings Omar. As for him, he should become a surgeon so that he doesn't talk to his patients; they should just wheel them in unconscious to the operating table, let him do the job, and then take them out again.'

In the end, though, it was decided that they were going to have to take Omar's situation seriously and try to encourage him in any way possible.

Next time Omar received an average mark in a physics exam, he complained that the teacher was ruining his future and asked him to be more generous with him. If he wanted to, Omar suggested, he could mark him down the following year when it no longer mattered. The teacher said that he understood his situation but that if he marked him up and then Omar got a really low mark in the Baccalaureate, he was going to be made to look like a fool. When Ahmad proposed that he donate some of his own marks to Omar, the teacher told him that since he thought so little of his own future, he should keep his already low marks and write them in his will to his children. Then Rola suggested that the physics teacher raise the whole class's marks; that way, if they all didn't get a good mark in the Baccalaureate, it would be the national examiners who would be embarrassed for being excessively harsh.

At break-time, Omar walked with Rola in the playground. He felt embarrassed within himself that he had fancied her for so long, yet the closest he could get to her was either through his antics or sometimes walking up and down the playground. Although she lived only three streets away from him, he didn't conceive of joining her for walks after school. She had her own friends; just to join them would be to impose himself. Not that she went out much for walks. So he let his heart simmer over the minor little exchanges he had with her.

Now Rola brought up the subject of his going to London, and offered to help him if he got stuck. He immediately wondered how that could happen: he couldn't go over to her house. Well, he could, but it was probably too much to ask her since he wasn't doing too badly overall. And then she said that he could ring her; he could ring her for a chat if he felt like it. He looked at her, trying to repress his excitement, and hoped that if he was drooling on the inside, it didn't show. He took her number and gave her his, then asked her if her phone would mind if it was rung by him.

'It's a very tolerant phone,' she said coolly. 'Sometimes we even get wrong numbers and it doesn't mind.'

Omar kept the number in the sleeve of Deep Purple's *Live in Japan*, not knowing how he was going to come up with an excuse to ring her. A few days later, his mother came to his room and said that he had a phone call, 'from a girl, and her voice was nice'. He accepted his mother's gentle teasing gratefully, knowing that had she pretended it was a call just like any other call, there would have been an uncomfortable unaddressed silence afterwards. He cleared his throat and tried to suppress his shyness. 'Hi,' he said, still trying to clear his throat.

'Hi, what are you doing?' she said gently.

'I'm very busy, but if you can't stand living with yourself, I'll talk to you.'

She laughed, and they ended up talking for about ten minutes.

Afterwards, when his mother asked him what the phone call was about, he said, 'Nothing', and was amazed that the conversation had mainly been about nothing and that all the mental strain he had put himself to, to create topics that would turn the conversation into 'something', was completely unnecessary. Then he turned to his mother to make sure that he hadn't dismissed her. 'There's this mentally handicapped girl in our class and I'm just trying to help her,' he said.

'She *would* have to be mentally handicapped to ring you, but it's good of her to let you help her,' she said with a smile. Then she added gently, 'Just make sure you don't help her too much.'

He turned back to his mother and said, 'Don't you worry; it's just the phone.'

He watched her refrain from answering, as she could have done, 'One thing leads to another.' Instead, she let him be and nodded her head.

A few days later, his mother and father told Omar that to encourage him to do better in school, and as a motivation not to sway in wrong directions, they were going to send him to Ziad for a few weeks during the summer. It would be too expensive for the whole family to go to Spain, but Omar needed the break the most as he was gong to be under a lot of pressure. It was an unexpected offer that made not studying a difficult option after all his parents' efforts. At first, he had a slightly clearer focus when he studied, and the promise of his summer break, along with the intermittent warm calls with Rola that lasted for about twenty minutes, meant that he was able to push himself past the desperate feelings of meaninglessness that he developed every time he faced his books.

A few weeks later, he tried to resurrect his previous motivation while praying along with his friends that the troubles would intensify so that the Baccalaureate would be officially cancelled and his school marks would hold as the only records for entry into university.

On the morning of the Baccalaureate, Omar decided to throw away all his little cheating notes; they were not worth the risk. Whatever happened, he would not have to go back to the horrible feeling in his stomach of waiting for the exam day to come, while hating himself for not having enough motivation to study more or to focus when he was able to drag himself to his books. He took in the crispy sun of the morning and wished he could hear Rola's voice before going in.

For the next three days, he struggled through the arts subjects, trying to bluff as much as he could, following the advice that not writing anything in reply to a question that he didn't have a clue about left the examiner no room to be generous with him. With the science topics, he felt a sharpness and a focus he wished he had had while he was studying; now that it was here, it could work only with what was already inside him. With the physics paper, he kept on struggling with the last question until he was inspired, and, when the class was met outside by the teacher, it turned out that he was the only one who had been able to figure out the answer.

On the last exam, as he walked out of the building, he let a shriek out from the ends of his toes. When he later met his friends, they told him that he had been heard throughout the hall, and everybody laughed especially that the examiners would not know who he was and, unlike school, there would be no consequences. They jumped up and down like children and started talking about going back home and burning their books, but after a few jumps, they looked at each other, considering the fact that none of them could be 100 per cent sure that they wouldn't be repeating the exams in three months' time if they failed.

They packed up anyway and tried to figure out how they could celebrate enough; there was nothing that they could do that would express their joy. They took taxis back to Azmi Street and then walked all the way to El-Mina for ice creams, as if they were kids.

Ahmad commented how everything looked beautiful: the uncollected rubbish with flies hovering over, the rusty old cars, the dust by the pavement, old men's wrinkles with the creamy sleep discharge at the inside corner of their eyes, the blue sky so clear with not even an aeroplane trail anywhere to be seen. 'Even the ice cream which has always been tasty is still not failing us now,' he said.

When they suddenly heard gunfire in the distance, George added, 'Even blood is beautiful: it is so red, just like roses.' He started genuinely giggling at how none of them had even flinched.

'Why can't we be like this every day of our lives?' joked Ahmad.

'Because you need to be fucked up all year to get this,' answered George.

'Yeah, it's like constipation,' added Ahmad.

'You know,' reflected Omar. 'It's almost as if, just for one moment...'

He looked around to make sure he was being taken seriously. 'As if it's worth it.'

'What's worth it?' asked George.

'Nothing,' interrupted Ahmad.

Omar looked around with a puzzled smile. 'I don't know,' he said, and they all laughed with him and at him.

Three days later, when he rang to say goodbye to Rola before going to Spain, she told him that her family was thinking of moving to Australia, and it could be quite soon. His heart sank. She said that it was very likely that they would be still in Tripoli for three more weeks, but she wanted to let him know, just in case. He said that he would ring her from Spain just in case they left early.

The following day, his father and mother travelled with him to Beirut and were joined at the airport by Amin and Zeina. He kissed them all goodbye and promised he would keep on ringing until the line connected. When he had gone through passport control, he felt an urge to go back and say goodbye to his father again. He stopped and wondered whether there would be newer eruptions and he might end up staying in Spain and not coming back to Lebanon. He looked back and felt disheartened, knowing that they were unlikely to let him go out for another goodbye. He turned his back and walked through.

The Holiday

At the airport, Omar met Ziad, Sana and Jamal to a cheer mimicking the chant for the Syrian President, Hafez Al Assad. 'Here nobody is going to get us in trouble for mocking,' said Sana with a smile. After about twenty kisses and everybody ending up embracing everybody else, and Omar even extending his hand to shake hands with other arrivals, they walked towards the car park.

'Oh no!' said Omar. 'A new car! Gone are the days of the Chevrolet *mtartaa*. Ah, this is no good; it will only transport us from one place to another. What kind of a car is that?'

As he moved to inspect the car, a water balloon whizzed past him, landed on Sana's jacket and bounced back on the bonnet. She grabbed it and whacked Omar, who put his hand out to shield himself. The balloon exploded on impact with his hand, and splashed the green bonnet.

'You got him back,' cheered Ziad.

'You've baptised our car,' laughed Jamal.

Sana shook her head. 'No matter which way you look at it, it's still our car that is getting it.'

'That's right,' confirmed Omar. 'You should remember our old saying: "He who digs a hole for his brother falls in it."'

On the journey from the airport, Ziad pointed out the dry, hilly scenery. 'See, just like Lebanon, but without the bullshit,' he said.

'And on top of that, the people here don't hate us,' enthused Sana.

Jamal agreed and said that Omar should meet their neighbour, Carlos. 'He talks about the Arabs with respect, and says it was a privilege to be occupied by the Arabs because unlike other invaders, they didn't loot and rape but respected what was there and even added to it.' If Omar liked, they would take him all the way to Al Hambra in Granada and show him all the beautiful Islamic art and architecture left there by the Arabs.

'I've just escaped from the Arabs and you want to bring me back to them!' Omar laughed.

'No, this is different,' Sana assured him. 'It's a site really worth seeing; you'll be proud.'

'It's funny how I have to leave my country to be proud,' mocked Omar.

Jamal looked at Sana. 'Forget about him for now; he's not worth talking to. Let the boy relax first, get home, change his nappies, and once he's done playing with himself, we'll see what he's up for.'

As they pulled up to the apartment, Sana excused it as 'not much', but said that they were still thinking of moving to the countryside where they might have a swimming pool; it would be much cheaper but they still had to be sure that they were going to make money. They were planning on opening a sandwich shop with the help of Jamal's brother.

'But at least we can choose to live wherever we want,' said Ziad casually to Omar.

His mother corrected him, saying that it did depend on the money.

He looked back at her with a playful arrogance, and replied, 'What I was saying to this poor fellow is that at least we can choose whatever area we please — no Kataaeb, no Syrians, no Israelis, no nobody to worry about; we just choose wherever our asses wish to sit.'

Ziad whizzed Omar to his room and showed him a few records. 'See, they're civilised here. They have their own Hard Rock; this is called Barron Rojo, in Spanish, and if you want to be really proud, then look at this.' And he presented Omar with a record that had a Spanish guitar player on the cover. 'Paco de Lucia,' said Ziad. 'It's both Arabic *and* Spanish, and it works. He plays like a Kalashnikov; he's so fast he drills the guitar.'

Then he went on to tell Omar of all the new foods he just had to taste: 'Horchata, it's like milk but it's not and it's sweet; you can't get it anywhere else in the world. Chorizo, red meat you fry and when you fry it, even the frying turns red just like the Mercurochrome we put on our cuts. It tastes so good, it is official pussy. Sobra Sada you have to get from a different part of the country; it's like a dead person's flesh but you put it on stick bread and it's amazing; you don't fry it or anything — you just eat it, and it lasts. And all the starters they have that you can order, just like our mezza, they call them, eh, ta-something, and they have so many of them, just like us, but they're different; they have calamari, they have....' After about fifteen minutes, Omar asked Ziad to remember everything that he told him because his head wasn't going to hold it all. Ziad assured him that in the next three weeks, they would eat everything he had told him about.

As Omar was shown around, Sana shouted for him to run to the phone. She had been trying to get through since his arrival and she had a connection. When his mother answered, Omar said that his plane had been hijacked and that he was stuck in an airport in Greece. Jamal spoke crossly to Omar, telling him not to joke with his mother and to tell her that he was fine. Omar look at him, a bit taken aback by his unusual temper.

'We've been trying to get a connection for half an hour,' Jamal said. 'If the line gets cut off now and we can't ring her back, how do you think she's going to be?'

Omar told his mother that he was fine; in fact, if she didn't hear from him, it was because he was so fine that he was not wasting his valuable time trying to reassure them that he was fine.

Later, when they asked him how Lebanon was, Omar said that he had heard a few people, Moslem people from Tripoli, saying that it was the Palestinians who had ruined them. 'The shame of it all,' they said. 'The war started when the Christian Maronites adopted that attitude and the Moslems sided with the Palestinians because they had been kicked out of their own homes, but now all beliefs and Arabhood have been lost into the sea; everybody has split on themselves; there are no more causes left, and the fighting just goes on endlessly.'

Sana shook her head in sympathy with the country, 'We stayed until we saw the sky turn black, then we left,' she said, sighing and looking at Omar. 'And just one more year for you, God willing, and you'll be out of there. I hope you'll be able to secure your future through some decent college that your brother will find for you.'

As the conversation dwindled, Omar looked around the living room and said that it felt a bit like Lebanon.

Jamal laughed. 'Please,' he said. 'We've just left.'

Omar shrugged his shoulders; he still had good times in their home, despite everything. Sana came over, kissed him on both cheeks and told him that wherever they went, he would have a home and, thank God, they had a home now, even if it was all cramped. She didn't have to worry about water or electricity and, more importantly, about anybody's safety. 'But, of course, my heart will always have some pain in it as long as you and my sister are still in Lebanon,' she said. 'But such is life.' She shook her head and said that she hoped that Omar's mother had forgiven her for leaving and that she didn't think of her as a traitor. Omar looked at her in disbelief.

Jamal cleared his throat and said, 'Poor boy; you're treating him as if his mother were a harsh and heartless woman.'

She shook her head and wiped a few tears from her eyes. 'It's just that I feel for everybody who is still left there,' she said.

'Yeah, including the insects and the mosquitoes,' interjected Ziad, hoping to shift her sentimentality. Then he looked at Omar and said, 'My mother hasn't cried in a while; she's just oiling her eye sockets — as if you need more of this.'

Jamal snapped his fingers and opened the discussion to include all the things that might interest Omar during his visit.

'Definitely food; he has to check out the paella,' Ziad said, remarking that even his fussy mother liked it. Meeting Jamal's brother was another definite.

'And that's a duty,' Sana said. 'He's family to Jamal, his blood.'

They had to meet the neighbours, too; they had offered to take Omar out for dinner. A bullfight was suggested, at which Sana objected to witnessing more blood. But Jamal said to leave the boy to think for himself. 'Spanish dancing,' Jamal continued. 'See them bang the floor as if they're furious with the cockroaches!'

Omar didn't know where to begin. He said that just not knowing which to choose first made him feel as if he were being treated already.

For the next ten days, Omar was introduced with the same title given by Jamal's brother when he first smiled at him. 'Oh,' the brother said. 'So this is the other son!'

'Yes, I'm the adopted one,' said Omar, smiling.

Sana took his hand and said with assurance, 'You're not adopted. Nobody's adopted. You *are* our son.'

When they met their neighbour, Jamal prompted Omar to ask him about the Arabs. Omar wasn't sure what question he needed to ask but the neighbour nodded his head confidently and with relaxed seriousness said, 'We are Arabs, yes. Look at me and look at you.' Omar raised his eyebrows and looked at Jamal in surprise.

Ziad smiled. 'See,' he said. 'I told you they don't hate us.'

As they approached the bullfight stadium, Omar saw people standing with placards, protesting against the cruelty of it. He admitted that he felt guilty about it and wasn't totally convinced about what he was about to contribute to. Jamal told him to allow himself to experience it once. 'It's part of culture and acculturation,' he said.

Ziad said he had seen it once and was glad to have done so; he would go again because of Omar but he would probably not go a third time.

Inside the stadium, Omar watched himself being excited as the bullfighters started slowly taking more and more risks with their own lives. At first, he felt for the bull: no matter what the bull did, he was going to lose; there was no way that he was going to come out of this alive. Jamal corrected him and said that there were times when the bull would be spared if the bullfighter made too much of a mess. 'What's too much of a mess?' Omar asked. 'More blood than—' and Omar was swept away by the oncoming action as the bullfighter stood face to face with the bleeding bull, sword in hand, and then, in a movement that seemed both slow and fast, he put the whole sword into the bull. To Omar's surprise, he felt an animalistic surge go through him. As they walked out of the stadium, Omar said that overall he had felt the futility of all the blood, but he admitted that there had been times when he had felt as if he was hurting the bull and, despite himself, he enjoyed it. He said that he felt like the men in the caves thousands of years ago must have felt but that he saw himself enjoy being sick and, for that reason, he did not want to do this again.

Jamal patted him on the shoulder, saying, 'Well, now you know.'

Ziad admitted that he felt the same and he wouldn't go again but he did enjoy watching it on TV and he had even got into the artistry of it.

As an extra present to Omar, Jamal's brother offered them his beach chalet for the last week of Omar's stay. Jamal and Sana could drive to nearby villages to see what kind of shops they lacked and maybe get ideas for a business. Ziad looked at Omar with excitement and motioned discreetly with his right hand to signify having sex. When Omar looked at him blankly, Ziad motioned for him to follow him.

'If they leave us on our own, who knows what can happen?'

'Are you serious?' Omar asked, with a hint of worry.

'Well, you never know; who knows anything?' Ziad shrugged his shoulders, and then stopped and moved his head back. 'Oh no, what's wrong? Don't tell me you're in love!'

Omar awkwardly tried to explain his situation. 'There's a girl that I like, well, possibly fancy, but that's about it. There can never be anything more to it, because if there was, she'd be ruined, so I wouldn't even think about it. Plus I like her. Plus she's also leaving to go to Australia.'

'Let me get this,' said Ziad, tilting his head. 'You're being loyal to a girl who you've never had anything going on with, you're never going to have anything with, and she's leaving, and, eh, and it's crazy!'

241

Omar nodded his head with gentle acceptance. 'Isn't it?'

Ziad looked at him straight.

Omar raised his shoulders. 'Look, you never know,' he said. 'She might stay for another year. I might tell her that I like her or something.'

'Oh no!' Ziad put his hand over his forehead. 'What happened to the king of porn?'

Omar slouched a bit. 'I'm still the king of porn; they're not related. I won't even think of her that way, but right now, she's not gone, so, eh, you know, and ehm.'

'What?' persisted Ziad.

Omar wanted to ring her to talk to her just in case she was leaving before his return. Ziad said that he could do it from the apartment later on when his parents were not around and Ziad could just say that it was he who was ringing his friends in Lebanon. 'But you have to promise one thing,' he said. 'If she's leaving Lebanon before you get back, you have to agree to chase women with me.'

Omar cleared his throat. He said that if that were the case, he couldn't promise, but he'd help Ziad with his quest.

When Ziad's parents left early next morning to get some shopping, Omar and Ziad alternated in trying to get a connection. It was Ziad who was dialling when the phone connected, and he screamed at the top of his voice for Omar. When Omar took the phone, he told Rola that Ziad was gay and couldn't handle speaking to a woman. She laughed hesitantly and told him that she was glad to hear his voice. He asked her what the matter was — was she leaving in the next eight days?

No, she wasn't, she said.

'Nine days?' asked Omar, because in that case, he would still see her before she left.

She cleared her throat and asked him how his dad was.

'As good as your dad,' he said. And she went quiet.

'Have you not talked to your parents in the last two days?' she asked.

'No.'

She told him that there had been an incident and his father had got hit and they had taken him to the AUB hospital in Beirut. She wasn't sure what his condition was.

Omar and Ziad were dialling impatiently when Sana and Jamal walked in with the shopping for the beach trip. They told the boys that there was no point in trying to dial Tripoli if Omar's parents were in

Beirut; they needed to contact either Laila or Zeina and then get the hospital number. Jamal played the situation down and suggested that Omar and Ziad go to town and they would take over the dreary work of dialling. Omar insisted on staying, but after half an hour of dialling, Sana approached him gently and said that dialling with more intensity was not going to make the lines connect any faster; he should go and take it easy instead of making himself tense.

He said he would walk down the street, and, if the line connected, she could give him a shout from the balcony.

When Sana waved for Omar, he ran up. His aunt was well composed and whispered that there was nothing to worry about. He talked to his mother and she immediately started crying, then she held back her sobs and told him that his father was getting better; he was in intensive care but he was coming out of it.

When he asked her what had happened, she said that there had been a shooting incident but the most important thing was that his father was going to make it. He asked her again what had happened and she told him that his dad couldn't talk; he needed the rest. Also, he should just clear his head and pray.

Omar immediately said that he no longer believed in all that stuff.

She said that she was going to pray; that was all she had left.

He suggested that he cut his holiday short but she told him that there would be no need. 'You'll just overcrowd the room in the hospital and your father wouldn't want you to do that,' she said. He had only about a week more and he could sit by his father when he came back. Then she said that he should ring one of his friends the following day because the results of the Baccalaureate were going to be announced.

After the call, Sana told Omar that his brother, Khaled, was flying down to Lebanon and there was no need to worry about anything. He should just go on with his holiday and he would be able to see his dad the following week. They suggested that, in the meantime, they still take up the offer of going to the chalet; it would be a change of scenery.

The following day when they reminded Omar to ring one of his friends to find out his exam results, he said that he couldn't be bothered wasting his time; whatever the results were, he couldn't do anything about them until he came back to Lebanon.

Sana asked him for the phone number of one of his friends and Ziad said that he'd take over that task.

Omar said that he was going to go in for a nap, and, if they found anything out, not to wake him up; they could tell him when he was up. Half an hour later, Sana opened the door ever so slowly and peeked in, trying to repress her happiness. Omar turned over in the bed and looked at her. She nodded with gentle pride. 'You've passed.'

Omar looked at her blankly, nodded in acknowledgement, and then turned back again. After about fifteen minutes, he got up and said that he would be back in a few minutes. He went to the beach on his own, felt the sun on his shoulders, looked at children running and laughing, and their parents smiling at them, and then sat down. He looked behind him to see Ziad standing a bit of a distance from him. He waved for him to come over. 'I don't feel anything,' said Omar.

Later on, at dinner, Jamal tried to celebrate his exam success but couldn't get much response from Omar. Omar apologised for his flatness and said that the only thing that would wake him up was if he got up and hurt somebody.

Sana put her hand over her mouth and said that she was scared they were breeding a killer.

Jamal said that out of fairness to his dad, Omar should at least have a bit of optimism. Omar felt himself about to argue back but stopped himself; he decided to make an effort and ordered a banana split with extra chocolate.

The next morning was unusually cloudy. Sana and Jamal suggested that Omar and Ziad come with them on their visits to nearby villages since they weren't going to be swimming. When Omar declined, Ziad did too. When they had left, Ziad said that Omar felt to him like a sprained penis; he didn't know what could cheer him up; everything he suggested was declined.

Omar said that he could just leave him alone.

Ziad shrugged his shoulders and said that he was going out to hunt for some good-quality sex magazines. When Ziad left, Omar sprang up and searched for the number of the hospital. After only the third dialling, the line connected. When a nurse answered at his father's room and Omar asked her how his father was doing, she asked him to hold on. He heard his mother mutter and then her voice faded. Then he heard Khaled's voice utter the traditional phrase, 'May God compensate in your peace.'

Omar asked him what it meant even though he knew what it meant. Khaled said that his father had seemed to be doing better but then he had got worse. He had passed away, and the doctors had done everything they could.

After he put the receiver down, Omar looked around at the white walls and started to move his head slowly. He glimpsed the cloudy sky and got up and headed towards the beach. It was empty. He walked over the sand and knelt like he used to kneel at the end of his prayers. He looked ahead at the frothy waves breaking to a cold breeze, and remembered the times when he used to feel a presence of beauty all around him, filling his chest and linking him in an unseen way to distances as far as his eyes could imagine. He felt nothing. There were just the clouds and the big endless sea.

From behind him, he heard Ziad shouting in the distance. 'King Omar, I've been looking everywhere for you. HEY YOU! I've got pussy galore for you.'

Omar let Ziad approach him, without turning. He felt Ziad's presence behind him, halting, then stopping, then heard Ziad's words through his breathlessness: 'Shit! The bastards.'

Omar turned around and asked Ziad who the bastards were.

Ziad tried to connect with Omar to see if what he was thinking was true.

Omar began to raise his voice, asking who the bastards were.

Ziad tried to calm him down, asking Omar to let him know what had happened.

'Yeah, he's dead,' Omar said. 'Now you're happy! Tell me who the bastards are. What happened anyway? How come nobody told me?'

Ziad told Omar to calm down a bit and just to take one minute out, but Omar started shouting and then lost it. He grabbed Ziad by his shirt and shook him.

'Tell me, you son of a bitch, tell me what happened.'

Ziad stood still with a blank expression.

'Tell me! I know you know,' Omar shouted, and he started yanking Ziad by his shirt. 'Tell me, you cocksucker, TELL ME!' As Ziad moved back gently, Omar pushed him and then swayed as he tripped.

Omar knelt down on top of Ziad and, with his right hand, gripped some sand and moved over Ziad's mouth, while frothing. 'I know you know,' he said. 'Tell me.'

Ziad closed his mouth and tried to stop Omar's hand from shoving the sand into him, then he pushed Omar back with all his might and got up. 'I didn't kill Abou-Khaled,' he said. 'Leave me alone.' And he walked off.

Omar looked at his hand and saw a tightened fist that was white from the pressure. As he moved back to his original position, he broke down crying. He felt his chest heaving as he cried his numbness out. He looked at the clouds and felt as if he could hear their silence and, at the same time, witness this physical body underneath him making all the those sounds and moves. He heard a voice behind him. As he looked back, he felt his movements in slow motion. He saw Ziad standing solemnly, with his right hand gripping some sand, and then he heard some words spoken softly: 'You can put sand in my mouth if you want.'

Omar's head moved slightly to the left, as if not recognising the speaker. Then he found himself turning back, looking at the sea. He felt the presence behind him approaching him. When the approaching arm behind him made physical contact, he knew it was Ziad. He softly remembered that Ziad was a person he knew, and then he felt as if a very quick and invisible elevator was coming in, and he felt his body and the piercing pain in his chest as it pushed out with his crying.

Over the next two nights, Omar would wake up at night, not sure whether he was still dreaming or whether what he had woken up to was really reality. He saw his father waking up from the bed and smiling and saying that he was OK. Omar believed it and then remembered that it was not likely that this would have happened. He then saw his father being buried with all the family around him, with Omar watching from the air above him, and then his father made a sound from underneath the earth and he was alive. By the third day, Omar remembered that this could happen only for maybe one more day after burial; after that, it probably couldn't happen. And then Omar would see the furniture around him. The furniture was the same as itself and it looked very much like what he was seeing and it was just there, as it was, being itself. There was the furniture and what was underneath it. That bit was the floor. He made as little noise as possible when he went to the toilet at night but usually Sana heard him and got up and sat with him. Those times, the furniture looked most like itself, but not the times when he was on his own. When he was on his own, the furniture had a presence.

On the third day, when they went out with the neighbour for lunch, he took Omar aside and said that what he was about to say was not intended to make him feel better. He said that his experience was different, but over fifteen years ago, he had had two friends — a couple to whom he was very close — who died in a motorcycle accident. He said that it took him about five years to feel better. He said that he wasn't sure whether hearing this could help Omar, but that maybe, if he knew that it was part of him and that it was not going to go away so quickly, he could let it take its time and not force himself to feel different.

To his surprise, Omar's face opened. He felt a certain ease within himself.

Afterwards, he went to Sana and Jamal and answered something that they had been asking him but not been able to get a definite answer about. Yes, he was missing the burial anyway, but he would like to make it back earlier, even if it was two days earlier than his return date. He thanked them for not letting him worry about the extra cost.

Omar took a connection through Greece and was met at the airport by Amin. They drove in silence, the scenery just as it was, just as he had always known it, until they got to Tripoli where he met his mother, Laila and Zeina, all in traditional black. His mother cried, unable to look at him. He kept himself under control, trying not to add to his mother's pain. When she got up to go to the kitchen, he looked at Laila and asked her how his father had died.

Laila began to weep and said, 'Leave the bastards alone. Some things are just not worth knowing about.'

He calmly turned his gaze to Zeina who cleared her throat and said that she was surprised that he hadn't been told. She said that their father had borrowed his working companion's car: 'Abed's old Mercedes, it was, and he was going past a Syrian checkpoint in the Ibbeh, a small irrelevant checkpoint guarded by just two Syrian idiots — it only led towards the plantation trees.' It seemed that their father thought that the soldier had let him pass, and he went on. 'He must have shouted for him to stop after he had already made some headway but our father mustn't have heard him. The soldier took out his machine gun and fired.'

Omar felt a quick movement through him and witnessed an intention within him to get up to go to the toilet, but his body didn't act. Then he opened his eyes and saw that it was he who had just thrown up on the floor.

The Black Boot

Omar felt on the brink of shutting off the whole world. After the first couple of days, just as his head was beginning to settle, he saw it clearly: Ahmad was Syrian; he loved Ahmad, and so, as simple as the basic maths he had first learnt years ago, he couldn't hate all the Syrians. He saw the temptation right in front of him; he had heard so many people make such sweeping statements that when they dealt with individuals they actually were held back by a prejudice. His own statements he witnessed emerge out of him and splash out in mid-air at the overall situation, never materialising — whether it was buying something from a vendor or leaving hope within himself that maybe there was even one soldier at a checkpoint who didn't agree with the way the Lebanese were being treated. Not even the Israelis could be completely blind. He could bet that there must be at least one person, one Israeli, who was like him, and could see what was around him and that what was being done in his name was wrong. Ahmad was tall, very thin, and was beginning to develop a moustache, and Omar felt his smell inside him, but mainly his giggle, even when there wasn't anything too funny going on.

He had expected that his family would be cursing the Syrians more, but they weren't. Before heading back, Khaled said that he would undertake the task of going over to compensate Abed for his car. But Abed's family said that the car was not important in light of the overall situation; a few bullet holes were not going to damage it beyond the years that had already been put into it. In any case, for the next while, it was going to be hard for any one to get into it. Khaled said that was why he was offering. No, he was told. It would be a shame for them to allow any compensation. His father was a lifetime friend. 'This is not how they do things in Lebanon,' they said. 'Over there, where you come from, insurance would take care of it, but here, everything is shared between people and God.' Khaled came home and said that he had done his duty, made sure that the family's name stayed clean. 'They are good people,' he said. 'Thank God there is something left in this country.'

'And why shouldn't there be?' exclaimed his mother.

'The war brings out those who are already corrupt, like shit to the surface,' added Amin. 'The rest live among the roots of the earth.'

Omar noticed that it had taken a disaster to make them remember the good that is there beneath the rubble. But soon everything would go back to how it had been and, like his family, he would go back to being shoved around each day, instead of directing himself. Before he left, Khaled told Omar that he had been impressed by the doctors in American University Hospital in Beirut. 'You should consider doing medicine,' he said. 'For the time being, it could raise your spirits to reflect on what you can contribute to what's going on around you.'

Omar was pleased to hear that there were standards in any area that had not completely disappeared, but did Khaled mean for him to go and specialise outside and then come back to this place? He wondered to himself whether there was anything in Lebanon that would make him come back. Not one thing.

He wasn't so sure what to do about Rola. When he met her, he oscillated between wanting to break down in front of her and feeling flat. What would be the point? She was due to leave soon. He had promised himself that he would make an effort to let her know that he liked her in more than a fancying way — not because he was hoping that something more than fancying could develop, but because he didn't want to live this pathetic life where he hadn't even said anything. There was something about saying the words that would have done something, something to the air — even he couldn't explain it to himself. But whatever it was, he no longer wanted to be under the air around him. But things had changed. To say something when she might leave the next day would leave the whole air with him, and especially now that she was going to go somewhere so far, as far as possible if he was going to England. He would be lumbered with that dead air. Better not make things heavier for himself. He could have rung her more, but he didn't. Her parents were supposed to sell a piece of land before they could take the final step of going but, as with everything in Lebanon, things could drag on and on. And who in his right mind would be living on Lebanese soil and want to buy more soil? It would be like buying more trouble. But Rola said that her parents were serious even though they had suggested she join her classmates when the year started, because it would give her stability for just two more weeks.

249

When school started, Omar strained to joke. He already felt the sympathy of those who knew him and those who half-knew him, but what was he going to do with all that sympathy? He didn't want it to cripple him. He knew that he could get away with more than usual but he didn't want to use his father.

'Your father will be glad to be still helping you in the spirit,' Ahmad retorted.

Omar grabbed Ahmad and gave him a kiss. 'I like your politics,' he said, realising that just as he saw Ahmad as his brother, Ahmad must have felt the same way for him not to be burdened by having to be defensive. He looked at George and admired him too; although nobody had come to him and said that all the Syrians were bastards, he felt as if it was about to roll off their tongues, with the exception of George. He wasn't holding anything back. Had he let himself go, he might have cursed the clouds out of the sky but he would not have said anything that would have added to Omar's burden; what each was carrying was enough. It was bad enough without putting extra weight on each other when it was not going to make anyone's load any lighter. Still, Omar felt that his joking was strained. His classmates were not laughing as much as they used to; he was trying too hard.

And then Rola left. He was about to say something, even at the last minute. Maybe it was hope itself that he didn't want to give up on. As he stepped back from her front door, she said, 'Yo, come here!' She pulled him by his arm and gave him a kiss on each cheek. 'You can go now,' she said.

He smiled. She was more relaxed than him; she could be because she was the girl. He thanked her.

'What for?'

'For not playing games like all the other girls.'

She shrugged her shoulders, and he realised that she didn't want to put any of her friends down. When he left, he felt a pain inside him: the pain of all that could have developed with her. But at the same time, he noticed a relief: the relief of all that couldn't have developed with her. He thanked God and the stars and whatever monkeys inhabited the earth that he hadn't tried to reach for her hand and profess all the romantic feelings he had for her. In light of all the social constrictions and the curfew climate, it would have been like asking for a certificate of idiocy.

He knew that there were others, probably only a few, who had taken things a step further with the ones they loved, but that extra step seemed silly to Omar. To make a move was taking advantage and trivialising the love into the physical, when it could not hold up to any future promises in such an unstable world. And then there were other perspectives, like that of George, who said that he wouldn't allow himself even to feel romantic about somebody; he just wouldn't do that to his heart. Although he could acknowledge that someone was fanciable, porn was enough of a reality to put things in perspective. For Ahmad, porn wasn't even an option; his younger brother was so curious that any small noise in the middle of night after everybody had gone to sleep would be the end of even the film title coming on. His situation wasn't even comparable to the option of fantasy that George had. It was an issue to be negotiated and sorted out between his palm and his penis; he wasn't even involved. Between all these positions, it seemed that Omar didn't have much option but to see what his eyes were showing him, and it seemed that he was somewhere in the middle.

After a few weeks had passed into two months, Laila asked Omar how he was doing. He said he was beginning to believe that his father had died, but generally, when he wasn't aware that his father was dead, there was a black boot above him, big enough to cover the sky, and it was always there, especially when he didn't look up. She agreed and said that everybody felt stepped on. He grinned, saying that he could see how everybody felt that way, but he was convinced that the boot was tailor-made for him. But then, maybe everybody felt like that.

Balcony

Omar noticed that lately he had been clenching the rails of the balcony every time he stood near it. He relaxed his fists and noticed a fear in him — a fear that he would jump. What surprised him about this fear was that over the previous two years he had been getting the impulse to jump, and when he heard nearby fighting, he often headed towards the balcony much to the near-hysterical objections of his mother; he had thought that there wasn't much fear left in him. Maybe it was because now that he really wanted to jump, there seemed to be something inside him holding him back — funny how there was so much inside that he hadn't a clue about. Maybe it was like another government on the inside, with some people wanting liberation and others wanting to be ruled.

One night, he drew the oldest chair in the house to the balcony and sat with his cup of tea, watching the steam flutter off the top of the mug. He was surprised how much he could see considering that all the streetlights had gone off a few years back; all that was visible was visible due to the sheer luminance of the moon. He slid his foot to the bottom of the metal rails and sat back. As he sat back, he felt a tap at the bottom of his slippers and instantly jumped off his seat, fearing that a ghost had tapped him. He got up, looked over the rails to the apartment below and saw that the balcony there was empty. He sat back down, shrugging off the incident, puzzled that he had never really considered the existence of ghosts as a possible reality, and then smiled at himself. That was all he needed now: for ghosts to be real and for him to have to deal with them. As he raised his mug, he wondered whether he would spill his tea on himself if he got another tap. Just as he brought the cup to his mouth, he felt another tap. A fright went through him but he held his mug steady, and then quickly put it down so that he could get up and look at the balcony beneath. Again, it was empty. He moved back while still holding the rails, and waited. Then with a quick movement, he moved forward to see his neighbour, Ali, holding a long broom and sporting a fractured smile. He let out a giggle although unsure how Omar would react to his antics.

'It's frightening, isn't it?' he said.

Over the years, Omar had often stopped for small chats whenever he bumped into Ali but there had been only a few times when they had visited each other and when they did, they talked about common school problems. They could have had more contact, especially as they were in the same school year, but because they were in different school systems — Omar American with English as the main language and Ali in a Jesuit school with French as the main language — they automatically veered away from even attempting to study together. For a split second, Omar considered pretending that he really didn't welcome that kind of joking. But he didn't know Ali well enough and might have sent him on a guilt trip and it would have been too much work afterwards for Omar to convince him that he, in turn, was joking.

'Yeah,' he said. 'You really did get me. I actually though it was a ghost.' Omar felt that he couldn't just leave the conversation there. Given that Ali had taken such a risk, either they were going to become friends or every time they met, there would be a doubt with Ali that maybe he had gone too far. 'Hey, come up,' he added.

'It's one o'clock.'

'You won't have to knock; I'll have the door open and we'll slip out to the balcony. You won't see anybody; they're all asleep.'

At first, when Ali talked about the desolation that his family had felt and how it was felt across all the families throughout Lebanon, Omar was impressed by his neighbour's ease in describing the general state of the Lebanese people, but then, as Ali went on recounting horrific scenes he had witnessed and others he had been told about, he continued with detachment, and Omar began to wonder whether Ali was making things up. He told of being at his cousin's house and hearing a lot of commotion in the street and then through the stairs in the building. There was knock on their door and they were asked if they could lend a hand. His cousin's parents weren't in so they ended up helping. It turned out that the whole family had gone to El-Mina to buy ice cream and they had waited in the car as their youngest, the twelve-year-old, was sent to bring the order as there was no need for the whole family to queue. As the whole family watched the child from a distance, a car bomb blew up right in front of the shop. Half of the boy's face was torn and his skull was split; you could see his brain. Ali and his cousin helped the father hold his son in their apartment while he stuffed his face with cotton just to hold its contents. Omar looked blankly at Ali, trying not to let his face contort.

Ali smiled. 'I bet you're thinking that I'm lying.'

'I'm nearly throwing up and you're telling me all this as if you were reciting your shopping list.'

'You're all emotional and stuff! What, you want me to start crying? As if you've just come in as a tourist?'

Omar wasn't convinced. Ali shrugged his shoulders. He said that part of it, just in relation to his cousin's neighbour, was that he was impressed by the father. He was a believer, a true Moslem and not a preacher, and when you saw somebody holding themselves together through a faith in God such as you'd never known, it became inspiring and you just wouldn't allow yourself to start acting all sissy; it was truly inspiring to watch this father not become blasphemous. Omar said that he was touched to hear about this father, that he himself had lost all connection to whatever faith this man lived, and that while he believed that Ali had been touched at the time, he doubted whether it had lasted long enough for him to take on this father's convictions. Ali smiled. He admitted that everybody said he was cold, but he said that he wasn't; he just didn't feel anything, because if you did, you'd end up burning out like a candle.

'But how do you not feel anything?' asked Omar genuinely puzzled. 'I'd love to learn how.'

'Look, I saw a—' Ali began but Omar cut him off.

'I don't want to hear one more story; just tell me how not to feel because I can't do it.'

Ali told Omar that if he didn't switch off, he would end up being melodramatic and wailing like the Bedouins every time a taxi beeped its horn.

'OK, fine,' Omar said. 'I'm not saying I feel everything. Like last week when the American Embassy was bombed, well, there's at least a car bomb a week and I'm definitely not going to be sympathetic towards the Americans although—' Omar paused before continuing, '...although of course it was Lebanese people who died as a result of that bomb ... shit ... I was switched off to car bombs because they happen so often but now look: when I think about them, I get all fucked up!'

Ali laughed and let his guard down. He said that he had been winding Omar up.

Omar jumped in his seat at Ali's audacity. 'You made up the stories!'

'Oh no, the stories were true, but when I talk to people, I tell them as if I'm cool just to make them feel small.'

'Make who feel small — the stories or the people?'

'Oh, the people. I just like fucking with people. What else is there to do?' He smiled. 'You know, it's good to shrink them.'

'I'm glad I didn't befriend you as a kid; I would have stayed eight,' Omar said, shaking his head. 'As if people don't feel small enough.'

Ali nodded serenely. 'I have to play with these stories,' he said. 'My head won't hold them. If you think of every horrible thing that you've heard since the war started. For example—'

Omar leapt forward and put his left hand over Ali's mouth. 'I'm going to drink your tea for you,' he said. 'And I'm going to keep my hand over your mouth until you go downstairs.'

Ali looked at his watch and raised his eyebrows as if alarmed. Omar kept his hand over Ali's mouth until Ali pointed to his watch. Omar leaned over to see it was 2.30. When Omar took his hand off Ali's mouth, they promised each other that they would go and play pinball together the following day.

Next day, when Ali came up, he casually asked Omar whether he had heard of the bombing of the pinball shop. Omar kept on shrugging him off but Ali continued to smile and challenged Omar to go over with him to see for himself. They continued to banter until Ali said that they had to go to the shop anyway to play, and if it wasn't blown up, they'd just play. Omar kept on telling Ali that he wasn't being had, that he should learn how to hide his sly smile because it was giving it all away.

When they got to Monla Street, Omar's mouth opened; the blast had been so strong that the wall directly opposite the shop on the other side of the street was black, and the glass fronts of the three shops on either side were shattered. The owner of the shop was casually kicking the debris with his feet when Ali whispered, 'Look, he'll be open again by next week.'

Within ten days, the pinball shop was open again, with the same non-décor as before, just the machines and a desk in the middle of the shop for getting change. George and Omar stood by the *ka'k* vendor, listening to the almost whispered conversation of their walking companions about why the shop had been targeted. It wasn't that the slot machines involved gambling, which is forbidden in the Koran and therefore a legitimate reason for the fundamentalist Tawhid to tell the owner to close down and then blow it down for him; it was more likely that he had refused to pay protection money. 'What?' Omar said. 'Their level of corruption reaches that level?'

He was laughed at again for being naïve. Over the previous few months, he had needed to be more hushed when asking for porn videos. The shop assistant had told the customers who he didn't know very well that porn was now banned by the Tawhid, and Omar had believed this. The videos were confiscated for themselves, his friends said, adding, 'There's a shop in El-Mina, right next to a Tawhid office. The owner is in with them; all you have to do is walk in.' They urged him to try it for himself.

Even though it was out of Omar's way, he made the trip. He looked through their selection, hoping to find some of the films not stocked in his own shop which held only a few of the old classical movies, but he found a poor selection. He waited until there were no customers and went over to ensure that the shop was right next door to the Tawhid office. Maybe this wasn't a wind-up, but if things had changed since the person who told him about it was last able to do it, he could just be handed over to the Tawhid next door. He walked out with three movies without even bothering to rent regular features. Back on Monla Street, Omar was told that most of what he saw with his eyes was not what it seemed: 'See this vendor who we've buying *ka'k* from for the last three years? Well, who do you think he is?'

Omar shrugged his shoulders. 'He sells *ka'k* — that's what he is.'

'Not quite. Abu-Steiff, the guy with the showy jewellery who shows up in his Mercedes every now and then — well, that's his brother.'

'What? How come one sells *ka'k* and the other is loaded?'

'He keeps a listening ear for him. That's what he's there for.'

Omar dismissed the explanation; if he were to go by everything he heard, more than half of the city was Syrian undercover. 'With that many, there's hardly anybody left to eavesdrop on,' he protested.

'No, he's not Syrian, just a lowlife embezzler watching his back. It's like this: half the city is Syrian undercover; half lowlife crooks; and half Tawhid; the rest are the insignificant common folk like us.'

'Hold on, that was more than three halves!'

'Yep, this is reality. Either you stretch your head to see it for what it is or you can stay blind in your comfy childish ways of seeing out.'

256

As he dismissed them, Omar jokingly turned his back and started to look upwards towards the balconies of the surrounding buildings. He squinted and then turned around. 'Guys,' he said. 'Look at all these holes at the top of the ceilings of the balconies. What are they?'

'They're from bullets. Every time two fuckers have a quarrel, they either shoot between each other's legs or up, to outdo each other.'

'Or from drivers with wounded passengers who are trying to rush to the hospital, shooting up in the air to clear the traffic.'

'Or from occasional celebrations.'

Omar looked up to the balcony and smiled in wonder. 'Amazing.'

'Yeah, amazing that it's so easy to get killed just by coming out on your balcony.'

When Omar got home, he looked at the ceiling of his balcony: it was clear, but his next-door neighbour, who shared the same ceiling, had three bullet holes. After his dinner, he came back out and looked at the stretch of the street from top to bottom. It was pitch black; the sounds of electricity generators emanated from lit apartments whose light did not reach the street. He went back inside, thinking that he could allay his mother's fears by telling her that he was going for a quick walk, no more than a few buildings away. The fighting had been easing off and it looked as if he would be going back to school after a three-week break. Things were getting safer, he assured her, but all this imprisonment was suffocating him. 'I'm tall now,' he said. 'I'm seventeen, no longer a kid. Just fifteen minutes.' He promised that he would not go to Monla Street but actually take a right in the opposite direction.

She consented. When he came out of his building, he walked past five buildings and sat on the side of the street in front of a tree. By leaning and gazing to his left, he could see his own balcony. He looked to his right and knew that a five-minute walk was likely to encounter a few gunmen. He looked towards the sky and let the quietness settle. There wasn't a single car in sight. Then he let his head slowly rest between his knees where he could see the ground between his legs, and he closed his eyes. Once, looking at the horizon could transport him to a place above himself. But no longer. He was here, and he wept. This was not a life, he thought to himself; this was not a life. He had oscillated between feeling like an innocent child, trying his damnedest to believe that it was all rot rot rot, and like an old man who had lived

257

a few of the same lifetimes. In school, he clowned and rioted himself into a frenzy, milking joy out of a stone, making more of something than it was in the first place, but when he got home, he ended up with himself again: this dreary, bland bulk of a weight that just pulled him down, and down, and further down, without ever hitting any ground — just a weight. And he wept.

As he settled into calmness, he remembered the times when, as a child, he would feel lighter after having cried. He let a sigh out; this was going nowhere. He had come out to feel a bit of relief but this confinement was endless. There were seven more months to go and then he should be out of Lebanon but the thought did not cheer him. He imagined a bitter long-distance runner realising that there was nobody else with him in the race, and slowing down to a halt. Still panting, wondering why he had run in the first place, having run out his respect for the finish line: *Fuck you! I'm just going to stand here; for this race to be over, you have to come to me.* Time stood still. When he looked back, it seemed as if time were yanking and pulling, sometimes flowing and sometimes stalling like a dying car. Whatever clarity he had come into was not showing him how he could be helped. It wasn't as if he were getting an insight; it was only a sight. In looked like out and neither could help the other. He remembered how he had been commended for maturity by his family but even wisdom was useless: what was he going to do with it anyway? He didn't need more; he needed less: he needed not to see. And then suddenly, he heard a car approaching and he felt fear emerge in him. An old Peugeot went past him, and, about twenty metres away from him, it slowed, then stopped. Then it reversed. It stopped a few metres from him and a young man tilted his head out the window. 'Are you all right?' he asked.

Omar nodded his head. 'Yes, yes, I'm OK. Thank you very much.'

'No problem.'

Omar saw a scared woman sitting next to the driver as the car moved off.

Omar was touched. This stranger didn't have to stop, and it wasn't as if he had been alone. It could have been anybody. It could have been an armoured car and all he would have needed was for some angry ignorant fucks to add to his pollution. He saw that things could always get worse, and no matter how bad they got, a drop of beauty could come his way for one tiny moment and glow amidst his misery. Then he sensed a feeling go through him, or was it a thought? *It is bastards like this guy who prevent me from being free.* He had thought of a way out: even his mother and Ziad and Amin were not a reason to live; you can't live for somebody else. *Maybe you just have to go sometimes,* he thought, *and it's bastards like him who have to show me that somewhere in the corner of the world, there is kindness, and, when it comes from a stranger, it's hard to ignore. It's fuckers like him who I'll never see again who don't allow me just to give up.* Omar pulled back. He had just been touched by beauty and that same touch had shown him that his bones had bitterness in them. *I must be filthy down to the core,* he thought, *down to this shit, foul, horrible, dreaded soul that still inhabits me.* He got up. He wasn't going to sort anything out, and, the way he was feeling, it was quite likely that the next car would fulfil his expectations.

As he walked back home, he got a whiff of the beauty he had just felt and then laughed at himself; maybe he needed to drop everything to be safe. *Maybe it's not that nothing matters; maybe it's that even wondering whether anything matters does not matter. Maybe even if things did matter, well, it doesn't matter. That's it:, whatever way you look at it, even not looking at it — well, none of it matters. Mattering doesn't matter and not mattering doesn't matter. Even maybeness itself, for sure, and not maybe, doesn't matter. And, matter matter doesn't matter when matter matter matter doesn't...* And for no reason at all, he felt as if his breath was lighter than it had ever been.

After he had been back in school for three days, fighting broke out again, and sounds of shelling were denser than ever. When shelling was at its worst, there would be no walks, not even balcony. Then, after a few days, maybe a bit of balcony, watching the empty street. He was seeing more of Ali than his friends but even Ali who was more than nobody was sometimes too much. Sometimes he felt as if his mother was invisible. He felt guilty for not trying harder to cheer her up, but then didn't he need some cheering to cheer somebody else? Added to which, she was now saying things she would never have said before. Once she used to reprimand him for using '*Tfeh*' — 'The sound of spitting is the most debasing expression you can use,' she would say. Now, quite casually and at least once a day, she would say, '*Tfeh* on this life.' It was hard to want to be near. He would see himself sit in his bedroom, thinking about her but not getting up. Then he would fantasise about the movies he had not seen: *Zardoz, Broadway Danny Rose, Easy Pieces...*

One day, he fantasised about *Papillon* enough to make him decide to risk going to the video shop even though it was unlikely to be open. He convinced his mother that he was going to the video shop near the house and not the one five streets down. Yes, it would be open, he told her, because the owner lived in the building opposite. He didn't even open for business; he opened to have coffee and talk about politics with his next-door neighbour. As Omar ran between buildings, trying to shield himself from bullets that might stray, he felt that what he was doing was ridiculous. If he died right there, he would have died because he was running to get a three-hour-long film about two people who were trying to get out of prison, and they weren't even cheery-looking people. The cover he had seen had shown Steve McQueen and Dustin Hoffman in the ugliest light possible. As he passed the video shop he had lied to his mother about, he saw that it was closed. Now what were the chances of his favourite shop being open? He ducked again and ran. When he got to his shop, he smiled. Yes, it was closed.

He had escaped his house and risked his life to see a film about trying to get out of prison — now, why had he done that? To learn something about escaping? If that had been his original intention, he had just learned that he could escape but what he was running to was not there. And the moral of the story was that his situation was different from all those movies, in that prison was the safer place; the world outside was the prison, not the one on the inside. Unless, of course, he went further, or rather deeper inside, and saw himself as the prison from which he could not run away unless one of those bullets he had been avoiding fell on him. Then he became aware of a voice inside him: 'Omar, you're trying to hypothesise about the meaning of life while putting yourself in danger. You're a fucking idiot; just run home.' *No*, he thought to himself, *I'm going to walk home slowly.* And he proceeded to figure the distance from the kerb at his feet to the one across the road. He closed his eyes and walked. There would be no cars; he would hear them coming from a few streets away if there were any. As he tried to gauge the next kerb, he felt a slight fear run through him, just like the one that used to come up years ago whenever he tried to swim across a swimming pool with his eyes closed, hoping that he wouldn't bang his head on the other side when he arrived. He opened his eyes and snapped out of himself. *What am I doing?* he asked himself, and then ran back as carefully as he had come. Just as he reached the video shop next to his house, he saw the owner come out of his building. Omar stopped in his tracks. 'Are you opening?' he asked in delight.

'Son, if I open, what mad man is going to rent movies?'

Omar smiled. 'I'm very mad.'

The man took his keys out and looked at Omar. 'I suppose you're not ... what else are you going to do?' Then he hesitated as if about to put the keys back into his pocket. 'Damn,' he continued. 'I'm more crazy than you are. Come on.' And he rushed over to the other side of the street, bent and unlocked the shutters. Omar bent down with him and started pushing but he was stopped. 'Only halfway,' the owner said. 'I'm closing down after you and I don't want more nutters.'

They went in and he put the lights on. As Omar browsed, he tried to repress a sigh. He didn't frequent this shop because the picture usually wasn't clear and the selection was shit. He quickly chose two films and took his money out. 'It's on the house,' the man said. Omar tried to argue, saying that he was privileged in the first place to have had the shop opened for him. As he ushered him out and bent to pull down the shutters with Omar, the owner turned and said, 'Son, no money in the world would make me open. Now go and enjoy them.'

Later that afternoon, Omar leaned over his balcony with Ali and let himself slowly sink onto the rails. They had run out of conversation, and there was silence apart from the occasional shelling in the distance. A soft whizzing sound went past them. Without budging and without turning, Omar said, 'That was a bullet, wasn't it?'

Making even less effort to talk, Ali answered, 'Yep.'

A few moments later, Omar mocked his previous statement: 'We could have died, right?'

Ali responded in the same tone, 'Right.'

Omar sighed. 'Life is cheap, right?'

Ali stalled then answered, 'Life is cheaper: it's free.'

George Benson
and the Middle East

$\mathbf{B}$ack in the school playground, Omar stood between Ahmad and George, arguing about whether the Baccalaureate was going to be cancelled. Unlike previous years, this one had involved the longest school disruptions throughout the whole country.

'Remember how hard we prayed last year? I'm not raising my hopes again,' George argued.

Ahmad giggled. 'You have to have hope. I kept on hoping they'd cancel them even up till the point I was doing them — actually, after doing them, I kept on imagining that a rocket would fall in the store where they keep them and burn them, but my imagination didn't succeed.'

'Yeah, and then they'd have you repeat the exams since they don't store all the country's papers in one place.'

'Oh, that's what was wrong with my imagination. God thought it would leave me more inconvenienced and he was just trying to do me a favour. I should teach him to take an extra step of correcting my plans in the future if there's anything wrong with them — he should've sent a rocket to *each one* of the centres.'

Then Omar turned to them. 'I wonder what would happen to me if they cancelled the Baccalaureate.'

'You'd just have to stay with us!' Ahmad laughed.

'Just get out,' said George casually.

When Ahmad remarked that no one would take them, George reminded him of what their maths teacher had said — that the second Baccalaureate was the same level as the first year of an American college; he knew because his wife was American and he knew the system.

'Well then, how come we're convinced our system is shit?' asked Ahmad.

'Because we've come to believe that everything we do is shit,' said Omar. 'And everything we do *is* shit, but maybe just no more shit than any other.'

Ahmad nodded his head and suggested, 'You know, you should emphasise to them that you've been through a war and you've got to this level despite the disruptions; they should take your perseverance into account.'

Omar shook his head and shrugged him off. 'Oh yeah, sure. Look, over there nobody talks to you; you just apply and that's it; you sit on your ass waiting.'

George held Omar's arm. 'No,' he said. 'Ahmad has a point. Your brother should approach them. Some of them have to be human; they can't just preach all this civilisation and not live up to it — well, at least in a couple of places.'

On the way back home, Omar ended up joining Walid even though he was walking with Jalal, a classmate he had found to be funny over the years but had avoided because he had been disloyal and a coward whenever the class had agreed to walk out on an unfairly scheduled exam. Jalal was recounting how the Sri Lankan housemaids who had been increasingly employed over the previous few years in Lebanon were worthless. Omar was about to interject and say that they had left their country because their situation was more desperate than theirs, and that they had no one to turn to when they arrived in Lebanon, when Jalal said that the other day he had 'done' a maid with two of his other friends. Omar had heard so many macho statements that he decided not to engage until Jalal said, 'We did her for five hours; in the end, she kept on falling asleep.'

At first, Omar couldn't believe what he had heard but having asked Jalal more about it, he said calmly and directly, 'What you are saying happened is rape.'

Jalal said that it wasn't his responsibility; it was his friend's maid and his parents weren't in. Besides, she wasn't going to talk to anybody about it: 'She hardly speaks English.'

After lunch, Omar was still disturbed by what he had heard. Normally, he would have argued but he had always dismissed Jalal as the only person he knew who was truly rotten, so he hadn't wasted his breath arguing with him. What disturbed him was that a few years back, when Zeina had been putting 'outside' down for not being more civilised than 'us', she had pointed to the level of sexual abuse and sexual offences that existed in the West, and had remarked that in Lebanon such behaviour was not as prevalent. Omar had come to see

263

that with all the war and its sickness there were other sicknesses which were more deeply shaming and at least there was one area where 'we' weren't 'lower'.

He rang Zeina to ask her whether in her studies there were any reports of an increase of rape because of the war. She said that there was a difference between rape and atrocities committed by soldiers or militia men as opposed to civilians. She didn't think there would have been an increase of rape in general. 'If anything, there's more of a deterrent than before the war because people are very ready with their guns; the rapist would think twice about being gunned down later on instead of waiting for the police to find him and verify that he did anything in the first place.'

'We can't be completely clean either,' she continued. 'What do you expect? We're human; there will be at least some rape, no matter where you go in the world, but we still have far less rape than all the civilised countries. Don't keep on looking for the worst in us just so that you can completely write us off.' While her comment was flippant and not totally directed at Omar, she added, 'When you get to your brother — and you've only got five more months — don't turn your back on us completely.'

'I'm done siding with anybody,' he said. 'I have nothing to do with anybody, neither "us" nor "them".'

'You still need to have some pride. Otherwise you wouldn't be talking to me about this...' and she gave a gentle laugh, 'Mr Freedom.'

'I wouldn't know what to do with pride,' he said flatly.

'Just remember my words: one day, you'll need them. You can't throw your whole heritage away. You'll need it one day; otherwise you'll find yourself with nothing. You'll end up feeling like you're completely on your own and you don't need to do that to yourself.'

After the conversation, Omar was reflecting on the Sri Lankan maid when Ali walked in, all excited. 'Guess what! You know the *ka'k* vendor who stands on Monla Street and has a crook brother? Well, yesterday — you missed this — yesterday, his brother happened to stop with his Mercedes and flash gold jewellery when somebody who must have had an old grudge on him pulled a gun, and guess what! His brother takes a whole Kalashnikov from his push cart — this little push cart; you'd think he was storing salt and plastic bags in it — and he whips up a Kalashnikov. Isn't that brilliant?'

Omar looked at him blankly.

'I swear to God! I know I'm smiling, but I saw it with my own eyes.' He looked at Omar and repeated, 'I swear. OK, I didn't see the whole event but I saw it just as it was finishing off. You can ask your friends; they saw the whole thing.'

Omar said he believed him but he had just heard something that had upset him. He went on to tell Ali about the Sri Lankan maid. 'You know,' he concluded. 'She needs somebody like this vendor. Imagine a country that is so poor that their people come to us, and she's probably not going to go back; she'll probably stay.'

Ali shook his head negatively and said, 'Oh no, not again; you've been fingering the asshole of your mind.' Then he looked at Omar determinedly. 'Just leave the rest of the world alone. I'm giving you gems from our own land and you're just throwing them away.'

Omar looked at him blankly.

Ali used a common expression that had been registering for Omar lately: 'Just leave it'. And then, as Omar didn't get it: 'Just leave the world alone and let it be.'

Over the next few days, Omar played with that expression, trying to find a way to apply it. He had heard it so many times before; he had seen so many old people make a hand gesture over their shoulder as if the problem were being thrown into the sea. But it was one thing to know something and another to be able to put it into practice.

During break-time at school, Ahmad casually said that he had made a tape of the bombing because he was living so near the green line that he had missed the sounds last time there was a ceasefire. Omar looked at him, sure at first that it was just a throwaway comment, but then Ahmad insisted; he said that he had found the silence unsettling. Omar looked at him again, doubting him, and Ahmad swore he wasn't lying. 'I'll get you the tape,' he said.

And then Omar heard that expression again — this time from George who was shrugging his shoulders. 'Leave it.'

Omar turned as if privately tickled. 'If we leave everything, there'll be nothing left,' he said.

'And so?' answered George.

Ahmad giggled his usual giggle. 'Otherwise, you'll end up carrying the world on your shoulder.'

'Leave him,' added George. 'He likes to carry the ladder sideways.'

265

Omar shook his head. 'What's wrong with you guys? It's like we can't have a conversation; you have to drop it in the middle of it. It's like you can't let anything go anywhere.'

'Four more months,' remarked George. 'After that, we'll be finished. You'll go to England, this undercover will go back to Syria to his headquarters, and I'll be in the American University in Beirut with the rest of the idiots, if I get my Hariri scholarship. No matter which way you look at it, it will be the end of this.'

Omar had been feeling the weight of the waiting getting heavier by the day. At home after school, he would sit at his desk, having thanked his mother for cooking his favourite meals now that she had nobody else to consider when cooking, and then he would count the days until June. He would take his usual hour's break for a walk around five, and, by the end of the night, he would be almost lifeless from the usual dreariness of despair. But the following day, just the thought of meeting Ahmad and George would be enough to make him walk in with a smile. But now he looked at them and realised that it had been like a fight to muster all his energy to be up. He looked at George and said, 'Look, if I drop it, if I leave it, there'll be nothing for me. This is the only place where I don't want to leave it.'

George looked at Ahmad 'What's with this guy?' he said, then looked at Omar and saw an intensity he had seen only when Omar was genuinely upset. 'I don't know what's wrong with you, but for you, I'll drop it.'

Ahmad tapped George on the shoulder. 'Actually, he wants you to carry it,' he pointed out.

Omar looked at Ahmad with annoyance, and then shook his head with a smile and lightly punched him on the shoulder. 'You are so fucking hard to be pissed off with,' he said.

Ahmad shrugged him off. 'Please, mister, go pick on somebody else. It seems like you're just looking for a fight and I don't want to be your way of letting off steam.'

Later, Omar thought of the two poles: leaving it, and letting steam off. It was as if the closer he got to June, the more heaviness seemed to be seeping in. There had never been a way to let steam off. The joking in school was managed in between trying to keep their attention on the subject — otherwise they'd fail. The walk at five was disrupted most days by witnessing one ugly situation or another. He definitely had to find a way to 'leave it'; otherwise, by June, he'd just crack.

It was as if instinctively he had to remind himself of what he had decided when, during his afternoon walk, he met a walking acquaintance he hadn't seen in a few months. When he asked about him at first, the others had said that being Christian, Michel had probably had enough of Tripoli and had left it. It was a joke because Michel openly made fun of Moslems in the small circles of friends and it was always obvious that there was no truth to his joking. When Omar asked Michel where he had been, he casually said that he had been detained by a dirty militia for six months. Then he asked Omar if they could take a walk off the main street; he just wanted to relax and not see too many people; his head was quite full. He had never come up to Omar's house and Omar couldn't make out whether he was genuinely agitated or just flippant, so he took the safer option and invited him over. Michel accepted gladly.

Omar's mother's face opened as if she had taken an immediate liking to Michel, but when she went to make tea, he asked Omar if they could go out to the balcony. Having excused themselves, they went out and Michel said that it wasn't that he been detained; he had been imprisoned in horrible conditions. His brother had been a member of the Qawmi party, which was neither a Moslem nor a Christian party, but a neutral one religiously, and that was why he had been held. 'It's a neutral party,' Michel said. 'But no, he was a Christian and they had an eye on him and believed that he should be with them, so they got me instead.'

'Imagine,' he said. 'My own people, Christians, and I've never believed in this bullshit in the first place. I won't bullshit you; it's not like I'm going to side with the Moslems because they're better — because they're not. I'm just going to hate them and the blood they come from.'

Omar looked at Michel, not sure what to say. 'Why are you not saying anything?' Michel asked. 'Don't you believe me?'

Omar was taken aback. 'I just don't have anything to say back to you,' he said.

'If you don't believe me, look,' Michel said, as he rolled up his sleeves. 'They put their cigarettes out in my arm. Six months I was in. By the end, I was begging them to kill me when they passed by.'

Omar looked at Michel's hand and saw a few circular marks, and then he noticed that he wasn't feeling anything. He hoped that Michel wouldn't ask him again whether he had any doubts because he wouldn't know what to answer. It wasn't that he was sure or not sure; he just didn't feel anything. When it started to get dark, Michel thanked Omar for '...just the something, the whatever, the, eh, just standing on the balcony with me. What am I talking about? Eh, thank your mum for the tea.'

Omar offered to go down with him to the end of the street but Michel declined. Late that night, Omar wondered whether he had managed to let go of what he heard or whether he had just not taken it in, in the first place. Whichever it was, the images of the circles on Michel's arms were just floating; they weren't in his stomach; he wasn't writhing in sympathy with Michel's suffering. Neither were the images completely out of sight; they just dangled in front of him. What was that? It didn't seem like 'leaving it' or 'taking it'.

Next day, Omar decided that he was going to take everything as it came and just enjoy the whateverness of everything. He even decided to try sitting next to Jalal — let all those years of seeing him as a bastard fall away. He even engaged with Jalal's joking. There was no doubt about it — Jalal was clever and he was fun. He thought to himself that by judging and taking a stand, he had missed out on some extra fun he could have had.

About a week later, when Omar tried to take his shoes off as he sat on his bed on arriving from school, he found his sock attached to his shoe. He pulled his shoe towards him and took a peek; he couldn't see anything. He slowly tried to take his foot out and saw that dry chewing gum was embedded between the fibre of his sock and his shoe. At first, he was mildly annoyed, but as he spent about twenty minutes trying to remove the gum from his shoe, he started to get increasingly angry. He looked at the sock and realised that it was hopeless trying to save it. Then suddenly he remembered Jalal bending down earlier that morning; he remembered feeling a slight pressure against his foot at the time. He fumed. When his mother asked him who would do such an unfunny thing, Omar shrugged it off and said that the gum had probably just slipped in.

Later that night, Omar couldn't sleep. He boiled with anger. He looked back over the years and saw how, like most people, he had had to hold his anger in; otherwise there was always a chance that things would escalate. Everybody had heard way too many stories about how one insulted person had later brought some armed people to beat up whoever had insulted them. Everybody either knew some people who were armed or had connections and could pull it off. He saw how it had been good for him to learn not only to pull back but also always to stay in touch with the goodness of people. For all the ignorance and the tempers that had often flared around him, he was able to see that beneath the anger there was a goodness that did not intend for things to flare up to that level, even when people did not admit this later. Based on his own misunderstandings, he had held that if you sat in front of somebody and you just looked at them and let everything fall away, there was hardly ever much opportunity to disagree, and even if you did disagree, there was enough heart for disagreements just to be. After about an hour of sleeplessness, he made a resolute decision.

The following day when he arrived at school, he walked slowly up to Jalal who extended his arm to shake Omar's hand. Omar gently pulled his right hand back and then, as he leaned forward, he brought the palm at full force across Jalal's cheek. Jalal's companions were taken by surprise: Omar had whacked Jalal without uttering even one word. The friends instinctively moved to hold Jalal back when he started to move forward. Omar stood his ground. 'Guys,' he said. 'You can let him go; let's just see if he wants the shit beaten out of him.' Jalal pushed forward but only enough to be held back.

Omar was still standing his ground when George ran over. He looked at Jalal and then took Omar by the arm. 'OK,' he said. 'Whatever he did, I'm sure he deserved the slap, but he's definitely not worth wasting more time on.'

Omar told George and Ahmad what had happened and confirmed that the only other time he had hit anybody in his life was when he was thirteen; it was a small slap and while he may not have verbally apologised afterwards, he had acted sorry within a few minutes. But slapping Jalal was something that he was not going to regret for the rest of his life. Ahmad commended him, saying that he had seen red watermelons before but none as red as Jalal's inflamed cheek.

As Omar passed in front of the video shop on his way home, he was greeted by the owner who had opened the shop for him a couple of months earlier. He received a casual invitation to come in and Omar decided to have a browse. As he looked through the movies, he heard a familiar conversation between the owner and his neighbour who were discussing the state of the middle east, how the bigger powers of

America and Russia had been playing them like pawns, how the oil played its part, how Lebanon did not have the economy to sustain such a long-term war — almost eleven years now, a country whose only income had come from tourism now long buried. 'Who's paying for all these arms?' one of the men said. 'Who's going to sort out what has given God a headache?'

Omar spontaneously turned around and said, 'George Benson. All he wants is the night. Give him what he's asking for; deal with him.'

He was met by blank faces, and then the neighbour asked, 'Who is this George Benson?'

Suddenly Omar felt ashamed and wasn't sure what to do. His reaction had come out of tiredness, weariness of hearing about politics, but it was a private joke. To apologise would be to say that he had made fun of them. 'Eh, it's a song,' he said. 'Eh, "Give me the Night". It's in English. He's, eh, he's a black singer from America.'

'Oh yeah, the blacks have been oppressed just like us. You think we're bad for being screwed by America? Well, the blacks are being screwed by their own country in their own country.'

Omar took a couple of films — after all, the reason he was in the shop was out of gratitude — and then walked out.

As he took the elevator, he felt confused. That feeling of justification for having slapped Jalal had ended up extending itself into cockiness. It was hard to balance. It seemed like something that could go too far and do harm. Omar shook his head in the privacy of the elevator; it was unlikely that he would have much opportunity to learn how to balance this thing that could flare up and go beyond where he wanted it to go.

The End

Omar asked his walking companions, 'How does one say he likes a girl and would like to walk with her?'

'Why?'

'What for?'

'You're not going to do something stupid?'

'Well, you tell her that you'd like to "go out with her".'

Go out with you, thought Omar to himself.

Half an hour later, Omar came back with a big red face and a smile wavering on idiocy. 'Oh no!'

He said that there had been this girl he had fancied for a while: 'She walks up and down Monla Street; I've been noticing her for a while and really like her.'

'And?'

He said that she had just come out of her house with two friends and he had walked right up to her and asked her if she would go out with him.

'What?'

He had asked her if he could have a word with her and so she had stepped back a couple of steps, no more, and then he had asked her.

'And what did she say?'

'She smiled apologetically and said that she didn't go out with people she didn't know.'

'Aaaaah, and why did you do that to yourself?' they asked.

'OK, I felt sick in my stomach before doing it, and I knew there was no way she was going to say "Yes" — well, it would have been a one in ten million chance, and I know the population of Lebanon is no more than three million — but still, I didn't want to have lived all this time and not asked this question once.'

'But you're going to be in London in less than four months!'

He admitted that it was probably the most idiotic thing he was ever going to put himself through, and he had known that before he did it, which made it more idiotic, and she didn't have much of a chance: 'It's not like I have experience in this kind of thing and can at least come out looking slick.' Still, with all the embarrassment and feeling as small as a piece of lentil, he still did not regret it. 'Actually, I'm so full of embarrassment that I feel bigger; I'm a bigger idiot but at least I'm not a nobody in this area.'

They commended him on his idiocy and said that although it was as purposeless an exercise as one could put themselves through, in Lebanon the only way to be courageous was through idiocy; at least he could say he had had a moment of courage.

In school, the sense of wanting to take everything to the limit and get the last drop before it all disappeared was permeating the class and taking hold in all of Omar's classmates, including those who would not get involved in antics but were happy to witness them develop. The teachers took a surprisingly relaxed attitude to the developing may-hem; it was as if they had talked about it among themselves, and their attitude was that the students could miss out all of the last two months if they wanted even if it meant that they were likely to flunk the Baccalaureate and waste it all, having just nearly made it after four-teen years of school. There was a feeling of generosity: this had been the most disruptive year and it was understandable as they had been under so much pressure. The teachers were willing to be considerate and not set very difficult exams, hoping that that might ease some of the pressure until the Baccalaureate exam dates were set.

The only teacher who did not promise to make any concessions with his exam paper was the chemistry teacher. He said that he did not want to rob them of the opportunity of being challenged and thus better prepared for the Baccalaureate; but he wasn't believed. The class generally agreed that there was an air of sadism about him. Omar and George tried to reason with him, saying that with all the dis-ruptions throughout all the schools in Lebanon, there was a possibility that the Baccalaureate would be cancelled, and if it were cancelled, the only results they would be measured by were the school exams. The teacher said that if people lived their lives hoping for things not to happen, their whole life would end up being a non-event; he told the class that they were wasting their time. When he left the class, he was fuming. Omar said that it was OK; with this kind of callousness, it just made it easier to take revenge. They had planned on expressing their gratitude to the other teachers for giving from their hearts and souls, especially the maths and physics teachers who often brought the class in an hour before school and kept them an hour after school, on their own time, and even put up with nagging resistant complaints. But this one was going to be different.

The problem with the stink bombs that you could buy was that they were clichéd, but then Ahmad proposed that he work on a natural stink bomb. He said that he knew how to rot an egg naturally, without breaking it; then, when you broke it, it had the foulest smell he could think of.

The problem with leaving a pin on the seat was that it would be visible, but then George said that he could find a permanent ink marker the same colour as the seat.

The problem with trying to humiliate somebody was that the more general and prepared the trick was, the more likely it was that the response could be repressed and brushed off as something to be occasionally expected, but then Omar suggested that if the board erasers were soaked in water, when the chemistry teacher came to wipe the board, you would see his expression change at the first wipe and it would be more difficult for him to stay cool as not only would he be tricked, but he would be carrying out the trick on himself.

The chemistry teacher responded to the stinking egg by naming the chemical responsible for the smell. He still looked annoyed but also smug, as if he had actually outsmarted whoever was responsible, although no one in the class thought so. The pin was a mystery: he did sit on the seat but he didn't jump up and, when the seat was inspected after the class, the pin was not where George had quickly but meticulously glued it. The wet erasers idea was a treat that evolved beyond their plan: having taken the eraser, the teacher noticed the smudge he created only after he had already taken two whole wide sweeps. When he stopped, the class had already prepared a silence for him. This time, his annoyance was so visible that he did not respond with a remark. He looked back at the board, then took the other eraser and tried it: it was also wet. Then he looked back at the class and said that since the blackboards were wet, no writing could be done, and thus it would not be possible to have a class. No one objected, and he was left in the position of having deprived them of something that they hadn't wanted in the first place. After a few minutes, he sensed that the class was happy in its awkwardness and so he shook his head and said that he would be generous and, as they were leaving soon, he would rise above their ways.

There was still one more class to come. Omar, Ahmad and George had prepared a trick but, for a more authentic effect, they decided not to share it with their classmates. They were not sure whether to leave it for the last class or do it in the class before and see the teacher come back uncomfortable the following week. However, when he seemed to be recovering after the trick with the erasers, pretending that he was unscathed, they looked at each other and, with a sign, agreed.

Ten minutes later, Ahmad slammed his book on his desk and, with a red, angry face, turned to Omar who was sitting next to him. 'I TOLD YOU BEFORE: PLEASE — AND I SAID "PLEASE" SEVERAL TIMES — DO NOT, I REPEAT, DO NOT DO THAT!'

Omar raised his fist as if threatening to hit Ahmad. At this point, George got up from his seat two rows back and proceeded to rush towards them, as if trying to diffuse an explosive situation. But at his second step, he fell, and, as he hit the ground, he let out a scream. He slowly got up and brushed himself off, while bending over with a contorted face. The teacher looked at Omar and saw blood on his lower lip. 'Omar, did he hit you?' he asked, indicating Ahmad.

Omar shook his head as if in surprise. 'No. Why?'

'Your lip: there's blood on it.'

Omar raised his eyebrows, wiped his lip and then looked at his hand. He looked back up with a blank expression. 'Blood,' he said.

In a low tone, the teacher said, 'You can go to the toilet and wash it off.'

'No, it's OK,' said Omar calmly.

As George stood halfway between Omar and Ahmad and his seat, he muttered, 'My watch is broken. My watch ... it is....'

The disruption was so quick and intense that most of class sat frozen in disbelief. It had been commented that not even God could split those three boys up, but, within less than a minute, it looked as if Ahmad and Omar were about to kill each other. The teacher was not sure how to proceed. There were three seemingly unrelated things hanging in the air: the question of what Ahmad and Omar had nearly fought over; Omar not totally wiping the blood off his lower lip but being determined that he did not need to go to the bathroom; and George's contorted face indicating that he was in pain. The teacher looked at Omar and Ahmad and said, 'I'm not even going to ask you what that was about. Just one question: are you going to stay in your seats?'

Omar nodded his head positively; Ahmad left a slight delay and followed suit.

The teacher turned to George and asked sarcastically, 'Do you need to go to hospital?'

George gave a guttural moan and said, 'I don't think so.'

When the class finished and the chemistry teacher left, the class looked at Omar and Ahmad. They looked at each other and Omar slowly got up and gave Ahmad a kiss, and their classmates shook their heads in relief. Ahmad explained that he had had to prick himself with a pin to muster an intensity that wasn't going to be broken by laughter. Omar said that he hadn't had that problem: he had already accidentally cut his lower lip the previous week and all he had to do was give it a slight bite, although to make sure it would bleed again, he had ended up overdoing it and being in more pain than he needed. George said that despite being in pain from having tripped himself, he was contorting his face to stop himself from breaking into laughter.

'So basically the three of you put yourself in pain to put him in pain,' someone said.

Ahmad smiled. 'Some pain is not painful; some is sweet.'

Later, they were commended on their trick. Someone said that it was true that had the class been told about it, they wouldn't have been able to feed off the real tension in the air. They didn't recognise what was happening when it happened, but it was something they could enjoy afterwards and it was still hard to believe that Ahmad and Omar hadn't been fighting for real.

When they came out of the chemistry final-year exam three weeks later, they were surprised that the teacher had not set it as hard as he had threatened. Before Omar could give him the benefit of the doubt, Ahmad suggested that maybe he didn't want to lose face by looking like a sore loser. Omar nodded his head and said, 'I've tried very hard to find his heart but I couldn't and now that he's gone, it's easy to imagine he had one. But he was a cunt.'

When they had finished all their exams, they were left with a muted feeling of jubilation: they would never have to do this again. But they still hadn't crossed the finishing line: the Baccalaureate dates had not yet been set by the government. Ahmad, George and Omar remembered Jamil and how he had dropped out four years earlier having pulled the gun on the English teacher.

Three days later, Omar bumped into him. The feeling of loyalty was as fresh as the old days. They had met each other only every few months over the four years but this time was different: it was clear to Omar that the others in the group were all going to go to college but not Jamil. It was something they had always known but now it seemed to be emphasised more than ever. Omar wished he could apologise for the difference in the opportunities they had been born into, but there was no way to say it. Jamil was a proud person; he had gone on to help his father as a car mechanic and he didn't seem to need to be patronised. As they sat beside a coffee shop, Omar tipped a plastic mug by his elbow but then quickly moved to save it. A coffee drop fell on his finger and he brought it to his mouth. Jamil smiled in surprise. 'You're not fasting,' he remarked.

It was a question usually asked shamingly. 'No,' answered Omar with confidence. 'You know, I really don't get it how people fast for the month of Ramadan and for the rest of the year they don't pray or have anything to do with Islam. They do it because everybody else does it. I'm not going to fall into that trap.'

'Oh,' Jamil replied. 'I thought it was because you're leaving that you no longer care.'

Omar told him that a few years before, he had got into Islam and had prayed five times a day; he had fasted seven days in his life — no more — and that was how it had been since. And then he added that leaving had nothing to do with anything.

Jamil smiled. 'Good,' he said. 'Just make sure nothing changes you.'

After they parted, Omar felt a dent in his chest. It was unlikely that he would see Jamil again before his departure. He wondered whether he would ever see him again.

The next few weeks passed with still no date set for the Baccalaureate. He saw Ahmad and George and they struggled to encourage each other to remain motivated. It was too tempting to fantasise that it would be cancelled. Ahmad and George said that they had no option but to persist but that if by any chance Omar could convince his brother in England to pull him out without having to do the Baccalaureate, he could be free without having to wait for the government to hand him his freedom.

When Khaled rang to say that there were two colleges that looked hopeful — one in Manchester and one in Ireland — he picked up on Omar's understandable wish. He said he should wait a bit longer: even if he could get in with only his school exams, it would be no harm to have the Baccalaureate as a back-up.

'Ireland! Where the hell is that?' asked Omar's mother.

A week later, as they watched *Live Aid*, Zeina told Omar's mother that she should encourage Omar to go to Ireland if he could. 'See all these people raising all this money for people in Africa,' she said. 'It was all started by an Irish guy. The British are so stingy, they would never think up something like this, but it's always the same: it's the poor who always have more heart than the rich. They have so much unemployment in his country but he still reaches out to a different continent.'

Without sarcasm, her mother answered, 'Shouldn't he be feeding his own people first?'

Zeina was not fazed. 'No mother,' she said. 'His people are no longer dying of starvation, but they did at one time, and that's why he is doing this now.' Then she told Omar not to dismiss the place just because he didn't know it; he should let his brother make the suggestions for him.

When Omar talked to George and Ahmad, they first thought it was Iceland, and then they laughed at themselves for having thrown geography out the window. 'I'll tell you why,' George said with conviction. 'It's because we have been fucked around by so many nationalities that we don't know where we're coming from and where we're going. Just yesterday, twenty-one Finnish UN representatives were held by some militia working for the Israelis. Now, which one of you knew that we had Finnish people on our own soil?'

'Finnish?' said Ahmad with a smirk. 'Is that like "crossing the finish line" or "finish your plate before I wash it"?'

Omar shook his head. 'Who the fuck let them in? And if they're UN and Israelis can have them captured, then why the fuck is the UN allowing itself to exist in the first place?'

'All these foreigners want to come and visit when we're dying to leave. Did you know that a father put his children up for sale the other day?'

'That's just typical,' answered George.

'The guy wasn't selling them. He said that he was willing to have them adopted by somebody from outside this country, for free, because he was heartbroken that he couldn't provide them with a life in this place.'

When Omar heard that they were not babies, but around five and seven, his heart sank.

'Hello,' Ahmad said, waving his hand in front of Omar's face. 'Where have you gone again?'

Omar would increasingly lose concentration even in the company of others. Khaled had rung and said that it was now up to Omar if he wanted to come over without doing the Baccalaureate: both the Manchester and the Dublin colleges would accept him on his school grades since they were good. But Omar wasn't so sure what to do. When his neighbour, Karim, bumped into them in the elevator and said that he was emigrating to America to finish a Masters, Omar's mother thought it would be a good opportunity for Omar to travel with him, just in case something went wrong; at least she would feel more reassured. At first, Omar pointed out to her that he had flown alone before but then he himself felt comforted by the idea. He would settle for Karim's departure date in three weeks' time, and, unless the Baccalaureate dates were set before they bought the tickets, he would leave without doing the exams.

The proceedings for the visa were already set in place but when Amin tried to get Omar his army exemption from an area outside Tripoli, he was told that he didn't need it that year. Omar was concerned: if he were stopped at the airport and he didn't have it, he would not be allowed to leave. Karim assured him that a cousin of his had been able to get it from the same place that Amin had gone to. Amin was reluctant to make the trip again because it always involved at least some risk on the way, especially if he wasn't travelling with somebody who had some connections. He returned to reassure Omar that he had received the same response as previously. There was still one more week before Karim and Omar were due to travel, and the dates for the Baccalaureate had still not been set.

Three days before he left, Omar was in George's car as he was waiting for his concierge to unblock the entrance to their garage. George got out of the car to look for the concierge in his ground-floor apartment but didn't' find him. Just as he was about to double park, he

278

saw the concierge and smiled. 'We've been looking for you,' he said. 'But you *are* here.'

Omar casually smiled at the confusion and then watched George get out of the car to calm the concierge down; the concierge had approached Omar to ask him why he was laughing and had then proceeded to walk off. When George returned, he calmly told Omar not to worry about the confusion, but when he got out of the car not to look the guy in the eye and especially not to smile. When they made it up to his apartment, George casually said that this concierge was a bit nutty: he had been insulted that Omar had smiled; he thought he was being laughed at.

'And where did he go off to?'

George laughed. 'To his apartment,' he said. 'He has a machine gun.'

'Are you serious?'

George nodded with a smile. 'Yep, I told you, he's nuts.'

'And what was he going to do? Shoot me?'

George shrugged his shoulders. 'Well, you know, who knows? But it doesn't matter now; it's fine; and on the way down, I'll be driving you, so it's fine.'

When Omar got home, he felt as if there was something inside him, something like a neon light that was flickering and was about to go out. He sighed: two more days.

On the last night before leaving, he fulfilled his promise to Ali, even though he had to rush as Laila was arriving from Beirut with Samer and Khalil, to say goodbye. Just after sunset, he sneaked with Ali behind the new Mercedes cars that were parked off Monla Street. Then they sprayed the cars with yellow and red paint, as Ali giggled with vengeance. He had been assured by Ali that anybody who made money during the civil war in Lebanon was a crook. But was there a chance that there was even one of them who was not a crook? As Omar sprayed, he felt his lack of conviction. Then he imagined himself being caught. What might be worse than being caught by a crook would be being caught by a good person. Not only would the embarrassment make him feel small, but he imagined a good man losing it. At the third car, he stopped.

Back home, he was still distracted by having put himself in a risky situation. He found it hard to believe that it was his last night. Just before putting Samer to bed, Laila heard a few gunshots and put her hand over her mouth. 'Oh no,' she said. 'Please God, make it just a small incident.'

Samer looked up at her. 'That's a Kalashnikov,' he said. 'It's nothing.'

Omar made a face. 'He's only seven and he can tell the different sounds?'

Samer smiled with pride. 'I know Kalashnikov is Russian, M-16 is American; then there's the RPJ and the B-7.'

'My God!' Omar shook his head. 'And he says them with all innocence.'

Laila bent over, kissed her son, and then kissed Omar. 'You used to know them too. Have you forgotten?'

'Me?' asked Omar.

'Yeah, you — you and Ziad. Remember?'

Amin smiled. 'Maybe it's time to forget everything and just go.'

Later, as Omar closed his eyes, he remembered the phone call with Zeina. They hadn't grown as close as he wanted, but that was just how it was. As for his mother, he couldn't feel sorry for her because if he did, he wouldn't want to leave. And then he thought of Amin's smile. He was going to miss Amin's smile. Throughout all his life he had never seen a person who could be angry, and even shout sometimes, and not make him feel at least a bit of either anger or fear. But no: on the few occasions when Amin had been angry, it was a white anger that polluted no one, even when he frothed at the mouth. When he smiled, his eyes danced. The way Omar had been praised over the years by his mother always left him connecting to his mother's love, but with Amin, whenever he was praised, he was left feeling good and hopeful about himself. He wondered how long it would be before he would see that smile again.

At four in the morning, he was woken up by his mother. Karim had knocked on the door. It was time to go.

Omar was hoping that the tiredness would prevent his mother from getting too emotional. As he moved through dressing himself, he felt the strange peace that comes with being awake at a time too late to be called night and too early to be called morning.

He let Zeina and Jamal kiss him, then sneaked in to take one more peek at Samer, promising not to wake him up. He tried not to look his mother in the eye until Amin told him to reassure her that everything would be fine, and better than fine: great. He looked at Amin and his eyes danced. 'Go,' Amin said.

As Omar walked into the elevator, his mother took Karim by the hand. 'You take care of my son, please,' she said. 'I'm begging you.'

Karim smiled. 'No problem. It will be an honour.' He kissed her. 'He's not a kid,' he reassured her. 'And there's nothing to worry about anyway.'

Just as the car pulled out, Omar looked up. They were all lined up on the balcony, waving: Laila holding his mother as she wiped her face, and Amin waving as if telling them to hurry away.

He kept looking back until the driver veered off.

At the airport, his and Karim's luggage were casually searched and passed on. Passports were checked for visas at the check-in desk. And then, at the emigration desk, the officer looked at Omar and said, 'You don't have a clearance from the army.'

'What?' he answered in complete bewilderment. 'My brother went twice and—'

'All I'm saying is that you don't have one, and you need one. Your friend has one.' The officer looked sternly at Karim and said, 'Tell your friend to calm down.'

Karim slowly looked at Omar and motioned for him to back off. Then he turned back to the officer. 'I'm sure there is some way to rectify this situation,' he said and asked for the passport to check it for himself. Then he discreetly put his hand in his pocket before slowly handing Omar's passport back.

The officer made stamping sounds. 'Have a good trip,' he said.

Karim held onto both passports until they got on the plane and then explained that he had got his clearance through somebody he knew in the army.

'And how much did you bribe him?' asked Omar in a hushed tone.

'One hundred dollars,' Karim replied, and then, as he looked into Omar's passport: 'Shit! he didn't stamp your passport.'

'What?'

'It's too late to go back. Don't worry about it: you have a visa to London and that's all that matters.'

'Are you sure?'

'I have a few hours' transit in London. I'll wait for you until you get out to your brother; it'll be fine.'

Omar looked out the window as the plane shifted gear towards take-off. Beirut. This is Lebanon. He noticed he was grinding his teeth.

...the story in this book continues into another book that has already been written. Its publication is aimed no longer than a year from the launch of this one, irrespective of this one's reception.

Acknowledgements

Thanks to: whoever taught me how to read and write; family for love and believing in me past the nappy stage; Angie Vinter for teaching me how to type as well as believing I had something to type; Katie Jennings for being a true teacher; Deirdre Conlon for nagging me to write and for generally being a suppa sista; Barbara Hannigan for putting everything aside and reading from the heart when we lived together; Sheila Greene for not reporting me to the Dean and seeing beyond my nuttiness; Eileen Halahan for spiritual something or the other where you end up feeling there is a divine something and the other somewhere here and there back then here and now and all along when I didn't know it; lots of friends who gave love directly and indirectly (this includes all the ones I have mentioned and the ones I have forgotten to mention but remembered later and the ones I still haven't remembered and might never remember despite my love for them); Claire Counehan for having huge ears each with a heart in it (no, no, she doesn't look one bit silly); Deirdre Conlon again because I feel like it; Wassim Eid the goat killer; Isolde Blau for having a huge heart with one big ear at its centre (again, could've looked really funny); Rachel Graham for Rachelness, Wael Wansa for telling me he was touched by it despite the number of books he has read, my mother Gilda Frakalanza for believing I have something to say to the world; Hugh Buckley for being Hu Bukli; Alan Peart with that Jesus smile; Maria Rawlins for spiritual guidance and mentorship; and Pat McCoey for those Soul workshops that are just about impossible to name while genuine life-changing shifts are felt; Aine McCarthy for believing in my vision and encouraging me to self-publish; Emer Ryan for typesetting and corrections. And everybody else directly involved in bringing this book into being, from the paper feeder in the publishing house to the van driver who brought the books to the shops to your hands holding it right now and your eyes for taking it in and all the places and spaces it might be welcomed in, to the bees and the trees and the stars and the sun and the wind, the pauses between the breaths, me for having the patience to be me so far, and to the one force that holds me down and gives me the strongest gravity to be on this planet; my daughter Samira, sunshine pure and pure...

(there are other people who continue to believe in me irrespective of whether I write like my brother Karim: Colm; Yannnis; Fadi; Souheil; Bassam, Ghada; Walid; me dad Oussama and me ganma Taita from some Heaven balcony overlooking our traffic; Maha; Uncle Assad; Salwa; Ghassan, Brendan of the Doyle family; Louay; Peter Quinn; Hilal; Kholeh; Ibbi, Andrew tall guy; Johnny B and numerous love givers... Those I won't thank because it gets silly after a while, like breaking a heart down to its molecules and atoms). David Kane I forgot to mention but it's too late now because it has already gone to print... Munir... Marw...*_ -..:)